The
Runaway
Girl

Elsie Mason is the pen name of Paul Magrs.

Paul was born in Jarrow in 1969, and brought up in the North East of England. Since 1995 he has published fiction in many different genres. He lectured in Creative Writing for many years at both the University of East Anglia and at Manchester Metropolitan University.

In 2019 he published his book on writing, *The Novel Inside You*. In 2020 Snow Books republished his Brenda and Effie Mystery series of novels. In 2021 Harper Collins published his book of cartoons, *The Panda, the Cat and the Dreadful Teddy*. In 2022 he won the Crime Writers' Association prize for best short story of the year.

Whichever genre he has worked in, he has always written about working class women from the north. In many ways historical and romantic saga fiction was the first genre he was aware of, as a child, when he eavesdropped on his female relatives telling tales around the kitchen table in South Shields.

Taking on a female pen name has been wonderfully liberating: he has loved writing as Elsie.

He writes and lives in Manchester with Jeremy and Bernard Socks.

The Runaway Girl

Elsie Mason

ORION

First published in Great Britain in 2023 by Orion Fiction,
an imprint of The Orion Publishing Group Ltd.,
Carmelite House, 50 Victoria Embankment
London EC4Y 0DZ

An Hachette UK company

1 3 5 7 9 10 8 6 4 2

A CIP catalogue record for this book
is available from the British Library.

ISBN (Mass Market Paperback) 978 1 3987 0895 2
ISBN (eBook) 978 1 3987 0896 9

Typeset by Born Group
Printed and bound in Great Britain by Clays Ltd, Elcograf S.p.A.

www.orionbooks.co.uk

For Georgina Hammick

Chapter 1

In later years, if you were to ask what Cathy Sturrock was like, just about everyone would give you similar answers. 'Why, she's always the life and soul of the party! She's strong. She's in charge. She's been here forever! She's the Queen of the Sixteen Streets, is Cathy!'

Such was the esteem that the denizens of that area by the docks in South Shields held her. There was no nonsense with Cathy. She was strong because she had always had to be strong. And she was glamorous, too. By! You should have seen her when she was a young'un, with her flaming red hair and those catlike green eyes. She still had her looks as an older woman, sitting in splendour by the bar in her beloved Robin Hood pub. For more years than anyone could recall she had reigned here, at the top of steep Frederick Street, at the heart of the community, overlooking the Tyne.

'But is that what she's really like?' the stranger might ask, watching this woman as she sipped milk stout and chattered with her usual gaggle of friends. 'Surely she couldn't always have been queen here? So secure in her place in the world? How did she even come to be here in the first place?'

Most of the locals would frown at this, as they would at anyone asking too many questions about a person's past. It was something that just wasn't done in the Sixteen Streets. People had to bide together so closely in these rows of two-ups, two-downs, and for the sake of a quiet life, it didn't do to enquire too much into the pasts of those who dwelled nearby. There was lots of speculation and lots of gossip behind people's backs, mind, but no one liked a nosy parker, asking questions outright about folks' secret lives.

Some people did speculate about Cathy Sturrock's origins. While most assumed that she had always been here, living by the dirty docks of South Shields, there were others who dimly recalled hearing that she had blown into this place, alone and starving and very young, back at the end of the Great War, all those years ago. With nowt to her name and desperate, she had shown up here in the Sixteen Streets, almost at random, back when all the men and boys were away fighting and there was a bereft and horrible feeling about the place. That's when Cathy fetched up in town. She was fleeing something or someone and looking for a place to settle in. That's what some of the old matrons said when the subject of Cathy's past came up. But they claimed that they didn't like to speculate or remember much more. Cathy had been good to all of them round here and the past was the past. If she wanted to forget it, then it was no one's business but her own.

Cathy sat by the bar and sipped her drink, feeling that familiar warm buzz from both the alcohol and the talkative hullabaloo of her bar. She was so at home here and so familiar with everyone that she could give a good guess at what every small huddle of drinkers was discussing. These people really were like her beloved subjects and there was nothing that Cathy didn't know about them. And she knew that sometimes even her oldest and most loyal friends would mutter amongst themselves about her past. She was a very familiar sight to all of them, in her velvet gowns that always seemed too grand for a sawdust-floored place like this. And yet there was still a mystery about her. One that she was still keen to guard, even all these years later.

How many years, exactly? Twenty or more she had been landlady here, ruling supreme. Twenty years since her great struggle to make the Robin Hood hers alone, and to free herself of the shackles of a loveless marriage. More than twenty years since she staggered into this place for the first time, with nothing to her name. Just the clothes on her back. Hardly a picking on her. Despair in her heart. Desperate to find a new place to hide away in and to simply forget everything that had already happened in her young and wasted life . . .

Sometimes she couldn't help herself from going back and dwelling on the days that had seen her first pitch up here in the Sixteen Streets. It was always mixed feelings she experienced then. Sadness and loss, but also great elation and joy. She had faced up to so much and triumphed, though there was always such great shame that she kept hidden deep inside.

It was the Biscuit Man who had brought her here, and it was he who she had to thank for finding her the right place in the world. It was all random though, and he'd had no idea the favour he was doing her, that day he'd offered the girl a ride in his cab back to the factory.

Why, she couldn't even remember that driver's name now. She remembered the horses that pulled his wagon better than she could remember him. He'd just been another gurning ne'er-do-well, looking at a bonny, helpless lass and figuring he'd have some fun with her. He let her clamber up into his cab to sit beside him not out of the goodness of his heart. Oh no, it wasn't for the sake of helping her out that he gave her a lift.

Even at the age of nineteen, Cathy had realised that. Cathy Carmichael as she had been known then. No, that fella with the wagon had just been after a bit of a feel. He'd fancied getting his leg over, somewhere between Morwick-on-Sea, where their fateful journey had started and his destination, South Shields, in the next county down.

'Aye, bonny lass, you just come and sit up here with me, then,' he'd laughed, and hoisted her up onto the seat beside him. 'Are you running away?'

She had nodded grimly and wouldn't be drawn any further. Her mouth settled into a thin line, as it often did when she was cross and determined. Somehow her stubborn quiet only attracted the Biscuit Man even more and he kept gazing at her appreciatively as he drove his wagon out of the small seaside town onto the main rutted road going south.

'It's biscuits I've been carrying,' he told her, almost proudly.

'Yes, I saw the writing on the side of the van,' she said. 'Shouldn't you be away fightin'?' she asked him cheekily.

'Dicky heart,' he told her. 'And I'm doing my bit by keeping these deliveries goin', if it's even any business of yours, young lady.' He growled at her, clearly put out by her questioning.

Cathy didn't care. She sat up straight on the shiny leather seat, looking as respectable as she could in her thin cotton frock. The only frock she owned. She'd had to leave her other few belongings behind in her lodgings this morning, as she'd fled without paying the past month's rent. All she had was a battered carpet bag on her lap, but there was bugger all in it. If robbers set upon her now they'd find themselves empty-handed, she reflected, and this thought made her feel braver. I've got nothing to lose, she thought. Not now.

She took a swift grip of herself. She had almost crumbled just then. She had almost submitted to the tears that were threatening to overwhelm her. They were always there, right behind her eyes. Her feelings lay in wait for her, patiently biding their time for her to drop her tough façade. Then they could get to her and remind her of everything she was leaving behind.

4

But no. She mustn't dwell upon things she could do nothing about. She had to follow her present course and make a future for herself.

'Wights Biscuit Factory,' the whiskery driver was telling her. 'That's who I work for. I take deliveries to all the big, fancy shops in all these towns. I go all over Northumberland, supplying the big shops with fancy tins.'

'Do you, now?' Cathy said, humouring him, watching the rows of townhouses rolling by. The streets were mostly empty this time on a Monday. There was no one around to see her leaving the town she had made her own for this past year. No one cared that she was absconding, penniless and no better off than she'd been when she arrived. There was no one to notice anything she ever did. Usually this thought made her feel desolate, but today she felt a surge of wonderment, almost excitement. I'm free, she thought. I'm free to make up the rest of my own life . . .

But for now she was stuck with this boring man, telling her all about biscuits and the history of the Wights Factory in South Shields. He was burbling on about custard creams and ginger snaps. Couldn't he even hear how dull he was being? She knew only too well that he was filling up the air with nonsense chatter, to cover the fact that he was excited and nervous at having her sitting there beside him. As he yammered about biscuits, his mind was spinning on dirty thoughts. She recognised the signs, of course, and knew that she'd have to fight off the mucky bugger before long.

'Aye, a lass like you, looking for work an' all that, you could do worse than knocking at the gates of Wights Biscuit Factory,' the driver told her. 'They're always after lasses to work in the baking house and on the production line. And with all the young fellas away at war still, they've been needing even more, or so I've heard.'

'Oh, really?' she asked. Actually, maybe he was giving her a good tip here. Maybe factory work was exactly what she was looking for. Not that Cathy Carmichael had ever seen a factory in her life, or even knew what factory work might consist of. She'd come from the country and had never seen a town bigger than Morwick in her life. She didn't let any of that ignorance show, however. She turned to look at her driver with interest and he leered at her, mistaking her querying glance for interest in him.

'I can drop you at the factory gates,' he told her. 'I'll be taking the van back to the depot and I'll have stuff to sign and my gaffer to see. But if you play your cards right I could introduce you and show you around. Make an introduction or two. It's hard and hot work, they say, but the living's good. Most of the folk in the Sixteen Streets work at the biscuit factory, they say. If it's good enough for all of them, well then, I imagine it's good enough for you too, lass.'

She blinked at him and asked, 'The Sixteen Streets?'

'Oh,' he grinned. 'That's the whole area on the hill above the factory and overlooking all the docks. That's what they've called it for years, all the folk who live there. It's like a rabbit warren, it is. It used to be a right bloody slum, back in the olden days. They were all crammed twenty to a house. And they're tiny little houses, too! In the bad old days it was a smoky and mucky old place. You'd choke on the fumes from the chimneys and if you walked up the wrong way someone'd slit your throat and chuck you in the dirty water. But it's better now, or so they say. It's almost respectable, is what I've heard.'

The Sixteen Streets, Cathy thought to herself, and liked the way the words sounded. Perhaps she was a little superstitious. Perhaps that was a bit of the Irish in her, that came down to her from both her ma and her da's sides, or so she'd been told . . . but there was a little shiver inside of her when she heard the name of that place they were headed to. It was like she could foretell something of the future and some special part of her knew that the place was going to be important to her.

More than important to her. The Sixteen Streets was going to become her whole life.

The driver had noticed her shivering. 'Are you chilly, lass?'

It was true, the breeze was whistling in through the sides of the van. 'I'm all right,' she said tersely, not wanting to let him know she was having curious thoughts about the future. For the first time in God knew how long, she was even letting herself feel hopeful . . .

'Listen, maybe we could see about getting you warmed up somehow?' the driver said. 'That frock you've got on is like a wisp of nothing.'

She glanced out of the corner of her eye at him. 'Aye, we'll see about that,' she said, as the road opened out ahead of them. They were on their way to South Shields and not even this horrible man could spoil her mood now.

Chapter 2

She managed to escape from the Biscuit Man mostly unscathed. When they arrived by the coastal stretch north of the Tyne he pulled up to the roadside and tried to give her a bit of a kiss and a cuddle. She found him to be a puny thing though and she thought, if this one oversteps the mark too much, I could break his neck, I reckon. She shuddered as he covered her face in slobbery kisses. I'll give him a dicky heart all right, she thought.

'That's enough now,' she told him firmly.

'Oh, is it?' he chuckled, moving even closer.

'Yes,' she said, and with that she reached out and took hold of the quivering hard flesh inside his mucky trousers and gave it a sudden, sharp yank. The Biscuit Man howled and leapt away from her.

'Yer little divil!' he screamed as soon as he could get his breath back.

'There's more of that if you keep on at me,' she warned him.

'Where did you learn to hurt a man like that?' he gasped.

'I grew up on a farm,' she shrugged. 'For years I watched my Aunt Linda pulling the balls off pigs and sheep. I always knew it'd come in handy.'

The Biscuit Man stared at her like she was a monster, his

breath still coming in jagged bursts. 'I was only trying to be nice to you,' he muttered.

'It wasn't what I'd call nice,' Cathy said. 'Now look, can we get moving again? You've had your fun.'

'Fun!' he said, in a strangled voice, and moments later their journey resumed.

The next hour was spent wordlessly and the girl was glad because it allowed her to concentrate on their new surroundings. North and South Shields were dense, smoky conurbations gathered round either side of a wide harbour. The whole place stood on tall cliffs overlooking the endless, shining expanse of the North Sea. There were massive ships and cranes in the harbour, and everywhere she looked there was a profusion of rooftops and chimneys, everything crammed in closely and sending up plumes of dove grey smoke into the early evening air. There was hooting of factory horns and ships' whistles and the cries of gulls. There was noise and stuff going on everywhere she looked as the wagon's horses clip-clopped through the cobbled streets.

Cathy could feel a rising excitement in her heart. All the sadness inside her had swelled into an enormous, unbearable burden in recent weeks but now, at the sight of this town she had never been to before, that tension had cracked clean across. It had vanished in the stiff salty breeze from the sea. Here was a challenge. This was a fresh start. Now she felt like she could put her anguish behind her for a while, as she faced up to the possibility of beginning a new life.

They trundled through the darker, dingier slum streets of town, where the gutters ran with filth, and women and kids sat on doorsteps or glared out of windows at newcomers. It was like entering dark ravines where shady, unknown creatures were dwelling. Lights came on as the twilight deepened and the streets took on a more cosy, welcoming aspect, lifting the girl's heart even further.

Soon they were outside the tall iron gates belonging to Wight's Biscuit Factory. Cathy stared in wonder at the hordes of women in aprons and hats that came flooding through the gates at the end of their shift. They looked exhausted and they were covered in glittering sugar. Behind them the tall chimneys were pumping out violet smoke into the burnt orange of the sky. Cathy filled her lungs with the most wonderful, ambrosial smell. The first time she caught a whiff of the sweet buttery smells of the biscuit factory was something she would never forget.

The whiskery Biscuit Man glared at her. 'Well, this is the end of the line for you, my dear. I've got to go and get these horses stabled and whatnot. You can get out now and good luck to you.'

She gave him a surprised look. 'I thought you were going to introduce me to the bosses? Help me find a job at the factory?'

His wayward eyebrows went up. 'Are you kidding, hinny? I said I'd help you if you played your cards right. But you didn't, did you?' He glowered darkly. 'In fact, you hurt me. I think you might have done me some permanent damage there, you horrible minx.'

'Ha!' Cathy burst out. 'I'm glad! You deserve it!' She clutched up her battered carpet bag that contained absolutely everything she owned in the world. 'I don't need your help,' she told him. 'I'll make my own way. I've always had to before, and I'll manage perfectly fine on me own! So, bugger you, you scruffy old git!' And with that she jumped out of the cab and onto the cobbles at the foot of Frederick Street.

She strode away from the Biscuit Man's van and didn't look back at him once.

'You made a monkey out of me, lass!' he bellowed after her. 'You . . . you used me! You should be ashamed of yourself!'

This made her laugh. 'Aye, maybe I should be ashamed about lots of things,' she thought to herself. 'But I bloody well refuse to be!'

Her instincts told her to head up the hill. The street she was on was one of many in serried ranks overlooking the docks. Her idea was to march up this road and get to the top and from there maybe get a good high-up view of her new town. And from there? Well, then she would see what she could see and she would decide what to do with herself next. One thing at a time.

Cathy swung her carpet bag and climbed up the hill, paying close attention to all the bay windows with their sparkling white net curtains and the whitewashed doorsteps and polished front doors. Maybe these were poor folk, but they were proud, keeping the outsides of their homes immaculate.

Kids were still out playing on the street in little gaggles and they stared at her as she breezed past. There were no men to be seen, of course. Well, that was just as well. Men only caused bother for girls like Cathy.

Perhaps strangers were a rarity round here, she mused. It was the kind of place where everyone knew everyone else and a new face stood out a mile. Part of Cathy longed to live in a place like this and belong to people like that. The kind of people who looked out for you.

She was so used to the quiet of the countryside and living with just a few all too familiar faces around her. Living up on the windy hilltop, looking down onto the moorland. Hearing nothing but her aunt's mithering tones. A bit of noisy confusion and crowds would be like balm to her soul. Even hearing these rowdy kids at their games did her good. She was only a few years older than them, really. She felt like she'd missed out on that childhood bliss of having loads of pals her own age and playing out like this lot. All that time had been robbed from her.

But there was no use letting the past get her all rankled and upset. She shook her head and felt her stomach rumble. It did more than rumble. It was growling. All she'd had all day was a broken custard cream offered to her by that mucky devil in his wagon. The lovely aroma from the biscuit factory made her hunger pangs even worse. Why, she could still smell it! But there was something else, too – a fried oil smell. A chip shop smell, golden and crispy.

Ahead of her there was a short queue standing outside bright windows. 'Betty's', the sign above the shop read, and some wag had supplemented it with the scrawled epithet, 'Swetty'. Cathy laughed to herself and realised that she hardly cared how sweaty Betty might in fact be, because she was starved and a packet of chips would fill all her immediate needs splendidly.

Feeling around in her carpet bag for the purse she'd had since she was a child, she joined the queue of those waiting for an early supper. Some of them acknowledged her with a shy smile, with the same cautious curiosity that the kids had done. So they weren't unfriendly to strangers here, then. They were intrigued and polite and slightly distant. That suited Cathy fine, she thought, as she poked around in her purse, finding only dark, ancient coins. One of them was an old Queen Victoria coin, smooth to the touch.

Others were getting glistening slabs of fish in golden batter. She watched them emerging from the steamy shop with their parcels. Men and women linking arms and eating the chips straight from the paper. Cathy knew she wouldn't have enough for fish. Maybe the chips would fill her up enough, and maybe if Swetty Betty was a generous soul, she could ask her for some scraps of batter . . .

'Eeeh, hinny,' said the woman in front of her in the queue. 'You look like you're drooling! Your tongue's hanging out!'

Cathy looked down to see a tiny old woman staring up at her. She was so diminutive Cathy hadn't even noticed her there. The woman had a smile that split her weathered face in two, it was that broad. Her eyes were dark and almost hidden inside the wrinkled folds of her face. A shapeless, ancient hat was pinned to her head by a glistening hat pin and she was bundled into a monstrous fur coat that looked like it was hopping with fleas. 'Oh!' gasped the girl at the sight of her. 'I never saw you there.'

'Ha!' the old woman chuckled. 'Well, you'd do well to keep your eyes peeled round here, lass. There's all sorts round here, and they're not all as friendly as me.'

Cathy felt herself warming to this strange old soul. She found she couldn't help herself. Her voice was booming, and she was only about . . . what, four feet tall? In her ratty fur coat, she looked like she could be a hedgerow creature out of the wild. 'I'm Cathy,' Cathy said. 'I'm new round here.'

The old woman looked her up and down. 'Aye, you are, aren't you? You look like you've wandered here from another world. Are you after chips?'

'I'm absolutely starving,' Cathy admitted.

The woman stared at Cathy's skinny frame through her thin dress and tutted. 'You look like you've not been eating properly for weeks. You've not been looking after yourself, lass.'

That was true enough. Her existence in recent times had been hand-to-mouth, ever since she had lost her job at the department store and her meagre savings had run out. 'I think I've got enough for chips.'

'Betty's prices are reasonable,' said the old woman. 'My name's Mrs Sturrock, by the way. I'm well known round here – I run a boarding house in Frederick Street. Number twenty-one. It's nothing grand, but I've a room free, if you're looking for summat.'

Cathy smiled at her. 'I do need somewhere, actually. I've pitched up here with nothing, no plan, and nowhere to go. I wasn't sure what I was going to do.'

Mrs Sturrock looked scandalised. 'Whit? You're here with no family nor friends nor nowt? You've no people to go to, hinny?'

Cathy shook her head. The queue inched forward and they came closer to the warm, inviting interior of the tiled shop. Now she felt rather foolish, admitting that she was essentially homeless here in South Shields.

'Eeeh, lass,' the old woman said. 'You know, the folk here are welcoming, good people. They might be a bit rough and ready in their ways but we're all right really. So you're lucky in that way. You've fetched up in a world that's mostly friendly. But that's not to say that there aren't bad buggers here as well. We've got bad'uns here, who'll kick you when you're down. Ones who'll nab your last crust off of you. We've got evil-minded souls here, just the same as anywhere.' Her voice had taken on a rich, dark timbre that made Cathy shiver involuntarily as she bent closer to listen. But then the old lady grinned once more, revealing her scanty brown teeth and letting out a blasting reek of bathtub gin. 'Ah, but mostly they're the kindest souls you'll ever meet, round here. Believe me, you've come to the best place in the whole world. I've lived here all my life, hinny, and look what it's made of me!'

Cathy smiled at her in bemusement, and then she found they'd reached the head of the queue in Swetty Betty's fried fish emporium. Mrs Sturrock patted her hand. 'You know what? This'll be my treat, hinny. I'll buy your supper for you tonight.'

Chapter 3

Mrs Sturrock told her that the best place to eat your fish and chips on an evening like this was right at the top of the hill. There was a bench by the railings round the graveyard and from there you could see right over the whole town and all the docks spread out around you. Cathy found herself following and tagging along after the tiny old woman and felt quite content to perch beside her on the bench, amused by the way the old lady's feet didn't even reach the ground.

'Isn't it grand?' she asked the new arrival and Cathy had to admit that the view was terrific. The ships in the harbour were vast, rising above the warrens of sloping roofs like tailor's dummies stuck with pins and veils of fabric. The cranes waded through the water and stood stock-still like gigantic fishing birds biding patiently for their prey.

The air was soft and cool, with just a tang of the approaching autumn in it. Cathy loved the reek of the sea in her nostrils. She found it made her nostalgic for her childhood, when she and her ma had lived closer to the shore, before she moved to live on the farm estate at Morwick. She shook her head to clear it of nostalgic thoughts. She simply had to concentrate on her present circumstances. Dwelling on the past would only send her into gloom and despair. She blew on a hot fatty chip and crunched it hard.

'You were right. These are the best I've ever had!'

Mrs Sturrock cackled. 'Swetty Betty has a secret recipe, but round here we all say her secret is that she never ever changes the fat or cleans out her fryer. That's why everything fries so dark and delicious.'

Cathy pulled a face but found she didn't care. The fish was fresh and melting in her mouth. Her insides groaned at the taste of it. She hadn't had a proper meal in several days. 'Thanks so much for this, Mrs Strurrock,' she said, through a huge mouthful. 'You're a lifesaver.'

The old woman was studying her keenly. 'You know, I've not got a gift. Not like my old friend Winnie does. Now, she has a real and genuine gift for presentiment.'

'What's that?'

'Hm? Oh, it's what Winnie also calls prognostication. But that's just putting long words to things in order to sound grand. What she's gifted at is getting glimpses of the future. For getting a feel of how things will turn out.'

Cathy smiled. 'Well, I could do with some of that. I haven't got a clue what I'll do next.'

'Well, like I say, I don't have our Winnie's gifts,' said Mrs Sturrock modestly. 'But I do have some few talents in that direction.'

'Oh?' Cathy was only half listening, really, relishing her chips and the sharpness of the vinegar she'd lavished on them.

'And do you know what I can see?' Mrs Sturrock's eyes crinkled up as she focused her thoughts, with a chunk of cod halfway up to her mouth. 'I can see you living here for a very long time. Yes, I can see you getting to be a woman who lives right here on this hillside . . . why, most of her life, just like I have done. I think you've found your true place in the world, Cathy. That's what I see when I open my psychical eye. I see a future for you here in the Sixteen Streets.'

Cathy's own eyes went wide. 'Well! Thank you . . . I mean, that's nice to hear. I'm not sure though – this is only the first place I've fetched up. I thought about maybe going in for work at that biscuit factory down the hill . . .'

Mrs Sturrock closed her eyes again and tried to concentrate as she chewed and smacked her lips. 'Hmm, I don't see you working in the factory, no. I see . . . something different. Something more . . . glamorous! I see people looking at you, and you all dressed up.'

'Dressed up!' Cathy laughed, thinking of the ragged dress she was wearing. 'Am I going on the stage?'

Mrs Sturrock pursed her greasy lips. 'It doesn't do to mock the talents of those gifted,' she warned, and Cathy felt reprimanded. 'You'd do well to heed my words. You belong in this place, Cathy. You must give your heart and soul to the people here. Do you understand?'

Cathy shrugged. 'I don't really, no. But it's nice of you to try to read my future. Do you do tea leaves, as well? The cook in the big house where I used to . . . work, she did tea leaves but she was always wrong, every time . . .'

Mrs Sturrock glanced at her like she thought tea leaves were a very low-class kind of thing. She carried on chewing and the two of them sat like that in companionable silence, watching the skies above the docks changing colours. Then all of a sudden Mrs Sturrock was crumpling up her greasy newspaper and jumping up from the park bench. 'Righty-oh. I've made a decision about you.'

'What's that?' asked Cathy, amused by this energetic woman in the ratty fur coat.

'Well, the first thing you need is somewhere to lay your head, pet. There's no use making plans for the future if you've nowhere to live. The answer's obvious. I've got a guest house with a room to spare. You need somewhere. We'd rub along fine, wouldn't we?'

Cathy felt a surge of gratitude. 'Oh, but I've no money. I mean, not enough for rent and—'

The old woman waved her clawed hands. 'We can figure that out as we go along. You can owe me. And once you're on your feet you can pay me back. What do you say?'

The girl felt relieved that she was going to be sleeping under an actual roof tonight, but she also felt a touch of dread. She wouldn't have been able to say why. It all seemed so quick and so rash. She hardly knew anything about this strange old woman who'd treated her to supper. Now she was delivering herself up to her and placing herself at her mercy.

But it would be rude to refuse Mrs Sturrock's generously offered help. She could hardly throw it back in her wrinkled, hopeful old face.

'That's extremely kind of you,' Cathy said.

The old woman looked delighted. 'Right! Come along now! Come and see my little palace on Frederick Street!'

Then she was dashing away and Cathy was forced to follow her, crumpling up her own chip paper and shivering in a sudden chill that came wafting up from the sea.

Mrs Sturrock's was just one more door in that steep streetful of doors, except hers was the only one with dull, peeling paint. Her net curtains were the only ones Cathy had noticed that were hanging like grey rags.

'Here we are,' cawed the old lady, unlocking the door. As she opened it, they were met by a waft of stale air and a sharp whiff of cats. Cathy forced herself to put a smile on her face as she followed the furry back of her new landlady down the dingy hallway. The whole passageway was fraught with side tables laden with dusty plants and odd trinkets. Bundles of newspaper and yellowed periodicals were bundled up on the shabby carpet. Cathy found she had to watch where she was stepping in case she stumbled.

Oh, what have I let myself in for? she thought. Why did I agree to come here without seeing the place first? But even as she thought this out, she knew the answer. I'm desperate, that's why, she thought unhappily. And I didn't want to hurt this old moo's feelings . . .

Now the old moo was leading her into a back parlour, which was just as cluttered and filthy as the hallway had been. Mrs Sturrock busied herself lighting lamps, which glowed softly and did very little to improve the look of the place. Every surface was heaped with tatty old junk. Bottles and jugs and dirty plates and cutlery. Cathy's stomach roiled as she sat down where she was bidden and realised she was looking at a clump of mouse droppings on the used tea plate in front of her. 'D-do you have many guests staying here?' Cathy asked politely.

The old lady shucked off her fur coat and revealed that she was even tinier and skinnier than Cathy had imagined. 'Well, yes! Yes, usually! Usually we're overrun!' She bustled into the scullery and put the kettle on the hob. 'Eeh, I'm parched for a cup of tea after me salty chips, aren't you, pet?'

'Are you sure you've the room to put me up?' Cathy asked, hoping to find a way out of her rash commitment.

Mrs Sturrock stood in the scullery doorway, pushing aside the bead curtain and sighing. 'To be honest, pet, we're not as over-whelmed as we usually are – it's been a tough time recently. It would be a godsend to have some youthful company in the place.'

Cathy's heart sank and she felt sorry for the old dear. She was alone here, wasn't she? This whole neglected house was empty apart from her, Cathy just knew it. And now Cathy had been trapped into staying here with her . . .

Oh, but this was ridiculous. She hadn't signed anything or given her word. All she'd done is accepted a few chips. She didn't have to do what this old woman said – even if she did claim to have had a prognostication.

Mrs Sturrock returned with a tray of tea. The teapot was vast and chipped, but the aromatic heat of that brewing tea made Cathy's rebellious thoughts subside for a moment or two. She accepted a cup and saucer – both mucky – and sighed. So what was wrong with a filthy house? This woman was kind. She had opened her door to Cathy and she wasn't doing it with any ulterior, awful motivations. She wasn't after something horrible from Cathy. How could she be? All she wanted was to help a new girl in town. A girl who had arrived with nothing to her name.

I must be more grateful, Cathy told herself. Mrs Sturrock has reached out the hand of friendship. I must be gracious and kind.

Oh, but the smell of cat pee made her nose wrinkle up. She couldn't help it.

'Drink that tea and I'll show you your room,' said the old woman. 'Why, I think you could have my best room. What do you think of that? The room at the front with the big window, overlooking the street.'

'Oh, you mustn't go to any bother,' Cathy said. 'I won't take up much space!'

Mrs Sturrock laughed. 'I tell you, pet, there's no other guests. You've got the pick of three of my rooms, but that one at the front is the best. It used to be my old mammy's room, before she took bad and died up there. Oh, but that was a long, long time ago. It's been aired thoroughly since then. Why, that must be ten years since. There's been no one slept in it since then.'

The whole place was getting worse and worse by the minute. Cathy sipped her tea and was surprised to find that it was delicious. Just right. Just as sweet and as hot as she liked it. Mrs Sturrock watched her obvious enjoyment with a sly smile. 'See? You're feeling at home already.'

'I do feel a bit more relaxed, yes . . .' Cathy said. 'I can hardly believe that I've come so far in one day. All that journey in the wagon with that horrible old man. That was just this morning – we started out from Morwick.' It seemed hard to credit that so much had gone on. 'I don't think I've ever travelled so far afield in all my life!' She knew it was true. She had never been more than a mile away from the estate or the little town of Morwick ever before. Her odyssey today was like the equivalent of her suddenly travelling up to the moon.

'We'll get you settled in so you can have a good night's sleep,' Mrs Sturrock told her. 'And then tomorrow we can start to think about what the future will hold.'

Cathy smiled. Yes, tomorrow would be soon enough to think about anything as complicated as the future. 'Thank you. You've been very kind to me.'

'That's quite all right,' Mrs Sturrock said. A fleeting worried look passed across her face. 'I dunno what my son will say about it all. But never mind, I'm sure he'll be fine.'

'Your son?'

'Yes, he lives here too. Thinks he owns the place, but he doesn't. This house is mine and only mine, and what I say goes. So he can like it or lump it, but if I want to take in a new guest, then the decision is mine. Oh, he's a lovely lad my Noel, of course, but he's strong-willed. He knows his own mind, but by hell I'll make him accept you as a guest, and even like you! You, my pet, are staying, and that's an end to the matter. So, drink up, and let's get you settled.'

Cathy gave her a sickly smile and found that all her misgivings were coming back. She swallowed them down firmly. I'm just going to have to be brave, she told herself. I've been brave this far. I've just got to keep going, whatever life throws at me . . .

Chapter 4

The bed felt damp and clammy, whatever Mrs Sturrock had said about airing the room. Cathy tried her very best not to mind, bundling herself up in the ancient bedlinen and seeking solace in sleep. At least no one besides her new benefactress knew she was here. No one else in the world had a clue where Cathy had ended up. There was a lovely feeling of liberation in that.

For the first time in my life, I'm actually free, she thought.

But the idea of no one depending on her, and there being no one for her to confide in, almost brought on the wave of sorrowful tears she had been fending off for weeks. No, she had to be strong. She had to keep all her feelings at bay. And she had to do her very best with this new hand she had been dealt.

She tried her best to sleep in the unfamiliar bedroom, with cats scratching at the bedroom door. She didn't even know how many cats Mrs Sturrock had, but it sounded like an army of them, sharpening their claws on the woodwork. Perhaps they were used to getting into this room and sleeping on the bed? There was certainly a rank whiff of cats in the room. Well, while Cathy was staying here, they'd just have to keep out.

Their plaintive cries and endless scratching went on into the night . . .

What was she going to do? She had no money and no ideas yet about how to make some. Already she was beholden to old Mrs Sturrock. She had fallen on the mercy of a stranger.

But the old dear seemed kind and benign enough. That was something, at least. Cathy wasn't used to kindness. She was more accustomed to the tight-lipped forthrightness of superiors telling her what to do. She was used to the emotional wrangles and blackmailing of her Aunt Linda. She still felt wounded from the way her aunt had betrayed her. It was something she would never, ever be able to forget . . .

Shivering on the damp sheets Cathy fell asleep at last, some time after eleven, but was then disturbed some time later by noise coming from the street. A pub on the other side of Frederick Street was spilling its rowdy occupants. Out they came tumbling after a late lock-in, sprawling and rolling in the street. They didn't care about the women factory workers trying to get their much-needed sleep. They shouted up at darkened windows and sang raucously as they went off down the hill. They sounded like older men, those exempt from the call-up. Old drunken sots. Cathy groaned and sat up, disturbed by the noise.

And her heart knocked loudly in her chest when she heard a key in the door downstairs.

Noel Sturrock didn't often fall in love. He was grudging and careful with his affections. He was careful to protect himself. He knew that the world was cruel and wicked, and that women were skilled at twisting and conniving at your feelings. It was better to keep out of that rat race of love completely. He'd been bitten once or twice in his thirty-eight years and no thank you, he wasn't ready for all that again.

That night he came back after a late one at the pub and he felt full of hell. It hadn't been a big night. It had just been a few of the old regulars staying back. A few games of cards. A few laughs. Just the familiar faces. He wouldn't say they were friends of his, especially. He'd just known them all for years. As a landlord of a licensed premises, he now had the kind of status amongst his fellow men that he felt he had always deserved. Look at the rest of them – labourers, they had been. Now they were mostly retired or they were wounded and had been shipped back from the front. He had risen to a different kind of sphere and was keen to let them know it. His largesse, it was, that let them stay drinking after licensed hours. He sat at his bar in the Robin Hood and watched these fellows getting sloshed and he could think, aye, I'm better than the lot of you all put together. And now you know it.

Noel Sturrock had laboured through much of his life with a raging sense of his own self-worth and ego. He knew that he was better than the world he had been born into. He knew he was only here because of some dreadful cosmic mistake. And at the same time he was cursed with several defects which, though they had saved him from going to war, had blighted his life. He was stooped with a curved spine. His mother had had him looked at when he was a child, when it wasn't so bad, but nothing had been done. Nothing could be done. He just had to put up with it. 'We all have our crosses to bear, Noel,' she had told him so many times over the years.

Sometimes he really hated her. That dirty old woman who he was so dependent upon. That mucky, lazy old slut. It was because of her that he had everything wrong with him. His height! That was all down to her, too. His dad – who he'd never clapped eyes on – was reputed to be a giant. A fine, fully grown man. But his mam was a dwarf and so was Noel Sturrock. Well, not an actual dwarf, but near enough. He felt like he was glaring up at everyone in fury and resentment. Like he'd lived his whole life in their shadows and in the shadows of the houses that the sun hardly touched here in the Sixteen Streets.

So on this night when, for some reason, he couldn't even manage to get himself drunk on the rotgut whisky he loved to sit sipping at his very own bar, he was in a worse mood even than usual. He swayed only slightly as he let himself into the stinking hallway of number twenty-one. The catty smell assaulted his sensitive nostrils afresh and he cursed his mucky mother out loud. Some days he fantasised about getting all her cats and shoving them into a burlap sack, tying it up with tarred rope and chucking them into the River Tyne. Ha! Maybe it wouldn't need a much bigger sack to stuff his old mother in there with them too? And then they could all go down together, screaming and clawing at each other, down into the drink?

These ghoulish thoughts cheered him as he slammed the front door and staggered down the passage. He wondered if the old cow had left him something to eat under a plate, in the oven? He bet she hadn't even bothered. There was bad blood between the two of them recently. They'd had some awful rows. She'd been refusing to cook for him most nights, saying that he didn't appreciate it when she did. Well, that was true enough. Her cooking was rank and inedible. But right now he was starving. He'd eat anything she might have left out.

But there was nothing in the scullery or the parlour. Not even a still-warm pot of tea with a few dregs left. He hunted around for a scrap of bread. He found a stale crust and gave the fry pan a quick wipe, knowing it would still be encrusted with grease. Yes, perfect. Disgusting but perfectly delicious. Noel stood in the scullery and hated his life all over again. What was he doing? What was he eating? He slurped water from the tap. God, those cats of hers ate better than he ever did. They got better attention and affection than he'd ever had from anyone.

He stumped into the hall and up the stairs. He was noisy and clumsy, traipsing like Frankenstein's Monster on the stair carpet but what did he care? His old mother would sleep through anything. She'd be under all her covers with her nasty old coat on top for extra warmth. She'd have her woolly hat on and she'd be dead to the world. He could be as noisy as he liked and she'd not come out and say hullo and goodnight and was he all right. She couldn't care less if he came home safely or not.

Noel was at the peak of his despair as he reached the top stair of the first landing and that's when he had his vision. That's where, against all his instincts and his bitter wisdom, he fell in love. It was something he would never have believed was possible, not that night or in any of the years that followed. But it was true. Something lifted inside his chest. When that door on the landing opened and out stepped a figure he had never seen before, something very strange happened to Noel Sturrock. It was like the coming of the first touch of spring to a cold and frosty garden. It was as if a window had opened in his skinny chest and let some warmth and light inside, kindling his frozen heart.

The cats scattered, disturbed by the humans. Some of them darted into the bedroom, scrambling out of the way.

He stared at Cathy Carmichael in that doorway of what had once been his old nanna's bedroom and he fell in love at first sight.

Not that Noel wasn't terrified, too, at this weird apparition in the moonlight spilling through the bay window.

'W-who are you?' he asked her. 'What are you doing here?'

He wanted to sound furious. He needed to sound outraged. Who the devil was this, floating about his home in what seemed to be an old Victorian nightgown? Her long hair was hanging down, looking like she'd been laying on it, tossing and turning all night. Her face was bleary with being half asleep and she looked just as shocked at the sight of Noel as he was himself at the vision of her.

But he was the one who was supposed to be here! He reminded himself of this. This house was his place in the world. He had every right to come home as late as he liked, pie-eyed if he pleased. He should be able to come in and not expect to be scared out of his wits by . . . by . . .

'I'm sorry,' she said. Her voice was wonderfully warm and deep for a young woman. Contralto, the word popped into his head from nowhere.

'Who are you?' he repeated.

'The old lady let me have a room,' she said, jutting out her jaw defiantly and holding onto the doorframe. 'She said it would be all right if I stayed. I had nowhere else. I'm new round here.'

Noel simply stared at her. 'Why are you wearing one of my granny's old nightgowns?'

'The old woman said it would be all right. I didn't have anything of my own . . .'

Noel growled at her, 'That old woman you keep referring to is my mother, Mrs Sturrock. You should be more respectful.'

'Oh, I am!' gasped Cathy. 'I am. And I'm so grateful to her . . .'

She was beautiful. Noel was saying words and not really listening to himself. He was barking questions at her like he was in command of himself and the situation. But he gripped onto the banister and, despite the cold, his hands felt sweaty. He was slipping. His resolve was melting away. He stared at her and tried to fathom out why her face seemed so familiar to him. Why did it seem so right that she should be here tonight? A weird and lovely spectre in a Victorian nightdress? Part of his cankered soul was rebelling inside and wanted to

27

throw her out on the street. How dare she spring out on him like this and turn everything upside down?

Because that's how everything was now, for Noel Sturrock, proud landlord of the Robin Hood public house.

Everything was upside down and he was hopelessly, bewilderedly in love for the first time. And it made him feel as sick as a dog.

'I'm Cathy Carmichael,' she told him. 'And I take it you're Mrs Sturrock's son that she told me about?'

The girl seemed much more confident, all of a sudden. He almost resented her for the calm in her voice and the way she introduced herself. No stammering, no quavering. She behaved like she wasn't frightened or unnerved one tiny bit, talking to a stranger on the stairs. Noel envied her this poise she was demonstrating, even as he admired it. Even as he craved it. He stared at her long, long legs. He stared up at the huge height of her and he found that he could hardly breathe.

'Just don't be noisy and don't be a nuisance,' he snapped. 'And just you stay out of my way! My mother never said she was taking in waifs and strays again. Bloody old witch! Flaming strange women!'

He hurried past her and thundered up the second flight of stairs, to his attic room, where he flung himself down upon his unmade bed and sobbed like a baby, knowing something huge had happened to him tonight. And he knew that he was going to have a hard time coping with it.

He was in love with Cathy and how he hated her for it.

Chapter 5

'Ah, here she is, look! My new little lodger.'

Cathy was met the next morning in the parlour by this welcoming shout from Mrs Sturrock, plus the avid stares of three old biddies sitting round the table. She had tried to comb out her long, tangled tresses and she was still in her antique nightgown. What she really wanted was a bath, but she wasn't sure what the arrangements were in this house. Presumably it would be a tin bath in front of the fire, but she'd have to ask Mrs Sturrock about how and when the water was available. There was so much Cathy didn't know about her new surroundings.

Now she was confronted by these woman peering at her as she stepped into the room. They weren't all as old as Mrs Sturrock, she realised. One of them was even quite young. They had teacups in front of them and this was clearly a regular meet-up to discuss the pressing matters of the day. Today Cathy was one of those matters: the new arrival in the Sturrock household.

'Well, she's a bonnie thing,' said the oldest of the women. 'That's true enough.' She spoke as if Cathy couldn't hear her.

'Isn't she just?' smiled Mrs Sturrock, as if taking credit for her new lodger's beauty.

'But where did she come from?' asked the youngest of the tea-drinkers. 'Did you get any sense out of her?'

Cathy frowned. 'Erm . . . I can actually talk for myself, you know. I'm not daft.'

Her landlady cackled at this and bade her sit down, pouring her a cuppa out of the giant brown teapot. 'Eeeh, I like that! She speaks up for herself, even to her elders. Now Cathy, these are my best friends from the street. This is Margaret, and that's Winnie and this young'un is Ada. They're a funny-looking bunch, but they're nice enough. I'd keep on the right side of them if I were you. Friends are what you'll be needing, having turned up with nowt to your name. No money nor clothes nor anything.'

'What?' gasped the woman called Ada. She was the youngest of the gaggle, care-worn and dumpy-looking. Her hair was scraped back into a bun in a practical style, making her look older than her years. She was very buxom, and she pulled her cardigan tight over her breasts as if she felt self-conscious. 'That can't be right! You really arrived here with nothing at all, hinny?' She sounded genuinely concerned. 'Well, I'm sure we can rally round and get you some clothes and stuff for your immediate needs, can't we, ladies? But tell us . . . how the divil do you come to end up with nothing at all like this? And how come you've ended up here?'

So Cathy sat in her borrowed nightdress, cradling her hot cup of tea in her hands, and told them her tale. She had decided on a certain, truncated version of the truth that she would tell anyone interested or nosy enough to ask for it.

'Oh, I used to be in service, when I was a kid. Morwick Hall, have you heard of it? In Northumberland. But then they were getting rid of staff because of the war . . . and I had to leave to find work in Morwick Town. I was at the new department store there for a few months and I quite liked it, but then I was getting bullied and I lost that job. So I made a decision, about heading south. I decided that I would aim for the bright lights of Tyneside, and I would try my luck there . . .'

'The bright lights of Tyneside!' laughed the oldest of them, Margaret. 'I think you mean Newcastle, pet. Not round here! There's not much that's bright round here.'

Cathy explained, 'I got a lift from a fella with a wagon and he was going to the biscuit factory. That's how I ended up here. From what he said, it sounded like a friendly and a decent kind of place.'

Mrs Sturrock frowned. 'Aye, well he was right enough with that. You'll be better off flinging yourself on the mercy of the Sixteen Streets than old Newcastle. The big city can be a frightening, heartless place. I've been there once and I didn't like it much.'

Ada asked, 'So what do you think you'll do with yourself now that you're here?'

Cathy felt helpless, but she sat up straight and jutted out her chin defiantly. 'I'll find something I'm good at, I suppose. It's about time I did.'

Winnie – who had colourless wispy hair and a vague expression – flapped a bony hand at the girl. 'Hurry and drink up your tea. I'll take a look at the leaves for you.'

When Cathy did, the woman who was famous for her fortune-telling peered at the dregs for several moments before letting out an excited gasp. 'Oh! It's not going to be easy. It won't be very easy at all. But I think you're going to like living here, Cathy Carmichael. I think you've come to exactly the right place.'

'Will I find my fortune?' the girl laughed.

'No,' said Winnie. 'And you won't find happiness . . . at least not at first. But I can tell you something here and now – you'll never be bored. Things are going to happen for you, Cathy. This is where your life truly begins.'

31

Cathy noticed Mrs Sturrock rolling her eyes at the dramatic way Winnie was carrying on. Later she told her new lodger, 'Pay no heed to Winnie. She gets daft with her psychical readings. They rarely come true.'

Cathy smiled. 'But I like the idea of my life beginning at last . . . and things happening to me! I love the sound of a bit of drama . . .'

Mrs Sturrock shuddered. 'Don't go wishing for drama. Not round here. You might get more than you bargained for, pet.'

Before that first morning was over, the short and dumpy Ada Farley from number thirteen had arranged to gather up a bagful of clothing from the local women. 'Eeeh, it's very good of you, pet,' Mrs Sturrock told her. 'You're busy enough with your three lads to look after and that husband of yours to see to.'

Ada scowled at the mention of her wayward husband. She was clutching a bundle of laundry to her chest and beaming at Cathy. 'Look, needs must. This lass can't even go out till she's dressed properly.' Ada was secretly keen to know what circumstances led to a girl leaving her home town without any belongings to her name, but now wasn't the time to go probing further.

Sorting through the bagful of jumble that now littered the dining table, Cathy was polite and enthusiastic in her thanks. Inside she was mortified by the charitable actions of her new friends. At least the clothes seemed clean, even if they were old and baggy and worn. Ancient combinations and bloomers that came out of Queen Victoria's day, by the looks of it. Thick woollen socks and gloves and a hand-knitted fisherman's jumper. 'Oh, but this is beautiful,' she said, reaching for a fine woollen shawl.

'Ah, that's my own contribution to the effort,' said Ada Farley, ducking her head modestly. 'I thought it would be nice for you to have something that was actually pretty as well as warm and useful.'

Cathy had never worn anything as splendid as this shawl. 'But it must be worth something . . .'

Ada shook her head. 'Never you mind, hinny. You just wear it with my good wishes.' Then, all of a sudden, she was gone.

'She's good-hearted, Ada Farley,' Mrs Sturrock commented. 'Worn to a frazzle by those noisy boys of hers, of course, and older than her years because of the life her drunken husband gives her . . . Have you seen the lines on her face? The poor thing. But y'knaa, she's one of the best souls you'll ever meet round here.'

Cathy put the shawl around her shoulders and relished its warmth and softness. It felt rather like getting a hug from one of these terse and reserved women. It was really the next best thing.

Mrs Sturrock urged Cathy to be slightly less formal, and to call her by her given name, Teresa. 'I already feel like you're part of the household,' the old woman smiled up at her as they ambled along the seafront.

This was later on that first full day in South Shields, when Cathy had dressed herself in a long cotton dress that was the colour of pale coffee. It had been in the bundle of donations and fitted her almost perfectly. She put on a pair of old, worn wooden clogs that she found surprisingly comfortable, and she tugged the shawl around her shoulders. The scent of the wool filled up her senses: a compound of woodsmoke and some kind of floral perfume. It was a homely scent that made Cathy's heart ache vaguely inside her chest. 'I like your friends,' she told Teresa Sturrock as they strolled along past the Marine Park at the bottom of Ocean Road.

'Ah, they're a fine lot,' Teresa smiled. 'We've seen each other through a lot of bother over the years. We've had all sorts going on. And it's been a tough few years, with the hostilities and all. And all us women have had to take a lead in things and keep the old place going, what with the men being away. Some of them who've come back are in no fit state to do anything anymore . . .'

Cathy nodded. Up in Northumberland the war in France had seemed so distant. They heard details from the papers and, of course, all the young men upped and left, some never to return. And there was the terrible impact that it had on the family that belonged to Morwick Hall of course . . . Cathy shook her head and took in deep lungfuls of fresh sea air. No, it really wasn't the time to go roving over all that past history now – the war to end all wars was over at last. It had been over for some time. And so was her life up in Morwick. She must do her best to forget all that had gone on there – and everyone who still lived there.

'Eeeh, lass,' Teresa chortled. 'Sometimes you've got such a faraway look. I think you must be a proper dreamer.'

'Not really,' Cathy shook her head, and her long dark hair streamed out around her. 'I'm very practical, really. I get on with what needs doing right now. I find it's best to leave hopes and fears and dreams all to one side. They never really come true, do they? We're best off concentrating on what we can do about the here and now . . .'

The old woman considered this as they walked and she carried on pointing out places of local interest. The beach and the fair. The boating lake in the park. The tall houses where the grand folk lived. The new ice-cream parlour that had opened up quite recently, where folk said the coffee was out of this world . . .

'Tell you what, I'll teach you to tie that hair of yours up in a fancy chignon, like mine,' said Teresa. 'You've got it blowing around your face like you live in the wild!'

Cathy laughed. 'That's where I'm from! Why, I come from the wild! I come from the moors and Northumberland coast.

I've told you that. Maybe I'm just wild in my soul, eh?' She spread out her arms and twirled about in the street, flaring her new shawl and enjoying the tug of the sea breeze.

'That's no good round here,' said the old woman. 'Specially if you're looking for work, as I suppose you'll be. You've got to look tidy, pet.'

Cathy composed herself. 'I know . . . You're right, Teresa.'

Teresa Sturrock looked gratified that the girl remembered to use her name. It was a bit like having a lovely daughter-in-law. That's what this felt like, this past couple of days. Teresa had been making believe that her poor son had actually managed to snag a girl as lovely and as vital as this one.

This thought reminded the old woman of something she had been meaning to say all day . . .

'Ah, pet. I saw my lad this morning. Before he went over the road to the Robin Hood. He told me he bumped into you last night on the landing when he came in. He said you gave him quite a turn.'

The girl felt herself flushing. She felt chastened and embarrassed by the memory of the encounter. 'I think he thought I was a ghost. I gave him a shock. In that nightgown . . . I think he believed I was a phantom standing there in the moonlight!'

'Well, he's very superstitious, is Noel,' Teresa sighed. 'When he was little I told him I named him Noel on account of how he came to me on Christmas Day. I tell him that Father Christmas left him in the fireplace and he's like a kind of wonderful pixie . . .'

Cathy laughed. 'Well, he can't still believe that!'

Teresa smiled uncertainly. 'I think he feels very different to everyone else. That's just him, though. That's the man he's grown up to be. He treats himself like he's something very special indeed, as well he might. Sometimes I think he really does believe that he was delivered to me by magic!'

When Cathy thought back to that figure that night – all stoop-shouldered and fearsome-browed – the only magical being she thought he looked like was a troll, or a wicked dwarf. Of course she didn't say as much to his mother.

'Anyhow,' Teresa went on, smiling, 'I think he's rather taken with you, Cathy girl. When I saw him this morning, on his way out to meet the brewery man, he couldn't talk about anything else . . .'

'He was talking about me?' Cathy asked uneasily.

'I think he's properly . . . what's the word?' Teresa chuckled. 'Smitten! That's it! I think my lad is smitten by you, hinny. So just you watch out!'

Chapter 6

The Robin Hood had been in business for many years. It was like a beacon at the top of Frederick Street. Many of the individual Sixteen Streets could boast of having their own public house, but the Robin Hood was known as the grandest and the best.

Cathy wasn't sure what to expect when she first stepped in through the front doors, at the landlord's invitation. The windows were all pebbled glass, so all that could be seen from outside was warm lights, flickering firelight and moving shadows. A great gabble of noise and raucous piano music came drifting out each time the door swung open.

'Oh, that's Aunty Martha on the piano,' old Teresa Sturrock laughed as they passed by the tawny glowing windows one evening. 'She's been banging away on that old piano since she was a bairn. I don't know why we all call her Aunty; mind, she's nobbut thirty years old.'

It turned out that many of the women in the nearby streets were known as Aunty to all their neighbours, as if everyone was connected in one all-encompassing family who knew each other's business.

Early Friday evening, as if lulled by the vamping piano music, Cathy went across the road in her new best frock and stepped inside the doors of the Robin Hood for the very first time – it was into a thick fug of tobacco smoke and a wall of noise. Male chatter and laughter assailed her ears. She squinted through the gloom, her eyes stinging, and tried to locate the landlord. It was his invite, after all, that she was accepting by coming over here.

'Oh, it'll mean so much to him,' the old woman had sighed. 'I told you, pet. He was smitten with you the first second he clapped eyes on you, no matter how grumpy he seems. Now he'll want to show off to you. He'll want you to see his precious kingdom over the road. He'll want to show you off, too, to his cronies and mates he always has propping up the bar.'

She wasn't all that keen, but Cathy found herself drawn across the road and into the smoky, boisterous bar. She had never really been inside a public house before. It was strange to think, but her life so far had never taken her into such places. The only time she had lived near a saloon bar was in Morwick, but she'd had no friends and no one to go with. Her hours at the shop had been so long anyway she couldn't even think of going out. And besides, such places were the preserve of men. A woman going in alone would be bound to raise eyebrows and draw attention. And so it had been easy never to go near these sort of places.

Now though, as she gathered her courage and moved through the crowded bar, Cathy felt her spirits lifting up. Maybe it was the warmth and the flickering light and the ragged singing that accompanied Aunty Martha's playing. Maybe it was the cheery rough and readiness of the place. But something in her responded to it all. All at once she was startled to feel herself feeling somewhat at home here at the Robin Hood.

The barmaid wasn't very friendly towards her, however. She was a beefy woman with teeth that stuck out and a dress that her bosoms were spilling out of. She was called Ellie and she dominated the whole of the bar, barely moving from the spot as she wielded pint pots and tankards. It was as if she was possessed of eight arms like a gigantic squid dredged up from the harbour, hefting the beer pumps up and down with great expertise. When she caught sight of Cathy, her elaborately painted eyes narrowed suspiciously.

'You're the new girl His Nibs was talking about, aren't you?' she bellowed at the girl.

Cathy flushed with embarrassment. 'Oh! I suppose so . . . I'm staying with the Sturrocks and Noel mentioned that there might be a—'

'Ooh, Noel, is it!' the barmaid laughed sardonically. 'It took me five years to be invited to use his Christian name. That old hobgoblin!'

Already Cathy felt that she had done something wrong. She had been too familiar. She had said the wrong thing. 'H-he just said that you were needing some help over here . . .' She felt shamed as Ellie the barmaid glared at her, up and down, as if examining every portion of her and finding her wanting.

'By, there's nothing to you,' was her conclusion. 'You've gotta be tough, working in a place like this. It's not very genteel, you know. They'll be pawing at you and grabbing at you as you try to go about your business. You'll have to learn how to fend the buggers off.'

Cathy lifted up her chin determinedly, gritting her teeth. 'I can do that.'

'Well,' said the barmaid doubtfully. 'We'll see how you get on. We'll keep you busy scrubbing and tidying. Bottle washing and collecting glasses. We'll try to keep you out of trouble.'

There was a hint of kindness creeping into her bellicose tone, and Cathy was glad of it. Their conversation had attracted the attention of some of the older men who were standing, slurping their pints of dark ale at the bar. They were studying Cathy with open appreciation.

'New barmaid, is it, Ellie?' asked one old guy, chuckling.

'She's just here to wash the bottles and pots,' Ellie glared at him. 'So just you pop your eyes back into your head, Frank Farley. And I'm the only barmaid you'll get to stare at round here, remember. I'm not planning on budging up for anyone!'

I thought I was only here to have a look at the place, Cathy thought to herself as she scrubbed at the pots and glasses in the galley out back. She was surrounded by a million things that needed washing. The water in the old stone sink was dark grey and the suds were thin and greasy. She felt like she had been shanghaied into menial work at the back of the pub. Ellie had bossed her about, slinging an apron at her to cover her clothes and setting her straight to work.

Cathy found herself getting on with the task she had been set, without complaint. Perhaps this is what Noel Sturrock had meant for her to do. She was due to start paying back some of what she owed them for being given a room. Part of her was glad to get stuck in, doing some actual work to pay her way.

Mind, the glasses weren't getting any cleaner as she scrubbed and rinsed and plunged them back into the scummy water. The hopsy smell of stale beer was making her feel a little nauseous too.

Then all of a sudden the landlord was standing in the doorway of the galley screeching at her. 'What the divil do you think you're doing?'

She jumped and stammered back, 'E-Ellie said I'd best get on with some work . . .'

'Ellie!' Noel cursed and spat on the mucky tiled floor. 'That one! I wouldn't listen to a word she ever says, pet.'

Cathy took her hands out of the lukewarm slop and felt relieved. 'You mean you didn't expect me to be washing the pots?'

'Actually, it's not a bad idea.' He pulled a face. 'We could do with an extra pair of hands. That busty old mare just stands out front batting her eyelashes at all the old gaffers and she barely does a stroke. But honestly, I'd rather put you out front than her, pet. Where everyone can see you!'

Suddenly he was all smiles. His shaggy eyebrows lifted up and his craggy smile filled his whole face, making him look for a moment rather like his elderly mum. Cathy returned that smile, suppressing a shudder. Really, Sturrock looked much more hideous in the daytime than he had on the landing where she had first spied him. But at least his tone was kindly today and he was bestowing a smile on her. That first encounter had made Cathy think he was crazy.

She wiped her hands on a filthy dishcloth and said, 'It's a really lovely public house. I wasn't sure what to expect, but there's something nice about it. I think it's welcoming.'

Now the landlord looked delighted. 'Do you really think so, pet? It's not everyone who does. Mother says it's a rough and ready sort of place and most of the women round here won't even step foot through the doors. But we've not had any fights or barnies for a few weeks, as it happens. It's all been very respectable.'

She accompanied him back into the saloon, where the little man made a great show of installing her in a seat by the blazing hearth. The drinkers took some notice of her, and Sturrock was flattered to see them taking note. He felt like he was putting on display some grand new possession that would do him great honour. Just look at her sat there, with that flawless complexion. Even reeking of soupy scummy water and beer slops from the back room she was like a goddess sitting there!

From the bar Ellie was glaring jealously at the fuss Sturrock was making. He took joyful note of her irritation. Well, Ellie had her chance with him a year or more ago, the landlord reflected. He had offered her his all and she had laughed in his face. She had scorned him. 'You? You can't be serious?' And he'd been so mortified by her shock and horror that he had back-pedalled quickly. 'Oh, yes, yes, of course, I'm joking, pet. I just thought I'd see what you'd say! Of course I don't mean it. How daft, eh? A big strapping girl like you . . . and me!'

Ellie had stared at him suspiciously – this was during closing time on Christmas Eve the year before last – and she saw that his proposal had been completely in earnest. She bit her lip and felt her heart crumbling softly in her chest. Oh, she had dashed his hopes in an instant. She had crushed him without even thinking about it. And, if she had considered things for half a moment more she might have boxed a bit more cleverly. Ellie would have forced herself to gird her loins and to think about the future. She would have made herself at least look as if she was flattered by his words and was thinking them over. No, instead she had laughed and spurned him on the spot. His feelings for her had died in a flash and all she'd felt since was his smouldering resentment. They'd had all this time since, months and months of working together and she had sensed every day that he was hating the sight of her. His loathing was much stronger than his love had ever been.

Now here was this young usurper. This lass who had landed out of nowhere. Younger than Ellie and so much more bonny than the barmaid had ever been. All at once Ellie could see the way this was going to go.

But I'm not about to leave, she thought. I'm on a cushy number, here at the Robin Hood. I'm not making way just because the landlord's got himself a new bit of stuff. Because that's what she is, isn't she? He's clearly found someone who can stomach the sight of him . . . Ellie stared in fascination as she kept on pouring endless pints of stout and ale, trying to picture that skinny old hunchback making love to this willowy stranger from the north. How could the lass even bear it?

Cathy knew she was being studied and scrutinised – not just by Ellie, but by all the men in the bar, too – and she found that she didn't really mind. Let them look! she thought. I've got nothing to hide. Then she thought again: oh, but I do indeed have things to hide, don't I? Things that I never want people here in my new home to know about me . . .

She took a long sip of the dark, delicious milk stout Sturrock had brought her from the bar. Well, I must conceal all that I don't want my new neighbours and friends to know about me. I must push it all to the back of my mind. There's no need for anyone to learn things that I don't want them to. No need at all!

She sat back and felt that blazing warmth of the fire and relished it. She found herself smiling. Sturrock caught her eye and smiled hopefully back at her.

This is the start of my new life, Cathy thought. This is day one and everything before this can stay lost in the past and in the shadows. Now I've got nothing to be ashamed of and nothing to hide. Let them all stare at me and I'll just grin back. I'm as good as the rest of them all put together! I've got bugger all to be ashamed of, and my whole life ahead of me!

She finished her drink and Noel Sturrock darted forth to take her empty glass. 'How about another?' he smiled.

Chapter 7

The early days of Cathy's stay at number twenty-one Frederick Street went by quite contentedly and she was more surprised than anyone. Even the chaotic mess of the house stopped bothering her after a little while and, in order to keep herself busy, she set to work cleaning and tidying everything she could lay her hands on.

'But you don't mind, do you?' she asked Teresa Sturrock first. 'If I go interfering with all your precious things?'

Teresa threw up her hands and laughed. 'Are you joking? Of course I don't care! Get cleaning, girl!'

All the tricks of the trade she had learned in service at Morwick Hall came in useful. She crumpled up balls of old newspaper (there were plenty lying about) and soaked them in white vinegar in order to remove the filthy streaks from all the windows. Up went the sashes for the first time in years and Cathy straddled window sills, hanging out over the street, scrubbing away at the glass in order to make every inch of the panes shine brightly. She set the grey net curtains to steep in bowls of detergent and the old woman gasped to see how white they turned. 'It's like flamin' magic! Who'd have thought it!'

Neighbours came out to see all this palaver. Look at the new, bonny lass cleaning up Ma Sturrock's midden! Here she comes now look, with her hair all tied up in a cloth, dragging boxes of unwanted tat into the street. Here she is smacking a huge feather duster against the side of the house, sending up smoke signals of ancient dust.

Teresa Sturrock propped herself up on her neighbour's outside wall, sipping tea and smoking woodbines, pleased to let the lass get on with it. Her neighbour was a widow called Mrs Patterson, a skinny, unhappy creature who had lost both her grown-up sons at the start of the war. The lads had signed up the first day they could and set off singing and marching with loads of the other eager recruits. Arriving in France they had been killed within a matter of days. Jillian Patterson had never been the same since. She barely said a word to anyone, but here she was sharing a cuppa with Teresa and watching on as Cathy dashed in and out of that house, lugging furniture and emptying her dustpan.

'She must be like a breath of fresh air round yours,' Jillian said. 'Top up for your tea, hinny?' She had brought a tray with a freshly refilled teapot. Sitting there with curls of steam coming off their mugs on a sparkling autumn day was like a tonic for the two of them, as was watching someone else doing all the work.

'Aye, my poor old house won't know what's hit it,' Teresa chuckled. 'Look at all them bloomin' hats!' Now Cathy had brought out armloads of hats – some dating back to the years before the turn of the century – and was bashing them against the wall to get plumes of dust out. They had all been shoved away in a cupboard in the downstairs hall and it did Teresa's heart good to see them all again. 'All my hats! I used to be right proud of them!'

'Aye, you did, pet. We often used to remark on Mrs Sturrock and her hats, coming down the street. What's she got on today, my Arthur used to say.'

Cathy was indefatigable. Out came all the loose rugs and she hung them on the low wall in front of the bay window. She gave them a thrashing with an antique carpet beater, until clouds of muck went rolling over the brow of the hill.

'What do you think about the Armistice then?' Jillian Patterson asked her neighbour. 'Do you think that'll really be an end to it all?'

'The what, pet?' Teresa hadn't been keeping up with the news at all. She rarely did at the best of times, but lately her mind had been elsewhere again.

'The end of the hostilities, man!' Jillian gasped. 'I can't believe you've not been listening to your radio or reading the paper . . .'

'Ah, I don't go in much for all of that,' Teresa shrugged, pulling her housecoat tighter about her chest as a chill wind swept up Frederick Street. 'All that war news was so complicated, I never really understood what was going on. And it was always so sad. Well, you understand that more than anyone. So I just stopped listening, I suppose . . .'

'But you must have heard all the hullabaloo and the cheering and all, when they said that the war is gonna be over?'

'Ah, but they said that before, didn't they? They said it'd be over and done by the first Christmas. Four years ago, that was!'

Jillian looked firm. 'Nay, this time it's over. It's really over. The Germans are done. It's the Armistice, pet. It's the end of it at last.'

There was a new sense of hope in the denizens of the Sixteen Streets. Teresa Sturrock could feel it in the air, just as tangible as all the gritty dust clouds that her lodger had beaten out of her rugs and cushions.

As the old woman made her way about the town, carrying out her usual visits and chores, she could feel that happier mood taking over everyone she met. She could feel them looking to the start of the next year with an optimism they hadn't let themselves feel for such a long time.

'Can it really be?' she asked her son. 'Is it really the end of it, do you think?'

Noel kept abreast with developments much more than his mother did. Working at the bar gave him time to stand there with the *Shields Gazette* and to overhear what the drinking men were saying each day as they jawed and chewed over global events. 'Aye, I do,' he said. 'All the servicemen are starting to come back. Well, the ones who've come through it alive. Things will be changing here, and it won't all be wonderful. I've seen a few of the lads already and you wouldn't recognise them. Young lads with arms shot off, legs missing, horrible scars and lumps out of them. We've had a few come into the pub already.'

'Oh, how horrible,' Teresa said. 'I'm glad you were unfit for service.'

Noel laughed bitterly. 'Too old, too infirm. Too broken before I even started!' His voice was harsh. 'Not that I mind being left out of all that. What was the point of it all, eh? All that destruction and all those young lives. And what's it gained anyone?'

They were out, walking down Fowler Street on a busy Saturday afternoon. Teresa – sporting an old, favourite plant pot-shaped hat – was embarrassed by her son's caustic words and tried to shush him. 'You mustn't say such things. It's the war! Sacrifices have to be made . . . for the sake of the country and . . .'

He sneered up at his mother. 'You know what I'd do? I'd get all the generals and high-up officers and the dukes and the queens and the kings. And I'd put the whole bloody lot of them on the battlefield. I'd give them all the guns and bombs and knives and I'd set them on each other. I would!'

47

His voice was getting louder as he loped along the high street, and his mother rolled her eyes and wished he would pipe down. 'Oh, you talk such rot. You always did . . .'

'I'd let those buggers fight it out for themselves, whatever beef they have with each other. Then all the ordinary lads could just stay at home, getting on peacefully with their lives. And meanwhile all the kings and dukes and what-have-you can just bloody well do each other in.'

'Eeeh, our Noel,' said his mother. 'You do come out with some terrible things.'

He scowled at her. She never really understood a word he said. Part of the reason for that was that she only ever half listened to him. As she scooted along in that tatty old rabbit fur coat of hers, she was more bothered about the people passing by and what they must think of her mouthy, embarrassing, crook-backed son. It had always been the way, and as a result Noel had deliberately made himself noisier and more obnoxious over the years.

'Well, that's world peace sorted out, then,' he snickered. 'They should put me in charge, shouldn't they?'

'You!' she laughed. 'I dread to think what the world would be like then.'

He pulled a face. 'We'll never know, will we? No one outside of the Sixteen Streets will ever know a thing about me. Like all the generations that lived and died here before us. We're none of us special, are we?'

'Special!' laughed his mother. 'He wants to be special, does he?' It was one of her most irritating traits, he thought. The way she started talking in the third person about you, even when she was stood there talking directly to you. It was like she was distancing herself from him even as they stood side by side in the street. Suddenly she gasped and grabbed his arm. 'Ooh, shall we have a frothy coffee? We could go and sit in that new place.'

Noel pulled a face. 'What new place?'

They had turned into Ocean Road, the long tree-lined street that led from the library all the way down to the seafront. Teresa stood in front of the shining Art Deco frontage of the new ice-cream parlour. 'Franchino's!' she said, in an affected accent. 'Doesn't it look cosy inside?'

It hadn't been easy for Teresa Sturrock, bringing up her boy alone.

In many ways the two of them belonged to an older age, a time long gone. While the rest of the world was all wirelesses and movie shows and information about the war getting relayed across the planet with what felt like lightning speed these days, the Sturrocks belonged firmly to the days of old Queen Victoria. All that stuff in Teresa's house – just as Cathy was discovering – belonged to the previous century. Mother and son went on living in the preserved wreckage of the past.

Teresa had been a lone mother in those dark and difficult days. It would be hard enough now, but back then she had slaved to keep them out of the workhouse, and they'd only ever been a few steps away from its confines. She was still haunted by the years she had dwelt there, in her early teens, when her parents had died and she'd had nowhere to go. Teresa swore that she'd never go back, and she'd see to it that her son would never live a pauper's life either. And so she'd come through, working every job she could, making money by fair means or foul, keeping her son safe and giving him a proper roof over his head.

The dad was long gone. He was an older chap. Never really very interested in Teresa or her sickly, squalling brat. He upped and went very early on and all the neighbours soon forgot there had ever been a man in Ma Sturrock's life. It was almost as if she had given birth to her malformed son in some curious act of virgin birthing.

He never said it very often, but the boy was very bitter about not having a dad. He was about seven before he even realised what one was, and what they were for. He came in from the street, where he had been fighting with the other lads from Frederick Street as usual and demanded of his mother: 'The bairns out there say I have to ask you what a bastard is, Mother. What's a bastard? Why am I a bastard and all that lot aren't?'

Her broken heart went out to him and she smothered him with kisses and cuddles until he shouted at her furiously. 'Gerrof, man! What's wrong with you? Why can't you tell me why I'm a bastard?'

She tried her best to explain. She tried to tell him that the two of them didn't need anyone else in their lives. They were enough to make a family. He mustn't listen to what the other kids said when he played out in Frederick Street. Sometimes they let him join in with their games, but mostly they shouted at him, saying he had grown up wrong. He was all bent out of shape. Unlike all of them, he'd never had a da'.

'Don't listen to them, pet. They're rough as guts, that lot. You're better than all of them.'

She could always see how much it hurt him, the things that others shouted and said about him. If she could have waved a magic wand, she'd have taken all the hurt away. But there was no wand and no particular words that could salve his wounds. All she could do – and this was where she went wrong, those who knew her would say – was to give in to her son's every whim and tantrum. All she could do to make up for everything was to spoil him rotten.

That was why Noel was like he was. Her quite imperfect little boy who, she said, had been left in the fire grate by Father Christmas.

Even now, with him in his late thirties, she could look at him and her eyes would well up. Her poor little lad, whose life was so disappointing to him. Who went everywhere wearing a bitter scowl.

Except recently . . . perhaps he'd been a little happier? Sprightlier? Maybe. And maybe his old mother knew what had brought these changes on.

Here they were in the new ice-cream parlour, Franchino's, and, as soon as they were seated at one of the swanky chrome and glass tables at the back, she was going to have it out with him. It was all down to Cathy, wasn't it? Their new mysterious lodger. That lovely lass had turned his head, hadn't she?

Her son Noel was in love. She just knew it had to be so.

Chapter 8

Was he really in love, he wondered? Is this how it felt? He knew he had looked at Cathy and felt something quite unexpected and unfamiliar to him. Perhaps she really had forced him to fall in love with her at first glance.

Obviously, his daft mother was playing daft and getting carried away. She was absolutely convinced she had done a miraculous job as a matchmaker. But Noel was more pessimistic than that. No, it was much too early to imagine that Cathy could fall in love with him. Wasn't it?

He wished he understood his feelings better. They felt turbulent inside him, tossing like the North Sea.

There was lust he was feeling, of course. Oh, that was definitely in there. And he cared about the girl, of course. She made his heart twinge in a funny way when he saw her. It was a feeling a little like a trapped nerve. A curious pang. Especially when he saw her working away at some daunting project, such as clambering up on furniture to pull down all the cobwebs that had gathered in his mother's rooms. Or washing the walls down. Really, whoever washed walls? All her efforts seemed to touch him in some indefinable way: the fact that she was going to all this bother for their sake.

And to think he had been so rattled by her, the first time

he had seen her! When she was like a phantom at the top of the stairs. She had unnerved him so much he had shouted at her, upset her, even! What he wouldn't give to go back and make a better first impression on her now . . . He could show her his gentler, more tender side, perhaps.

Still, it was good to keep them guessing, wasn't it? It was good to keep them on the hop, never quite sure what your true feelings were. He knew he would have to be very careful with all of this business. He could still hear Ellie's raucous, jubilant laughter ringing in his ears. How that blowsy madam had mocked him when he had declared his feelings for her! But those feelings were nothing to those he was developing for Cathy Carmichael.

But slowly, slowly, he thought.

Now though, here was his mother with her wide, almost toothless grin and her avid eyes under that ridiculous hat, staring at him across the café table. 'Well then?' she prompted. 'Are you going to start courting her? Are you going to ask her out? That's the proper way of doing things, in case you've forgotten. You've got to treat her special and take her about the town. Dancing, and all of that carry on . . .' His mother was in a strange kind of reverie, as if she was imagining herself being wooed by some long-ago beau.

'I can't be bothered with all that,' Noel sneered. 'I don't have the time or energy to go courting. As for fancy dancing about in draughty halls, no thank you! We'd look ridiculous, her towering over me as I try to lead her around. She'd be ashamed to be seen with me.'

His mother gasped. 'Don't you ever say that! Ashamed, nothing! She'd be glad, I'm sure, to be seen on the arm of my son.'

He shrugged. 'I don't think so, Mother.'

They were both drinking strong Italian coffee out of heavy china cups. The brew was potent, bitter and sweet, and exactly to Noel's taste. He glanced around at the busy café and nodded approvingly. 'This place is all right, isn't it? Seems to be popular.'

'An actual Italian family run it,' his mother informed him. 'The Franchinos. They live over on Jackson Street. They moved here before the war. Seem like nice, clean-living people.'

He laughed sourly. 'Clean living! What does that even mean?'

'Clean in their habits. Smart. She has her bairns immaculate. And the old lady who lives with them seems like a nice, respectable kind of woman, though she barely talks any English. No, they seem like a good lot to me.'

Noel shook his head at his mother's curious values. He felt like taunting her: if you're so keen on cleanliness being next to godliness, how come our own house was so bloody mucky for years? It was taking Cathy days and days of constant work to get it anywhere near decent. Even she was looking like she regretted taking the whole filthy enterprise on . . .

But he didn't say anything like this to his mother. He didn't want to upset her in public.

'Good coffee, anyhow,' Teresa said. 'I don't really mind the Eyeties. They seem like the right sort of foreigners. The nice ones. Not like the Germans or the Arabs.' She pulled a face and he had to shush her. There were always a lot of Arabs on Ocean Road. There always had been. South Shields had been a world-class trading port since the time of the Romans and as a consequence was filled with faces from all over the world.

'Mother!' he said. 'You shouldn't let your prejudices show like that.'

'Why not? I speak as I find. It's a free country, isn't it?'

The two of them continued relishing their coffee in quiet, until Noel said, 'Has Cathy mentioned anything to you about how long she plans to stay living at ours?'

'She can stay as long as she likes, for all I care,' Teresa chuckled. 'Free of charge! Everything's been so much better since she's been with us.'

'Aye, I'll not deny that,' Noel said. 'I just wondered if she had plans for the immediate future.'

His mother narrowed her eyes at him, 'I see! I know what you're up to! You're going to start, aren't you? You're going to take my advice and start courting that lovely young woman.'

He sucked at the molten sugar and grounds at the bottom of his cup. 'Actually, I was going to offer her a job. She can come and work each night at the Robin Hood. Collecting glasses and that. If she can put up with us. I'd like to keep her where I can see her. Keep an eye on her. And maybe see about training her up to be a barmaid.'

'Oh, I can just see her there!' Teresa said. 'She'd be lovely, standing at the bar. Mind, that buck-toothed Ellie won't like being shoved out of the limelight, will she? She won't like it one bit . . .'

'Who cares?' snapped Noel. 'I've made my decision, and what I says goes. I'm the landlord, aren't I?'

'I don't want to spend hours with my hands in that greasy grey water,' she frowned. 'Not that I mind mucking in. Well, you know that. I actually like hard work and getting everything clean. But I don't want to be washing scummy glasses the whole time . . .'

Noel reassured her. 'Don't worry, pet. I'm gonna train you to be a proper barmaid. All the skills you need at the pumps and dealing with the punters and taking money and proper measures and all of that. It's a whole world of things to learn about, but I think you can do it. You're bright, aren't you?'

They were sitting in Ma Sturrock's back parlour with the radio playing on Sunday afternoon and Cathy found herself smiling at him. 'Well, that's very generous of you, Noel. I'd be glad to start learning the skills.'

He beamed at her. 'I can just see you, standing at that bar of mine. Trading quips with the regulars and looking bonny in a new frock. It's like the place you were born to be.'

She laughed. 'I'm not so sure about that! But I'd be grateful for the work. Then I could pay my way here . . .'

He waved his gnarled hands at her. 'You do plenty, pet. My mother was just saying to me, the other day when we were out in town, you're a boon to us. This house has never been more spick and span.'

Cathy looked pleased. 'Honestly, if I hadn't bumped into your mam at Swetty Betty's that first day I fetched up here in Shields, I don't know where I might have ended up . . .'

'Could have been anywhere!' Noel chortled. 'Someone could have grabbed you down the docks and taken you off in their ship! The Arabs might have got you! They could have sold you into the white slave trade!'

'Eeeh, shut up!' she laughed.

'It's true! It happens! I've read some awful stories in the *Chronicle* and that. There's criminals and gangsters and slave-traders and all sorts that carry on their murky business round here. Look at that Mad Johnson lot!'

'Who?' Cathy asked, intrigued.

He shuddered. 'Ah, just a rough family you'd do well to avoid. They're allus up to no good, that set.'

Cathy looked worried, laying it on thick for Noel's sake.

He said, 'But you've lived a sheltered life. You don't know anything. You might have ended up in anyone's clutches!'

She stared at him with a strange, bemused expression. 'Instead I've ended up in yours. Yours and your mam's. Not clutches, exactly!' She laughed. 'I've ended up in your care, and I'm very grateful.'

Now Noel seemed to be blushing. 'Aye, well, I'm glad you're here. Me and my mother are very pleased. And you'll make a smashing addition to the staff at the Robin Hood, I'm sure.'

Teresa came bustling in from the scullery, her face bright red from cooking on the stove. 'I've burned the bloody tatties,' she growled. 'But I think the black bits will mash in and you'll never taste them.' She realised she had walked into the middle of a scene. 'What have you young'uns been chattering about, then?'

'Noel's offered me a position,' Cathy told her. 'Did you already know what he was going to offer me?'

The old woman's jaw dropped. 'Eeeh, son, you've never asked the lass to marry yer?'

He leapt up like a scalded cat. 'Nay! Divven't be daft, Mother! I've offered her a job in the pub! That's all! Just a job!'

Ma Sturrock saw that she had jumped the gun and fanned herself embarrassedly with the tea towel. 'Eeeh, the daft things I come out with! Don't pay no heed to me, hinny. And congratulations on the job, eh? So you're going to be his barmaid, are you? That's smashing. That's lovely, pet.'

Cathy sat there with a fixed smile on her face. A strange feeling came creeping over her. So, he was planning to ask her to marry him, was he? That's what was really behind all of this? The barmaid thing was just a step on the ladder . . .

She didn't know quite how she felt about any of it.

But it was a bit of security, wasn't it? It was knowing where her life was going. For the first time in ages – years and years – she would know where she was supposed to be.

The little man with his squawking voice and those fiercely flashing eyes . . . well, if she was quite honest, he wasn't exactly Prince Charming. She didn't feel exactly revolted by him, but she didn't feel like this was someone she wanted to spend her whole life with, either.

If she was honest with herself, she had seen this place as a stopgap. Somewhere to lay her head and to get her bearings. She was relieved to be taken in and looked after, and she was grateful to both Teresa and her son.

Cathy was no longer running away from her previous life, and that was a huge relief.

Sometimes she would wake up in a panicky muck sweat. She woke up reeling and panting, having dreamed of what she had run away from. She felt sick to her stomach when she was reminded of what – and who – she had left behind.

But she pushed all of this to the back of her mind.

She had to concentrate on now. No, she might not know what the future held, but she was determined to make the best of what she had to hand. Right now, that meant keeping both Noel and his mother sweet, and perhaps learning to be a barmaid at the Robin Hood.

All her secrets and her hopes, her dreams and her nightmares – all of these things she would keep locked up safely inside. Cathy was extremely good at covering her true feelings up. She had had to be.

All she had to do was keep herself calm. Don't panic. Don't give herself away too soon – and never, ever let her true feelings out.

But already Cathy felt like a wounded creature on some woodland path that had lost its way. She had wandered into the wilderness and somewhere along the winding path she had fallen into a trap. Maybe it was a good trap, and a safe place, but nevertheless she felt stuck here.

'I'll not stand for it! You're trying to get rid of me! You're trying to chuck me out!'

'Now, now, Ellie man,' Noel tried to assuage her. 'It's nothing of the sort. I'm just trying to take some of the burden off of you. With a bit of help behind the bar . . .'

She swore at him. 'Rubbish! I knew it, I just knew it! The first time you brought that young floozy in here. I thought – aye, that's my days numbered now. He's got some young tart he's picked up off the streets. He's managed to get some dopey young chit of a thing to suck up to him. I'll be out on my ear. I knew it! That'll be the next thing!'

Luckily the saloon was rather empty at this time on a Monday evening, but there were still a few regular punters hunched over their pints of ale. They cast a sardonic glance at their host being bawled at by his one-time favourite employee. He gritted his teeth and told her, 'I'll thank you to keep your voice down.'

She looked like she was ready to strangle him. 'Bugger you!' she yelled and threw down the towel and the pewter tankard she'd been wiping. 'Up yours, Noel Sturrock. I've broken my back keeping this bug-hutch of yours going, and what thanks do I get? I get offered the chance of training up my own replacement! Well, thanks a lot!'

'Oh, don't take on, Ellie pet . . .' His tone became wheedling as he watched her grabbing her coat and her scarf. It was only halfway through her shift and it looked like she was off already! In high dudgeon and showing off to her small audience. 'Here look, come through to the galley, and I'll explain to you . . .' he promised.

She sighed dramatically and followed him into the back room. Maybe he was going to offer her a rise in her pay. It was only right if she was expected to train up this new girl. Ellie joined him in the close confines of the galley. She leant against the dirty sink and felt the clammy, whitewashed walls pressing in close around her.

Noel smiled at her and stepped closer. And all at once his tone wasn't wheedling and plaintive anymore. It was harder, snider, nastier. He went up to her and stared up into her face.

'You just listen to me,' he said. 'You owe me. And you'll do just what I say.'

'What?' she tried to laugh him off. The daft sod, trying to sound sinister.

But now he had hold of both her arms at the wrists. He was twisting them. The skin was tightening and making her gasp all of a sudden. The little bastard was giving her Chinese burns! 'Hey!' she squealed, and he tightened his grip. He was like a vice.

'I can really hurt you,' Noel told her, and she could taste his bitter breath in her face. 'So just you do what you're told, lady. I could really hurt you a lot – and I'd enjoy it, too.'

She tried to wriggle away from him, but Noel Sturrock wouldn't let go.

Chapter 9

She found that she was excited about the challenges of her new job. It wasn't something she was expecting, but Cathy was actually excited to be learning new skills. It was like when she got her first glimpse of the big store in Morwick, and she started to imagine working in the ladies' department, helping women to choose outfits and hats. She had been so keen to learn and to fit into that role. That, of course, wasn't to be and she'd had to move on, but she realised now that there was something inside her that longed to take up a role and for that to be one in which she served the public. She wanted to stand in front of customers, all dressed up, serving them with just what they wanted.

'Hoy, you drunk old beggers! Hadaway with you!'

It turned out she loved joshing and messing with the loyal customers, too. In her first few days at the pub, she received umpteen proposals of marriage and almost twice as many proposals of a muckier nature.

'You should be so lucky, you daft old get!'

She let fly with her mouth and the insults came thick and fast. How the old gaffers lapped it all up!

Cathy felt that she was doing good work and being of use to her newfound community. She felt like she was holding court and that gave her a frisson of pleasure, even if she was merely working in a back-alley pub in the warren of streets above the South Shields docks. Even if she was just a lowly barmaid, it was still a role in the world and Cathy was proud to adopt it. She was glad to dress up and stand there at the bar where she could polish a glittering array of bottles and pint pots. It was like she had been offered a kind of salvation in the idea that she actually belonged somewhere. For the first time since she was a child, she really felt that she had a place in the world.

Noel Sturrock was her trainer, her employer and her mentor. He taught her everything she needed to know, unveiling each new piece of knowledge as if he were bestowing the great secrets of the kingdom to her. Cathy was a bright girl and really, as far as she was concerned, it was all fairly straightforward. She soon got a hang on how everything worked. She learned to pull the perfect pint, with just the right amount of foam on top. She was amused at how both Noel and the initially somewhat surly Ellie treated the business like a mystical experience when surely it was simply a question of having the right touch?

She learned about measures and quantities and all the tricks of the trade. She absorbed knowledge like a dishrag sopped up spillages on the shiny wooden bar. She learned about ordering and how to deal with the brewery, and about taking deliveries each week from the man with his wagon and the huge dray horse. All those huge, heavy barrels that had to be lugged by their pot man down into the cellar! Yes, there was lots of work to be done, and there were lots of rules and procedures, but there was nothing that Cathy couldn't get the knack of. She was apt and willing and she learned very quickly. Her landlord was delighted by her progress and even Ellie had to give her grudging credit for her aptitude as those first few weeks went by.

'Aye, you're not doing too badly,' said the older woman, smoking a tab end and gazing at the girl. She had slowly come to see her as less of a threat. 'Maybe you're a bit mouthy with the punters. They don't all appreciate getting lip off a young lass like you.'

Cathy smiled demurely, knowing full well that all her drinkers were thoroughly enjoying the bit of backtalk and banter she was giving them. Truth was, Cathy knew that she was already more popular than Ellie, but some instinct told her that modesty would be the best policy here. She wanted to stay on the right side of the more experienced woman.

As for Ellie, she wasn't too gutted to be sharing her space behind the bar. She wasn't as territorial as Noel had expected her to be. He had assured her that there would be enough work for both of them and, gradually, Ellie had the realisation that Cathy's competent presence meant a lot less work for her own rather lazy self. Her wages would stay the same, but she would have a junior colleague who was only too happy to throw herself into doing all of the heavier grafting. So, Ellie was assuaged somewhat, even if Cathy – in the new frocks that their boss provided for her – cut a very glamorous figure at the bar. Even if all the punters were remarking on her looks and getting excited over her novelty, leaving Ellie feeling a bit old hat as a result. What did she really care? She was happy to have an easier life and to let someone else do all the work.

Also, Cathy was taking up old Noel Sturrock's attention, too. No longer had Ellie need of fending the old crookback off. Neither had she forgotten the way he'd twisted her wrists, burning the skin and nakedly threatening her in the galley. His cruel streak had emerged fully that day for the first time, and it still made Ellie cross to remember it. Yes, she was glad not to be the only barmaid here in his sights these days. And she was glad not to be the favourite anymore. She even felt that there was something unhinged and deeply nasty about the man. It would serve that bonny usurper Cathy right to discover one day just what the old devil was really like . . .

'I'm glad that you think I'm fitting in and doing all right,' Cathy told her colleague. She sounded humble and pleased, quite deliberately. Cleverly she had learned that the way to deal with Ellie was to defer to her greater wisdom and experience. Treat her like the oracle and take away all her more onerous tasks. Pay tribute to her faded beauty and tattered grace, and it seemed that they would rub along fine.

'The punters seem to like you even if you're cheeky,' Ellie said, tossing the nub of her woodbine into the grey washing up water, where it landed with a hiss. 'That's the important thing. You've got to draw them here and keep them. This has to be the heart of their world, and that's what it's always been like for more than half the blokes who live in the Sixteen Streets. There are so many other boozers round here. There's one on every other street and there's a ton of them down by the docks. And then there's all the ones down Ocean Road. There's no shortage of places for these daft fellas to spend all their wage packets, getting pie-eyed of a night. So what we have to give them is a home from home. Somewhere that's much better than home. We have to become the wives and mothers and girlfriends and everything they want, all rolled into one.'

Yes, Cathy understood all of that. These fragments of hard-won advice from a veteran like Ellie really were nuggets of wisdom. Cathy was very glad of them.

'Thank you. This is very kind of you. You've let me into your world,' she told Ellie.

There was something so earnest and grateful in the girl's voice that Ellie – tough nut that she was – couldn't help but be touched. 'Ah, get away with you,' she laughed, flapping her tea towel. 'You're okay, you are. I thought you were an uppity little cow at first, but I've decided you're all right, really.'

Cathy grinned. 'And so are you.'

It felt like acceptance at last, it really did. It made her realise how seldom she had felt accepted during her previous life. Cathy couldn't deny it – the feeling was good.

At home, too, she felt more at ease. Number twenty-one Frederick Street really had become her home. Its unaccustomed cleanliness and tidiness were the stamp she had set upon the place, as if she had marked it out as her own territory. Old Teresa Sturrock didn't mind one whit. She was proud of her new-style house, where there was nowadays enough room to get moved about with ease, and where she could even entertain more visitors in the convivial surroundings of both her back and front parlour, depending on how grand she was feeling that day.

Cathy became a kind of angel in her house, brewing up the tea and baking delicious dainties in the stove. The girl would impress Ma Sturrock's aged pals by feeding them up and treating them like they were smart ladies visiting a tea room. She used up all the supplies of eggs, sugar and flour she could lay her hands on, baking in her spare time and bringing out a fancy, never-ending supply of baked goods. She even baked her own stottie bread, which was so light and fluffy that Teresa almost fainted at the first savoury mouthful.

'Eeeh, pet,' the old woman said. 'I've not tasted food like this in years. Where did you learn to bake like this, hinny?'

And so Cathy found herself disclosing a little of her carefully concealed past. She spoke a little about going into service at Morwick Hall at the age of thirteen. How long ago was that? Seven years? Something like that. Her first job had been dashing around after that crazy head cook. The woman had been a monster. She was a martyr to the endless miracles she had to perform on a daily basis, but she had been a wizard with pastry and cakes. Cathy had weathered the storms of her tantrums and had kept a keen eye on her techniques. She had learned to cook and bake in fairly short order and to a very high standard. These were lessons that would stand her in good stead forever.

Mrs Barnett, the head cook, had told her: 'You master these things and you'll always have work. You'll be the mistress of any place you go. You bake like I do and you'll have everyone enslaved. I mean it, dearie. You'll be the one calling the shots. If you can feed people, then you've got them at your mercy.'

It seemed like such a peculiar, grandiose thing to say! But now, all these years later in South Shields, Cathy was coming to appreciate the wisdom in the cook's words. She was using all the skills she had learned to create a whirlwind of confections and fancies and she had ensnared her landlady plus all her visiting friends.

'Oooh, I bet you're glad you took this one in,' Ada Farley laughed, munching on a vanilla slice. Custard came oozing out of the pastry as she chewed with relish. Flakes of pastry dropped onto her cushiony bosom.

Winnie, the fortune teller, wagged her finger as she devoured a delicate cream horn: 'I told you that she had a future here, didn't I? I told you she'd find her niche!' Cathy pursed her lips at this, smiling slightly, remembering that this hadn't been quite how Winnie had seen the future. However, she didn't quibble. She was happy to be made a fuss of.

'I didn't think I could fancy anything sweet at tea time,' Ma Ada said, dabbing crumbs off her lips and her double chin. 'Not after a full day's work at the biscuit factory. The smell of that place puts me off wanting anything sweet. But, by! Everything you bring out of that kitchen is irresistible, lass.'

Cathy blushed with pleasure. Making yourself indispensable, that was the way you found a place in the world. She remembered the head parlourmaid, Esther, telling her that, back at Morwick Hall. In those days, with money dwindling, they had been cutting down on staff all the time. Esther had known that the way to survive was to be the only one they could never do without.

That's what Cathy intended to become for the Sturrocks.

Noel was a tougher audience. 'I can't stomach all that sweet stuff. It's women who love all that sugar and cream. I can only tolerate so much.' He sneered at the multi-coloured cakes and sweets that stood on doilies on the antique cake stands that she had found tucked away unused in his mother's cupboards. All that Victorian finery was out on display and in use every day and Noel Sturrock did his best not to be impressed by any of it. 'You make me some savouries,' he challenged Cathy, smirking. 'Bring me something to tempt my appetite, girl!'

So she had made him sausage rolls. She bought the best pork meat from the butchers and seasoned and peppered it up and wrapped it in the most delicate, melt-in-your-mouth pastry. She brought the rolls out of the oven and watched with great interest at the changes in Noel's expression when she set them before him.

'Look at him!' his mother laughed, as Noel gave in with a hungry groan, gobbling up every hot greasy scrap on that rose-patterned plate.

Yes, Cathy laughed. The way to enslave people was by feeding them. By giving them exactly what their tastes were craving. Find the key to what they loved to eat or drink and then you had them. You understood their desires, and you could make them want to keep you as part of their lives permanently.

Cathy only wanted someone to say: 'You can stay here forever. You belong here, pet.' With all her skills and planning and learning and all the efforts she went to that autumn, that was all she was trying to achieve.

It was all about the art of fitting in. And by the time the colder mornings arrived and the winter winds came creeping down from the north, she really felt like she was starting to do exactly that.

'Well done, lass,' Noel said proudly, and he really meant it.

Chapter 10

Teresa Sturrock's usual cronies were not the only visitors to the tea table at number twenty-one Frederick Street that autumn. The old woman had succeeded in forging a friendship with someone new. A much younger woman, some forty years her junior, who lived in the next street with her young children, husband and mama. The Italian woman, Sofia Franchino, had become one of the regular visitors to Teresa's house.

Neither were sure how it had come about, exactly. Despite the differences in their ages and the fact that Sofia was still only just learning to cope with the language, they became firm friends. Teresa had the thickest northern accent of anyone in the Sixteen Streets – to the extent that even Cathy sometimes had problems understanding her gabble – but even so, the two of them would sit quite happily in the back parlour, nibbling cakes and slurping tea.

'It's very kind of you,' Sofia told her new pal.

'Ah, it's all so's you'll bring the babby round,' the old woman laughed, poking her finger into the infant's startled face, pinching the soft flesh between her gnarled knuckles. Immediately he started to cry and had to be passed back to his mother, to everyone's amusement.

Sofia Franchino had two very young children: a little girl called Bella, who was solemn, well behaved and immaculate in a Sunday-best frock every time you saw her, and the baby, Tony, who seemed like an angel to Teresa, even if he did cry lustily every time she tried to grab him for a cuddle. His vast brown eyes and already thick curly hair made him look like an angel from an old Renaissance fresco.

'Ah, you've got the loveliest bairns,' Teresa told her new friend. 'You can tell you're foreign and that you've got a bit of class.'

Sofia looked dismayed. 'Foreign? Why, I thought we were fitting in better than that . . .'

Teresa winced to see her bonny face crumple. 'Nay, nay, it wasn't an insult, pet. I was just saying that you can tell that you're a cut above the folk round here. Your bairns are like angels! Not like the bloody waifs and guttersnipes who run raggy-arsed round the Sixteen Streets!'

'Oh . . .' said Sofia, half understanding. 'A cut above?'

'Superior,' said Teresa, pouring fresh tea.

'But we are not,' Sofia shook her head firmly. 'If you could see the town we left, if you could see what Naples is like . . . It's a port, just like this. It has streets and streets of messy houses, just like the docks here. It has many families under each roof and the streets are filled with dirt and . . . what did you call them? Guttersnipes.'

Teresa smiled. 'But it sounds so exotic. And it's abroad, isn't it? It's bound to be much nicer than here. And warm, too, I bet? I bet it's lovely and sunny all the time.'

'That's true,' said Sofia. 'I do miss that. South Shields can be so chilly.'

The girl was careful never to insult the town she had settled in, nor criticise anything about it too much. She was eager to fit in, and something about her modesty and sweetness touched the old woman's heart.

Teresa knew that not everything was rosy round at the Italians' house on Jackson Street. The landlord hadn't kept the place maintained, despite the eye-watering amount he was charging the Franchinos to live there. The back walls were damp and seething with black mould. Teresa had seen this for herself and was shocked. The outdoor privy was forever blocked, too, and there was a problem with the pipes. But still Sofia wouldn't moan about the things she had to put up with. 'I am glad to be here,' she kept saying. 'Is better for all of us to be here than in Naples. This is where we belong now.'

There was a story behind that, Teresa suspected. She was sure she would hear it sooner or later. Something about the Italian girl and her family intrigued her.

'How's your mam doing, pet?'

Sofia pulled a face; her mother really didn't hold back with her complaints. The old nonna hobbled around with an ebony cane and she wore widow's weeds and what looked like a nun's veil almost every time she set foot out of the door. It was as if she was in mourning for her previous life and bitterly resented being here in the north of England.

'She hasn't been so well lately,' Sofia shrugged. 'One of the reasons I'm out and about this afternoon – to get out of the house while she's coughing and complaining. She won't go to bed while she's ill. She says she has to be up and about.'

'Not well, is she?' Teresa looked sympathetic. She had met the old woman several times and had felt judged by her. That scowling old face glaring at her from under the veil! She didn't know how Sofia put up with it. Still, she supposed she was her mam, and blood was thicker than water, and all that. As far as Teresa was concerned, the old madam had nowt to complain about. The young couple had brought her with them, hadn't they? They'd given her a home. They were devoted to her, just like Noel was dedicated to his own mam. But still that old woman went shuffling around with a face like thunder, reeking of Parma Violets, the particular kind of sweets that she sucked continually and crunched into when she was annoyed.

'Mama has got this terrible chest that's growing rounder,' said Sofia. Her English was good, Teresa thought, but her grip on local idiom sometimes slipped, with amusing results. 'She is coughing all the time and won't have the doctor in. Waste of money, she says. She's been brewing remedies on our stove. Recipes from the olden days. Horrible smells are coming out of our scullery all the time.'

'Oh dear,' Teresa said. 'The cough, eh? She hasn't got the flu they're talking about, has she?' A tiny niggle of fear started up in Teresa's chest. A tickle at the back of her throat. She glanced at the wriggling baby and the calmly sitting little girl. Imagine if they all got this terrible cough. That's how it began, wasn't it? The flu they had been talking about in the *Gazette*. She had read the piece in the paper last night. Well, it was mostly down south, but it was spreading fast. People moved around the country so much these days. What was in one place soon got everywhere. And with all those fellas coming back from the continent, who knew what was being shared around invisibly with every breath they took and breathed back out?

She shuddered and kept her thoughts to herself.

'I think it's just a cold,' Sofia said. 'The house is so damp, as you know. The walls, they are made of damp sand, it feels like. We are not yet used to winters here in South Shields – I don't think Mama will ever get used to the weather. She curses us for making her come here with us!'

'Curses you!' chuckled Teresa. 'Why, I think she ought to be glad. To be living with a lovely young family like yours. And with these lovely kiddas!'

Sofia shrugged and laughed. 'She'd complain about anything. She is like what you call people . . . a moody old crow?'

Teresa almost spat her tea out. 'Did I call someone that? You mustn't repeat it, hinny. It's quite strong. It's quite rude!'

'Ah,' Sofia smiled. 'Well, she is quite moody. Especially with this cold on her chest.'

The front door clattered then, and Cathy was home. She was tired and her face was glowing with exertion and the fuggy heat of the bar over the road. 'Here, squeeze the pot,' Teresa told her. 'There's still a cup left in it for you.'

Sofia poured the tea for the newly appointed barmaid, laughing at that phrase, 'squeeze the pot'. 'As if the pot itself was soft. When it's the leaves inside you are squashing and squeezing,' she said.

'Aye, that's right, pet,' Teresa said. 'Put a last dribble in my cup an' all, will yer?'

As Cathy sipped her tea, she fussed over the bairns. The babby went to her no bother and lay in her lap with nary a complaint. 'How was your shift, pet?' asked her landlady.

'Are you liking being a barmaid?' Sofia added. 'I think I'd like to try it, as well. Seeing lots of new people all the time.'

'Aye, that's true,' Cathy grinned. 'Though a lot of the time you're seeing the same old faces. The same craggy, red-nosed, leering faces of all these bloomin' awful old gaffers. But it's all right, really. It's not that much hard work, whatever that Ellie says. She makes it sound like the hardest job in the world.'

'Her!' Teresa snapped. 'I never liked that one. I had my suspicions at one point that she was trying to get her claws into my Noel. I think she set her sights on him . . .'

Sofia caught Cathy's eye at this, and the two younger girls almost made each other laugh out loud. The very idea that Noel was some kind of prize! The thought that his mother had to watch out for all the women flocking to his door, avid for his attentions!

Teresa noted a fleeting smirk on their faces. 'Hey, he's got a lot to offer, has my lad!' she protested. 'He might not look much like Rudolph Valentino or that lot, but he's got a heart of gold and he's worth a few bob. When I pop my clogs he'll be getting the lot. It would be quite a windfall for the right lass who'd chucked in her lot with my lovely, sweet, considerate lad . . .'

She sat there beaming at the two of them, looking sentimental and pleased with herself.

'Oh, Teresa, we meant no offence,' Cathy said. 'And you're right about Noel, of course. Why, he's a man of means. He's a really lovely chap.' She smiled and kept her actual thoughts about Noel private. He may be many things, she thought, but sweet and considerate he really wasn't. And he really didn't have a heart of gold. He was snappy and bad-tempered and sarcastic and he had the sharpest tongue Cathy had ever heard.

Teresa drew herself up and looked pleased. 'Why, I just knew you were getting to know him properly, Cathy Carmichael! I knew that you, of all people, would start to understand what my boy is really like.'

Ah, now the old woman was looking rather glad and chuffed with herself. Her face was reddening and her words were coming out in a flustered fashion. Cathy realised she had perhaps made the old woman believe that she thought rather more of Noel than she actually did. Perhaps Cathy would have to take back what she had said. She saw now that it was impossible to praise Noel in even the mildest of ways in front of his mam without getting her hopes up.

'Well, he's been like a saint to me,' Cathy said. 'He's taught me a trade. He's given me that chance to pick up skills that I never had before. I'm a barmaid now and I feel like I've been put in charge of the little kingdom that he's built.'

'That's right,' Teresa Sturrock was nodding firmly. 'You'll always remember that, Cathy. Don't pay any heed to all those who go making fun of my lad. He's come through a lot, that little monster of mine. He's had to fight his way to survive and yes, he might be a bit of a crosspatch now and then but he's as loving and as kind as any man. More so, in fact. So, there you go, Cathy Carmichael. I'm so pleased that you can see the best in him!'

Cathy smiled, but she felt her cheeks blazing hot with embarrassment. She didn't want to rock the boat with Mrs Sturrock, and she didn't want to lose everything she had built up here in this new home. She had gained their trust and even affection.

But she really didn't want to get any closer to Noel. The matchmaking his mother was doing was a dreadful thing. There was excitement ticking away under the layers of cardigans and foundation garments that the old lady wore. It was the excitement of imagining her son getting settled with a bonny lass of his own. Maybe one day having bairns like these two running about the place. Ma Sturrock's heart was set upon Cathy as a daughter-in-law; suddenly Cathy could see it all too plainly in her keen old eyes.

She had suspected as much for some weeks but now the suggestion was clearly hanging in the smoky air of the back parlour. You must take my son, for all his faults, and you must make him your own. Ma Sturrock's feelings were as plain as the coarse black hairs sticking out of her chin.

Chapter 11

The first big change that Cathy brought to the Robin Hood was the Women's Table.

'If you must, you must,' Noel Sturrock scowled at her. 'But if all the squawking and shrieking puts the men off their ale, then it's over. They're out again.'

Cathy was bold enough now with Noel to laugh at his objections. 'It's more money coming in. Women's money is just as good as men's, you know. And they won't be squawking and shrieking, they'll be very respectable.'

As it happened, the corner of the bar that was reserved for Cathy's Women's Table was indeed the noisiest part of the whole saloon that autumn.

The women had a lot to talk about. They were very vocal about goings-on in their local community, but there were world events to discuss, too. Their world was changing. Men were coming back from the front, broken and damaged, some beyond repair. New jobs and new lives were to be found for them. Women's roles would have to change yet again as the men returned home. And then there was this flu going round, too. There was indeed a great deal to discuss at the Women's Table.

'I wouldn't mind if they were in a separate room, or behind a little partition,' Frank Farley complained as he propped up the bar.

It was just a table by the fire, in the warmest spot in the room, with four wooden chairs set around it. Here the women sat and drank milk stout or sherry, pretending that they belonged here in the Robin Hood just as much as any of the fellas.

'Ah, shut your trap, Frank Farley,' Ellie told him robustly. She snatched his pewter tankard off him and swiftly refilled it with foamy beer. 'You're just bothered because now there's women to see you acting daft when you get pie-eyed. Now you can't behave as badly as you usually do.'

'Bollocks,' he snapped coarsely.

'And you'll have to mend your language, too,' Ellie warned him. 'What with ladies present.'

'What? Them bloody women swear worse than any blokes ever do! I've bloody heard them!'

Ellie simply laughed at him, but a part of her was worrying that Cathy might have gone too far, and Noel may have miscalculated with this business of encouraging women to come inside. What if all their drunken regulars got up and defected? There had already been mutinous mutterings about the Mudlark, down on the docks and how it was suddenly looking more attractive . . .

The thing that Frank Farley was most upset about was the fact that among the women coming to sit by the fire was his wife, Ada. She brought her knitting, and her best friend Winnie and she sipped black stout and kept an eye on her fella as he drank at the bar.

'It's not like she or Winnie is here every night, though,' said Ellie.

'She's cramping my style! She's spying on me!'

'Rubbish!' Ellie jeered. 'Isn't she allowed out to have a little drink? Isn't she allowed to have a bit of a social life of her own?'

'She should be home watching all them bairns. She should be cooking our supper.'

But the Farley boys were getting old enough to look after themselves. At least, the oldest one Tony could keep the others in check. Their exhausted and diminutive mother was surely entitled to one evening a week of being out in the world.

'It's all going upside down,' Frank and his cronies opined bitterly. 'Women working at men's jobs, women down the pub. The whole bloody world is going crackers, man.'

Over at the table by the fire, the women were becoming boisterous at some private jest. They looked completely at home, shrugging off their shawls as they basked in the warmth of the hearth. Cathy had joined them for her short break and it was striking how the new girl seemed to be completely at home amongst them. There she was, sat among some of the most senior matrons of Frederick Street: Teresa Sturrock, Ada Farley and that young Italian woman from Jackson Street, Sofia Franchino. Her whose fella owned the ice-cream parlour. Cathy was the one making them roar with laughter with something she had said. Something cheeky, no doubt.

By, Ellie thought. In just a few weeks that Cathy had certainly come out of her shell! The first time she'd met her she would hardly say boo to a goose, and yet now look at her! Why, the very first day behind the bar she'd started answering back to the men!

It almost made you think that the quiet, shy version of herself before she got behind the bar had all been a put-on, lulling everyone into a false sense of security. This poor homeless lass . . . why, we must all pitch in and help her! Only now that she was settled could she let out this louder, more confident self. Brassy, is what Ellie would call it.

It wasn't hilarity and laughter all evening at the Women's Table. When Cathy asked Sofia about her mother's sickness, the conversation suddenly took a much more serious turn. The women lowered their voices and crept together in a conspiratorial huddle.

'She's taken to her bed,' Sofia told them. 'Nothing will send her to her bed usually. But she lies there now with a poultice on her chest, coughing and coughing night and day. Her temperature is like the oven.'

The others were frowning with concern. 'It's this flu,' Teresa said. 'It's definitely the flu. It's come from abroad and it's raging through the whole country, the way I hear it.'

Ada Farley said, 'There's been a few women off at the biscuit factory. Mr Wight is very worried about it bringing production to a halt if it runs rampant through the workforce.'

'Eeeh, is that all he's worried about, the old twister?' gasped Teresa.

'The work rooms are all so hot and unventilated, you see,' Ada explained. 'Well, we get colds running through the place every year.'

Teresa frowned. 'One gets it, everyone gets it. But it'll pass. All these things pass by, don't they?'

'Aye, that's true,' Ada said darkly. 'And I've seen some horrible sicknesses coming through this place over the years. We've seen some terrible things. But I tell you, I don't like the sound of this one. Not at all. It fills me with dread, it does.'

The women laughed at her. 'You talk to that daft old Winnie too much,' Teresa chuckled. 'Her with her prognostications!'

'Maybe I do,' Ada said, and drained her half-pint glass. 'Shall we have another?'

'Nay, not for me,' said Teresa. 'That's me supped up, lasses. Time I got home.'

Teresa Sturrock would always be grateful to Cathy for opening up the Robin Hood to her. Leaving the bar that evening and crossing the cobbled street, she could hardly credit it. I'm a customer at the bar! A regular! She actually breezed in and out of the place that had always been an exclusively male preserve. Even though it was her own son who ran it, she had never felt like it was a place she could simply pop into.

But in just a matter of weeks this autumn, Cathy Carmichael had changed all of that. The women had a place by the fire, away from their homes, and this had made all the difference. Confiding together like that, discoursing on the vital news of the day, hunched over their drinks, it felt to Teresa that the women could set the whole world to rights!

She was daft, she knew . . . and maybe a little tipsy after a couple of halves. But it made you wonder, didn't it? What if it *was* women ruling all those countries that had all been at bloody war until very recently? What would the world look like then?

She was musing fancifully about what she would do if the world was hers to rule over as she brewed up a pot of tea in her scullery, back at number twenty-one. There was still some lamb stew on the hob from last night, and that would do them all for their supper tonight. She could make her cuppa and put her feet up with the radio . . .

Then there came a soft tapping on the back door. This was followed by a pitiful mewling voice. For a second Teresa thought that one of her many cats had suddenly learned some manners for once and was actually asking permission to enter. But then the voice spoke through the door, sounding pathetically weak: 'Eeeh, Mrs Sturrock. Is that you there, hinny? Can you help me, please?'

Teresa hobbled over to unlatch the scullery door. Behind it stood her next-door neighbour, Jillian Patterson. She was generally a rather tidy woman who kept herself clean and neat. This evening she looked half dead. Whey-faced with her hair all greasy, squashed under a hairnet. She was in her oldest, raggiest cardigan and her eyes were watery and unfocused as she met Teresa's questioning stare.

'By God woman, you look terrible! What's the matter with you?'

'I don't feel well at all,' Jillian said. 'I've not been able to do a thing for two days. I've not kept anything down and me head is banging. When I lie down the room starts spinning around . . .' She gripped the doorframe for balance. 'I shouldn't even be out. I tried knocking on the wall to attract your attention but I couldn't make meself heard . . .'

'I was . . . out,' Teresa said, not liking to say that she'd been down the pub. 'Come and sit down, hinny. I've got the kettle on. You need looking after.'

Just this small show of kindness reduced the lonely old woman to tears. 'I wouldn't ask anyone for help. You know that. I've always looked after myself and my own. Well now, with my lads gone, as you know . . . I've got no one.' She slumped down on the padded pew underneath the back window, dislodging one of Teresa's many cats. 'I just realised, lying there tonight. I thought, I've got no one. No one in the whole world. I could lie there dead in my own mess and no one would ever know!'

Teresa brought her tea and tried to be sensible and forth-right. 'Now come on, Jill. You know that you've friends round here. Everyone's looking out for you. Everyone looks out for everyone else. That's what it's like in the Sixteen Streets.'

The old woman clutched her tea and sipped it like it was the elixir of life. 'Aye, maybe. But I lay there next door for three nights and two days. I was coughing me guts up in that bed. I couldn't eat nowt and I couldn't get up. I didn't set foot out me front door. And who noticed, eh? Who even bloody noticed that I was bad?' Her rheumy eyes threatened to spill with tears again. 'Tell me that, eh? I could be dead before anyone even knew there was owt wrong with me!'

Teresa felt chastened. 'Well, I'm sorry to hear that. And we'll take more care in future. Just to make sure you're all right.'

'Eeeh, I divven't wanna be a burden, hinny,' the old woman moaned. 'It's just that I've never felt as bad as this in me whole life.'

Teresa pursed her lips. 'Aye, I've heard tell that it's a bad bug going round.'

'*Bad!*' cried Jillian. 'I feel like death warmed up! But I think . . . I might be over the worst of it now . . .'

Noel was outraged when he got back home that night, just before midnight. 'What? You fed that old bag my flaming supper?'

Teresa was at pains to mollify him. She could see his temper rising as he stormed about the scullery, clashing the dirty pots. 'There's still a bit of cheese left, pet . . .'

'I was looking forward to finishing off that bloody stew,' he yelled. 'And you've gone and given it to that skinny bitch from next door? What was she doing begging round here, anyway?'

Teresa tidied up her pots and pans. They could wait till the morning for a scrubbing. After everything she was too worn out to do them tonight. 'Look, there's still the bone from the stew, if you want to pick at that, son . . .'

He turned on her, fuming, his eyes blazing. 'Pick at the bloody bone? Are you joking? What do you think I am, a bloody dog?'

She fussed around him, knowing how to calm him when he flared up like this. She found him some cheese and a crust of bread and sat him at the table in the back parlour. He chewed crossly at his cheese.

'This is what we've come to, is it?' he growled. 'Laughing women in the pub and me mother giving me dinner to the neighbour . . .'

'Just eat your cheese,' she told him. 'That's nice cheese off the market.'

'Bloody cheese,' he grumbled.

'You'd have been shocked if you'd seen her,' Teresa told her son, picking up her knitting. There was relish in her tone as she started tale-telling. There was no malice or schadenfreude in it; it was just passing on news and Teresa always enjoyed relaying a good story.

'Seen who?' Noel asked. 'Hey, is Cathy in? Did she go straight to bed?'

'Aye, she was knackered. You're working her too hard over there.'

He crowed with laughter. 'Too hard! Ha! She spent most of the night gassing on with all the old bags she's encouraged to come cluttering up the place.'

'I bet your takings are up,' Teresa said. 'I bet the women are spending, aren't they?'

'Aye, maybe,' he said. Then his eyes hardened and he stared at his mother. 'So the old witch next door is bad with this flu that's going round?'

'Aye, I say so, aye,' said Teresa.

'What, and you let her come in here tonight, did you? Breathing the same air and sitting in the warm with you? Eating off our plates and using our cutlery?'

His mother stared at him. 'W-well, yes, love. Why? Is there something wrong with that?'

He looked alarmed. 'But she could have brought it in here. That old crone – whatever filthy germ she's got – she might have brought in here with her!'

He stared at his mother. She knew he was just doing it to be horrible. He was putting all the melodrama on, just to panic her. It was revenge for her giving away his supper like she had. 'Why, we could be breathing in her nasty disease right this very minute!' he cried, and then laughed horribly at his mother's dismay.

Chapter 12

'Mrs Patterson next door upped and died.'

That was the abrupt way Teresa Sturrock put it, and the dying had been just as quick and brutal as that.

'She never did!' gasped Ada Farley.

'I went round with a bit of broth on the Friday night, to see if she could manage some proper food, and there she was. Cold as the grave in her bed.'

'Eeeh, the poor old thing.'

It was a gloomy gathering at the Women's Table as they discussed their neighbour's demise. Suddenly it seemed like there was illness everywhere amongst the people they knew in the Sixteen Streets and beyond. Word of deaths all over town had been relayed to the women.

'They say that you can tell you've got it because all your extremities start turning blue.'

'What are your extremities?' asked Sofia.

'Fingers and toes. They go blue and then you know you're done for, apparently.' Teresa was thinking about the pale blue tinge to her neighbour's skin when she found her. The poor old thing had been lying there alone for half the day.

'Down at the biscuit factory, that old supervisor was showing us how to sew together bits of old fabric to make little masks to cover up our faces,' said Ada. 'Like our noses and mouths, kind of thing. Like bloomin' Zorro gone wrong.'

'What?' gasped Teresa. 'You're going to have to wear masks when you're in work all day? How are they gonna get everyone to do that?'

Ada shrugged. 'That's what they reckon. And not everyone can sew, so muggins here has to make half a dozen of the things before bed tonight. Out of old bed socks and sheets and bits and bobs. All quite fiddly.'

Sofia looked nervous. 'But is that what they are saying? That we should be wearing these things all the time, indoors?'

The women shrugged at her. 'I've seen folk on the trolley bus with similar things on, looking like bandits riding the stage coach,' Ada said, fiddling nervously with her hair bun, twisting stray strands in her fingers. 'But it makes you wonder, don't it? How does this thing really spread? Is it with us all the time as we sit in close spaces like this?'

The women looked around at the busy, cosy bar at the Robin Hood. With Cathy's encouragement the pub had become busier and busier in recent weeks. It had never been quite as full as this. She and Ellie were a blur of activity pulling pints and taking money. They looked damp and flushed with sweaty activity. The air was smudgy with smoke as everyone puffed away on their tab ends and Teresa shuddered at the thought of all that mingled breath in the stuffy air that surrounded them.

'Well then, we don't stand a chance, do we? We'll all get it,' Teresa said, slurping her drink. 'Look at how we live our lives! We're all hugger-mugger and squashed together in our houses and our crowded streets. This is where we live! All pressed together and breathing the same air – which was never very fresh in the first place, was it?'

Sofia was shaking her head. 'It doesn't make sense, though, because my mama, she barely went out. She sticks to the house mostly, and she doesn't work outside, she doesn't go to the pub . . .'

'Same as poor Jillian Patterson,' said Teresa. 'Why, she hardly ever left her own house. She was in deep mourning for her lads. Had been for years. I mean, she'd stump down to the general store to buy her few bits of groceries, but she wasn't a great one for mixing.'

'She were old, though,' said Ada. 'That's the thing. Mrs Patterson's body was probably weakened by years of hard living, I reckon. And this thing, this flu, just got to her and that's it. She's gone. How's your ma doing, Sofia?'

The Italian girl looked sickly. 'She's better than she was. She says she's getting over it. She's beating it with her home remedies and she'll soon be fine.'

'Well, I hope so,' said Ada. 'This is a terrible thing. When's Mrs Patterson's funeral, Teresa?'

Teresa shrugged. 'It were never gonna be a fancy do – she's got no one and hardly any money to her name. And from what I've heard there's a bit of a backlog with the gravediggers. They can't get them in the ground fast enough at St Jude's or any of the other parishes . . .'

The women drew in a sharp, horrified breath at the sound of this. They hated the thought of bodies queueing up to go in the ground.

The weather turned dreary and nasty, which only added to the feeling of doom that hung in the air. The factory horns blared, sounding the regular hours, and the fug of sweet biscuit-scented smoke came rolling up the hill, just as usual. The sugary aroma was almost like the sweet smells that doctors were said to spray in Elizabethan times in order to purge the plague in the teeming streets of London. But this was a modern-day plague and the whiff of custard creams and ginger snaps did absolutely nothing to fend off the insidious germs that coursed through those narrow streets.

'The Spanish Lady' some folk called it, deciding that the likeliest place of origin was somewhere in Iberia. Some of the newspapers aided and abetted this kind of speculation, and there was a touch of animosity towards foreigners in the smoky air. When she was out and about, Sofia tried to soften her accent, to sound less Italian, in case anyone started thinking she was actually Spanish. She felt hounded and harassed, moving between her chores at home and her working days at the family ice-cream parlour. Also, she was nursing her aged mother through the final stages of her sickness.

'I am getting well again!' Nonna bellowed. 'See! I am made of strong stuff, eh?' She would sit up in bed and bang her ebony cane on the floor to attract her daughter's attention. 'Now I am starving! I need to build myself up. Bring me ice-cream. Did Tonio make the fior di latte this week?'

'Yes, Mama, he did,' said her daughter, with a tired smile. Fior di latte was the magical family recipe for ice-cream. The simplest, most delicious ice-cream in the world. Recovering from the flu, with her sense of taste gradually returning, the old woman found she was craving this treat. 'And grappa, too!' she shouted. 'Strong spirits will revive me – you know that, Sofia!'

'Yes, Mama,' nodded her daughter. At first she had been alarmed by the sight of her mother downing stiff drinks in her sick bed. But there was no arguing with her when she got an idea into her head. Recently it had been in the papers, too – the suggestion that drinking whisky might help keep the flu away. Well, Mama wasn't going to touch Scotch or Irish, but a glass of grappa or two was apparently very welcome.

'Your mother is on the mend, I think,' Tonio smiled that night, as a volley of bangs from the old woman's cane rattled the rafters again. Sofia was in the midst of feeding her children.

'I am so relieved,' she told her husband. 'She is a pain in the ass, but I thought we might lose her. You hear about so many dropping dead lately . . .'

Tonio didn't like to tell her about the names he had heard mentioned during his gambling nights at the Mudlark. This was the insalubrious pub right on the seafront where he whiled away most evenings playing cards. Some of the names mentioned there, of people who'd breathed their last and who were now waiting patiently for their place in the churchyard, were rather young and comparatively fit people. They had nothing seemingly wrong with them, so this disease coming over from the Continent wasn't just something that stole in and took away the old and the infirm. It was invisible and capricious and, if Tonio were to allow himself to think about it much at all, he'd say that it terrified him.

'What if they say we have to close our ice-cream parlour?' his wife asked him. 'If people are told not to mingle. If we get told to stay at home and not go out . . . what will happen to our business?'

'No, no, no, that will never happen,' he waved his hands dismissively. 'How could they do that? They can't just tell everyone to shut down and stop. The war is over and everyone is home. Everyone is keen to get back on with life again. We can't just halt all of life in its tracks . . .'

Sofia was in the scullery, reaching into the cold store and making up a little dish of homemade milky ice-cream for her mama. 'You really think so?' she asked him. 'Not even to save lives? You think they will let this thing just tear through the whole country like a flood and take away who it will?'

He looked troubled. 'I think that is what it is already doing, my love. Like the war took away people and its impact was felt everywhere. This illness is like . . . like the ghost of a war. It is a mad and hungry ghost, rampaging through the world . . .'

Sofia shivered at his words and spooned out small helpings of the precious ice-cream for her young ones. What about the children? she wondered, as she watched them eat with relish. Have we brought them into a world where their wonderful lives will be simply snuffed out? Can the world really be as cruel and as dreadful as that?

Cathy found that she was keeping her head down and trying not to think about the flu. The news about the old woman next door had shaken her, but she tried to push it to the back of her mind.

'Look, let's face it,' Ellie sighed, voicing her usual pragmatic approach to the world. 'This pub is a sweat box and we're here every night, so we're bound to pick it up sooner or later. To me it seems like a kind of lottery. Some get a slight cough and others drop down dead. It's the luck of the draw, like so many things, and there's bugger all we can do about it.'

'I suppose you're right,' said Cathy. She was polishing the tables and sweeping round in the dreary daylight that came filtering through the pebbled windows.

Ellie carried on thoughtfully, 'I mean, it would be different if there was a magic solution or a miracle pill or an inoculation, say, that could protect us. Or if there was something we could do to protect the weak and the vulnerable besides keeping them at home and away from the crowds . . . But there is no magical cure, is there? We just have to brave it out. And we have to hope for the best.' Ellie laughed harshly. She had her hands on her hips and her generous bosom thrust out, just as if she was holding forth to a busy bar load of punters. 'What else is life all about, eh? Being brave and hoping that things will turn out for the best.'

Cathy smiled at her. 'You're right. That's how I feel about life, too.'

'Ha!' squawked the older barmaid. 'I knew there was something I liked about you from the first, Cathy Carmichael. We think in a similar way, I reckon!'

For the first time, Cathy felt that the senior barmaid was actually becoming something like a friend to her.

When they finished for the afternoon, there were a couple of hours until opening time and Cathy suggested that they wander down into the town together, and maybe get a lovely frothy coffee at Franchino's. It seemed like a natural step forward in their friendship.

As soon as she made the suggestion, she saw it was the quite the wrong thing. She watched Ellie's expression curdle into something spiteful. 'What? Go and drink coffee made by bloody wops? You must be joking, Cathy Carmichael! What are they? Eyeties? Spicks? I'm not mixing in with likes of them, no matter how nice their coffee's meant to be. I'll have a nice cup of British tea instead. It's them who brought it over, you know! The foreigners! They brought the germs here with their dirty ways!'

Cathy gasped at the woman's ignorance. 'But the Franchinos have been here since before the war, according to Sofia! They've got British nationality on their passports and everything!'

But Ellie was firm in her prejudiced stance. 'I don't care. I don't even like you letting that Sofia sit at the Women's Table, but I don't say anything about it. I don't want to cause a scene. But I'll be buggered backwards if I'll sit in their mucky place and drink frothy bloody coffee! No, thank you kindly, lady!'

Chapter 13

Later it was Winnie who got the blame for it all.

'Which isn't fair, really,' Ada Farley said. 'The flu was every-where. Winnie wasn't solely responsible for spreading it through the Sixteen Streets . . .'

'Aye, but she was in and out of everybody's houses all the time,' said Teresa. 'Same as always.'

'It's not the first time I wished our fortune-telling friend was better at seeing the future than she really is,' mused Ma Ada grimly.

It was true that Winnie hadn't changed her behaviour at all through those months of the flu germs running rampant through town. Most people stopped going out and socialising as much, and many wore the masks sewn by the biscuit factory girls in their spare time while at work or on the trolley bus or in the shops. As winter deepened and darkened, everyone went into a kind of semi-slumbering hibernation in order to spare each other the worst of the disease's spread.

Only Winnie carried on, going from door to door, spreading tittle tattle and being incredibly gloomy about everyone's chances of survival.

'Eeeh, all the poor lads coming back from the frontline,' she cried. 'Expecting congratulations and parties in the streets! And what do they get? Long lines of funeral corteges and coffins being carried out of houses. Eeeh, it's awful, isn't it? I know one lad who came home – one of the MacKay lads from Winterton Street – but found that almost all his family have been struck down by the flu. There was only half of the buggers left, and they were too ill to welcome him home. It's a tragedy, man.' This was Winnie sitting in the Sturrock back parlour, sipping a mugful of tea plentifully laced with medicinal Scotch. 'This is champion, this. I can feel it doing me good.'

Winnie herself – for all her gadding about – didn't get a single day's sickness throughout the whole of the pandemic. ('Typical!' Ada Farley crowed. 'If she fell in sh-you-know-what she'd come out stinking of roses!') She eventually put it down to all the whisky she enthusiastically imbibed during the visits to her neighbours. As far as she saw it, the old gypsy woman was raising their spirits and keeping up morale.

'But it was her to blame for this!' shouted Noel Sturrock, late in November. His voice was bitter and streaked with panic. 'It's all down to that ridiculous Winnie woman. She brought the germs in here! And my daft mother was too flamin' polite and kind to tell her to bugger off! She should have said, "Hadaway home, you nosy old witch! We don't want you round here, coughing and spluttering with yer woodbines!"'

But Teresa had never turned anyone away from her door. This was something that Cathy was glad about, of course, for she herself had benefitted from Noel's mother's welcoming largesse.

It was alarming to see Teresa come down with the Spanish flu, though. Cathy would remember it for a long time, that moment in the parlour when she saw her elderly friend coughing and unable to catch a breath. She looked like death as she sat back in her chair, her whole body shaking as she fought to control the wracking spasms in her chest.

Cathy had helped her to her room and got her settled. She had tried to feed her, to bring her hot drinks and whatever else she could find to ease her suffering. She didn't think twice about her own chances of catching the sickness; Cathy knew she herself was fit and resilient compared with Teresa. But she was ashamed to find herself thinking: what if the old woman dies? And I'm left alone here, living with Noel? Just what would that be like?

'I'm sure she'll be all right, Noel,' Cathy tried to reassure him. They were sitting in the back parlour late on a Sunday night, with snow falling past the lace curtains at the back, making strange shifting shadows in the shrouded room.

He glared at her. 'What makes you think so? Why would you think she'd be all right? She's old, Cathy. My mother's stooped over with a nasty chest and inflamed joints in the first place. A bout of the Spanish flu could well be the finish of her. You know it just as well as I do!'

She shushed him and begged him to keep his voice down. What if his mother in her sick bed just above their heads could hear his terrible words? She was up there, pressed under the weight of all the heaviest blankets, breathing harshly and glowing with feverish sweat. She had been bad for three days now and it was only getting worse.

'I could murder that Winnie,' muttered Noel furiously.

'You can't blame anyone,' said Cathy. 'It's just the flu. It doesn't care who it infects and there's no one to blame . . .'

Suddenly she saw that her intemperate landlord had tears in his eyes. 'What am I going to do, Cathy? What if it's the finish of me mam? What would I do without her?'

There was such helplessness in his tone that her heart went out to him. All she usually saw was mother and son carping on at each other. She was used to their caustic banter whenever they were in the same room. Now she could see that this was all a cover for a deep and abiding love and a fierce loyalty. This man in his late thirties really couldn't imagine a life without his mother there in the house alongside him. The very thought was sending him into a panic.

'Noel,' Cathy told him firmly. 'You have to be strong. For your mam's sake. She doesn't want to see you going into a flap over this. She doesn't want to see you getting all teary and soppy when you take her supper up to her.'

He tried to rally. 'Aye, I guess you're right. I'm taking on like a bloody woman, aren't I? She'd be ashamed of me.'

Cathy smiled at him as she watched him pull out a huge, none-too-clean handkerchief from his waistcoat pocket. He wiped his face and let out a horrible groan. 'That woman's all I've got in the world – she's my whole world. I know she's an argumentative and idle old besom, but she's my whole world, she is.'

Cathy reached out to take his hand. 'I'm sure she knows that, Noel.' Then she gasped as he snatched his fingers away from hers.

'What are you doing?' he cried. 'Touching me! Grabbing me hand!'

Cathy was flustered. 'I was just . . . trying to . . .'

He snarled at her like an angry dog. 'I know what you're trying to do. It's what you've been doing the whole way along! Worming your way in with us. Making yourself into part of our family. Or so you think! You've just been taking advantage of us. Of me mother's good nature! And now . . . now you're grabbing me! You'll be trying to kiss me next!'

She stared at him, shocked by this outburst. There was a mounting hysteria in his tone. 'I don't think so!' she shouted back.

But he was up and out of the room, mumbling and grumbling as he stumped away upstairs. Cathy was left in his wake, marvelling at the sudden shift in atmosphere. The man's completely crackers, she thought. And it wasn't the first time she'd thought it, either.

The next afternoon she was confiding in Ellie at the Robin Hood about their boss's weird behaviour.

'He vanished up into that attic of his. He left his mother's supper for me to do. I saw to her and checked she was all right before bedtime. He'd have just left her there while he thumped around angrily upstairs in his room.'

Ellie rolled her eyes, leaning against the immaculate bar and paying close attention to Cathy's tale. 'Thumping around was he?'

'Aye, it was like he was throwing around the furniture up there. He was in a fury all night long. He was still making a racket when I eventually dropped off to sleep. Well, how's that kind of carry on supposed to help his mam?'

Ellie let out a sigh of commiseration as she rolled herself a cigarette. 'Well, you know Noel, Cathy. I mean, you've not been here that long, but you know that he's a special case, don't you?'

Cathy's shoulders sagged, and she accepted a cigarette from her new friend. 'Yes, I do. But he's so volatile. He can be nice as pie one moment and the next, he's up the walls, screaming at you. All I did was reach out to take his hand. I was just being friendly, that's all. I don't see why he should react like a scalded cat . . .'

'But that's just it,' Ellie said. 'Being friendly. He isn't used to having friends. How many friends has he got, to your knowledge?'

'He's always surrounded by folk in here. All his drinkers and cronies . . .'

Ellie shook her head. 'They're not friends. They're just drinkers. They'd be here whoever was in charge of that bar, with their names on the licence and over the front door. They pay lip service to him and say hullo and pass the time of day, but none of them round here think very much of Noel Sturrock. They think he's a freak and a mama's boy and a crookback. No one would ever go near him if they didn't have to. Haven't you noticed the way that people go on around him? And he knows it, too. He knows that he isn't liked.' Ellie picked bits of loose tobacco off the end of her tongue and flicked them into the slop tray. 'It's a shame. But he's a twisted one. He's grown up all twisted and there's nothing to be done about that. He can't change his ways, and nor would he want to. He prefers keeping people at a distance.'

Cathy was amazed by Ellie's words. She knew there was lots that was different about Noel, and things that were downright unpleasant about his behaviour. Clearly, though, Ellie had spent a good long while close to him, observing his ways and the manner in which others behaved around him. 'But what a shame . . .' Cathy found herself saying. 'To be a kind of outcast like that. While still living in the middle of everyone.'

Ellie shrugged. 'Noel doesn't make it easy for himself. Sometimes, too, he enjoys it. He loves his reputation for being a bad-tempered bugger. He likes to put the wind up people . . .'

All of this was quite foreign to Cathy. She was used to having people warm to her. When she decided that she wanted to have people notice her and take a liking to her, she found it natural and easy to make herself appealing to them. She was warm and friendly. She could turn on what she knew was not inconsiderable charm. The very idea of purposefully turning people against you and putting their backs up seemed crazy to her.

Why would you turn people against you? Why, you might need them some day. You might have to turn to them for help.

'Listen,' Ellie cut into her reverie. 'I've meant to say this for a while, pet.'

'Oh?' What's coming next, Cathy wondered.

'I just think you ought to watch out for Noel Sturrock. He's the kind of man who you don't know where you are with him, one day to the next. There's a lot of anger and resentment in him. I don't think he's quite right in the head.' As Ellie puffed away on her skinny tab end, she was wondering whether to tell the younger girl about the moment in the galley kitchen when Noel had taken hold of her wrists and twisted the skin until it blazed with pain and almost bled. There had been other instances of casual cruelty over the years, too. Moments when, as they worked together, he had pinched her hard on the bottom or nipped a portion of her flesh between his hard fingers. Once he had even grabbed at one of her breasts, making her cry out in anger. 'Ah, divven't get excited, pet,' he'd jeered at her. 'It's just a friendly little pat, that's all.'

But she knew that there was both a nasty kind of cruelty and a twisted desire in him. He was grabby when he thought no one was looking. She remembered with shame that day he'd seized her belly in both hands and pulled at it through her blouse like he was kneading dough. 'You're getting fat, you!' he had cackled into her face. 'Feel all this! All this pudding! Eeh, or are you up the duff, eh Ellie?' And he'd hurt more than her feelings as he tugged at her folds of skin. That episode hadn't been all that long ago. Just a matter of weeks before Cathy turned up on Frederick Street.

'Just watch out for Noel Sturrock,' Ellie warned her bleakly. 'He was reacting weird because you took hold of his hand! He's got a bloody nerve. He's weird about touching people and I think you should watch out for yourself.'

'I can fettle him,' Cathy promised, though really she wasn't too sure about that. 'The thing I'm most worried about is his mother getting worse. If she goes downhill God knows what he'll be like . . . I don't think he can manage without her.'

Putting out her fag, Ellie returned to bustling about the bar, making busy work until the first of the afternoon drinkers came in. 'If she snuffs it, he'll just have to deal with it. Same as everyone else has to. Life rolls on, and that's all there is to it.'

This seemed a bit callous to Cathy. She already knew to take everything Ellie said with a slight pinch of salt. Life had made her hard and the harshness of the things she said sometimes made Cathy flinch.

By the end of that night at the Robin Hood, Ellie was coughing and spluttering and trying to catch her breath. That's not just because of the cigarettes and the smoky air, Cathy thought. She's gone and caught it, too.

Chapter 14

Often during those weeks it was left to Cathy to look after the ailing Mrs Sturrock. She fed her and sat with her, changed her crumpled, stale sheets and washed her. Very gently, very patiently, she made sure Teresa was comfortable.

'You're being like a daughter to me,' the old lady told her gratefully as she sipped the hot broth that Cathy had made. 'Did you put a touch of whisky in this? Winnie swears by it.'

'No, it's just broth. I really don't think the whisky helps,' said Cathy patiently.

'Where's that lad of mine?'

'Over at the Robin Hood. I've took the evening off.'

'Is it that time already?' gasped Teresa. 'I'm losing all sense of time in here. Do you think that's the sickness?'

Cathy hated to see her friend going downhill like this. She sat with her when she coughed and couldn't catch her breath. She held a bowl for her when she thought she was going to be sick or had to bring up something from her chest. She felt grateful to Ma Sturrock for taking her in, a day that seemed like a whole lifetime ago. Looking after her in this time of need really seemed like the least Cathy could do in return.

'I-I haven't seen much of that lad of mine,' said Teresa,

stirring her spoon in the thin soup. 'It's like he's scared to see me like this. Or scared of catching it from me . . .'

Cathy shrugged. 'He says he's very busy, which he is. Now that Ellie is off sick he has less help in the pub.'

'Ellie's sick too, now, is she?'

'It'll pass,' Teresa told her. 'She's strong, is that one.'

'But you feel all right, don't you, pet? And my Noel hasn't caught it?'

'We're both fine. It seems to have passed us by, or we got such a mild case it didn't do us any harm . . .'

'Aye, aye, that's good.' She struggled to sit up straighter against her fresh linen pillows and handed her tea tray back to Cathy. 'That was lovely, that, thank you.'

'You've only had the smallest drop . . .'

'But I can still feel it doing me good. Good beef stock, wasn't it? That's the other thing they say is good at fighting off the germs.'

Cathy had heard a dozen of the old wives' tales that had sprung up about the flu and how to combat it. Lots of bed rest seemed to her to be the best thing that worked, but that depended on the person having folk to look after them, and to tend to their needs.

'I don't think that your Noel is keeping away exactly,' Cathy said thoughtfully. 'I just think he doesn't like to see you not very well. He's used to seeing you up and about, strong and hearty . . .'

Teresa nodded sadly. 'Aye, well, I can't always be like that. He should realise. I think I've brought him up a bit wrong, haven't I, hinny? He's a bit selfish and foolish. He's still like a boy, really. He expects everyone to dance to his tune . . .'

Cathy didn't say anything, but she thought that Teresa had hit the nail right on the head. The old woman saw from Cathy's expression that this was so.

'But what was I supposed to do? He was my whole world. He was my little prince who I had to protect when the whole world was calling him names. They used to treat him so badly. Just because he looked different and wasn't a bonny lad. He'd come home from the big school and they'd have rolled him in the muck and kicked him around. I'd put the old tin bath in front of the fire and take hours filling it with steaming hot water. I'd have to put him in the bath every night because he used to come home in such a state. And by God, the bruises and cuts all over his body! It was like all the lads in his school had kicked him around like a pigskin football in the mire.'

Cathy found her sympathy for Noel growing when she heard tales like this. She thought she could partially understand why he had grown up to be the defensive, sometimes snide man that he was now. 'He should have learned to fight back,' said Cathy. 'That's what those lads were expecting. That's the only way to deal with things like that.'

'Ah, my Noel was too little. He was as titchy as a bairn! And there was so many of them. No, he was afrit of the whole lot of them and he made it worse by turning tail and running away. He pelted as fast as his little legs could carry him. They'd follow and laugh at him . . . all the way here. He'd fly inside the house and come looking for me. As if I was going to fight all those big boys on his behalf!'

The stories were rather pathetic, Cathy thought. Imagine Noel hiding behind his tiny old mother's skirts! Had he no sense of shame or dignity? If it had been Cathy she'd have come out fighting. She'd have grabbed the broom or the pan shovel. She'd have clattered them, one after the next! She'd have shown them a bloody lesson about coming after her!

But Noel wasn't like Cathy. And he had run away as fast as he could.

Now Teresa had a different thought on her mind. She was stretching over to her nightstand, feeling around in the drawer for her shiny leather purse. 'Here, hinny, would you do me a special favour?'

'Of course,' Cathy said, and waited while a new coughing fit subsided. At last Teresa took out a folded five-pound note and pressed it into Cathy's hands.

'Oh no, I don't want your money . . .' Cathy assumed she was being given some kind of reward for looking after the old woman.

'It's not for you,' Teresa said tetchily. 'If you'll listen, I'll tell you, hinny. Look, it's Christmas coming up, and I don't know whether I'll even last that long . . .'

'Of course you will!' Cathy protested.

'Hmph, we'll see.' Teresa was getting impatient with being interrupted. She wanted to get to her point. 'I wondered if you'd go into town for me? To Bells Brothers, the fancy store? And buy my lad a present for Christmas for me? Choose something nice for him, would you? Something that I might have chosen for him meself . . .'

Cathy invited Sofia Franchino to go with her to do the shopping. Sofia was glad to get out of her own sick house. As they wandered down the slippery, snow-encrusted Fowler Street, Sofia explained, 'Oh, everyone is mending now.'

'On the mend,' Cathy corrected her. 'We say "on the mend".'

'Ah. My mother and the bairns and Tonio. We are very lucky. We had a horrible week when we were all very poorly. I was the least bad, so it was me running around like the blue-arsed fly, of course . . .'

'Of course,' Cathy smiled, reflecting that looking after Sofia's fierce old mama would be much harder than seeing to Teresa. And with small bairns and a man to see to, as well! Sofia must have been run ragged. She'd had to close the ice-cream parlour for almost a month and they were losing money every day.

'So it is a very nice relief to go out today like this and just look at the displays and forget everything . . .'

Despite both the war shortages that still dogged the country and the effects of the pandemic, South Shields had still managed to dress itself up for the festive season. The shops were all aglow with tinsel and lights. The grocery stores smelled deliciously of fresh fruit and other seasonal comestibles, some of which hadn't been in such fulsome supply since the beginning of the hostilities. Apart from the masks being worn by some of the shoppers and staff, it almost felt like life was getting back to normal.

The two women wandered through the shining halls of the store, peering into glass cabinets and rummaging in bargain bins of fabric. The richness of everything overwhelmed them at first.

'There was a store like this in Morwick, where I used to live for a while,' Cathy confided in her friend. 'I thought I might get to work on the shop floor, like these women here. I thought that would be a lovely way to earn a living. But they had me doing the bins and all the heavy jobs round the back. They said I'd have to work myself up through the ranks to being out on show.'

Sofia laughed at her young friend's impatience. 'What a shame!'

'Well, I thought – bugger that. I'm prettier than all these dowdy old boots they had out front dealing with customers. They were wasting me, hiding me round the back! And it was back-breaking work. They had me working like a packhorse! So I left. I upped and left them in the lurch. I got talking to one of the delivery fellas with a wagon round the back of the store. He was bringing fancy tins of biscuits from the factory here and he said I should try out a new town – and here I am!'

'Ah,' smiled Sofia. 'So that's how you came to be in South Shields.'

They were in the menswear department, looking at fancy waistcoats and shirts. Cathy had the idea that, deep down, Noel Sturrock was something of a fledgling peacock. He liked to strut around, despite his physical handicaps, and she thought that maybe he might like something bright and showy as a present.

'So how did you come to choose South Shields?' Cathy asked the Italian girl. 'You left somewhere wonderful and exotic. How on earth did you choose here?'

'I'm not sure Naples was so wonderful,' smiled Sofia. 'Though I must admit, I do miss home more than I let on. Sometimes it is almost unbearable when I think about the people and the faces that belong there, and the life that we once took for granted.' She was stroking silk ties as she examined them. 'This blue! Have you seen a blue like this? This is what the sea is like at home.'

Cathy laughed. 'Here it's like a sludgy kind of grey, isn't it?'

'We make beds,' Sofia said wisely. 'We make beds and we lie on them. That's what we do, isn't it?'

Maybe one of those bright silk ties would be a good gift for Teresa to give her difficult son. That azure blue might suit him. Weren't his eyes a particularly bright kind of blue? Cathy tried to picture them. They were shrouded by overhanging brows and bushy, untamed eyebrows and they were set in a constant, fearsome scowl, but nevertheless she had the idea that Noel's eyes were this exact shade of blue. Funny that she had noticed, really.

'And we didn't so much *choose* South Shields,' Sofia was laughing, continuing her reminiscences. 'You'll never believe this, but we pinned the world map to the wall and my husband Tonio, he threw a dart at the world. He said – wherever it landed, that's where we would go to live.'

Cathy could hardly believe her ears. 'What?! And you went along with that foolishness? It's just the sort of thing a daft man would suggest!'

The Italian woman was laughing now, as if it was really occurring to her for the first time – several years later – just how foolish that moment had been. 'It seemed like a very good idea at the time. When there is the whole world to choose from, how do you narrow that down? My Tonio, he likes a game of chance.' She rolled her eyes at her own words. 'Oh boy, does he like a game of chance . . .'

Still sorting through the rippling silks of the fancy ties, Cathy was listening intently to her friend's words. She caught the bitter ruefulness in her tone. Yes, she had alluded before to the fact that Tonio was a bit of a gambler. More than a bit of one. He had a habit that had caused some bother in the past, from what Cathy could gather.

'And so he stood across the room from the map on the wall, taking aim. We were all watching, holding our breath. Even my mother was quiet for a moment as Tonio prepared to let the arrow fly. Then . . . whoosh! And thud! Our decision was made. We hurried over to see where the dart had landed.'

'And it was here?' Cathy smiled.

'On this obscure bit of coast, high up on this tiny island in the North Sea. We all gathered round and stared and stared. Tonio took the dart out and read the name aloud. "South Shields".'

'My mama gasped. "It's Roman! It's a Roman town! It's where our Emperor Hadrian finished his wall . . ." My mother is a fountain of knowledge like this. Especially about things long ago in the past. The excited way she was jumping and down, you would think she remembered the place personally from Roman times!'

What about a bow tie? Cathy picked out a sliver of silk in that same shimmering blue. Yes, this was it! How distinguished

Noel would look in a bow tie. Suddenly she felt she had exactly the right present picked out.

Sofia wasn't so sure. 'There's a saying about how you can't dress up a pig to be fancy?'

Cathy was fetching out her money and leading them to the counter. 'You can't make a silk purse out of a sow's ear?'

'That's it. I don't think Noel Sturrock will thank you for trying to dress him up like a silk purse.'

But Cathy wasn't so sure about that.

As they waited to be served by the snooty-looking sales assistant, Cathy said: 'You still haven't explained why it was so necessary for you to leave Naples at all? How on earth did you end up with Tonio throwing a dart at the map anyway?'

Sofia looked slightly uncomfortable. 'Oh, didn't I say? Sorry, that's the vital bit of the story. You see, we had to get out of Naples, Tonio said, or we were all going to be murdered.'

Cathy gasped. 'You're kidding?'

Solemnly Sofia shook her head. 'Would I joke about a thing like a vendetta? We take these things very seriously in the south.'

'But . . . *murdered*?' Cathy said, and suddenly they had reached the head of the queue. The assistant gestured impatiently for her to hand over her goods for wrapping.

'I can't tell the whole story here in public,' Sofia said. 'I will tell you it all, later on. The whole shameful saga . . .'

Chapter 15

There was one brighter, crisper winter's day when it seemed that Ma Sturrock perked up somewhat. When Cathy took her a crust of toast for breakfast and a pint of steaming tea the old lady was sitting up waiting and her eyes were gleaming.

'I think I fancy getting out and about today, Cathy hinny. Will you help me?'

Cathy was chuffed to bits to see the old lady looking so much better. She helped her get washed and dressed that morning. Standing up, Teresa felt a bit swimmy and sickly for a moment or two, but that was just because she was out of practise, she said. 'Too long lying about in here,' she laughed. 'I just need some fresh sea air in me lungs . . .' On cue, she started coughing then, and had to grasp hold of the bedpost for balance. She waved Cathy back. 'Nay, lass. I'm all right.'

The plan was to take their time, taking the whole day if necessary, and walk all the way down Ocean Road and get as far as the sea if they could manage. Teresa loved the idea of getting right up to the sea, feeling sure that the freezing salty winds would be somehow healing. 'I'd love to walk as far as Marsden Rock,' she said. 'But I realise that's probably too far for my first day back out . . .'

Cathy made sure she wore layers and layers of woollens underneath her shapeless fur coat. She took out the mittens she had been knitting for her for Christmas box, presenting her with them early.

'Eeeh, lass! What's these? By, this is a lovely surprise! You really made them for me?'

They were lumpy, hopeless-looking things, Cathy realised as her elderly friend turned them over in her claw-like hands. She had used oddments of wool in different colours and, even though mittens must be the easiest thing in the world to knit, Cathy had still made a mess of them. There were tattered ends of wool sticking out here and there. None of this appeared to matter to Teresa Sturrock, who clutched them in her purple fingers and held them up to her heart. 'I shall treasure these forever, pet. You made them for me. That's so lovely. I don't think I've ever had owt knitted for me since I was a little lass . . .'

Downstairs – after much huffing and puffing and swaying down the stairs – they stood for a while to rest. 'It's my joints have stiffened up,' Teresa said. 'I'll be right as rain in a moment.'

Cathy was starting to doubt that they were going to get very far at all on this walk of theirs.

She opened up the wooden cupboard filled with hats and joy lit up the old lady's face as she chose just the right one for their trip out today. Absurdly she picked a kind of battered spring bonnet that seemed to belong to the previous century. It had a little posy of wilting silk flowers sewn to its brim and, once she was wearing it, Teresa simply beamed with pleasure. 'Perfect! I do hope it's not too breezy out . . .'

When they stepped out onto Frederick Street, they found that it wasn't too windy or too frosty or slippery at all. Much to Cathy's relief it was dry and still, though chilly. It was the perfect day for them to venture out for their walk.

'I feel quite giddy with excitement,' said Teresa, stamping on the well-worn pavement. 'I feel like I'm back in the world at last!'

The friends and neighbours they saw on their walk that day waved and called out. Some of them hurried over to have a word. They congratulated Teresa on getting over the illness – so many had not! And it wasn't always the older, weaker, ailing ones who had been struck down, either. Some of the younger, hale and hearty folk hereabouts had been wiped out by the flu. It was a very curious, horrible thing.

The wave was passing, however. That's how it felt to Cathy. These past couple of weeks, you heard less and less about the flu, as national and local attention turned to other matters. Jobs, strikes, everyday misery and misdemeanours. Sometimes it seemed to Cathy that it wasn't so much that the sickness had gone away, or stopped having an effect, it was more like everyone had collectively decided to talk about it less. People were still getting ill, but if they elected not to discuss it so much, the Spanish Lady would somehow lose heart and fade away . . .

There were fanciful thoughts, Cathy realised. The best way of looking at it was to assume that the danger and the worst of it had passed. Those dark late autumn days had dwindled away and even Ma Sturrock was rallying, look! She had fought off those fatal germs!

They took little steps together, with Cathy chattering brightly all the way. When she glanced sideways at the old lady gripping her arm, all she could see was the top of that ridiculous faded hat and the shoulders of her tatty fur.

They got as far as Ocean Road and paused at Franchino's for a coffee, where Tonio and Sofia made a fuss of the sick woman.

'Drinks for you is on the house!' Tonio announced, firing up the steamy coffee machine.

Teresa waved her mittened hands at him. 'Nonsense! We'll pay our own way! You can't afford to chuck money at us – not with the way you gamble everything away!'

It was meant to be a gentle gibe, but Tonio stiffened in alarm at her words. Beside him Sofia was horrified at the easy way Teresa had let out the confidence that had been shared with her. 'Erm, go and sit down,' she urged them. 'I will bring your coffee over.'

Cathy winced as she took Teresa to a table. She could hear a whispered argument breaking out between the Italians in their wake.

Teresa said, 'I didn't realise we were meant to keep his gambling a secret,' she shrugged, and decided to keep her hat and coat on as they sat in a booth.

Cathy rolled her eyes. She had forgotten how tactless and forthright the old woman could be. This is what it was like having her out in the world again! She was causing bother as soon as she got out of the house. Things had almost been back to normal.

Sofia came over with their coffee and smiled at them so warmly. 'It is so good to see you again, Teresa. We thought you were going to leave us.'

'Leave you?' she gasped. 'You'll not be getting rid of me as easily as that!'

Cathy told her landlady the daft tale of how Noel had intercepted her with the parcel from Bell's department store. The bow tie had been all wrapped up by the sales assistant and Cathy had been instructed by Teresa to stash it away somewhere safe in the downstairs dresser, ready for Christmas. 'If I hide it away in my room, it'll just get lost amongst all my bloody old jumble,' the old woman had explained.

Anyway, as it happened, Noel had slipped home from the pub just as Cathy was putting the fancy, beribboned package away. She was stowing it in the back of a drawer that no one ever went into – not even Cathy when she had been tidying the place up.

'Well, Noel caught me red-handed, didn't he?' Cathy said ruefully.

'What? You never told me this!' Teresa said.

They were wandering alongside Marine Park, drifting along beside the evergreens that poked through the iron railings. By now they were almost within sight of the seashore. The slight breeze brought the smell of the brine to them, luring them on at their leisurely pace.

'It was about a week ago,' Cathy said. 'I didn't tell you at the time because you didn't look too good . . . and I was worried because Noel sort of spoiled the surprise for himself.'

'Eeeh, that lad,' Teresa said. 'When he was a bairn he used to go hunting round the whole house for his presents, weeks before Christmas began. He's always been a spoiled little bugger. It's my fault!'

Why am I even telling this tale now? Cathy wondered. She was turning it into a funny, silly diversion. But at the time it hadn't been funny at all. Noel had leapt at her and seized her hands. He had yanked the parcel off her and held it up in triumph. 'Aha! I see it! I know what you're doing! This is for me, isn't it? You've bought a present for me!'

There had been something so manic and gleeful about him, she had felt alarmed. He was making so much fuss that she couldn't even get to explain to him that it wasn't from her, but his mother . . .

'I'm going to open it now,' he gabbled. 'I'm going to rip it open now and spoil the surprise. How dare you keep surprises from me in my own bloody house?'

It was midday but there was a reek of drink on his breath, Cathy realised. He'd been tippling over at the Robin Hood, and this was the result. She had to beg him to stop. His fingers were poised to rip open the expensive paper and to tear away the delicate ribbons. 'Please,' she had to beg him. 'Please don't do that, Noel. You mustn't!'

He snarled at her. 'I mustn't, eh? And why not? It's for me, isn't it? It's a gift just for me?'

She had to admit that was true. 'Yes, but you must save it till Christmas.'

His eyes gleamed and he laughed harshly. 'But I want it now!'

There was a chance that he thought he was being playful. She thought about this afterwards. Perhaps he thought this whole scene was fun. They were dallying and bickering and he was taunting her. Clearly he was enjoying himself, and maybe he assumed the same was true of Cathy.

But Cathy hadn't been enjoying it at all. He was like a horrible little goblin, the way he was jeering and snickering and threatening to open the small parcel. All she could think about was the effort it had taken his mother to get out that money and, when she could hardly catch her breath, ask Cathy to go into town to find something to give her boy. Cathy thought about her own efforts, searching out something that might be just the right gift for Noel.

All at once she had felt furious with him. Why on earth were they all thinking about what *he* wanted? Why was he the centre of their worlds? She wondered if he'd stirred himself to go and choose a gift for his mother? Or even one for Cathy? None of it really meant that much, did it? It wasn't that important, surely?

But there was Noel Sturrock, clutching that gift to his chest. He looked just like Rumplestiltskin, Cathy thought. In that moment he repulsed her.

Of course she didn't say anything of the sort to his mother as they ambled along, closer to the beach.

'Eeeh, so the little beggar ruined the surprise,' Teresa tutted.

'Well, no,' said Cathy. 'I managed to get it back off him before he could rip it open. He gave in and saw sense. I hid it again, where he'd never find it.'

'He can be impossible,' his mother chuckled. 'You'll have to watch out for that. He has his funny little ways.'

'Aye, I've learned that already,' Cathy said.

'But any woman taking him on would see that he really has so much love to offer them,' Teresa said. 'No one is more loyal and loving than my lad. Some of the time it comes out all wrong, and he gets annoyed, but the temper is all at himself, really. He gets furious at himself, and that puts some folk off.'

Panic was starting to grip at Cathy's innards as she listened to her friend burbling on. Surely she wasn't talking to Cathy as a prospective daughter-in-law? Suddenly Cathy was feeling queasy. What kind of conversations had gone on behind her back between mother and son? What was Teresa really trying to say to her?

'I think Noel gets along fine without a woman in his life,' she found herself replying awkwardly.

'No, no,' said Teresa. 'He needs a wife. The time has come. He needs someone there at home just for him. I won't be there forever. This sickness has made us both aware of that. And before I pop me clogs, I want to see that lovely lad settled with a nice girl. Then I can go to my glory with contentment. If I could only see Noel happy.'

'Well,' said Cathy. 'I don't think you'll be going to your glory any time soon, do you?'

The old woman shrugged. 'Maybe not before Christmas, anyhow. I feel proper revived by all this lovely fresh air. But you mark my words, Cathy Carmichael. I've decided that life's too short to go beating round the bushes. You have to come right out and say these things.'

Oh, help. Cathy thought. What's coming now?

Teresa said it quite plainly: 'You have to take my son off me. You have to marry that little monster and make a man of him. That's what I say has to happen, and I'm always right, hinny, aren't I? I'm always right!'

By now they had a view of the vast expanse of the pale beach and the endless sea. The vista before them was huge, but Cathy was starting to feel trapped.

Chapter 16

Was it wise to be gathering in one house over Christmas? With those horrible germs still doing the rounds and all? Probably not, but Teresa Sturrock wasn't going to be deterred.

'I've had quite long enough confined to me bed,' she said thunderously, as she prepared a feast for Christmas Day. 'I reckon it's time for us all to get back together again.'

Whatever misgivings Cathy might have had were swept away by the force of the old woman's feelings. This was her house, after all, and Cathy, though she'd proved herself indispensable, was just a guest, after all.

So, the Franchino clan were all invited, grandmama and kiddies and all. Sofia Franchino had become such a good friend, plus they could surely be relied upon to bring a wonderful dessert, Teresa reasoned.

Naturally there would be Winnie in attendance. It took some reorganisation of the parlour and some chairs had to be brought from the front room, but eventually there was seating for everyone around the table. A new cloth was put on and all the cutlery was polished until it shone.

'It's to be a proper, fancy affair,' Teresa said. 'We've had such a miserable time of it. We all want to kick up our heels and celebrate, don't we?'

She havered over what to cook for the grand repast until one night her Noel came back from the Robin Hood with a burlap sack over his shoulder.

'Help! Has he been poaching?' his mother cried, in a flap.

'Shut your trap, woman,' he grumbled, thumping his burden down on the kitchen table. 'Have a look inside there. Go on! It's a rare treat, that.'

Teresa untied the sack and thrust her hands inside. Cathy felt herself shrinking back, thinking that she'd never be so bold. Why, there could be anything in there! It might even be alive still! She wouldn't put such mischief past Noel Sturrock.

But the fowl was quite dead, luckily. Ma Sturrock gasped in something approaching awe as she dragged it out of the bag. She cradled it in her arms and stroked its soft, white, feathery neck, looking almost reverential. 'It's bigger than you are, Ma!' her son laughed.

The bird's eyes were squeezed shut, as if it was trying to block out the noise. Cathy felt her heart twinge for it, and then cursed herself for being daft. 'A goose! Who else round here will be having a goose?' she laughed. 'Do you know how to cook it?'

'My mother knows how to cook anything,' said Noel proudly.

'There'll be something in old Mrs Beeton's book,' Teresa said. 'I don't think it's much different to any other bird.' Still she was stroking the soft feathers of its neck. 'Eeeh, won't we be fancy, offering them goose?'

'Only the best for my mam,' Noel beamed.

She shot him a shrewd look. 'Where did you get it? How did you come by a bloody goose, lad?'

He preened himself. 'Why, I have my contacts, don't I?'

'Not that rough lot who go drinking down at the Mudlark, Noel?' she said, eyeing him carefully. 'Tell me you're not making yourself beholden to any of that lot down there . . .'

'Now, you don't have to worry about me,' he chuckled.

Her eyes widened. 'Not the Mad Johnsons, son? Say you haven't taken anything off of that Johnson clan?'

He carried on laughing and tried to wave her fears away. 'Just you cook your goose, Ma. You just feed the five thousand and enjoy the season.'

His mother kept muttering about the Mad Johnson clan, who came from the rough end of town and held court at the Mudlark. Cathy didn't like the sound of them at all. 'What's so bad about them?' she asked Teresa as the two of them manhandled the goose into the cold store.

'They're not the kind of people to get in debt to,' the old mother said. 'They've caused havoc and mayhem in this town for years. The current crop of young'uns are the most vicious yet. I just hope our Noel isn't getting himself tangled up with them.'

Of course Noel Sturrock was getting tangled up with the Mad Johnsons. It wasn't long before Cathy became aware of the shady deals he was striking over at the Robin Hood. Usually their supply of bottles and barrels came on the back of the cart driven by the brewery's old dray horse, but some deliveries had started to come after midnight, brought to the back door by a ginger-haired fella called Alec.

'Alec Johnson, that is,' sighed Ellie the barmaid. 'Nasty piece of work, just like all his brothers and his uncles. What a family they are!'

Alec Johnson was tubby and hard-faced, with a ratty little tash that somehow made him look even more belligerent. He offloaded shining bottles of whisky and rum in the storeroom of the Robin Hood. Cathy saw her boss furtively peeling money from a fat roll of notes to pay him on the spot. She could see a mile off that this was dodgy stuff. Stolen supplies, surely.

All those extra bottles were red-hot. The two men looked so furious and guilty when she coughed and squeezed past them, going about her business in the back of the pub.

'You never saw nowt,' Noel warned her later.

'Ellie told me that the ginger fella is one of the Mad Johnsons,' Cathy said. 'Your mother warned you about them. Not to get involved with them!'

Noel spat on the cement floor of the storeroom and swore nastily. Cathy was taken aback by his vulgarity. 'What does my mother know about the world out there? She knows bugger all about the things you have to do in order to keep afloat in this day and age. She's been protected. I've been the one protecting her! The harsh realities of this life have never touched her for years, whatever she says. Me mam belongs to the last century. And she knows nowt.'

Cathy had never heard him speak so harshly of his own mother, but she thought he might have a point. The world of Teresa's concerns was very limited. She had no idea how the pub was run, or all the work that Noel had to put into it. She didn't know how he broke his back every week just to bring money home for them. In recent months Cathy had started to appreciate just what a struggle it was for Noel, and the effort he went to in order to conceal that struggle from his mother.

'Don't tell her that the Johnsons have been round here,' he asked Cathy, and there was almost a pleading note in his voice. 'She'll only worry. I'm just trying to bring in a few extra bob to see us through . . .'

The girl nodded slowly, keeping her eyes on him. 'Aye, all right, I'll say nothing,' she agreed. It would do her no harm to keep hold of a secret or two. She knew something about Noel that he didn't want spreading about. That gave her a little bit of power, maybe. A bit more stability, perhaps . . .

'You're a good lass,' he told her, and turned away.

*

He wore his peacock blue bow tie on Christmas morning and his mother glowed with pride at the sight of him. Noel stepped into the back parlour with his bony chin thrust out, as if to display his new piece of finery.

'Oh, very handsome,' his mother cried, clapping her hands.

'So, is this my birthday and my Christmas present all rolled into one?' he said.

Cathy had forgotten – of course, Christmas Day was his birthday, too. She remembered Teresa once telling her how she had pretended he'd been left in the hearth by Father Christmas all those years ago. He was her festive immaculate conception!

'Eeeh, will you listen to him?' Teresa laughed. 'Aye, it's your only present from me, you greedy little beggar. Do you think I'm made of money?'

He bent to kiss her glowing cheek. 'I love it, Ma, thank you.'

She was grinning with pleasure, already draining her first little glass of Christmas sherry.

Cathy came forward then with a parcel for Noel. He mimicked great surprise and joy as he took it and unwrapped a scarf that she had knitted for him. It was in shades of orange, purple and green and really about as expertly knitted as those mittens she had made for his mother. There were loose ends of twine sticking out and it looked a bit snagged and tight in places. But Noel held it up to his face and smiled at its softness. 'Eeeh, it's champion, lass. Thank you.'

She had never heard him say anything as heartfelt without following it up with something snappish and sarcastic. This was a day to remember, indeed!

'I have gifts,' he told them, and from a bag in the hall he brought them clinking, unwrapped bottles. Rum for his mother and port for Cathy. A blushing, confused smile was all she could offer him as she stammered out her thanks. Port? She didn't even like port. And he very well knew that she knew that these were nicked! These bottles were clearly part of the dodgy consignment that Alec Johnson had delivered to the Robin Hood.

'Ah, lad, how lovely!' his mother grinned. 'Ooh, I do love rum.'

Noel patted her hand. 'Only the best for my mother.'

Cathy bit her tongue. The cheap little bugger! Purloined bottles! He hadn't even made the effort to go down the bloody shops and choose something for his gifts!

Suddenly furious, Cathy returned to the scullery and all the hundred and one jobs that needed doing. She had a colossal pan of potatoes bobbing away, and she'd have to fish them out soon so she could roast them in the oven.

After a mammoth session of plucking, the bird was ready in a vast dish, all larded up and stuffed with sausage meat and chestnuts. Dealing with the thing had been quite a palaver, and there was a whole sackful of white feathers to show for her efforts.

'Here they are!' Ma Sturrock was calling out then excitedly, as the Franchinos stepped noisily into the parlour, with the baby screaming and Tonio singing some kind of foreign carol in a lustily off-tune voice.

Rubbing the grease off her hands with a tea cloth, Cathy went to welcome them. The back parlour was suddenly full of life and people hugging each other, wishing each other the compliments of the season. It was quite overwhelming at first and Cathy stood there beaming at them all.

Even Noel seemed pleased to have a houseful of visitors on Christmas Day. 'Let's have a drink! Shall I open the port, Cathy? Do you mind?'

But Tonio Franchino interrupted him. 'No, I have the perfect drink for this time in the morning!' From under his heavy docker's coat he produced a large, dark blue bottle. The liquid that he poured out of it was very thick and cloudy. Cathy, Noel and Teresa examined their glasses thoughtfully before downing it. 'This is my mother's famous limoncello,' Tonio told them. 'It's so powerful and delicious, it will knock all your blocks off.'

The tiny old woman in the black mantilla and shawl shrugged modestly and tipped her own schooner into her mouth with a gasp of relish.

Cathy did likewise and grinned. 'I've never tasted anything so lovely in my life,' she told the old lady, as she felt the lemony heat of it blazing down her gullet.

Sofia laughed and hurried through to the scullery. 'I will help you in here, love,' she told Cathy. 'I can see they're making you do all the work.'

Sofia herself had brought a lovely dish of baked fish, in a cream sauce with discs of lemon and cucumber slices arranged on it like scales. 'It's too beautiful to eat,' Cathy said.

'Nonsense,' Sofia laughed, and came to look at the mammoth bird in its roasting dish. The long neck was folded around one side of it. Cathy had left the head on, not quite sure what to do about it.

'Oh!' Sofia said. 'Shouldn't this be in the oven already?'

'I think I've got my timings wrong,' Cathy admitted. 'I've never cooked a whole Christmas dinner before. At Morwick Hall I was in charge of the potatoes, so I've got no bother doing *them*. It's just the rest of it all . . .'

'I will help you,' Sofia smiled. 'And we'll let the old ladies get drunk in the parlour, shall we? We'll just take our time in here.'

'Thanks,' Cathy said. 'Is there a lot more of that lemon stuff?' Suddenly she felt a bit teary with gratitude. 'This feels like proper Christmas today. Last year, I was all on my own. I was in that horrible boarding house in Morwick, all by myself. I never thought I'd have friends around me again . . .'

The Italian girl hugged her friend, alarmed at how emotional she was suddenly being. It wasn't like Cathy at all, this. They hugged and she watched her friend dabbing her eyes dry with her pinny.

'I'm letting myself get upset,' Cathy said. 'I know it's not like me. I don't mean to alarm you. But I have my reasons. I'll tell you some time . . . Later on, maybe. I'll tell you why Christmas is so hard for me.'

'It's a deal,' said Sofia. 'In the meantime, we better get this swan into the oven.'

Cathy's jaw dropped. 'Get this *what* into the oven?'

'Your swan. It'll take at least three hours. We better get it in there.'

Cathy was still staring at her. 'It's a goose!'

Sofia shook her head sagely. 'That is definitely a swan.'

Chapter 17

'Look, just don't tell anyone what it really is, and everything will be fine . . .'

Cathy bowed to what she felt must be Sofia's greater knowledge of wildfowl and the pair of them spent the rest of Christmas pretending that what they were eating was actually goose. They sat and smiled and nodded when Teresa exclaimed over the succulent roasted flesh of the bird.

'It has quite an unusual flavour,' she said. 'Sort of tangy.'

'Tangy?' frowned the old nonna, who stared suspiciously at her plate.

The children ate with gusto, as did Noel and Winnie.

All Cathy could think was: how on earth did Noel manage to come by a swan? Someone had been out in the boggy waterlands south of Sunderland, maybe. What kind of poacher nabs a swan?

She picked at her own meal, sticking to the potatoes mostly.

Between courses, as party games began in the parlour, Cathy and Sofia retreated to the chilly back yard to share a cigarette and to get some air.

'I never smoke much really,' Sofia said, laughing. 'Tonio says it isn't very ladylike. But I enjoy it so . . .'

'Me too,' Cathy smiled and they smoked in contented silence for a while, enjoying the Christmas Day quiet of the back lane.

'That bottle of brandy!' Sofia exclaimed. 'It is much too generous of Noel to give us such an expensive gift. My mother is delighted.'

Cathy shrugged. 'You're more than generous to us, pet. And besides, all that drink – as well as the bloody swan – it's all Noel's ill-gotten gains.'

The Italian girl frowned. 'Ill-gotten?'

'Nicked. Robbed. I think it's all stolen goods.' Cathy winced as she took a long drag of the shared cigarette.

'Ah, criminal,' whispered Sofia knowingly. 'And you aren't happy about it?'

'It's nothing to do with me, what the foolish man gets up to,' she said. 'But I live here and I work with him. I'm sort of dependent on the Sturrocks now. And I absolutely love old Teresa. When I thought she was about to peg it because of the flu I was devastated.'

'These old ladies are made of strong stuff, I think,' Sofia said. 'My mother also. And we must be made of strong stuff, too.'

'I think you're right, love,' Cathy smiled. She passed the cigarette over and thought about how much she was enjoying having Sofia as a friend. Had she ever really had a good friend before? There had been other chambermaids at the big house. There had been people she'd chatted to at work, even confiding in a few. But had she ever really had a friend of her own? Someone she actually trusted? With a gasp of surprise, Cathy realised that Sofia was most likely the first actual friend she'd had, close to her own age. An old biddy like Teresa didn't really count, and she suspected Ellie would stab her in the back, first chance she got . . .

'Listen,' said Sofia, breaking into the flow of her wistful, tipsy thoughts. 'Remember I said I'd tell you why we had to leave Naples?'

Cathy nodded. She remembered their day of close confidences as they had wandered around the shops of South Shields in their masks, carrying their baskets of wares. Already it seemed like weeks ago.

'Well, it was all because of Tonio. He was mixing in bad company. That was the reason we had to get away from home, fast. He had bad men coming after him. Men who would stop at nothing. Ones who would gladly kill his young wife and his mother-in-law, anyone connected to him. It was a vendetta,' Sofia sighed.

Cathy's eyes were out on stalks as she listened. 'But, why? What had he done?' She thought about that stocky, rather boastful man currently singing noisily in the back parlour. They could hear him all the way through the scullery. Had he murdered someone? What was he capable of?

'My husband has a kind of sickness. An addiction,' Sofia explained. 'To gambling. He cannot stop himself. If there is a game of cards, or chance, or anything happening somewhere in town, he will find it. He will lay down money and promises and anything he can think of. He would gamble away his home and his life in an instant. Nothing matters to him when he's at that table. And back in our home town, he got himself into trouble.'

'That's awful, pet,' said Cathy. A part of herself had been hoping for something more deadly and melodramatic, perhaps. She had to remind herself – this was real life, not some gory tale she was reading. This was Sofia and her family's actual life.

'He borrowed money from here and there and everywhere. Even from the worst family in our whole town. They were loaded and could afford it. But they never let a debt go unpaid. Tonio ended up owing them such a lot and the interest just went up and up . . .' She shook her head, laughing bitterly. 'He gambled with the sons of that family. That was how close he liked to sail to the wind. And he tried to win the money back from them! He was so certain of his good fortune . . .' She said a few words in Italian, and Cathy just knew they were rude words.

'But you're safely away from all of that now, though, aren't you?'

'He still owes them money,' Sofia said. 'Hundreds of pounds. Maybe thousands by now. We slipped away and managed to escape. He threw that dart and chose this place at random. It's all those years ago now, almost ten years ago.'

'There you go . . .' Cathy tried to laugh encouragingly. 'That's ages ago. By God, there's been a war since then. Who'd even think about a measly gambling debt after all that time?'

'I would,' said Sofia. 'And they would – the family that he robbed. Tonio might never think about it anymore. He might wave his hands and shush me when I try to talk about it, but I know it's true. One day we'll see one of those men. They will find us. They'll send the Man in the Black Hat after us.'

Cathy's eyes widened. 'Who?'

'That's what they did,' said Sofia. 'When they were going to . . . you know . . .'

'Bump someone off? Do away with them?'

'Yes, bump off someone. They would send their deadliest assassin to their door. The man who wore a black fedora.'

Cathy couldn't help it. She shivered in the cold, thrilled as well as chilled by the brick wall of the privy at her back. 'You're making all this up. It's just a story! You're having me on!'

'I wish I was, love,' she said. 'I've spent these past few years expecting at any moment to see that man in the black hat. Standing on our doorstep. Or seeing him from afar down the lane . . .'

She really believes it all! Cathy gasped and wondered whether to light a second cigarette. What other tales might Sofia tell her if they stayed out here for another?

Then the scullery door swung open and out tottered the ancient grandmother in her black shawl. 'What are you two gabbling about?' she cackled, heading for the toilet at the bottom of the yard.

'Oh, just old family tales, Nonna,' Sofia told her, adding something in fluidly musical Italian.

Shuffling along, the old lady chuckled and replied harshly, tapping her cane on the frosty ground.

'My mother says unless we want to listen to her bowels thundering like the day of judgment, we better go back inside the house now. Also, she says well done on cooking that swan.'

The two women hurried back indoors.

The rest of Christmas Day passed in a sweet blur of alcohol and fun. Noel kept the drinks flowing, playing at being the perfect host. Later the Italians and even Winnie – who had known the surly malcontent all his life – commented on just how welcoming and genial Noel had been.

Even when Winnie started telling the future for everyone, peering into their tea leaves and reading the lines on their hands, Noel had simply let her get on with it. He never complained once as she pretended to peer through the veil of future years, speaking quaveringly of the great good fortune that the Franchinos would soon enjoy. 'I see a big house by the sea! I see you all being very happy there!'

Tonio's eyes went wide. 'But that's amazing!'

'Ooh, yes . . . I see you having great success and moving up in the world,' Winnie promised.

Sofia whispered to Cathy, 'Oh, great. He's been talking about this new house. A huge thing, at Seaham. Looking at the sea. It's beautiful, but we can't afford to live that way . . .'

Now Winnie was clutching the small, soft hands of the Franchinos' daughter, Bella. 'Now, here is the clever and beautiful one. She will be the one carrying the name on into the future. She will have a whole empire of ice-cream parlours one day. And she'll have an army of red-haired children. I can see them!'

The adults laughed at the face of the little girl as it twisted in non-comprehension.

Winnie went on, 'I see these little vans, selling ice-cream out of the windows! They play music as they go round every street in town. There will be a whole fleet of them! The Franchino family will be everywhere!'

There was a round of applause from the collected company at Winnie's excited prognostications.

'And what about our Cathy, eh?' Teresa Sturrock cried out. 'She never lets you look at her palm, Winnie. She never wants anyone getting an insight into her!'

'Oh, no, no, really,' Cathy said. She got up and protested. 'Look, I'll go and cut up that fancy cake that Sofia brought.'

'Sit down,' Noel barked at her. 'Let Winnie take a look at your lifeline!'

Very reluctantly Cathy sat back at the table, and as the old woman grasped her hands in her own cold fingers, a wave of sickness went through the girl. I've mixed my drinks. I've nibbled on swan. Now I feel nauseous . . .

Winnie took longer than usual, staring into her subject's palms. Everyone was waiting with bated breath for a few moments. 'Well?' said Teresa. 'What do you see? Are there great things in the future for our lovely Cathy?'

They could sense Winnie equivocating. It was as if she could see something there but was dubious about whether she could actually share it with them. 'It's all right,' Cathy leaned forward to tell her. 'If there's nothing there, it's doesn't matter.'

'But there is!' Winnie burst out. 'I can see all sorts of things here. Maybe I can see too much . . .'

Teresa Sturrock chortled with glee, rocking back in her dining chair. 'Oh, good! Winnie's going into one of her funny trances! I love it when she goes into a spell like this!'

Across the messy table the old Italian grandmother was

muttering under her breath. 'This isn't godly,' she was saying, though only her daughter understood her words. 'Perhaps we should stop this?' Sofia suggested.

'Cathy . . .' said Winnie in a voice that suddenly became much louder and grander than her usual wheedling tones. 'Hark at me, Cathy Carmichael!'

There was such a weird shift in the atmosphere that the Franchinos' young son Marco started to grizzle and cry. Sofia hugged him closer and even she had to admit that there was a clammy, uncomfortable feeling in the air.

Teresa was encouraging Winnie to go further. 'What do you see, hinny?'

In that queer, booming voice, Winnie went on: 'You have had terrible choices to make, Cathy. I can see that now. You are hiding great sadness. More than any of us know about.'

All eyes were on Cathy and she cringed at the unwanted attention.

'You keep all of these secrets locked inside,' said Winnie. 'Even your new, good friends don't really know anything about you, who your people are or where you come from – not really. No one here really knows what it is that you've left behind . . .'

They were staring at Cathy again now and she felt like snatching her trembling hands back from the old gypsy woman. Damn her! Who did she think she was, playing daft games like this? Embarrassing her? Drawing attention to the things she'd never talked about? What business was it for anyone else? Why should they care about the things and the people Cathy had left behind?

Instead of getting angry Cathy kept her voice pleasant and tried to laugh it off. She said, 'I thought you were supposed to be looking into my future, not trying to see into my past?'

Winnie's head snapped up and she stared into the girl's eyes. 'You have already found your future, hinny. Your whole future is here, in this street and in this house. You have found everything you will ever need.'

The whole room seemed to sigh at her words.

'Eeeh, is that true, Winnie?' cried Teresa Sturrock. 'Is out Cathy gonna stay here with us, forever and ever?'

Winnie's face cracked into a huge smile. 'She has found everything she needs, right here, in the Sixteen Streets. And now, my dear Cathy, you have no need to run away ever again.'

Everyone seemed delighted by this reading of Winnie's. They all agreed that it was a lovely, gentle kind of foretelling of the future.

So why did Cathy suddenly feel sick?

Chapter 18

New Year's Eve had its own share of dramas.

Noel declared that he wanted to pull out all the stops and to have a great big party, just as they normally did at the Robin Hood. He wanted the place to be packed to the rafters, he wanted singing and carousing, and everything back to normal. Aunty Martha was engaged to play the piano all evening once more, even though she was still recovering shakily from her own bout of the flu.

'Are you sure you're up to playing all evening?' Cathy asked her.

'Of course,' the skinny young woman retorted. 'I wouldn't miss this for the world!' There was a feverish determination in her eye as if, during her bedridden weeks, all she'd been able to think of was one day bashing out the old songs once again on the pub's tuneless piano.

Ellie and Cathy were scrubbing down the tables and the rough wooden floors, discussing the coming festivities. 'Noel wouldn't be so cavalier about everything if he'd caught the bloody germs himself,' Ellie muttered. 'It was no bloody picnic, I'll tell you that much.'

Cathy didn't point out that both she and Noel had seen suffering close at hand, in the person of Ma Sturrock. She didn't say anything because sometimes it wasn't worth quibbling with Ellie. She became flustered and cross very quickly if you argued with her.

For her own part, Cathy found herself looking forward to New Year's Eve very much. She had a new dress and felt like she had been cooped up in the house far too much in December. When she'd worked at the pub it had been slack and quiet. Now Noel was putting up posters everywhere, advertising his New Year jamboree – 'A chance to see the back of this rotten old year!' he kept saying. Cathy felt that the danger from the flu had peaked and ebbed away; they had surely seen the worst of it in South Shields by now.

She and Ellie polished the glasses and wiped down the beer pumps and the bottles displayed on the shelves behind them. They enlisted Sofia's help to make dainty little sandwiches and sweet buns for a fancy buffet. When the doors were thrown open early on that final, snowy evening of the year, a happy crowd came surging indoors.

Cathy grinned. Noel's instincts had been correct, it seemed. A big night out was how everyone from Frederick Street and beyond wanted to finish off this year.

Later that night Noel's instincts were telling him something else, too.

For him New Year's Eve began quite happily. He had marched into his saloon bar like the perfect host, wearing a freshly ironed shirt surmounted by his peacock blue bow tie. He tried his best to stoop a little less and to hold up his head and to smile at his regulars and all the other punters. Look at me! I'm a success! I've filled this place with all these people and they're looking at me to give them a good time! He went strutting around and his new silk tie elicited a round of comments, not all of them sarcastic. In fact, many of the people who knew him mentioned that he had a lightness to him, a spring in his step and a touch of what – had they not known Noel better – they might have called gleefulness.

But Noel found that he was, in fact, happy. The emotion was unusual and didn't sit quite well with him. He endured it, nonetheless.

It's all to do with the lass, isn't it, he told himself. He also told himself he was foolish for letting himself rely on another person for his happiness. Why, they always let you down, don't they?

Except his mam, of course. She had never let him down.

As he went about his hosting duties he kept his eye on his mother, who was installed at the Women's Table by the fire. That was Cathy's idiotic name for it, of course – as if the women had ever needed anywhere special and exclusive to sit! Now it looked like a den of old harpies. His mother and her closest cronies were hogging the warmth of the fire and sending up shrieks of laughter. Well, he should be glad to see her happy and well, he thought. He should be glad she'd made it to the end of the year alive.

But Noel still wrestled with the conundrum of his own contentedness. He didn't trust it. He knew that happiness was something fragile. It depended on so many things. It could so easily be whisked away . . .

The den of harpies were discussing their Christmases and various Christmases of the past. They were discussing the changes brought by passing of the years, and the young men who'd never returned from the war, and all those folk who'd been carried off by the flu. It rather felt like the women were determined not to be maudlin, though; they all felt it incumbent upon them to enjoy this night for the sake of those who no longer could enjoy themselves. The women at their special table suddenly felt the need to live for the moment.

Teresa Sturrock sipped strong, dark beer with her friends Ada Farley and old Grandma Franchino, whose first name she had never quite caught. The old woman spoke very little English and seemed to respond to the name 'Nonna' from everyone.

'I was run off me feet the whole time this Christmas, of course,' Ada Farley sighed ruefully. 'With all my boys. You couldn't get them to behave or calm down, they were just so excited. Of course Frank did absolutely nowt to pitch in. He was in bed most of the time. He had a skinful of booze each night and was passed out through most of the days of Christmas. It was mostly just me and my lads.'

'You're best off without him,' Teresa counselled the younger woman from number thirteen. 'Just you and your boys.'

'One day perhaps. He'll drink himself to death or just go wandering off. I don't know . . .' Her eyes were glistening as she told these tales about her home life, trusting that they'd go no further than the Women's Table. 'Eeeh, but if you'd seen the boys. I mean, I couldn't afford to get them much. All they had was a couple of sweets in their stocking, a balsa wood plane to make up, a handful of nuts and a penny wrapped in a new hanky each. They had one book of stories to share between the three of them. But they were glad, man! That was the thing that breaks me heart. They were bloomin' glad of everything they got.' She was weeping openly now, dabbing her eyes with the sleeve of her old cardigan. She chuckled, adding, 'And you'll never guess what they put their moneys together to buy me?'

'What was that, pet?' asked Teresa, who was getting fed up by now with Ada's stories.

'Bloody biscuits! They'd put together their pennies to buy me a little tin of biscuits!'

Teresa cackled. 'Not Wight's biscuits? Not from where you work?'

'Aye, they did – like I don't see enough of the things! Like I don't spend almost every day getting sick to the eye-teeth of them, seeing them in their hundreds at work!' The women laughed at this, with Nonna Franchino joining in, even though she hadn't understood everything that was being said. Ada sighed and added, 'Ah, but they mean well, the daft little buggers.'

Soon they were joined by Cathy, taking a short break as she collected up drained pint pots. She had to shout over the raucous noise from Aunty Martha, who was playing her favourite music hall songs. The singing had become noisy as the evening wore on. 'How are you all getting on, ladies?'

'It's good to be out,' Teresa beamed at her. 'And you're doing a smashing job, love. I can't tell you how different it is in here since you started here. You've made it into a place I actually want to go!'

'Me too,' Ada piped up. 'Well, before it was like the Wild bloody West in here. You'd see them come stumbling and flying out of the saloon doors, out into the street. I mean it! It was like the OK Corral or something!'

Cathy laughed at this and felt pleased with herself and the changes she had brought to the Robin Hood and number twenty-one Frederick Street in the few months she had been here. Yes, she had set her stamp upon the place. And it was just as well, for if what Winnie had said on Christmas Day was true, then she was set to stay here for quite some time yet . . .

This thought didn't disturb her as much as she thought it might, however. In the past month or so she had really come to think of the Sixteen Streets as her home ground.

She realised that there were some fellas over at the table opposite, and all three of them had been glancing over. One in particular was taking a good long look at her. Brazenly staring at the barmaid now as she took her break. Cathy caught his glance and returned it boldly. God, he was handsome, she thought. Very pale and red-headed. A very angular face, almost bony. He seemed startled and turned away. She laughed at his sudden shyness.

The three blokes were in their smartest suits, especially for going out. Their clothes looked almost new, or at least well looked after. Something about their bearing told Cathy that they were servicemen, recently returned from the front, perhaps. The lucky ones, in that case, because the three of them seemed healthy and undamaged by their experiences. They were laughing and clearly set upon having themselves a good time.

'Who are they?' Cathy asked Teresa, leaning back in her chair and trying to be subtle.

'I've never seen 'em,' Teresa frowned. 'Nice-looking lads, though, eh?' She peered over her spectacles, studying them openly. 'Ah, that one is the youngest Johnson lad.' She pulled a face. 'Best avoided, that lot, hinny. You know what they say about that lot.'

As luck would have it, the fella who Ma Sturrock had identified as the wrong sort was precisely the one who had been admiring Cathy. The handsome one. She sighed and took in a swift inventory of his looks: he was strong, hearty and tall. He was flushed pink in the smoky warmth of the pub, wearing just a white vest under his smart going-out jacket. Auburn chest hair could be seen curling over the neck. He had thick curls of red hair on his head too and it looked smashing on him, Cathy decided. She'd never felt attracted to a ginger fella before, but there was something powerful about this bloke's looks. It set up a tingling in her breast that slowly sank down through her body and went somewhere she wasn't quite expecting it to as she sat there in a public saloon bar. It felt very like drinking that potent limoncello the old Italian lady had brewed.

'Hmm,' Cathy said, and collected the empty milk stout glasses from the Women's Table. 'Same again for you ladies, eh?'

As if on cue, just as Cathy was offering drinks, Winnie came in from the cold, unwrapping her snowy overcoat and headscarf. 'I'd love one, pet,' she grinned toothlessly.

Ada Farley said something caustic about Winnie's prognostications being useful for knowing when rounds of drinks were being bought, and the evening rolled gently on in the twinkling, amber bar light.

Towards midnight the music became even louder and the singing more raggedly enthusiastic. People were up on their feet and the tables and chairs were dragged back. The bare boards of the floor were exposed – a waxed and shining expanse for everyone to dance upon.

Aunty Martha's endless, bottomless repertoire was almost exhausted by the time that midnight came around. Her fingers were chapped red and her joints felt like they were swelling, but still she played on and on, hammering at keys that were yellow with decades of tab smoke. They were yellow as Winnie's few remaining teeth. Martha had a good view of those beige stumps as Winnie stood by her side to belt out the perennial favourite, 'The Blaydon Races':

> *'Ah me lads, ye shudda seen us gannin',*
> *We pass'd the foaks alang the road just as they wor stannin';*
> *Thor wis lots o' lads an' lassies there, aal wi' smiling faces,*
> *Gannin' alang the Scotswood Road, to see the Blaydon Races!'*

Even though the words were gabbled fast and Winnie sang in an exaggerated Newcastle accent, the whole pub managed to keep up with her through numerous verses.

Cathy – who'd never heard the traditional song sung like this – stood by the bar grinning, listening hard to every word. Then she laughed to see Ma Sturrock and Ada Farley gathering their long skirts in bunches at their knees. They linked arms and danced up and down the bare boards, jaunty and daft like Cathy would never have believed. Teresa was sprightly, too! As if the spirit of the dance had entered into her, animating her weakened limbs and lending breath to her tired lungs. Mind, it could have been the effect of all the stout she had put away, too.

As she laughed, Cathy became aware of the presence of a tall man at her side. It was like his whole body was giving off this special kind of heat. She knew who it was without even turning to look him in the eye.

'You've crept over to say hello to me,' she said, laughing at him. 'You've got up the courage at last, have you?'

'Courage, nothing!' he said gruffly, grinning back at her. 'And have I buggery crept over anywhere. I've come over here quite boldly, you knaa. And I've come over to ask if you'll dance with us.'

'With you?' she asked, feeling herself growing bolder under his obvious attraction to her. She was chuffed to see that, close too, he was even more bonny-looking than she had first thought. There was something compelling about him. 'Who are you anyway?'

'I'm Matty Johnson,' he said. Then he grinned at her in a way that made her stomach squeeze up into a ball. 'Now come on, lass. Come and dance!'

And there was nothing for it but to do just what he said.

As they rushed out into the open space at the heart of the pub, Cathy failed to notice the crooked figure manning the beer pumps. He was staring at the two of them as they grew hot and merry with the dance. He stood staring, his expression curdling, wearing his new peacock blue bow tie.

Noel Sturrock watched them whirling around and laughing like dizzy fools, and as he watched, he was growing more and more furious.

Chapter 19

Snow kept falling past midnight and into the early hours of the new year. By the time the partygoers at the Robin Hood came tumbling out of the pub, it was lying quite thickly in the shallow canyons of the Sixteen Streets.

The vast skies above were soft and opaque and no stars could be seen, but the fallen snow was bright enough to light the way for the revellers. Bursts of song and tuneless choruses could be heard drifting down the hill as the celebrations ended.

Teresa and her friends had left some time before the end, pleading exhaustion. 'You've done us all proud, son,' she told Noel, patting his cheek as she hefted on her itchy old fur coat and tottered off.

In the early hours there was only Noel and his two barmaids left, surveying the wreckage of the bar. 'They've drunk us dry!' Ellie exclaimed. 'And by the heck, haven't they left a bloomin' mess?'

The whole saloon was in a dreadful state. There was beer slopped on the floor and tables. Tab ends and mounds of ash were strewn everywhere. The last remnants of that lovely buffet had been scattered and ground into the floorboards by all those hectic, dancing heels.

'They know how to carouse round here, don't they?' Cathy smiled.

'Carousel!' Ellie laughed. 'Aye, that's a fancy word for it, lass.'

Over at the bar Noel seemed to be in a strange trance. His eyes gleamed with triumph at the night he'd hosted, but as Ellie turned to study him, she thought there was something else in his expression. Something hard that she didn't like the look of. His jaw was thrust out as he smoked a cigarette. He loosened that tie of his that he'd been so proud of. He was beetling his brows and she thought: I've seen that look on him before. He's bridling about something. Underneath it all, he's furious . . .

'What did you think, Noel?' Cathy asked heedlessly, whirling over to the bar, where he stood frozen. 'Did you think it went well? Did you have a good time?'

He seemed to have trouble meeting Cathy's eyes. 'It doesn't matter whether I had a good time, does it? I was one of the workers. It was my job to make sure it was a good do. I wasn't the one who was supposed to be having a good time.'

Ah, Ellie thought. She could hear the implied criticism there; the bitterness was leaking out of him. Clearly he had thought that Cathy had been enjoying herself far too much tonight. And look at her there! With her curls springing out of the chignon she'd fashioned. Her face all flushed with excitement and tiredness, her colour high even through the make-up that had been rubbed off her face by exertion and sweat. She looked lovely, even after all these hours of work and fun. Her gleaming face only seemed to make her boss's sudden sour mood even worse.

Time I was going off home, then, Ellie thought. He's working himself up into a temper tantrum, and I don't want to be around for that. Cathy needs warning, too, that he's about to blow his top . . .

'Well, I had a smashing party,' Cathy was grinning. 'Even though it was all hard work, all night. This lot can certainly put the drink away, can't they?'

There were empty pint pots and glasses everywhere you could look, all of them streaked with spirits and dried foam and lipstick smudges. The amount of cleaning and scrubbing involved made Ellie's stomach sink into her shoes. 'Shall we leave all this till the morrow?' she suggested. 'We can't stay up all night cleaning up. Don't we usually get it done later in the day, after we've had a sleep?' She was trying to think back to last year, but right now anything in the past was just a blur. 'I'm dead on me feet, here.'

Suddenly Noel was all gallant and solicitous. He swept into action, fetching Ellie's shawl from the room at the back. He took out his own wallet and pressed money into her hand – a bonus for all her sterling efforts. 'Yes, yes, you must get yourself home and into your bed. You're quite right, pet. Tomorrow's soon enough to shift all this mess. Off you go and get your beauty sleep!'

Ellie was quite alarmed by his sudden switch of tone. He ushered her towards the door, and she felt like she was dragging her heels. 'Well, all right, if you think that's the best way. But I want to do my share, mind. Don't you go staying to tidy up all night . . .'

The landlord chuckled at the very idea. 'Nay, lass. I'm not doing another stroke tonight. Why, of course not! Let's all get to our homes and get a proper sleep and I'll see you tomorrow afternoon, how's that?'

'Well, all right,' smiled Ellie, gathering her woollen shawl around her. She opened the saloon door, peeping out at the tumbling snow out there. 'Eeeh, just look at it! I'm glad I've not got far to go. Is it slippy? I'll be falling arse over tit . . .'

Then, blowing kisses to Cathy and Noel, she staggered off into the snowy night.

Noel closed the saloon door on her heels and Cathy said, 'That was kind of you. She looked really worn out. You're quite right. There's no need to make this place shipshape straight away. It can all wait till tomorrow.'

There was a curious pause then, as Noel shot the bolts on the front door and turned the large key in the lock. Then he turned very slowly to face his one remaining member of staff. There was a strange light in his eye as he studied her. 'You think so, do you lass?'

Bemused, she smiled at him. 'Well, that's what you were just saying. It can all wait, can't it? No hurry . . .' Her thinking was foggy with all the dancing and the drinks she'd taken. An odd sip here, and a little glug there. The fellas had been buying her drinks all evening. Since it was a special night, she'd actually taken them, rather than putting the coins in the tips jar. Now she was having trouble following Noel's shifting moods. 'Noel?' she frowned at him. 'Are you all right there, hinny?'

He stiffened slightly. 'Don't you call me hinny,' he said thickly. His voice was harsh and loaded with spite.

'Hey, what's the matter? Why are you talking like that?'

She watched him make his way back to the bar, limping on his bad leg, scowling all the way.

'Noel, have I done something wrong?'

He didn't answer her directly. Let her suffer, he thought. Let her just think over all the things she's done wrong tonight. Acting like a hussy at work. Prancing about like a trollop. Toying with people's affections! Just let her think back and she would surely realise how cavalier and careless and cruel she had been . . .

'Right,' he said. 'I want this place *immaculate*.'

She blinked at him. 'What?'

'I want all the glasses gleaming. I want all the tankards polishing. I want the floors swept and mopped and the tables wiped down. I want all the rubbish swept away.'

'I know, I know, we can do it tomorrow, the three of us, after we've had a proper sleep.'

The little man put his foot down. 'Oh no, Cathy. That's not good enough. Not for a proud landlord like me. What would everyone think, seeing the place in this state? What would they think of me, going home and leaving it like this?'

She gazed around at the wreckage of the Robin Hood, feeling flabbergasted by his sudden attitude. 'No one would mind! There's no one here to see it!'

'*I* can see it,' he said, hauling himself up onto a barstool and tutting. 'And I think it would be a bloody disgrace. You see, Cathy, what I've got – the thing that I have that sets me above other fellows round here – is self-respect. Dignity. I've got such a lot of it. And standards, too. And I must keep them up.'

She had no idea where all this was coming from, but she didn't like it. He was acting so strangely, he was starting to give her the creeps. 'All right Noel, hinny. I've had enough of this now. Let's get ourselves home and we'll do all the work tomorrow. We'll have your lovely pub neat as a new pin . . .' She set her jaw determinedly and went to fetch her coat.

'Not good enough,' he snapped.

'What?' Now she was getting annoyed with him. He wouldn't let her pass through the bar to get her jacket. He'd put his stool directly in her path. 'Let me through, Noel.'

'No,' he said. 'I won't. And do you know why?'

She was going red with frustration and annoyance. 'Why? What are you playing at?'

'It's because you're the junior member of staff here. You're the newest and the youngest. Sometimes the worst and the dirtiest jobs fall to the likes of you.'

'Look, what are you on about?' she said and, for the first time, wished that there was someone else on the premises besides him and her. Noel had turned peculiar and she didn't like it one bit.

'You, my lass, are going to stay up all night – if it takes that long – and you're going to set this place to rights.'

'What?' she gasped. 'I'm not doing that! I'm knackered!'

'You're young and strong,' he countered. 'And I thought you loved cleaning and tidying up anyway? That's what you kept saying to my mam, didn't you? When you were sorting out our house? Do you remember all that? When no one asked you to do it, you just got it into your head that we needed tidying up and cleaning and sorting out? Why, you were dusting and mopping and you were all full of energy. And by, didn't my mother think you were a miracle worker? I never heard the last of it! Young Cathy this and Young Cathy that! Why, I'd have thought that cleaning up was your special passion, Cathy. I'd have thought you'd love to stay up all night making this place perfect.'

She drew herself up to her full height. She towered over him and clenched her fists. 'You let me out of here, right now, Noel Sturrock. You can't keep me here. I won't work against my will. Don't be bloody stupid.'

'Oh!' he chuckled. 'Feisty, isn't she? Knows her own mind, doesn't she?'

She let out at aggravated sigh very slowly. 'I am not staying up all night, helping you do all this work.'

'Helping!' he shrieked. 'Helping, go hang! I'm doing nothing! I'm sitting here and I'm going to watch you. I'm going to sit up and supervise you for as long as it takes.'

'Hadaway,' she snapped. She relished using a local, dismissive epithet she had picked up recently. 'Hadaway and shite, man. There's no way I'm staying up all night here. Now, get out of my way.'

Noel narrowed his eyes at her. She was behaving all wrong. By now she should have been rushing into action and doing as she was told. He had hoped to browbeat her into doing what he wanted. But he should have known! She was so naughty and rude. It was typical of her to answer him back like this!

She reached forward with both arms and, to his great shock, pulled his stool to one side. Even with him sitting on top of it, she moved it quite easily with a hefty yank. Noel was mortified and let out an undignified squawk of rage. 'You filthy tart!' he cried as she tried to pass through the bar into the back.

His words brought her up short. '*What?!* What did you call me?'

He thrust his bony chin at her and spat flecks of saliva as he repeated: '*You filthy little tart!*'

She widened her eyes at him. 'I'm going home now,' she said in a shaking voice. 'I think you've had too much to drink. I've had enough of your rubbish.'

Oh, have you indeed, he thought to himself. All his thoughts were rocking crazily inside his mind as she turned her back on him. He didn't even consider what he was doing. He hopped down from his stool. He barrelled after her through the bar. She retreated into the back still muttering crossly to herself. She was livid, he could tell. But she wasn't as livid as he was.

Noel was little and puny-looking, perhaps. But he was compact and strong. He had spent years hefting barrels about in his cellar. He mightn't have looked as powerful as most other fellas, but he had a lot of strength in his arms and, when he crept up behind her and gave her an almighty shove, the force was enough to knock her right off her feet.

There were two stone steps down into the galley from the bar. Taken by surprise by his flat-handed shove, Cathy lost her footing. She gave a wail of terror and flew headfirst into the dark.

He watched as, in slow motion, her arms flew out to grab hold of something, anything, to support her. He flinched at the sound of her cry of shock. And then there came a sickening thump as her head connected with the damp concrete of the floor.

Cathy lay crumpled on the ground and Noel just stood there staring. He was fighting off panic, fear, fury and remorse all at once. All he could think was: 'It serves her right! This is what happens! She shouted at me! She shouted back! And this is what happens when *you don't do what I say!*'

He stood there frozen and huge silent moments ticked by.

Cathy lay face down with her new dress crumpled around her. Completely still.

Chapter 20

'Eeeh, lad! Whatever's gone and happened now?'

Teresa came thumping down the stairs in her nightgown and hairnet. She had been fast asleep, swimming tipsily in the milk stout fumes of her evening at the Robin Hood. The crash of the front door had woken her with a shock and now both her heart and her head were pounding.

There was her Noel, struggling in through the front door into the hallway and he was carrying their Cathy in his arms!

He was barely big enough to manage her. He looked swamped by all the folds of her green dress. Her limbs were splayed out helplessly and he staggered under the weight of her as he reached home.

'Noel, man! What's the matter with the lass? Tell me!'

'Help me get her indoors,' he gasped. He was purple in the face from the effort of dragging her home.

'Oh no! Oh, look!' Teresa's hands flew up to her mouth as she saw the mess that the girl's face was in. There was a dark contusion on her forehead and one of her eyes had almost vanished under a nasty-looking swelling. There was just a single trickle of shining blood down her face.

Together mother and son manhandled Cathy into the back parlour, laying her awkwardly on the pew by the window. 'It's not very comfortable. We should get her up to her room, lying down,' the old mother said. 'What happened, Noel? How did she do this?'

'Get a cold wet flannel or something. A cloth to compress the wound on her forehead and over her eye.' He snapped at his mother and she found herself dashing to the scullery to do his bidding. She wrung out the dishcloth and held it under the tap. Was it clean enough? It smelled a bit fusty maybe, but it would have to do. What else could she use at short notice? She hadn't been expecting to turn her parlour into a field hospital tonight . . .

And the evening had been so lovely! Everything had been so perfect. It was almost as if life was getting back to normal – and now this!

She came back into the parlour and Noel snatched the cloth off her. He dabbed gently at the girl's face.

'Eeeh, Noel,' fretted his mother. 'I don't like the look of the colour of her. She's gannin' green, man!'

'That's just the light in here,' he tutted. 'Get a proper lamp lit and shut up.'

Under his careful ministrations, Cathy was beginning to stir and moan.

'Here now, you're all right,' he told her gently. 'You're safe now, pet. You're not badly injured. Nothing broken. Can you hear me? Can you see me all right?'

Cathy was confused and starting to panic. She tried to get up, but Noel got her to sit back on the rigid pew. He propped cushions behind her back and laid the cloth over her forehead. 'The dishcloth, mother? Is that the best you could find?'

'You had me in a bloody panic!' she burst out at him. 'Is she going to be all right? Shall I run for the doctor?' Now that she offered to, Teresa thought better of it. Their old doctor was dead and she didn't even know the young one. Would he take kindly to being knocked up in the night on New Year's Eve? And what did he even charge? They didn't have money to go throwing away on unnecessary doctors. 'Is it just a bruise, then? Has she hurt herself bad?'

'I don't know, I don't think so,' muttered Noel. 'I reckon it looks nastier than it is.' He pursed his lips and glared at his patient. 'The stupid lass. She wouldn't watch where she was going. She was dashing around . . .' He shook his head, tutting. 'Those couple of stone steps into the back. They were sheeted with ice, it was so cold back there. Well, this one, she was so determined to get the place clean and tidy . . .'

'Aww, was she?' Teresa gasped, coming to sit at the other side of Cathy. She grasped her hand and patted it warmly. 'Why, she could have waited till tomorrow, couldn't she? You wouldn't have minded, would you, son?'

'Why, of course not,' he said, hoping that Cathy couldn't hear through the fug of her pain. 'She knows that. But that's what she's like, isn't it? She loves making everything just perfect for us. She loves to get things tidied up. And there she was, dashing about, and she slipped on the icy stone steps, didn't she? She went right over. I was behind her but look at the size of me! I couldn't do anything. I darted forward to grab her, to pull her back before . . . before she hurt herself . . .' His voice broke as he related the distressing details to his mam.

He's going to cry! Teresa marvelled at this rare show of tender affection. She had never seen the like! Noel's hands had flown up to his face, muffling his words. His humped shoulders were shaking as he sat there on the other side of Cathy. The pew rocked slightly as he sobbed into his hands, wracked with shame and terror.

'Ah, now, son!' his mother cried. 'Don't take on. You'll start me off, now! Look! Look, she'll be all right. You did your best. You'd have helped her if you could. I know you would . . .'

'It was horrible,' he said, in a heaving tone. 'Seeing her fall like that. I felt so helpless. And the sickening, horrible noise when her face hit the concrete . . .'

Teresa was examining the girl's face. 'Aye, I reckon she'll have a proper shiner there in the morning. She'll look shocking!'

'She's breathing all right, isn't she?' he said. 'Is she awake?'

'Hmm,' mused Teresa. 'I reckon she's going to have a nice sleep now. We should try to drag her up the stairs to her room. She'll be better in her bed. Come on, lad. Let's get her upstairs. We'll have to get this gown off her, too, else it'll spoil.'

'We will, will we?' Noel asked, with a strange note in his voice. 'We'll *have* to undress her, will we?'

'Oh, I should think so,' his mother said. 'She's not going to be comfortable in all this velvety stuff, is she?'

'Right,' said he. 'I think I've got my strength back. Help me, Mother – you take her feet . . .'

Later Cathy would remember having the most peculiar dreams that night.

She was on the back of a huge, snow white swan. Vast, powerful wings were spread out either side of her and they were beating very slowly as the bird soared through a dark, tumultuous sky. Snow was falling thickly and she could barely make out the details of the land below, but then she could see the tossing sea with its white caps of foam. She could see the pale sands and the crumbling cliffs and rocks of the shore. Then the smoking chimney pots and clustered houses and winding streets of South Shields.

She was soaring above the town, far above the land. Leaving it all behind and heading north. Home again to the far north, across the rivers and fields and moors. The strong neck of the swan stretched out straight ahead as it forged through the wintry night. The creature was so strong and dependable. She felt the need to apologise to him. She felt terrible, having eaten swan on Christmas Day . . . She called out into the raging wind and snow: 'I'm sorry!'

But of course the swan didn't say anything. In the absurd logic of dreams, Cathy suddenly somehow knew that this swan was the exact one that she had cooked on Christmas Day. This was her punishment, perhaps, being whisked away like this, and being carried off into the night on his back . . .

But the swan was kinder than that. All at once she knew that he was taking her home.

All her concerns were falling away from her. All her fears and pretences. The defences that she kept walled up around her and the secrets that she carefully kept hidden. They all melted into nothing like the snowflakes that landed against her skin. She knew she was going home again and this time – for once! – she was going to be welcomed.

Someone very special would be there waiting for her. Someone very special indeed . . .

The girl woke up, her face wet with tears.

The morning sun of New Year's Day was piercing and cruel, flooding through the gap in the curtains.

She tried to sit up in her lumpy bed and didn't quite manage it.

Simply everything was hurting. And this wasn't just a headache and a hangover, though that was there too. This was a livid, pounding, bloody pain right up to her temples. One of her eyes was welded shut. Her face felt hot and tight and bruised like a plum, like an overripe piece of bursting fruit. She couldn't help it: Cathy cried out in fright.

After a few moments the door opened and in lumbered Teresa Sturrock in her dressing gown, fussing and concerned.

'Lass! Lass, are you all right, hinny? How are you feeling?'

Cathy didn't even know. She had never felt like this before. 'W-what happened to me?' But even as she asked, she knew the answer. The events of the previous night were starting to come back to her. '*Noel* . . .' she said, in an urgent tone. 'He . . .'

Ma Sturrock came to sit on her counterpane, patting the girl's arm with her clawed hands. 'He's all right, pet. He's fine. He's just having a little lie in, after all the panic and palaver of the night. Eeeh, how good of you, though! How selfless and kind of you! Fancy thinking of him before yourself like that! Rest assured, my lass, he's quite all right.'

Cathy was confused. '*What?*'

'Well, he almost did himself a mischief, didn't he? A little bloke like him, and with his back as it is. You're such a strapping big lass, you know. Yet still he managed. He managed to get you up from where you fell and out of the pub. Why, he carried you – all by his self – through the snow across Frederick Street, back home. I came running down from me bed – and there he was in the downstairs hall. You were dead to the world! You were just a dead weight on his shoulders. But he managed to get you home! He was like a little hero!'

Feeling as if she was going mad, Cathy put her hands up to her face. The room was whirling round and she gasped with sudden pain as her fingers touched her swollen flesh. 'Oh, my god. What do I look like? What have I done?'

The old woman said ruefully, 'I wouldn't look if I were you, pet. It's just a black eye. Nothing to worry yourself about. It'll all go down again in a little bit. You'll see. But I wouldn't look in the mirror for a bit. Not just yet. You'll give yourself an awful shock.' She patted Cathy's shoulder and stroked her hair. 'Eeeh, lass. You gave us both such a scare. What were you doing, dashing about on slippery steps?'

'What?' she gasped. 'I . . . I don't know . . .' But she did know. It was all coming back to her. There was bugger all wrong with her memory. She could easily recall every detail of what had led up to her fall. She knew exactly what had caused her to land face down on that cold concrete.

Then she realised she was in her nightdress. 'Who undressed me?' she demanded.

'Why, we both did,' said Teresa. 'We had to get you out of that gown. It was a job that took both of us.' Suddenly the old woman sounded almost tetchy, as if she felt piqued that Cathy wasn't being grateful enough for the effort she had been put to. Teresa had been fast asleep in her warm bed. Had she asked to be rudely awakened and forced to help some lass who couldn't even watch where she was going?

'Th-thank you,' Cathy said, but as she said it, she felt the gorge rising in her throat. The fiery burn of all last night's drinking was roiling in her gullet. The very thought of Noel and his mother pawing at her while she lay here unconscious last night . . .

Her pounding head blotted out her thoughts. She cried out in anguished pain.

'You need to sleep,' Teresa told her sternly. 'That's the only thing for it, pet. You get your head down for an hour or two. I'll come back in the afternoon and bring you some tea. Something to eat, if you can manage it. And by then our Noel will be up and about. Then you can thank him. You can tell him how grateful you are that he came to your rescue. Why, he's your saviour! I'm sure he'll be eager to see you when he wakes.'

Teresa got up and hobbled for the bedroom door, moving through the pearly snow light filtering through the thin curtains. Cathy let her go and couldn't summon up the will or the energy to say another word.

She closed her eyes and let the waves of pain roll over her and wished with all her heart that the swan in her dreams would come soaring back down and fly her away.

Chapter 21

It was a relief when Sofia came to visit.

A couple of days into the new year and the Italian girl heard the news about Cathy's nasty fall. She came dashing round with a lemon cake smothered in icing and four bottles of milk stout.

'Drink up, it's good for you.'

'Aye, it'll put hairs on me chest,' Cathy laughed, trying her best to sound cheery. It did feel funny and wrong, sitting up in bed, eating delicious cake and supping beer!

Sofia sat on the wooden chair beside her, drinking from her own bottle. 'It's proper food, this, Cathy. You need to get your strength back.' Her visitor had looked critically under the dressing that Teresa had put on her head wound, and she had visibly flinched at the livid bruising.

'I look pretty bad, don't I?' said Cathy ruefully.

'How did you manage to do that to yourself?' Sofia felt embarrassed and annoyed that the news of Cathy's fall had taken so long to get to her. She had been pegging out her white sheets in the back yard when she'd caught the whispers of the other women over the back walls. That young lass at the Robin Hood has come a cropper and had a nasty do!

Now Cathy seemed reluctant to discuss it. She sipped her beer and sighed.

'Everyone's saying that Noel was your hero that night,' Sofia went on. 'They say that he found you after your fall and carried you home across the road through the snow! A little fella like that! He found the strength somehow and got you home. Apparently he's been like the cock of the walk, crowing all about it ever since.'

A dark look passed over Cathy's face. It was almost as dark as the bruising over her brow and round her eye. 'That's what they're saying, is it? And that's what he's got them believing? They actually believe him, do they?'

'Why, Cathy? What's wrong? Is that not right, then?'

Cathy tossed her head. 'Of course it's not right! He's lying through his stinking rotten teeth, the little bastard!'

'Cathy!' Sofia was shocked by her vehemence.

'Why, he had the brass-neck to come strutting in here on New Year's Day – when I was still delirious and sick to me stomach – and he was going, "Eeeh, pet, are you all right? Are you seeing double? Can you hear us, hinny?" He was making out he was all kind and concerned about me.'

Sofia listened to her friend with consternation. She had never heard her sound so angry or bitter before.

'And then,' Cathy went on, 'his bloody mother was there and she was prompting me. Actually grabbing me elbow and saying, "Cathy, man. Don't you want to say thank you? Don't you want to thank Noel for bringing you home to safety? Why, you could have been lying there for hours on that cold stone floor. You could have died there, hinny, if it hadn't been for our Noel."

Sofia said, 'Well, she is right, isn't she? It would have been a terrible thing if you had been lying on the cold floor like that until the morning. He did help you, after all.'

Cathy interrupted with a savage whisper. 'He pushed me, Sofia! That man bloody well pushed me down on the floor!

I lost me footing and went over on me face only because he gave me a flat-handed shove from behind!'

'What?!' Sofia gasped. 'But what would he do a thing like that for?'

'I don't know, I've been turning it over and over in my head as I've been lying here . . .' Cathy tried her best not to sob and bubble and let all her feelings out. Even though she was with her friend, she was determined not to cry and to show how scared and upset she really was. 'But the way he talked to me that night . . . God, he really hates me, Sofia. He hates my flamin' guts!'

'No, no, that can't be right.' Sofia shook her head. 'He adores you. I've watched him, watching you. You're wrong, Cathy. He doesn't hate you . . .'

'But look what the little bastard's done to me!' Cathy said. 'Look at the state of me . . .' A great wave of misery rolled over her. After a couple of days in bed she felt stale and dirty and exhausted with it all. She didn't need to hear from Sofia that the man who'd caused this really loved her. Everything had gone topsy-turvy and mad. 'I just want to get up and get out of here. I'm sick of these two round here.'

Sofia was decisive. 'Then you must come and stay with us.'

That was exactly what happened, that very afternoon. All in a flash, Sofia became business-like and would brook no argument about taking Cathy home with her. Not even when Teresa flapped and protested and said that the girl should stay right where she was.

'She needs a change of scene,' Sofia said kindly, but with a firmness that made the old woman back off. Sofia didn't add that she thought Cathy needed to be somewhere cleaner and more hygienic, too. She needed feeding proper food, and not just the endless mugs of beefy tea Teresa seemed to bring her.

Cathy merely gave in to the Italian woman's commands, with only the feeblest of protests. 'You've already got two small bairns, your old mother and a man to look after!'

'Then one more won't matter,' Sofia shrugged. 'And besides, it will be nice for me to have company, too. Someone I can actually talk to. My evenings are so dull, with my mother and the bairns going to bed early. Tonio is out most nights, playing his cards . . .'

The trip round to the next street was quite arduous for Cathy, even as she pretended it wasn't. The cold wind coming up the steep hill was severe and there was still ragged, frozen snow making the pavement slippery. She clung to her friend's arm and made her way woozily to the end of Frederick Street. Sofia was carrying the old carpet bag that had comprised Cathy's only luggage when she had first arrived in South Shields. Now it had a few essential items stashed hurriedly inside, just enough to see Cathy through a few days' respite care at the Franchino house.

Teresa Sturrock stood on her front doorstep, calling worriedly after them as they left her home. 'I don't know what our Noel will say about all this! When he comes home and finds you gone . . .' She looked quite upset as she stood there, clutching the door. Cathy's heart almost went out to her. 'What shall I tell him, Cathy? Why shall I say you've gone?' Another terrible thought seemed to strike Teresa then. 'And you *will* be coming back, won't you, sweetheart? You won't be leaving us for good?'

Sofia answered for her tired friend, just before they rounded the sharp corner at the top of the street. 'I'll send her back in a couple of days. Don't worry!'

Cathy felt relieved to get out of sight of Teresa and number twenty-one and the glowing windows of the Robin Hood.

*

Her days of convalescence with the Franchinos on Jackson Street were like a little holiday for Cathy. Although she was only one street away from the place she usually lay down her head at night, it was like she had travelled a thousand miles to be somewhere brighter, warmer, happier. She was surrounded by happy family members – and the children, too, were like a godsend. She sat with the baby on her lap and the girl Bella kept besieging her for attention.

'Let her alone,' Sofia laughed. 'She's supposed to be resting . . .'

'No, no, I love the bairns,' said Cathy. 'It's so nice here. So full of life. It makes me realise that living with the Sturrocks is like a bloody mausoleum. All that old furniture and all the old woman's collections of things. And us both stepping round so carefully in case Noel gets upset and flies off the handle!'

Tutting, Sofia told her: 'Well, just forget all about it now and enjoy being here with us lot. It isn't quiet and tidy, though. Maybe you won't be able to relax here at all . . .'

Actually, Cathy found their home very relaxing indeed. Even when old Nonna came after her with a poultice she had made especially to fade the bruising on her face. It stank to high heaven, and so did the scullery after the old woman spent a morning brewing up the herbs and God knew what else in a saucepan. Gamely Cathy let her put the smelly thing on her brow and was amazed at how soothing she found it. 'And blow me, but I think she's right! It's looking less bruised and nasty . . .'

The old woman brought out a leather-bound album of tinted postcards and she flipped through the faded pages, making sure that Cathy was paying close attention to each one. Nonna sighed deeply every few minutes as they studied these views of Italy together. Cathy was astonished by the etchings of the hills and mountains and that beautiful painted sea.

'You must be very honoured,' Sofia told her. 'If Mama is showing you Naples . . .'

The old woman sighed and kept turning the pages.

'It looks so lovely,' said Cathy. 'I really had no idea. And this is what you all left behind . . . to come here! To cold and smoky old England!'

Sofia's expression darkened. 'I explained to you about all of that. We really didn't have a choice.'

'One day you'll be able to go back though, won't you?' asked Cathy.

'I really don't know,' Sofia sighed, and sounded for a moment just like her mother. 'It all costs money. And what do we have? Tonio, whatever he makes, he just throws it away. What's the word? He piddles it away.'

'Aye, piddles is a good word,' Cathy smiled. She made appropriate noises as old Nonna turned yet another page and pointed out an etching of Mount Etna. 'Is he still gambling then?'

Sofia nodded. 'And all his plans, all those ridiculous ideas he had about us moving to somewhere bigger and nicer than this, it's all sky pie.'

'Pie in the sky,' Cathy corrected her. 'The house down Seahouses way, you mean?'

'Aye, we'll never be able to afford it. That's all gone. The money – he never really had it. So now we will stay here, in the Sixteen Streets.'

'Ah, I'm sorry to hear it, pet,' said Cathy. 'I know you were keen on the new place. But look. There's nothing really wrong with your house here, is there? It's not so bad in the Sixteen Streets, is it?'

Sofia pulled a rueful face. 'He promised me better. That man . . . he only got to keep me by promising me everything. I ran away with him and I threw away everything I knew. And I believed his promises . . .'

She waved her hands and drew herself up, as if determined not to sink further into despair. Her old mother had little to say on the subject. What she did was typically frank and pithy: 'Tonio is a good man. But he's got the sense of a horse and he can kiss my ass.' She had other, more colourful phrases to describe him, but she was too polite to repeat them in front of Cathy.

When she felt a little better and the bruises were turning acid yellow and green, Cathy accompanied Sofia on a trip out of the house to Franchino's ice-cream parlour. It was Sofia's regular working hours, but she didn't mind Cathy coming to sit at the zinc counter beside her, sipping endless coffee and passing the time of day.

Cathy felt terribly glamorous, with a patterned silk headscarf tied around her hair, covering up the worst of the bruising. She felt ready to face the world again at last.

'It's done me a power of good, staying with you lot,' she told her friend. 'You've got such a wonderful warm and lovely family. And the food! My god, I've never eaten so well in all my life!' Just the thought of those rich sauces and those peppery steaks and the buttery pasta was enough to make Cathy feel hungry all over again. She felt like she must have put on several pounds in just a few days.

'You deserve to be looked after,' Sofia told her, with a strange, rather stern glance. She was working at the complicated coffee machine that was her husband's pride and joy. 'You know that, don't you? You deserve to have someone care for you some-times? You can't carry on and do it all by yourself. You must depend upon those who love you.'

Though Cathy smiled at these kindly meant words, she didn't really understand them. Not really. She was appreciative of her friend's care and affection, but she didn't really understand what Sofia meant. Not yet. As yet she had no concept of depending on someone else's love. The very idea was new to her. She had always felt very much on her own.

'And now what?' Cathy asked. 'What do I do now? Where do I go? Back to live with the Sturrocks?'

Chapter 22

Was Matty Johnson a kind and decent bloke?

He hoped he was. He certainly felt like he was. Deep down, perhaps.

But it was hard to tell, wasn't it? Some of the things he had to do, some of the little jobs he had to carry out . . . Well, maybe they weren't all the type of thing you could go bragging about. Some of those things he'd rather not have the whole world knowing about. But that was the family business, wasn't it? Certain things needed doing.

But all the same Matty Johnson wanted to be thought of as a decent bloke.

His older brother Alec laughed at him. 'Eeeh, man, you and your mithering! You just have to get on with the job and not worry about it.' A portly little fella, Alec was. His complexion had gone the colour of the meat in a well-stuffed pork pie. His gingery little tash got on Matty's nerves, as did his natty tweedy suits and ties. He remembered when his brother was someone he looked up to. Out of all his older brothers, Alec was the one he used to idolize, once upon a time. Nowadays, though? Alec seemed just like a conniving, greedy little man. A ratty little devil given to whoring and gambling. He thought more about the tarts he knocked about with than anything else.

Matty Johnson was back from the war and the scales had fallen from his eyes. He'd seen awful things in the time he'd been abroad. Things he still saw when he closed his eyes at night. He'd never scrub those pictures of death and suffering out of his brain, and he'd never find a reason for it all. He came back home thinking that all human ambition just amounted to stinking carnage and misery.

It was wounding to get back home to find that his family's business was just more misery, just creating more suffering and terror – and all for what? Mounting up piles of money and rubbish and material goods. His mother liked jewellery and shiny things. She was like an old dragon sitting on her hoard of gold. She sent her boys out to bring home all the glittering things they could . . .

And Matty Johnson hated it. He hated his family and what they did in their home town of South Shields. They were nothing but wretched bullies and thugs, taking everything from those who couldn't afford it. Taking it because they are weaker than us.

He longed to stop. He wanted to throw it all in. But how to escape from the crushing, despicable arms of his family? His three older brothers and all his uncles . . . they were all hard men. They were annealed in rusty armour thick as the hulls of any of the ships in South Shields harbour. They knew no remorse nor pity for anyone who didn't belong to their clan. What were they going to say if they felt that Matty was ashamed of them? If they knew that Matty wanted to stop, and leave, and do something honest instead?

He really didn't know. There had never been an honest and decent soul in the Johnson clan. He felt that he must be the first.

His old mother watched him with a beady eye, knowing that he was different. 'Ah, son. You have to toughen up that hide of yours. You're much too soft, man. You went away to war, didn't you? You saw more fighting than any of my lads ever did. You should be tough as old boots.'

But he felt weak inside. He felt like something had broken. No amount of goading from his chain-smoking mother, fuming in her enormous chair in the parlour, could make him feel the same as his brothers.

Some of his regular little jobs were easier than others. Rounding up money from the lost souls down in the old pubs by the docks. Places like the Mudlark with its skulking clientele clutching their grubby cards. Hollow-eyed and shifty buggers, the lot of them. He found it easier to take from them. And it was indeed easy pickings, too! None of them would put up a fight. They acted like it was natural, that the Mad Johnsons would swing by and take a good slice of their paltry winnings. They knew that there'd always be a Johnson brother there, too, to lend a fistful of coins when they needed it – all for an exorbitant interest rate. Most of those soft-headed bastards couldn't read or count anyway, and much of the time was spent explaining the figures to them. Truth be told, Matty spent just as much time showing them how to do sums as he did twisting limbs or breaking heads in the alley out back. Really, he was educating them. That was a better way of looking at it.

But all the while, he knew that what he was doing was wrong. Even when it was gamblers and drunken sots he was roughing up and taking money from. He knew it was all a murky, miserable business.

His worst moment came early that January. He felt his worst pangs of regret and came closer than ever to throwing in the towel, not that long after New Year. Maybe it was his best moment? The moment when he really started to make changes in his life?

It came about when his mother sent him with his brothers Alec and Jan to collect their dues from the establishments on Ocean Road. It was easy enough in this dingy, disreputable pub, say, or that seedy knocking shop, or that illegal book-maker's. But it was different when it came to Franchino's ice-cream parlour. The place was packed out with old women drinking coffee and spooning up desserts. They all looked up with interest as the three strapping blokes came striding in, asking for the owner.

Anyone can see what we are, Matty thought darkly. We're just three hooligans on the rob: Alec so sleazy and twitching with eagerness to make his demands; Jan the size and shape of a coffin, and just as thick. Matty was ashamed of himself and his brothers and never more so than that day, as they went up to the counter and glared down at the Italian bloke serving there. A fussy, bald little fella. Full of pride and defiance. Bristling at them, knowing that they were here to extract cash from him.

Matty knew him. He knew Tonio Franchino from the gambling den at the back of the Mudlark. He'd taken money from him before and lent it to him, too. Here they were, meeting in the bright light of day, in Tonio's place of everyday business and the little man looked scared. He looked like all his shameful secrets were coming out to haunt him. He was furious and terrified all at once.

Ma Johnson had known this would be the case. When she had learned that the biggest gambler, the most hopeless case at the Mudlark, was the man who ran the ice-cream parlour, she had crowed with glee. 'Good little earner, that place must be. A lovely money pot. Get yourselves down there and put the menaces on him. Bleed the place dry!'

And so they were here, to set up a regular payment day with Tonio Franchino. 'Twenty per cent,' Alec told him, shrugging carelessly. 'Not so bad, is it? And then your lovely wife need never know how much debt you're in.'

Tonio was flustered. 'Will that scrub my debts out?' He felt idiotic and out of his depth. Truth be told, he didn't even know exactly how much he owed the Johnson boys.

Alec took out his neat little book from the inside pocket of his silk-lined coat. He made great show of licking his finger and turning to the correct page. From where he stood Matty could just see rows of incomprehensible figures. Somehow he knew that it was all a lot of rubbish. Alec didn't keep proper records or figures of what he extorted from people. He scribbled down any old nonsense and simply took what he wanted. It was rank cruelty to have the likes of Tonio Franchino hanging on like this.

'W-will that pay it off?' he said. 'A regular payment? But for how long?'

Alec glared at him. 'It won't pay off anything. Not even the interest. Do you know how much you've had from us these past few years? We've been very generous. When you've been pissed and showing off. Playing every night, hour after hour. You enjoy your game, don't you? And you lose count, don't you? You're lucky that we keep proper records . . . and know just exactly what you owe.'

Matty felt terrible, watching the older man cringe behind his counter. Taking twenty per cent off him would cripple him, surely?

'But . . . but what am I paying for? If I'm not paying off my debts?' The Italian was struggling to understand. His accent was coming in more thickly too, as if, in his distress, his second language was starting to fail him. 'Oh god,' he said, imagining what Sofia would say if she could see what was going on here today.

'What are you paying for?' Alec laughed. 'You're paying to keep yourself safe. And to stop this lovely place from getting smashed up. There's some right crooks and ne'er-do-wells round here, surely you know that, Mr Franchino? All this lovely glass and these shiny counters and your fancy coffee machine . . . You wouldn't want to see it all smashed to smithereens, would you?'

Alec's voice was so purringly oily, Matty felt sick. He watched the Italian bloke quail.

'And you've got a lovely family, too, haven't you?' Alec asked, smiling.

Tonio's face drained of all colour. 'All right, whatever you want. Just keep down your voices. I don't want any of my customers knowing any of this . . . or my family . . .'

Alec held up both pudgy palms. 'We are nothing if not discreet, Mr Franchino.'

Just as Tonio shuffled to his old-fashioned brass till they were interrupted by his mother-in-law. She had been upstairs in the store room, catching forty winks, as she often had to in the middle of the afternoon. No one begrudged her vanishing for a little snooze. It really wasn't as if she did much vital work in the ice-cream parlour anyway. Mostly she just shuffled around with that stick of hers, mouthing hellos to the regulars and smoking a cheroot with her coffee.

Now here she was, blundering into the middle of Tonio's shameful scene. She stared up at the three Johnson brothers and they were like three armoured tanks surrounding her. 'Well?' she frowned. 'Tonio, why are these gentlemen not being served? Shall I find them a table? What do they want?' She fished around in her pinny for her pad of paper and stub of pencil. Her shaggy eyebrows knitted together in consternation.

'These gentlemen aren't having anything today, Nonna,' Tonio said, sounding nervous. 'They're just leaving.'

Alec told the old woman, 'We just came by to give you our best regards for the new year.'

She frowned up at him. Matty was amazed to see his wicked brother flinch at the old woman's stare. Something he saw in her eyes had knocked him off his stroke, for just a second.

'All right, hinny?' Alec asked her blithely, mockingly.

The truth was, the old woman had seen straight through Alec Johnson. She had taken one look at him and his brothers and she had known right away what they were about. They were hoods, plain and simple. A quick glance at her slump-shouldered son-in-law told her everything about what was going on here. They were bullies and gangsters and they were trying to do a number on the Franchino family. The old woman drew herself up to her full height and stared at all three of them like she had nothing to lose.

'*Get out of here*,' she told them.

There was a pause and then Alec laughed. 'I beg your pardon?'

The old woman ground her tiny, worn teeth together and jutted out her whiskery jaw. 'I'm telling you now. Get out of here right now.' This is what she intended to say, although half the words were in Italian. But the three Johnson brothers instinctively knew what she was saying. Her bold defiance was coming at them in waves.

Alec chortled out loud. 'Oh, wonderful! The old woman is priceless! She's tougher than you are, Franchino! She's not afraid of us, are you?'

She stuck out her turkey neck and asked, 'What?'

Alec was in fits of laughter by now. 'Deaf as well as daft! I said, dear, I said, you're not afraid of us, are you?'

Indeed she wasn't. And, as Alec carried on splitting his sides at the old lady, Matty could have warned him of what was coming next. For he had seen the way the old woman was clutching that stick of hers. She was grasping it in front of her with both hands. She'd dropped her pad and pencil back in her pinny pocket and she was hefting her cane like it was a swordstick . . .

It was an ebony cane she'd had for years. It had a silver top to it. The kind of thing that could do some damage. In a flash it was up in the air and, before anyone knew what was happening, she had brought it down, with all her might, upon the crown of Alec's head. On his sparse, gingery pink pate.

Oh, how he howled.

How he bled, too! There was a kind of bloody flash like an explosion coming out of his skull. His brothers could hardly believe it – the old witch had drawn blood with just one blow! As if she'd known exactly how to strike him to garner maximum effect.

Everyone in the place was up on their feet. They were staring in appalled horror. Almost everyone in there knew who the Johnson boys were and what they had been doing to Tonio. They had all chosen to keep their heads down. No one wanted to get messed up with those mad lads.

Now everyone was silent – including Matty and Jan – as they watched their brother Alec screeching with pain and clutching his head. Blood ran freely down his sweating face. He spat out a gobful as he howled.

Nonna Franchino knew no mercy. She knew that with people like this, you had to hit first and hit hard. You had to keep hitting them until they went down.

To Matty's astonishment, up went the ebony cane once more, and in a flash she brought it down again into the selfsame spot on Alec's head. He shrieked in pain and flailed out with both arms. '*Get it off her!*' he squealed.

Jan tried to grab for the cane, but she adroitly smacked him away.

'Now get out of here,' she warned them. 'Before I *kill* you all.'

Matty felt like cheering. He felt like laughing. He wanted to hug the old woman more than he wanted to break all her bones. Oh, to see his brother Alec brought low like this! He'd never live it down!

'We're going,' Matty told the Franchinos. 'We're going now. And . . . I'm sorry, I'm sorry for all of this.'

The old nonna was gleaming with triumph as she heard him say this. Jan was confused and didn't know what to do. 'Help Alec,' Matty told him. 'Come on. Let's get him home before he bleeds to death.'

Alec was sobbing with pain now. The blood had run freely into both his piggy eyes and his brothers had to lead him back to the door. Oh, the shame and the ignominy of it all! The Mad Johnsons would never get over this!

Matty felt glad. We deserve this, he thought. This is all our rotten just desserts . . .

As he helped his brother out of the place he turned to Tonio, who was standing shocked behind his counter. 'Keep the money. Just keep it.'

The old woman waved her walking cane in the air in a vaguely threatening motion and Matty nodded with respect. 'We're going,' he promised.

And as he went home with his brothers that day, Matty Johnson felt like he'd done his first decent and good deed of his whole life. He had left the Franchinos in peace.

Chapter 23

For a few days the old nonna of the Franchino family was the talk of the town. Everywhere Cathy went she heard whisperings about the old lady who had stood up to the Johnson boys. 'They'll never live this down, the bad buggers! And it serves them right, too!' This was in the queue at Swetty Betty's at the top of the Sixteen Streets; Cathy was eavesdropping on two unfamiliar women discussing the fracas.

'Them boys have run amok for years,' the other woman said. 'They just take what they want and think they can get away with it.'

'Aye, but from what I hear the old woman gave them hell! That Alec Johnson's got a cracked skull!'

'It'll take more than vinegar and brown paper to fix that!' They laughed at this, and then it was their turn to put their order in. 'Is there any skate, petal?'

Cathy didn't know what to think about the to-do at the ice-cream parlour. At one level she had been just as shocked and horrified as the rest of the Franchino family, to hear what Tonio had had to endure. And then she had been terrified by the danger Nonna had placed herself in. But then to hear how she'd fettled them like that! With a few good raps of that cane of hers!

However, Cathy knew that they hadn't heard the last of this. She imagined that the Johnsons' pride was wounded far more deeply than Alec's skull. They wouldn't let this episode lie, surely.

The other thing that gave Cathy pause for thought was that Tonio had described the three men who had menaced him. He named the three Mad Johnsons who had stood at his counter that day: the moustached Alec, the immense Jan . . . and the third had been the younger fella, just back from the front – in his demob suit and his white vest. Matty. Yes, Cathy had quite a vivid picture in her head of Matty Johnson. Ever since he had kept staring at her on New Year's Eve. She could still feel what his strong arms had felt like when he'd danced with her so clumsily on the sawdust floor of the pub. She could still catch the scent of him, the warm, not-unpleasant tang of his perspiration.

Cathy hated to hear how he'd been there in the midst of this scene. He had been one of the bad buggers making Tonio's life a misery.

Sofia's reaction to the events had been dramatic. She had turned on her husband, blaming him for everything. She had rushed protectively to her mother and refused to see anything amusing about any of it. 'She could have been killed! How dare you put her in danger like that!'

'She wasn't scared!' Tonio protested. 'They were the ones in danger! Look at the damage she did! They fled, Sofia! Those buggers fled!'

But Sofia wouldn't be assuaged, and Cathy had found the scene awkward to witness. 'Is all your fault,' Sofia said, her accent thickening as it always did when she became emotional. 'I know it's you and your gambling behind all this. You're a horse's ass! You are piddling our money away and you bring danger to our door!'

Their row was the reason that Cathy had come to the fish shop, in order to escape the argy-bargy and to fetch something for their supper. Perhaps hot crispy food would calm them all down? She didn't know. All she knew was that she had never been in the middle of a household of arguing Italians before and hadn't reckoned on how fierce the noise would be. Both bairns were screaming at the hullabaloo and the old lady was, of course, shouting excitedly about her own part in the dramatic story.

It was a relief to be standing in the hot fragrant steam and the endless gossip at Swetty Betty's.

Then Cathy clapped eyes on Teresa Sturrock, who came shuffling into the tiled room in her hideous, mangy fur coat. 'Eeeh, there you are, hinny!' she cried, and squashed past the people between them. 'You don't mind me pushing in to be with my friend, do you, love? She's like a daughter to me and I've not been well.' Somehow Teresa got them all to let her through and Cathy's heart sank into her boots. She felt guilty for not feeling more pleased to see her friend from number twenty-one.

'Hello there, Teresa,' she said.

'Eeeh, hallo stranger!' Teresa greeted her mockingly. 'Why, we've not seen hide nor hair of you for weeks!'

'It's not been that long,' Cathy frowned. Unconsciously her hand went up to touch the borrowed silk scarf that hid the still-fading bruises on her face. 'Just a few days.'

'Aye, well, it's not been the same round at ours with you gone. The place is like a morgue! Our Noel's disconsolate! He's shuffling about like his heart is broken . . . and the cats! All the cats are going crackers, man. They're yowling and scratching at the furniture, like they know something's wrong. Like they're missing you like the rest of us are. So when are you coming back hame then, hinny?'

'*Hame*'. Cathy smiled at the way the old woman pronounced the word, and the way she looked up at her so hopefully. That familiar, crab apple face, with its broken teeth. At that moment Cathy remembered the very first time she had met Teresa Sturrock, and they had stood here in this very fish shop. Cathy had been starving, lost and needy. She had looked and felt like one of Teresa's stray cats. Teresa had come galumphing to her rescue. By, that seemed almost like a lifetime ago already.

But it was important to remember how old Ma Sturrock had helped her in her hour of need. Who knew where Cathy might otherwise have ended up? She reminded herself solemnly: she owed a debt to this tiny old woman.

'I reckon I'd best get home tomorrow,' she promised. 'If you'll have me back?'

Teresa's face lit up. 'Lass! You've made me day! You've made me year, in fact! That's wonderful news.'

Others in the queue were looking with interest to see what the lively, raised voices were about. 'Don't be such a nosy parker!' Teresa snapped at the woman in a headscarf in front of Cathy. 'It's nothing to do with you, beaky!'

As the queue shuffled forward, Teresa kept gabbling, making plans, telling her what it was going to be like now that Cathy was going to be hame again. Cathy smiled and felt queasy at the thought of living under the same roof as Teresa's son.

Because he had pushed her, hadn't he? She hadn't imagined it, had she? Those knotted, gnarled, pan-shovel hands of his had reached out and pushed her over. They hadn't reached out to catch her or pick her up . . .

He was like a split personality, he was. She had seen him spitting and snarling at her. And other times she had seen him being so nice and smarmy.

But she was starting to doubt herself. He had been so shocked by her accusation that he'd pushed her. And he'd been the one who'd carried her home. Was she wrong to think bad of him?

Right now she didn't know at all. She just knew that she hated to hurt his mam's feelings, and so she had to return for at least a little while. Lord knew, she couldn't stay around the Franchino house much longer. Not while they were all still at war. She'd been there long enough already.

'I'll pack up my carpet bag and I'll come back round tomorrow morning,' she promised Teresa, as it came her turn to put in her order for supper.

'Champion, lass!' beamed Teresa.

Meek. That was the word.

On the Tuesday that Cathy went back to number twenty-one both her landlady and her son behaved very meekly around her. She knocked at the front door and was led into the parlour, where Teresa insisted on plying her with fancies from the little bakery on Frederick Street. Pouring the tea she said, 'I thought we'd have proper elevenses together so we can catch up with each other.'

Even the numberless cats had been treated to dishes of sardine heads and tails from the wet fish shop. They ate and then they slinked around Cathy's ankles as she sat at the parlour table. 'Well, this is a very nice welcome,' she smiled.

'Hey, your bruise is almost healed, that's good,' said Teresa. 'You must have good healing skin.'

'Ha! I've got a thick skin, if that's what you mean.' Cathy sipped her tea. 'That's good tea, that.' There had been no tea at the Franchinos, which had been weird. They had coffee with everything. Or grappa, or the old woman's lethal limoncello.

'Noel's been asking when you'll be ready to go back working at the pub?' said Teresa. 'They're run off their feet he reckons, and that Ellie one is carrying on right funny lately. He says the goofy mare's moods are all up and down and she's not pulling her weight.'

Cathy had been thinking about it for the past few days. Of course she had to get back to work. She had to bring money in. But when she thought about being in that place again, all the good times and the happy memories of the past few months broke up and dissolved in her mind like a biscuit dunked for too long in her tea. All she could think of was the shock of her fall. The head-splitting pain of it. The way the room swirled around until she thought she'd gone and died . . . It was hard trying to push aside those kinds of memories.

'I suppose I'm ready to go and get back to work,' she said uncertainly. 'If they're needing me over there . . .'

Teresa poured them more hot tea and looked tremendously pleased with herself.

Later that day, once Cathy had been up to her room and unpacked her small bag, she heard the front door clash downstairs and knew that Noel had come in. She steeled herself for seeing him again.

'Bonny lass!' he greeted her, in a voice she hadn't heard him use before.

'Noel,' she nodded to him as she came down the staircase. Just running her hand down the banister, she could feel how dusty it was. She'd been away only a short time but it felt like the Sturrock house was returning to its habitual mucky ways. It was like nothing could hold back the smothering tide of dust.

As Noel kissed her chastely on her cheek, Cathy felt herself longing for the noisy warmth and brouhaha of the Franchinos' place. There was nothing weird and twisted about them and she didn't feel like she was treading on eggshells when she was with them. Last night's fish supper – when they had saluted her with their limoncello and told her how happy they'd been to have her visiting – already seemed like a hundred years ago.

In the parlour, Teresa Sturrock announced the fact that Cathy was happy to return to the Robin Hood.

'Marvellous! Me profits have dropped without a bonny lass behind the bar!' cried Noel.

'Don't let Ellie hear you saying that,' Cathy winced.

He scowled. 'That one! Why, her face is droopier than her drawers these days.'

'What's the matter with her?' Cathy asked. 'When I saw her last on New Year's Eve she was happy as anything.'

'Aye, she was happy for a couple of weeks. Happier than I've ever seen her. But this week she's been bloody awful. She's murder to work with. Sighing and moaning all the while. To tell you the truth, I think it's man trouble.' All at once Noel sounded like a chatty old wifey. He hunched over his tea and lit a tab end. 'Aye, I reckon that's what it is. She's got a bit of bother in the romance department.'

'It's not romance I'd call it,' said Teresa ominously. 'Beasts in the field have more romance about them.'

Cathy realised she'd been missing out on the latest developments. 'Is she courting then, our Ellie?'

'She's running around with someone,' said Noel. 'And you'll never guess who.'

'It's the fella what brings the hooky bottles of booze,' Teresa put in. 'That's who she's knocking about with. That ginger fella. The Mad Johnson fella. Alec. Him who got clonked on the head by whatserface, Nonna Franchino.'

Cathy gasped. 'Ellie's going out with *him*? Why, he's a *horrible* man!'

Noel shrugged. 'There's no accounting for taste, hinny.'

'Any road up, it's not making her very happy,' Teresa said. 'She's got a face like a mucky weekend.'

'The phrase is "long weekend", Mother,' Noel rolled his eyes.

Teresa shook her head. 'Nah, it's a face like a mucky weekend she's got. Eeh, you should have a word with her, our Cathy, when you go back to work. Find out what's been going on. All the ins and outs.'

The nosy old buggers, Cathy thought. They just love shoving their noses into other people's business!

Still, she was intrigued to know what her fellow barmaid was getting up to. And she also wanted to know just what it was like to walk out with one of the Johnson lads.

Chapter 24

No one cared about Ellie Mackenzie. That had been true for several years, at least.

She wasn't upset about that fact. There was no point, was there? It was simply true. I mean, yes, she had friends who thought about her occasionally and wondered how she was. That was certainly true. There were drinkers at the Robin Hood who thought the barmaid was a grand lass. They often raised a glass to her and wished her well. But no one actually *cared*. It was a simple matter of fact.

The truth of it was Ellie had no one close to her. Once her mother died, almost ten years ago this spring, she had been left on her own. There was no one close to her. No more family. There had never been anyone else close. It simply meant that there was no one in this world who put Ellie Mackenzie first.

But that, she truly hoped, that state of affairs was changing, wasn't it?

Oh, he wasn't perfect. He was a bit of a rough diamond. Some might have said he was sleazy. Some would say he was downright criminal but he was *hers*! He was her chap! Her actual lad!

Ellie Mackenzie, after all these years on her tod, clinging to life in the same dingy room in the rooming house at the top of the road by Westoe Cemetery gates, well, in these past couple of weeks, she had gone and got herself a bloke.

For the first couple of weeks of this love affair Ellie had clapped the fact of it to her bosom as she went about her duties at the Robin Hood. Mopping tables, swabbing floors, emptying ashtrays. Her insides had sung for a fortnight with the joy of it. Her lips were sore with kissing. She had bruises on her arms where he'd held her so fervently.

She'd never felt like this for years. She was thirty and she was sweeping about like a young lass who'd just discovered the joys of spring.

Noel had noticed what was going on at once.

'You're smiling a lot,' he said, one day more than a week ago, chewing on the damp end of a Woodbine and peering over his *Chronicle*.

'Perhaps I am,' she laughed, waltzing about the saloon.

'Hmm,' he said, and studied her covertly. Was that a bit of a glow about her? She was being secretive and saucy, answering him back. She was being pert in her manner. Noel had known her for many years. How long had she been working for him here? Why, ever since her mother had gone to glory. Was it that long? Before the war at any rate. Noel had never seen her like this. He'd seen her bold and flirtatious, raucous and sometimes even rude. But not like this. 'Have you gone and got yourself a fella, our Ellie Mackenzie?' he asked her.

She threw back her head in the middle of polishing the tables and laughed. 'Maybe I have! And what would you say to that?'

He shrugged and found himself saying, 'Well, I'd wish you all the best in the world, pet. You deserve a bit of happiness, you do.'

She was amazed by his kindness, the sudden softness in his tone. 'Why thank you, Noel. That's very good of you to say.'

'Aye, well,' he turned the page of his paper. 'Is it true, then? Is there a bloke on the scene?'

'There is!' she beamed. 'And it's Alec Johnson!'

Noel almost swallowed his cigarette end. 'Aw, nae, hinny. Not *him!*'

She had first become aware of the dapper red-haired fella when he started making deliveries at the pub in person. That was proper service, that! He was a businessman who didn't mind getting his own hands dirty. He came knocking on the back door with his clinking, sparkling crates of spirits and what-have-you.

Sometimes Ellie answered that door to him and he chattered away all charmingly, using the kinds of words you didn't hear in these parts very much. He was a sophisticate, was Mr Alec. That's how he himself put it. He loved the finer things in life and wasn't ashamed of that. And he had his sights set higher than a life round here in the Sixteen Streets.

Ellie had watched, sceptical at first, but with increasing admiration, as he delivered his bottles of booze and came out with all his patter. 'And how's my lovely lass today?' he'd ask her.

Ellie wasn't daft. She knew all the bottles were nicked, or they'd been procured through some risky, shady business. But that was nothing to do with her. In her eyes Mr Alec was a successful businessman. Why, just look at his fancy suits! He said he got himself togged out in Newcastle, at the finest gentleman's outfitter in the city. Gentleman's outfitter! Just the sound of that phrase felled Ellie. How fancy did that sound?

Well, maybe he was nowt much to look at, with his piggy little eyes and his bristly pink chops. And maybe that red hair of his was just a few straggly strands underneath his trilby hat, but that hardly mattered to her. He spoke well and he put all his attention onto her when they spoke. She found herself being thrilled by that.

Of course her dizzy happiness hadn't lasted forever. After a fortnight, a certain gloom had descended over Ellie. The switch in her mood aggravated her boss and surprised her customers at the Robin Hood. 'What's gone wrong for Ellie?' folk asked.

'How the hell should I know?' Noel growled at them. 'Women are all loopy, if you ask me.'

She confided in her young friend and fellow barmaid, Cathy Carmichael, the very day that Cathy returned to working at the pub.

'Do you think I'm being daft running around with Alec?' Ellie asked her, once all the tale – such as it was – was told. 'Am I acting the giddy goat?'

Cathy was rather stiff in her reply. But she warmed up as she realised that Ellie had been genuinely happy at one point and was starting to question that happiness. Her uncertainty was making her gloomy. 'But why aren't you still happy, Ellie? Noel has told me that you've been right down lately. He said you were happy for a bit, then you've been cast down again, these past few days.'

Ellie was surprised to hear Noel had been keeping such close watch. 'Well, I've been very happy since . . . you know, Alec and me, we started walking out. But this past week, I've not been so glad. Maybe I've let that show a little bit.' She could have kicked herself for being so transparent.

'Everything in the garden not so rosy?' Cathy asked.

'It's not the garden that bothers me,' Ellie frowned. 'That's even if I had a garden. No, all I've got is that one room of mine. A bedroom, if you get my drift.'

'Ah, I see,' said Cathy. She braced herself to be told more than she wanted to hear about Ellie's love life.

'I'll put a brew on and I'll tell you what's what. Don't worry! I won't embarrass you with details!'

But she did.

Cathy's ears burned as they sat there with a mid-morning cup of tea.

Ellie was rather frank when discussing sexual matters. Some of the things she made reference to during this chat, Cathy had simply never heard of before. I grew up on a farm! Cathy thought. And I'm no innocent. I know what's what! But there was a tawdry sophistication about the things Ellie talked about that set her to shame.

'So the woman who owns your rooming house doesn't mind if you have . . . a gentleman to stay?'

'Ah, usually she does. But Alec has charmed her, of course, and she just melts when she sees him. She shoots out into her hall to see who it is coming in the front door and then it's: "Ooh, Mr Alec. How marvellous to see you again, dear." And he's like, "Good evening, Florrie. Here's a florin for your trouble." He slips her a coin and a bottle of Portuguese forti- fied wine. Then she brings hot water in a jug and extra clean towels, just to make it seem like she's running a tidy house. Well, she's such a slattern usually. We have to fetch our own water, all the boarders in her place. But she puts on such a show for Alec. "Ooh, Mr Alec, will you be here for breakfast?" she giggles. Then, when he's not there and it's just me, she sidles up with a face like a furious monkey and goes: "You whore! You jezebel! I should toss you out on the street!"'

Cathy hardly knew what to say. It sounded as if things between Mr Alec and the buck-toothed barmaid had been moving rather fast. She had given him – presumably – her *all*.

'Is that why you're upset, then? Is that why your mood has changed? Because the landlady called you a jezebel?'

'Why no,' Ellie laughed. 'I couldn't give a stuff about what she thinks. No, it's Alec and me . . . in the bedroom, like. I don't think it's working. I don't think we go together, kind of thing. I don't think we *fit*.'

'Oh, I see,' said Cathy, not really understanding at all.

'Well, he tries his best. And it's all busy and huffing and puffing and some of that can be quite pleasant. But I don't know, somehow it's just not working and he's looking crosser each time. He says I don't relax! Well, how can I relax with that old bugger Florrie listening at the door?' She shook her head sorrowfully and daintily sipped her tea.

'Ah,' Cathy commiserated. 'It must be hard.'

Ellie scowled. 'It so rarely *is*. And he blames me. That's the problem.'

They were interrupted then by Noel, hefting a barrel of ale up from the store room. 'Eeeh, is the Mothers' Union having a good gossip then?'

'It's nowt to do with you, Noel Sturrock,' Ellie told him beadily.

'Aye, well I hope you're happier today than you've been these past few days,' Noel snapped. 'Now that you've got your bosom buddy back.'

'Who, Cathy?' Ellie smiled. 'Why aye, it's smashing that she's back at work with us. We've missed you, pet!'

Smiling, Cathy reflected that she'd never have said that she and Ellie were bosom buddies, exactly. They rubbed along fine these days, but that was about it.

'So are you gonna be cheerier now, hinny?' Noel admonished Ellie. 'You've been right snappy for days. I'd have thought you'd be happy as owt! What with all your courtin'!'

Ellie rolled her eyes at him. 'What would you know about romance and courtin', Noel Sturrock?' She laughed at him as she got up to help him with the pumps. 'What woman's ever looked your way? What would you know about any of it?'

The words were harsh, but her tone was kindly enough, Cathy thought. She caught Noel's eye then and the old devil winked at her.

She rubbed the fading bruise on her brow. Well, this evening she'd have to face the public in the saloon with her war wound on show. She didn't look so bad, she decided.

Later that afternoon she found herself on the steps into the storeroom – the very place where she'd had her fall on New Year's Eve. Noel was there behind her, all of a sudden. 'N-Noel,' she said. 'Listen, I've been thinking while I've been away. I should have said this before I went to stay with Sofia and them . . .'

'Oh aye, pet?' She could tell he was bracing himself for whatever she might come out with next. What would she accuse him of now, he was wondering.

'I should have thanked you,' she said, surprising him. 'For picking me up off this frozen floor. For dragging me home. For seeing me into bed. You and your mother looked after me and probably saved my life.'

'Aye, lass,' he said.

'And all I could do was act all delirious and daft. I was saying all kinds of awful things to you. At one point I even thought you'd shoved me down the steps! I believed that you'd shoved me over on purpose!'

He shook his head sorrowfully. 'Your wits were scrambled. You'd had a nasty bump.'

'That's true enough,' she said. 'I could hardly think straight, and I thought all sorts of awful things about you . . .'

'That hardly matters, pet,' he smiled.

'I just wanted to say, now that I'm back here at work, I'm sorry, Noel . . . for ranting and raving at you like that.'

He closed his eyes as if her words were like sweet balm to his troubled soul. 'It does me right good to hear that, petal. You know, I'd never do anything to hurt a hair on your head, don't you?'

They smiled awkwardly at each other and went about their work again.

What had changed? Why had Cathy seemingly decided he wasn't really to blame for her fall? She, who'd been so sure at the time?

Cathy had decided to give him the benefit of the doubt. For the sake of where she lived and where she worked, she would have to believe the best of him. She had been very tipsy and mistaken, that was all. Of course he had never set out to harm her! It made her tremble to think of the possibility that he had wanted to harm her. No, she refused to be frightened of him.

Now, look how happy he was after just a few kind words! He must think an awful lot of her. Of course he'd never hurt her. Why, he blossomed with just a handful of sweet phrases from Cathy. He was like putty in her hands now!

Wasn't that better than fighting?

When the doors were open in the early evening and the saloon fire was perking up nicely, the Women's Table filled up. Ada Farley was there with her knitting and she was joined by Winnie, of course, and that old Nonna Franchino, who sat there with her infamous silver-topped cane on show. She was looking very pleased with herself and her recent notoriety.

Every now and then one of the fellas would offer to buy her a drink. Everyone had heard the tale of how she'd bested Alec Johnson, and there was no love spared for that vicious ginger bloke round here. Soon the old nonna was a little tipsy with the extra half pints of stout she had graciously accepted from them. She shared her good fortune with her two pals and the talk at the Women's Table grew jolly and loud.

Cathy was aware that Ellie was bridling with fury. She hissed into Cathy's ear: 'That old bitch could have dashed his brains out! Does anybody think of that? They just think it's funny. But I don't think it is. What if it was the other way around? What if he'd hit *her* like that on the head? She wouldn't be laughing then . . .'

Cathy tried to stop her fellow barmaid from sidling across the busy bar to stand in front of the old Italian grandma. Quick as a flash Ellie was over there, with her hands on her hips, and she was yelling at the whiskery avenger: 'Aye, laugh all you want, you nasty old besom! But Alec will have the polis onto you! It's common assault, what you did! He could have you locked up, he could!'

Well, there was a roar of laughter from all corners of the pub at these words. The very idea of Alec Johnson calling in the polis! And calling them onto an old lady, at that!

Ellie flushed red with shame as they laughed at her. Winnie and Ada were laughing, too. Even the old woman was cackling at Ellie.

They were laughing at her. Not just at the daftness of what she'd said about the copper, but at her relationship, her new fancy fella and even her hopes that she might at last be happy. Even just the hope of that tiny bit of happiness was making them all laugh like broken drains.

No one cared for Ellie Mackenzie. Not really. No one had cared for years.

Chapter 25

Life returned to its everyday pattern for Cathy both at number twenty-one with the Sturrocks, and at the Robin Hood, where she worked at least a few hours almost every day. It was a golden period, in many ways, with Noel in a genial, tolerant mood almost all of the time, and Ellie gradually becoming content with her ongoing relationship with Alec Johnson. Seemingly, their intimate problems had been resolved – or, at any rate, Ellie made no further attempts to explain them, much to Cathy's relief. Perhaps they had found they fitted together after all. Cathy didn't feel compelled to ask.

The strange thing, though, was when Mr Alec next paid a visit, bringing his usual crates of contraband liquor, he hardly spared Ellie a glance. He stood at the bar with Noel and took a nip of Scotch with him, and he only spared the slightest of nods for the woman he was supposedly squiring about the town. Why, he paid Cathy more attention than he did Ellie!

'Oh, he likes to be discreet,' was how Ellie explained this afterwards. 'He keeps all his passion for when we're alone together.' She sounded almost smug as she said this, but Cathy felt slighted on her behalf. 'What did you expect?' Ellie chuckled. 'For him to go slobbering all over me in front of you two?'

Cathy pulled a face. She would hate it if her fella just about ignored her like Mr Alec had Ellie! Not that Cathy had a fella, mind! And not that she was looking for one!

As the wintry days became milder, there was an early hint of spring in the air. Another wave of flu came through the town, and there were whispers of panic and a few coffins and corteges coming out on the streets, weaving their resigned way down to the churchyard at St Jude's. It was a reminder that, though the snowdrops were poking out their brave little heads, the dangerous winter wasn't over and done with yet.

Then Ellie was swanking about in a new dress and showing off a fancy bracelet her beau had gifted her. She started dropping hints that she might be moving soon. 'Moving house?' Cathy gasped. 'Surely you'll still be living round here? You'll still be working here with us?'

There was what could only be called a simpering look on Ellie's face. She looked like the cat that was quite confident about getting the promised cream. 'Well now, I quite fancy being a . . . what do you call 'em? A proper lady of leisure . . . Sitting about in my nightie all day and eating a fancy box of chocs for breakfast . . .'

'Get away,' laughed Cathy. 'You've got too much go in you! There's no way you could sit around all day doing nowt! And if you ate chocs for breakfast, you'd soon get fat!' Actually, now that Cathy turned to study her friend she realised that Ellie was, in fact, looking rather stouter than she had since she'd known her. Why, perhaps a bit of love and attention was making her happy?

They were working together to make the saloon shipshape for Friday night. It was amazing how much crud and dirt could accumulate through the week. It was tiring work, getting the old place gleaming in time. Ellie often pointed out how these tasks would go neglected before Cathy started here. Noel always said: 'No one sees the muck by gaslight anyway! And who needs a beer parlour to be clean?' Standards had gone way up in the past six months.

Ellie paused as she stood with the mop in its tin bucket of scummy grey water. 'There's talk of Alec putting me in my own little place. He's got a house, he says. Way over in Boldon Colliery. It's posher over that way. There's someone living in it now, but it's time for them to move on. Some woman he used to know. Eeeh, he says it's a fine little palace, Cathy. He says he can just see me there, like a queen in my own kingdom.'

'A house of your own!' Cathy gasped, though she knew better than to believe a word of it when a bloke offered you anything. A whole house! Of course, it was far too good to be true, wasn't it? 'Is he going to marry you, then?'

Ellie looked scandalised. 'Hush! Don't say that! You'll jinx it all, Cathy!' She sloshed the mop in the dingy water and sighed heavily. 'But you must know, I've got my hopes up. He keeps talking about what a lonely life it's been for him. He's not getting any younger. Now, that sounds like a man wanting to settle down, doesn't it?'

'Aye, maybe,' smiled Cathy. But she was thinking, what with all this talk of a house – where was it? Miles away in Boldon Colliery, had Ellie said? It was more likely that Mr Alec just wanted a fancy woman. A bit on the side, tucked away in a house that he owned, waiting on him when he deigned to show up. But how different was that to ordinary marriage anyway? Cathy wondered.

Eeeh, fellas had all the power and all the luck, didn't they? In some ways Cathy felt herself lucky that she herself wasn't running around with men and getting tangled up in their awful schemes. They were all bloody selfish, as far as Cathy could tell, and she was best off out of it!

Look at old bucktoothed Ellie there, all buxom and thickening at the waist! Going all moony and soppy about her little ginger bloke as she swabbed down the floorboards! She'd do anything for that man, just to be able to say that he was hers! Just so she'd have the pride of saying she belonged to some man.

It was a funny old business, Cathy thought.

'Well pet, I hope it all works out for you,' she told Ellie firmly. 'And I hope you get your house in Boldon. I can imagine coming to visit you and you'll be sat there like Lady Muck!'

Ellie beamed. 'Oh, to have visitors! I can't have visitors in that one-roomed place at mucky Florrie's. I've never been able to have anyone round. When you come we could have tinned salmon sandwiches, pet! We'll be sat there like duchesses, nibbling dainties off china plates.'

'Aye, we will,' Cathy said. 'I'll hold you to that, mind!'

Something about Ellie's brightness and hopefulness cast a dark pall over Cathy that afternoon, though. She couldn't say exactly why.

With the sun starting to make more of an appearance, Teresa Sturrock felt like she might be coming out of hibernation herself. She was ready for a bit of an airing at last. She shrugged on her tatty fur coat and chose a shapeless cloche hat from her cupboard in the hall. 'What do you say to a walk along the seafront, Cathy? And a turn or two around the park?'

It was a perfect way to spend a couple of free hours forgetting about work and all their concerns. They linked arms and paraded down Ocean Road, breathing in the stiff breeze that came in from the sea. It was almost a bit too bracing at times, but it felt grand to have that cool air against their faces.

'It's blowing away all me cobwebs!' Teresa laughed. 'Isn't that how it feels, pet?'

The park was busy with folk who had much the same idea. At the first sign of bright sunshine with a hint of warmth, they had come out to stroll around the lake, where the birds were squawking like mad in the trees, wood pigeons and gulls acting like they too thought that spring had come early.

Teresa was pointing out the small fairground over the road, with the tops of its swings and rides looking like a fairy tale castle hidden behind tall fences down beside the sea. 'It's not been open since the war was on. Maybe they'll get it going again this year?' the old woman set to musing. 'If you'd only seen it in its heyday. When I was little we'd go down and spend all day at the fair. A few pennies would last you all day long. Whole families would be out, and all the women would have their great big hats on and the fellas were in three-piece suits, even just for sitting on the sands. You've never seen owt like it, man! By, we knew how to have a good time then, Cathy! All the fair, and this park, and all the miles of sand – you'd hardly see a spot that was empty for all the people who had flocked here!'

She smiled at the old lady's happy memories, but to Cathy it sounded much too busy. She didn't like the sound of all those crowds. 'Where I grew up, we were right by the sea,' she said. 'But we had miles of it all to ourselves. That's what it felt like. All this golden sand and the sea went out leaving it all shining silver as far as you could see. And there was a castle – a real castle! Right out on the front. We used to say that the castle was ours, all us kids from the village. We made believe that it belonged to us and we were in long ago times . . .'

Teresa was studying Cathy as she reminisced aloud, strolling around the bronze boating lake. 'Where was this then, hinny?' Teresa asked. 'You know, you've never really talked much about your upbringing and all that. In fact, you never really tell us anything much about your life before you came to us.' She gave a funny kind of laugh. 'It's almost like you've put aside everything that ever happened to you before you came to South Shields. Like you were trying to forget it all.'

Cathy pulled a face. She looked reflective and much more serious than Teresa had ever seen her. 'Perhaps I am. Perhaps that's what I've been trying to do. Why, that's what a new start is all about, isn't it?'

'Aye, pet, but you don't have to be secretive about your past,' Teresa said. 'You don't have to go hiding it all. Not from someone like me, who's been your good friend since you first got here . . .'

Cathy couldn't help laughing at Teresa's obvious fishing. The old wifey was nosy as anything! She was avid to find out about Cathy's past. For months now she had been convinced that Cathy was fleeing from something when she first met her. For months Cathy had been keeping her secret intact. Once or twice Teresa had tried to wheedle it out of her, but with absolutely no success whatsoever.

'Eeh, pet,' she was saying now, as they passed the boathouse on their third lap around the lake. 'If you ever feel like talking it all over, you know where I am. You know that it's hopeless keeping it all bottled up. The past will find its way out, you know! And secrets are no good, curdling up inside of you!' Teresa laughed. 'That's something you'll learn about the Sixteen Streets, pet. There's lots of secrets, and some of them get kept a long time. But everything comes out in the end! Everything comes out in the wash!'

The stiff breeze from the sea was a good drying wind, and Teresa's mention of the wash made Cathy wish she'd thought to put the wet sheets out on the line in the alley before they ventured out. It was a good drying day and they weren't taking advantage of it. She looked down at her reliably nebby but loyal landlady. 'Honestly, Teresa, I've nowt much worth telling about my past. No scurrilous secrets, I'm afraid!'

Teresa looked like all her hopes had been dashed, and she tightened her grip on Cathy's arm. She said, 'Well, never mind, pet!'

But both women knew that Cathy was lying. Both women knew for a fact that Cathy had secrets she wasn't telling anyone about – not if she could help it. They could stay buried forever as far as Cathy was concerned.

'*Hoy, man! You great gawky buffoon!*'

Teresa's sudden shout of annoyance startled Cathy. Some great big bloke had swerved by them on the path and he'd trodden on the old woman's foot as he went by. Her poor, bunioned feet were tiny things, crammed into old lady's plain shoes. Cathy had washed and rubbed her feet for her and she knew how much they pained the old dame. Teresa had been so grateful for that washing and that rub! It was something that no one ever did for her, and she couldn't reach to do it properly herself.

Now here was some great hefty ninny striding past and treading on her sore toes! No wonder she let out a honk as loud as any of the geese on the lake. No wonder she let fly a volley of rude epithets at him.

The clumsy bloke simply stood there and took all her insults, and he tried to get a word in to apologise. 'I'm truly sorry, missus, for stepping on your toes . . .'

'Yer great clod-hoppin' bloody fool!' Teresa screeched. 'Ooh, they feel like bloody hell! They feel like they've been cut off, me poor toes!' She grasped Cathy's arm for support and now other strollers were taking note of the noisy scene. Some were pausing to watch and there were titters of laughter as Teresa continued with her verbal assault.

'Look man, I'm sorry,' said the clumsy, big-footed fella in the path. 'What more can I say? What more can I do?'

Cathy looked at him more carefully then, taking in properly his thick red curls of hair in the bright afternoon sun. She stared at his muscular arms and chest through his open-necked white shirt. Why, she knew just who this was who'd gone stamping on Ma Sturrock's poor delicate toes!

'Matty Johnson,' Cathy said, almost under her breath, and locked eyes with the bloke who'd danced her around the saloon on New Year's Eve. Together they had made those shining boards tremble and shake!

Teresa Sturrock was still shouting: 'I'll tell you what you can do! You can treat us both to a cup of tea to get over the shock. I need a sit! I need a cup of tea! You can buy us a piece of flamin' cake, too, you great clumsy oaf!'

Matty Johnson had recognised Cathy by now, too, and his face broke into a warm, winning smile. 'Aye, all right then, I'll buy you both tea and cake, will I? And I'm sorry about your foot, missus. I hope some cake will make up for it?' He glanced in Cathy's direction. 'Hullo again, you,' he said.

Chapter 26

They went to a small tea room, not far away, where they could still get a glimpse of the sea from the window where they sat. Matty Johnson was behaving like the perfect gentleman, putting in their order with the young waitress and smiling at them when the girl hurried away.

'Well, this is very nice, very nice,' said Teresa, looking around at the other afternoon tea drinkers. Cathy knew that it was somewhere that she would never come of her own accord: 'What? Spend all that money when we've got perfectly good hot water and tea leaves at home? Folk only go to places like that so they can sit and swank about it.'

Today she seemed quite content to sit there, being seen in her fur and her shapeless hat. When the tea came, out popped her little finger when she raised the cup to her mouth. She looked comically genteel as she sipped and fluttered her eyes at Matty.

'I was hoping I'd run into you again,' Matty was telling Cathy.

'Oh aye, been looking for me, have you?'

'Just keeping me eye open, since New Year's Eve, that's all.'

'Well,' said Cathy, sipping her tea and critically examining the plate of fancy cakes. 'I've been out of circulation, really.'

Through a mouthful of sponge, Teresa burst out: 'She had a nasty fall on New Year's Eve and spent a little while recovering from a bump on the head. You can still see a bit of the bruise, if you look . . .'

Cathy pulled a curtain of dark hair across her forehead, wishing that her landlady hadn't drawn attention to it. 'It's all right now. It was nothing . . .'

'If you'd been with me, you'd never have come to any harm,' he told her.

There was an awkward pause for a moment or two then. Cathy nudged the plate of cakes at the Johnson fella, but he shook his head quickly. 'You should look after yourself better,' he told Cathy. 'No more falling about.'

She grimaced at this. 'I'll try.'

'She was a bit pie-eyed,' said Teresa, through a mouthful of icing and buttery sponge. 'Eeeh, these are champion, these cakes. Aye, she'd had a skinful that night, drinking all the tip money away, my Noel said.'

'Why, it was New Year,' Matty smiled indulgently. 'She had a right to get a bit drunk like the rest of us. Seeing out that terrible year . . . well, we all had a wonderful time, didn't we?'

The old woman smiled at him. 'That we did, lad. I suppose we did.'

Later, after they'd finished their tea and Matty had paid up, they left him on the pavement outside. He caught Cathy's hands between his as she turned to go up Ocean Road. 'Look, I want to see you again. Properly, pet. Like . . . going out for a dance in the evening. Would that be all right, do you think? Would you like to?'

His question caught her out. She hadn't been expecting him to be quite so formal and old-fashioned. He made her smile. 'All right then,' she said.

At home that night, spooning out mince and dumplings, Teresa Sturrock was merciless to Cathy. 'Eeeh, she was so demure with him. Like a princess or something, playing it cool. You should have seen her, our Noel! She was proper putting on airs with this young fella!'

Noel sat hunched over his dish of mince, slurping up gravy in a desultory fashion. 'Oh, aye?' he said.

'He was being a proper gentleman, mind, to give him his dues.' She fished around with her spoon in the pot and popped another golden dumpling onto Noel's supper. 'Have another one, petal. Aye, if he'd asked me to go out, I'd have said yes, too, he was so gallant! And by, he's a good-looking fella as well, Cathy! Watch out – he'll go whisking you off your feet! Well, I suppose he might as well, if there's no one else on the scene. He's after you, Cathy!'

The girl shrugged, chewing the gristly mince. 'I suppose he is.'

'Suppose nothing!' Teresa laughed. 'Your eyes were out on stalks, drinking him in with your tea.'

Across the table Noel stirred and muttered unhappily. 'So this is the fella who was dancing you around the pub? This is him, is it?'

'Aye,' said Cathy, and wished they'd just stop talking about it all.

'Well, you know who his people are, don't you?' Noel glared at her. The intensity of his look almost made her gasp. There was sheer anger there, but there was more besides. She saw that he was both hurt and upset, too. 'You know he's one of the Mad Johnsons?'

'I don't care about that,' said Cathy. 'I don't care where people come from, or who their people are. I judge folk on their own merits, and on the way they treat me.'

'Well said, hinny,' said Teresa hypocritically, through a mouthful of suet and grease. It had to be said, she was the worst one in the world for prejudging simply everyone from gossip and hearsay.

'You might say that and mean it.' Noel twisted his face. 'But wait till you hear just what those Mad Johnsons get up to. Why, you know that they were trying to get money out of your precious Franchino lot. You know that the old woman cracked Alec Johnson on the bonce with her cane?'

'Yes, I've heard all about that,' said Cathy. 'Everybody has.'

'Well, your lad was there as well,' Noel told her smugly. 'I have it on good authority that your precious Matty was there as well as Alec that day. Trying to extort money off your foreign friends and threatening to do them over. So that's the sort of fella you're saying yes to going out with, Cathy! So what do you think of that?'

Cathy didn't know what she thought about that at all. But she was damned if she was taking Noel's word for anything. Like she said, she took people as she found them, paying no heed to tittle-tattle or rumour.

So at the end of that week she put on the dress she'd worn new on New Year's Eve (having brushed out the scuffs and mended the slight tear from her fall) and she went out on the town.

Matty came knocking at the door of number twenty-one, with his hair smarmed down with some kind of oil that smelled wonderful. He had on a neatly ironed shirt with no collar, opened slightly at the throat. When she stood surveying him on the doorstep, her eye was drawn to the expanse of collar-bone and the curls of red hair that the open neck of his shirt revealed. He wore no jacket nor overcoat, even though it was still early in the year and that wind coming up the hill from the docks was deadly. 'Eeeh, you must be frozen!' She let him in and took him through to Teresa's parlour.

The old woman and three of her cats on the settle all sat up straighter to get a good look at the visiting gentleman. 'You look proper bonny,' she told him, with a rakish grin. 'And doesn't our Cathy look magnificent tonight? I helped her put all those curls in her hair. We were tying rags onto every lock until about midnight last night.' Teresa was proud of her handiwork, and she was glad of helping Cathy, but at the same time she would rather it was her Noel that was taking the girl out tonight. But what more could she do to matchmake? The girl knew her own mind. She would make her own choices.

Cathy laughed and shook out her dark red hair, feeling very proud of the way she looked tonight. She'd taken every effort with her appearance, even using a fancy bar of fragrant soap that Teresa had gifted her. 'It's special this, from Paris before the war. Just sniff that perfume – it's bloody irresistible!' she'd said to Cathy.

She had taken a longer, more pleasurable bath than usual, in the tin tub in front of the range, lavishing herself with this wonderful Parisian lather. Listening all the while in case Noel came bursting in, though luckily he hadn't. Tonight her skin felt wonderfully soft and fresh and gleaming. She knew that her complexion was marvellous in the soft lamplight of Teresa's parlour.

'You look smashing,' said Matty Johnson and his dark eyes were gleaming with what looked like adoration.

They danced that night like Cathy had never danced before!

He took her across town to a dance hall she'd heard other women talk about – the Alhambra, where the interior decoration made her feel like she had been transported into another world. To Cathy, all those white plaster pillars and swags of plush velvet were like something out of a fairy tale. The nooks decorated with gigantic potted palms and other exotic plants imparted the feeling of being in something like the *One Thousand and One Arabian Nights*. Everyone was dressed up in their finery, ladies and gentlemen she had never seen before. No one she had ever seen propping up the bar of the Robin Hood, at any rate.

'Ooh, it's magical, Matty!' she gasped, forgetting to play her part coolly almost at once.

He was delighted by how chuffed she was to be there. 'Aye, it's not bad, is it?'

'Not bad, he says!' Cathy laughed out loud, squeezing his arm as he linked with hers. 'I've never been anywhere like this. Well, I saw the ballroom at Morwick Hall of course. And once they had an actual ball and I saw them all going in and I watched from the stairs, but I was never there for myself. I never . . . never *danced*!'

But she danced that night in Matty's arms. She didn't really know how to, simply because she had never had the opportunity to learn. But it seemed that Matty knew all the steps to every kind of tune that the band played for them that night. He didn't dance showily or with any great aplomb, but he knew the steps and he kept to the rhythm. Tightly held in his arms, Cathy was a quick and eager study, following his lead. It was easy, just treading with him through dance after dance, round and round on that sprung and shiny floor, weaving in and out of endless swirling patterns amongst all those other happy souls done up in their finest. They were all having a whale of a time and Cathy could feel her heart glowing inside her chest. Her breath quickened with excitement and joy. She really didn't think she'd ever been happier than she felt that night at the Alhambra.

They tried to cool down with paper cups of fruit punch, served out of a silver salver at a table by the palm trees. They managed to find seats, sitting pressed wordlessly together in the crowded corner.

'Are you having a nice time?'

She turned to smile at him. 'You know I am.'

'I suppose you've got your pick of all the fellas, a beautiful girl like you,' he said. 'I bet you're out dancing all the time. Fancier places than this, an' all.'

She shook her head. 'Why no, no, not at all.' She lowered her eyes, almost embarrassed. 'To tell you the truth, this is the first place I've been to like this . . . with a boy . . . a man . . . friend.'

He smiled in amazement, and at the way she'd stumbled over calling him a man and a boy. 'Really? Your first? And yet you seem like such a woman of the world!'

'I'm not at all,' she said. 'I've not had much time for going out and enjoying myself, really. It's been one thing after another, making ends meet, trying to survive.'

'You've not had much fun, have you?' he asked softly. She felt his hand on her back, rubbing the velvet nap. She was so intent on the feel of him it was almost as if his fingers were brushing over her bare skin. His voice was lower as he said, 'No one's ever really taken care of you, have they?'

She had to admit that that was true. Cathy had always had to look after herself. Her life had been a helter-skelter, hand-to-mouth kind of affair. There really hadn't been much fun or enjoyment and she hadn't been able to really rely on anyone at all. Not family nor employers nor friends. But nowadays things were getting to be different. This all felt quite different.

'Maybe this is where my real life begins,' she found herself saying.

He looked startled at her words, just for a moment. 'I think you're really special,' he told her, and then, without pausing to think about whether it was the right moment or not, he leaned forward and kissed her.

Chapter 27

'His hair's not really red,' said Cathy. 'Not carroty red, not really. It's more like golden red . . .'

'Aye, it is,' Ellie agreed with her. It was the next evening and they were hard at work at the Robin Hood. Nowadays they were doing sandwiches in the early evening – home-baked stottie bread with cheese and onion. There was a giant jar of pickled eggs on the bar for those who fancied a snack. The idea was to keep people in the pub, to stop them sloping off to get fed, and to keep them spending. It all meant even more work for the barmaids. 'These stotties are selling as fast as I can put them up!'

'He looked so handsome in his clean white shirt,' Cathy was still going on. 'I can't believe he never had a coat with him, though. When we came out he was soaked through with sweat from all the dancing, and we were out in the freezing air again. It was midnight and there was snow coming down.'

'It's a wonder he doesn't get pneumonia,' Ellie said with a shudder, recalling her own recent bout of flu, lying feverish and aching in her bed.

'Ah, he's tough as anything,' smiled Cathy. 'Strong as an ox.'

Ellie studied her. 'You're really smitten, aren't you? I've never heard you go on like this.'

Buttering yet another flat loaf, Cathy looked abashed. 'I suppose I am going on daft, really. It was just one night out with the bloke. Why, he probably has loads of girls on the go at once . . .'

Ellie shrugged. 'Not according to his brother. Alec says that since he's been back from France, Matty's been living pretty quietly. They were all worried about him for a while, there. He was too quiet. Having nightmares and that. They thought he was never going to be the same as the lad they all remembered before he went to the war. But they say he's perking up now. You're the only lass on his horizon, Cathy, and Alec says you're bringing his brother back to life.'

Cathy quietly absorbed this piece of information and glowed with its import. She had known it already, though. She knew there was a special connection between her and Matty.

'Urgh, these pickled eggs give me the creeps,' Ellie was saying. 'They're like eyeballs in a jar, sitting on the counter. I can't bear reaching in to fish them out . . .'

The two girls were in charge at the Robin Hood tonight, since Noel had given himself the night off. He was at the variety show in town with his mother. As a special treat he'd encouraged her to dress in her finery to see the show. He'd worn his best suit and bought a large satin-covered box of chocolates. It was high time they treated themselves, he had announced at breakfast that morning.

Cathy had found herself thinking: he's only doing it because I had a night on the town the night before. He's showing that he can just as easily have a night out too! Uncharitably she followed up that thought with a chuckle. Aye, but the only person he's got to take out is his mother!

Eeeh, but Cathy knew she was being unkind. She should be glad that Teresa was getting an evening out at the theatre. Some singer she really liked was doing a turn on the bill tonight. And it was lovely of Noel to think of his mam like that, but still Cathy found herself thinking: he's just jealous that I was out dancing last night. He's not happy about it at all . . .

Well, there wasn't much she could do about that. She had her own life to live and it felt like – at last – she had started to live it.

'Three cheese savoury stotties for the Women's Table,' said Ellie, handing Cathy a loaded platter. 'Would you take them, pet? That old Italian woman keeps trying to put a bloomin' curse on me.'

The Evil Eye had indeed been trained on Ellie several times in the past couple of weeks. Nonna Franchino did some kind of obscene-looking gesture with her fingers at her eyes and then her throat, muttering under her breath whenever Ellie swayed nearby with her heavy breasts and hips. 'Is an old Neapolitan curse,' the grandmother confided to her friends. 'She deserve it. Running about with that bad man. And shouting at me like she did, in front of everyone! Just for defending myself. No, she should suffer, that Ellie.' The old woman's eyes would blaze as she waggled her fingers energetically and even Ada Farley felt alarmed at the venom in her tone. Luckily, no one really put any store by superstitious curses, not really – though Ellie kept her distance from the Women's Table if she could help it.

So it was Cathy who took over their soft, floury stotties stuffed with crumbly orange cheese and green onion. She set the plate down with a clatter and grinned at them all. 'How are our lovely ladies tonight, then?'

Ada, Winnie and Nonna Franchino all studied the glamorous barmaid carefully. 'We've heard you've been out on the town,' said Ada, with a smirk. 'You were seen, young lady! Out dancing at all hours.'

'Oh, I was seen, was I?' laughed Cathy. 'And who's been spying on me, then?'

'By all accounts you stood out in the crowd,' Ada told her. 'That's what I've heard, hinny. They say you looked right bonny. They say you were having the time of your life.'

Cathy beamed. 'Aye, it was lovely. I've never had a night like it.'

Winnie was tucking into her stottie sandwich, narrowing her eyes as she tried to concentrate to see what the future might bring. But the mists of time seemed impenetrable just at that moment. 'By the heck, this onion's strong,' she said.

Turning to go, Cathy was struck by the thunderous look on old grandma Franchino's face. Her dark, wiry eyebrows were tugged down over her blazing eyes and her mouth was twisted into an expression of disappointed rage. 'My daughter isn't happy with you,' she growled at Cathy. 'Sofia feels the same way as I do about the Johnson men. All our family feel that way about all the Mad Johnsons.'

Her heart plummeted to her feet on hearing these words. Cathy hated the thought of disappointing or upsetting the Franchinos. The Italian family had been so good to her. They had given her shelter, so nicely, just recently . . . She had felt like an honorary member of their noisy clan. The idea of falling out of favour with them was terrible. Especially when it came to Sofia. She couldn't imagine not having her as her good friend.

'But I was out with Matty last night,' Cathy tried to explain to Nonna, who glared at her stottie and refused to touch it. 'He's not the same as the rest of his brothers or his uncles. He's a good man. He's not mixed up in everything like the others are . . .'

Nonna clicked her fingers imperiously. 'Ha! That is all you know, Cathy Carmichael. You know nothing! He was there with the others. He was there with that one I struck on the head, and the other one, the dumb big one. Your Matty was part of their gang, when they came into the ice-cream parlour and started saying their awful things and menacing our Tonio.'

Cathy stared at her, not wanting to believe what the old woman was saying.

'Ah, that's shut you up, hasn't it?' the old woman jeered. 'That's taken the fun out of last night for you, hasn't it? Your man you were seeing – he's just the same as the rest of them. He was there with them, Cathy. He's just as bad as the rest!'

Without another word, Cathy left the table by the fire and returned to the bar.

'Hey, you were a bit bloomin' hard on the lass,' Ada Farley told the Italian woman, fiddling with her hair.

'She need telling!' Nonna growled. 'She needs to be warned who she is mixing it up with. She's a good girl, but I think she is having her head turned . . .'

Over at the bar, Ellie took note of Cathy's precipitous mood change. 'Who's said something to you to put you in the doldrums?' When Cathy explained, Ellie narrowed her eyes. 'That old witch needs taking down a peg or two. Have you seen the way she keeps putting flamin' curses on me?'

There was a glimmer of tears in Cathy's eyes, Ellie was alarmed to note. 'Is it true though, Ellie? Is Matty really as bad as the other Johnson men? Was he really there trying to extort money out of the Franchinos?'

Ellie tossed her a clean dishrag. 'Come on, let's get these glasses shining. And look, Cathy, this is men's business. It's best if the likes of us keep right out of it. But I think there's something you should understand about the Johnsons, and that's the fact that they are a business. A family business and they all stick together. Now, you might not like the kind of things they're involved in, but that's your choice. You're not going to change any one of them. No way, no how. If you get involved with one of those men, there's lots of advantages, but you might just find yourself having to turn a blind eye . . .'

'Is that what you do?' Cathy asked. 'Do you have to turn a blind eye to the things your Alec gets up to?'

Ellie's lips tightened into a hard line. 'Aye, sometimes. But he tells me so little about what he gets up to anyway. I see him when I see him and we never really talk about much. He never confides in me! So it's not too hard for me to forget the kind of nastiness he's involved with . . .'

Cathy knew she would have to go and see Sofia, in order to try to put things right between them. She hated the very thought of there being any tension between them, since Sofia was probably her favourite of all the friends she had made since moving to South Shields.

But it wasn't to be as easy as all that. Sofia wasn't angry with her, nor did she shout or demand that Cathy stop seeing her fella. She just went cold and clammed up. She refused to discuss any of it. 'Is your business,' was all she'd comment, when Cathy went to see her at the ice-cream parlour. 'All I'll say is that you know who he is, and the people who he comes from.'

Really, Cathy would have preferred it had her friend exploded furiously and turned that famous hot temper onto her. Instead this felt very much like the cold shoulder. Sofia brought her frothy coffee, said her little piece, and then left Cathy alone, sitting there in her booth.

So, was this how it was going to be? Was this her future if she carried on seeing one of the Johnsons? And if that was the case, was it really worth it?

Oh, but her answer to that came just the following evening, when she saw Matty again for another date. It was a clearer evening, though still chilly. This time he had a coat, but he insisted on giving it to her, draping it over her shoulders when they took a stroll along the coastal path. The wind was picking up, making it harder and harder for them to converse. The light was fading and it might have been romantic, were it not for that keening, savage breeze from the incoming tide.

Cathy pulled the dark woollen coat tighter around her, pausing to appreciate the quality of the cloth and the lovely silk of the lining. Aye, the Johnson men seemed to have a bob or two, she had noticed. She sighed at herself for thinking this. She needed to be honest with herself. Wasn't that apparent wealth part of the attraction for her? Was she really that shallow? A bit of money, a bit of security . . . was that really enough to lure her in? To start seeing a man that none of her friends could abide? She shivered, and it wasn't just because of the sea breeze.

'Shall we go in somewhere and get a drink?' Matty asked her. 'You're looking frozen, petal.'

She smiled up at him and thought: I'm being daft about a fella, aren't I? I'm as bad as Ellie. I'm happy just to have the attention. I'm happy to feel as if I belong to someone. But what if I lose everyone else as a result?

They went to a hotel on the seafront and sat at a table in the bay window, where they could watch the sea beyond the cliffs battering against the shore. Darkness came down quite quickly and the rain started to lash.

Cathy sipped a port and lemon he'd bought for her.

'You're looking gloomy?' he said. 'Are you having such an awful time?'

'Why no,' she smiled. 'It's all just new to me, all this. Going out with a fella . . . you know.'

He supped his amber pint. 'But you'll have had boyfriends before, in the past?'

She blushed at his words. 'Oh, aye. Nothing serious, mind . . .' This wasn't something she wanted to discuss with him at all. Better to have him think she was a total innocent, a daft ninny or an old maid than have him know anything about the truth.

'Look,' he said. 'You don't have to be afraid of me. I'll never do anything to hurt you. You need to know that, lass.'

She nodded and smiled. 'I believe you.'

And she did. She knew that he was gentle, really. She knew – somehow – that he was a good fella, whatever anyone else thought of him.

Chapter 28

Something she really liked about Matty was that he wanted to take her out to places and to spend lots of time in her company. Those first few weeks, as the year opened out from its early weeks of frosty hibernation, Cathy accompanied him to the Music Hall, to the races, and even to the fairground over in Gateshead. There was something almost giddy and carefree about those days and nights with Matty Johnson. She had almost forgotten what it was like to stop thinking about work and making a living and just getting get by from day to day. Here, instead, was life and at last a sense of relishing and enjoying it.

They laughed together a lot. Afterwards, she'd have been hard-pressed to say what had been said by either of them that was so hilarious. Perhaps it was just the way they said things, or the way they saw the world; they seemed to chime in with each other, falling about helplessly at the same things. They watched other people and the way they carried on – at the theatre, at the racetrack, at the fairground or the park. It all just seemed so funny to them. Matty and Cathy lived in a kind of bubble that carried them along, separated from the world, but somehow still in the thick of it.

Happiness, she thought – that was the element she was floating in. It was thicker than normal air, sweeter and warmer than the usual atmosphere she lived in. It felt rather like the molasses-thick scent that came rolling up the hill from the biscuit factory. Perhaps it was love? Cathy didn't even know whether that was possible . . . so quickly, so soon? Could what she was feeling really be described as love already? All she had done was watch this man bare his arms at the tin can alley at the fair, winning her a coconut in the process. She had been whirled about the room by him at the dance and she had sat at his side as they had rocked with laughter at the antics of the comics at the Music Hall.

It was at this point that she longed for someone that she could confide in. Only by telling these stories out loud would she be able to measure the full impact of her feelings. Was this really love? In the sharing of the tales – aloud, to an unprejudiced witness – she would find out the truth. She would know where her heart was in all of this.

But her heart was battered and bruised. It was numb from years of being treated wrongly. It was hardened through all her habitual self-protections. And none of the friends she had made here seemed ready to listen to her happy and confused ramblings. Obviously Sofia was out of the question as a possible confidante. Teresa Sturrock was Noel's mother and she wouldn't want to hear of Cathy's affections going to anyone but her darling son.

There was Ellie, of course, but theirs was a friendship based on their being flung together at work rather than anything else. She'd never have chosen to spend so much time with the blowsy and volatile barmaid otherwise. But then there was a curious coincidence of their both walking out with Johnson brothers, so maybe that was a point in their favour. It was surely something that ought to draw them even closer together . . .

But lately, Ellie was off in a world of her own. She was in a strange and rather dazed state that Cathy found her words could barely penetrate. The older barmaid had left her Frederick Street lodgings at long last. The place she had spent years living in, both with her mother and without, was long behind her, and she knew nothing but relief about that. Now she was dwelling in a place of her own – a whole house! – over in Boldon Colliery, a couple of miles away, just as Mr Alec had promised. She was living a grown-up life with lace curtains at the windows, a cloth on the dining room table and a fancy rug on the living-room floor. She spent all her wages – and the bit extra that Alec gave her now and then – on nice things for her new home. She was forever down the market on her afternoons off, picking up odd bits of crockery and doillies, napkins and bedding.

Determined that the two of them become better friends, Cathy went with her round Shields market one Wednesday afternoon. After all, if things continued on the way they were heading, was it impossible to imagine that they might one day become sisters-in-law? Cathy castigated herself silently for bringing up such a rash idea. Look, it was all very early days, wasn't it? She was letting her silly imagination get away from her. Cathy had always prided herself on being so practical and sensible! But here she was, daring herself to hope.

The two women were togged up in their warmest coats and scarves for the afternoon round the busy stalls. Cathy was in a sea green hat she had knitted for herself – another shapeless piece of knitting that she was nevertheless proud of. Bustling along beside her was Ellie in a brand new sheepskin coat. 'It's a late Christmas gift from Alec. Isn't it wonderful? I've never had anything like it before.'

She had given a little twirl on the pavement. While admiring it, Cathy wondered whether Alec had guessed his lady friend's measurements quite wrongly. The buttons down the front seemed to be straining slightly against Ellie's girth.

'He's very generous with me,' Ellie said, as they perused a stall of glass and china oddments. She turned over fancy figurines and decorative, colourful bottles. They were eye-catching things that were of no practical use whatsoever. Cathy could see no point in owning such things, but Ellie was avid for them. She said that every shelf and windowsill in her new home was already lined with what she called her 'precious things'. 'We never had much space before, what with living in one room, me and Mam,' she explained, with a sigh. 'We just had the odd vase and that. But now, thanks to Alec, I can really spread out my wings and feel at home. I can really feather my nest!'

Cathy smiled encouragingly and found herself following along in Ellie's wake, amused by the image of her as a great big bird, sitting in her nest with her bits of glass and china and tat. Why, that was really what she was like: a big biddy hen on her nest!

Suddenly Cathy felt herself short of breath. She stopped short in the street and a shock went through her. She looked round for her friend in her new sheepskin coat and suddenly she knew.

She took her elbow and drew her aside. 'You! You're expecting!'

Ellie was feathering her nest and preparing to lay eggs! Cathy could hardly believe it. Was she mad? What would Alec say? With a sudden burst of horrible intuition, Cathy knew that he wasn't going to be pleased about this. All at once Cathy knew that this was a disastrous turn of events.

Ellie was glowing with happiness. 'You guessed! Why, I've been dropping hints like mad!'

'But aren't you . . . I mean . . . terrified?'

'And ashamed?' Ellie kept her voice low, as they discussed these intimate matters in the middle of the market place. 'I know it's crazy. I'd never have chosen this or set out to do it on purpose . . . oh no, indeed not. You may look sceptical at me like that, Cathy, but I've never set out to entrap Alec. That's just not something I would do. I'm not some hard, crafty, greedy girl – I hope you realise that?'

'Of course I do,' said Cathy. 'Oh, but Ellie, you're not married to him. There's no sign of you ever being married to him. What are you going to do? Have you told him yet?'

Ellie shook her head and, for the first time in this conversation, she looked scared. 'I'm waiting for the right moment.'

'Oh my god,' said Cathy. She had gone cold all over, even despite her new hat and scarf. Her skin prickled and her stomach was turning over.

'Eeeh, Cathy, are you all right?' her friend asked her, suddenly worried. 'Why, you're gannin' green in the face, hinny!' She put her arm around Cathy's back to hold her up, as if it were she who was in the fragile state. 'Whatever's the matter, love?'

Waving her concern away, Cathy tried to straighten up, but another wave of sickness coursed through her. It was a physical reaction to the shock of Ellie's news. It made her breath come raggedly and her stomach felt like it was shrivelling. 'It's just the surprise,' she gasped. 'It made me think . . . made me remember about . . .' But she forced herself to bite down on her words and say no more.

'Let's go inside and have a cup of tea.' Ellie led her towards a tea room, where a girl in a starched pinny sat them down at a table in the window.

Later that day, after the girls had parted, Cathy could hardly believe how calm and happy Ellie seemed. That large and grouchy woman she had worked at the pub with – the one who had been so territorial and unhelpful at first – had somehow transformed herself into – what? A deluded fool, is what Cathy couldn't help thinking. Ellie wasn't thinking straight. She wasn't seeing her fancy man Alec for what he really was.

Ellie clearly didn't understand the role he had put her into. There in her little house in Boldon Colliery, Ellie was meant to be nothing more than just a bit on the side. A good time girl who he'd pay for, and occasionally visit, but she was meant to look after herself and give him no trouble.

Cathy had seen her off on the trolley bus to Boldon Colliery. Ellie was laden down with packages of useless bric-a-brac from the market. 'Next time you'll have to come and see me at home!' Ellie cried. 'Will you do that, pet? You'll love how I've got the place. You'll be mad with jealousy!'

Watching the bus trundle off and waving to her friend, more than anything Cathy felt sorry for her. She was going to be so disappointed, Cathy was sure. She was going to be bitterly hurt.

At home later that evening Cathy longed to talk to Teresa about Ellie's predicament. Of course she couldn't, what with Teresa being the worst gossiper she had ever met in her life. Also, there was no love lost between Noel's mother and his oldest employee. The old woman would have gladly – even maliciously – spread this delicate news about Ellie all over the town.

So Cathy had to keep very quiet about it all.

'Oh, there was a message for you earlier,' Teresa suddenly announced, as they sat with a last cup of tea in the parlour that night. Cathy was just back from her late shift at the pub, where it had been quiet and dull all evening.

'Oh, yes?'

'It was shoved through the letterbox, no stamp nor envelope or nothing, so I'm afraid I've read it.'

Cathy tutted, smiling at her elderly friend's incorrigible nebbiness. She took the sheet of paper – it looked like it had been torn out of an old book. She didn't recognise Matty's careful, practised hand, but she knew at once that it had come from him.

'Eeeh, well, there you go,' Teresa Sturrock watched her absorbing the short message. 'So his mother's invited you round to meet her, has she? Well, you're honoured indeed, Cathy. The old Johnson woman is famous round here. She's like royalty to some! And there she is, requesting the pleasure of your company! And so what do you think of that?'

Cathy felt nothing but nervous at the very idea of meeting this woman, who – if the rumour were right – was some kind of queen of crime and murky goings-on. But at the same time she was pleased and excited; her fella Matty wanted her to come and meet his mam! He had said so right out, in plain words and clear handwriting. Cathy felt like hugging the curt missive to her chest, she was that pleased. 'I want you to come to our house on Tudor Avenue,' he had written. 'What with things being so serious and good between us, I think it's about time, Cathy love.'

Chapter 29

During the course of her young life, Cathy had had to face up to lots of people. She had been brave and unbowed, tackling each new encounter as she went along, thinking: I mustn't be daunted – I'm as good as they are! She had been in service in a big house and met all kinds of people, back when she was very young. She had lived in Morwick and met a whole different set of grown-up people going about their own business, and she'd had to contend with them, too. Contend with them in more ways than one. And in her months here in South Shields, life had brought her all kinds of challenges to face, and folk to impress.

Tonight though, as she took the trolley bus with Matty, wearing her smartest new blouse bought with her meagre wages from the pub, she was feeling nervous. Cathy hardly ever felt nervous when she was meeting people! What was the worst they could do to you? Why, all you had to do was give a good account of yourself, don't mumble or look miserable. All you ever had to do was be yourself and look the other person in the eye. That's all there was to it.

As the trolley bus lurched and rattled through the streets, guided by the wires that stretched and sparked overhead, Cathy felt nauseous. She felt Matty's hand squeeze hers through her glove and he said, 'She isn't really an old dragon, you know. No matter what everyone in the town might say. She's my mam.'

His mam – Gracie Johnson – was infamous throughout South Shields, even across all of Tynemouth. She was the head of a family that was feared throughout the region. No one could say what exactly their business was, but all those brothers and uncles kept themselves busy day and night keeping it going, and keeping those pennies rolling in.

At the centre of their empire was the old mother's house on Tudor Avenue, where all the boys had been brought up, amid the streets where they had first cut their teeth as bullies and thugs, extorting money out of their school friends and fighting and doling out thick ears and learning simply to seize all the things they wanted.

The streets in this part of town were even shabbier and more run-down than the Sixteen Streets known to Cathy. When she stepped off the tram car, it was into an unfamiliar area, where the tilted chimney pots were pouring thick smoke, the roof tiles looked loose, and all the curtains at the dark windows were shabby and tatty. There was something rather unwelcoming about the place. It was quite different to Frederick Street, where the women took a pride in scrubbing their front doorsteps, polishing the windows and boiling their net curtains until they were sparklingly white. They might be poor, but there was no excuse for muck. Apart from Teresa Sturrock, of course, Cathy thought ruefully – she stood out as the muckiest in her street. Eeeh, but Cathy wished she was back there with her again tonight. Her insides were curdling and turning over with trepidation.

'I've never known you so quiet,' Matty laughed gently, still holding her hand as she led her to the house where he'd had his youth. 'All my mam wants is to get a look at you. I've told her all about you.'

She bit her lip and wondered what he had said. 'I hope she won't be disappointed by me . . .' Inside Cathy recoiled at her own pathetic words. Disappointed, nothing! The old wife could take her as she found her. She should be glad to have Cathy visit! She should be proud to see her son courting Cathy! There – that was just the bit of boost she needed. Yes! She needed to feel proud of herself. She jutted out her chin as they approached the front door and Matty fetched out his key. Cathy was – just as she always was – ready for anything!

Of course, these things were never as bad in the event as you feared beforehand. Especially if you went in with the right attitude. You had to face up to people and show them that you were just as good as they were. This was Cathy's attitude and it had stood her in good stead.

Still, there were some bumps in the road that afternoon. A couple of awkward moments . . .

The old lady was sitting in her living room, which was rather dark and filled with lumpy furniture. It looked like Victorian artefacts all around her – armoires and cabinets. The kinds of things that Cathy recognised from the big house she had worked at. But here all those massive pieces were crammed into a small, terraced house.

The room was lit by flickering candles and Cathy had to squint as she eased herself between narrow gaps. Matty showed her to a low settle where she should sit. He perched himself beside her and smiled at the tiny but fierce old woman on the armchair in the middle of the room.

Eeeh! She might have got dressed up! was Cathy's first thought. There's me taking all me trouble with ironing a new blouse and polishing me shoes, just to make a good impression. And get a load of her!

Old Gracie Johnson was still in her nightie. It was a mass of delicate ruffles in ivory white. Over her small, shapeless body she wore a pink matinee jacket and a frilly mob cap. To Cathy's astonished eyes she looked exactly like a large and wrinkled baby.

'So,' Ma Gracie said, in a wheezing voice, 'this is your new lass is it, our Matty? Let me get a good look at her.' At this she produced an old-fashioned lorgnette from under her covers and held it up to her startling, pale blue eyes. Cathy did her very best not to flinch beneath that gaze. 'Aye, aye, very nice,' the old woman said at last. 'She looks healthy and strong. She's bonny, too. I'd say she's the most promising lass you've ever chosen to go out with, Matty. But what does she talk like, eh? What's she got to say for herself?'

Cathy was growing irritated at being discussed as if she wasn't present, as well as being studied like she were in the cattle market. 'I'm very pleased to meet you, Mrs Johnson. It's nice to put a face to the name and to meet Matty's mam.'

'Oh aye, oh aye,' Gracie Johnson chuckled, still peering through those antiquated spectacles. 'I'll bet you've heard some horror stories about me, haven't you? About how I'm a hard and evil old bitch, eh? I bet you've heard all the stories they whisper about me in town. About how wicked and cruel I am? How I set my boys doing all my terrible work for me and making me a pile of money?'

Cathy considered how to reply to this. She decided she would play it cool. 'Why, no, Mrs Johnson, I've heard nothing of the sort! No one's ever said a bad word about you – not in my hearing, anyway. They've all said you're a wonderful person. A lovely lady.'

Gracie laughed until flecks of spittle shot out of her toothless mouth. 'Hahaha! I'm sure that's true, petal. I'm sure you're telling the truth. Why, I'm a paragon of bloody virtue, aren't I, Matty? And everyone knows it!'

Cathy smiled at her. 'You're held in very high regard by the whole town.'

The old lady's expression soured. 'They're *scared* of me. That's what it is. They're scared of my lads. And so they should be.'

It was Matty's turn to seem nervous, as he leaned forward and patted his old mother's ruffled arm. 'Don't get into all that now, Ma. Cathy doesn't want to hear about all of that.'

'She should! She should hear about it all!' Gracie raised her voice querulously. 'If the lass is thinking about having anything to do with our family, then she needs to know what we're about.'

Cathy shrugged. 'You can tell me what you want.' She tried to sound nonchalant. A woman of the world.

'Eeeh,' sighed Ma Gracie, and suddenly her bright blue eyes were fixed elsewhere. They were trained on some earlier, and immeasurably superior, time. 'It used to be that everyone in this town really was scared daft of the Johnsons. It was back in my dada's time. Way back when. He ruled his family with a rod of iron, and he'd clatter and belt them all to keep them in line. He sent them all out to do his bidding and woe betide any of those boys who didn't bring home the bacon.'

'It was all a long time ago,' Matty said gently. 'Things are different nowadays. You're going on about Queen Victoria's time!' He laughed at the very thought.

His mother snapped, 'That's the time I belong to, Matty Johnson! And don't you forget it. Back then we had values. We had proper family values. And the head of the family was in sole charge of everyone. He told them what to do and how they were to do it. And those are the traditions that were handed down to me. That's how I've tried to run my family and the business, too. Do you see, Cathy? That's how it has to be.'

The girl nodded, struck by the fervency in the old woman's voice. 'I think I do, yes.'

'So that, even though I'm just a woman – and a weak and feeble one too – I've got the responsibility of all these lads around me. All me brothers and sons. And I've got to be tougher than them. I've got to be tough for all of us!'

'Shall I bring some tea through?' Matty asked, determined to get their afternoon visit back on track.

'Aye, you do that, son,' she laughed at him. 'Go and do lasses' work, why don't you?' She tutted, shaking her head as he left for the scullery at the back. All at once Cathy felt exposed and vulnerable alone with Gracie. 'They're soft, the lot of them. They're not hard like my uncles and my dad were hard. I feel like it's me who's made them soft. Do you think that could be true, Cathy?'

'I-I don't think they're soft,' Cathy told her. 'Why, look at Matty! He was away in the war! Look what he had to face up to!'

'Aye, maybe not Matty. Matty's always been different and special. Matty's always been my favourite. No, I'm talking about the rest of them. I've got five boys, did you know? I'm talking about that bloody Alec. Letting the side down. Becoming the laughing stock of the town. You must have heard? How he got hit and beaten up by some old widow woman on Ocean Road?' She wheezed with difficulty, laughing at her eldest son's shame. 'By God, if I was well, I'd tan the soft bugger's hide for that!'

'Aye, I've heard the tale,' Cathy said, deciding not to let slip that the Franchinos had been good friends to her.

'So I'm hoping you're a tough lass,' Gracie told her fiercely. 'I hope you're from good stock. Maybe you'll bring some fibre back into this family.'

Cathy gulped, feeling like Gracie was going too far. It was like she was interviewing Cathy about actually joining the firm!

Then suddenly Gracie was asking, 'So, who are your people? Who do you belong to? Where do you come from?'

It was the kind of direct question that Cathy always dreaded. Usually she flummoxed her way out of giving straight answers.

But those pale eyes were trained implacably upon her. Gracie Johnson wasn't the kind of woman you could fob off with vague answers.

'Just farming folk,' Cathy said. 'Up in Northumberland. Near Morwick. Do you know it?'

'Who have you still got alive? Have you got a mam?'

'An aunt. I have an aunt.' Cathy was surprised at herself. This was more personal information than she had volunteered to anyone since leaving home.

'And does she know you're here? Do you keep in touch?'

Cathy shook her head. Absurdly, she felt a tickling in her tear ducts. She felt a swelling in her throat, like she couldn't swallow. These questions were getting to her. She felt like she was being mesmerised.

'Are you not in contact with any of your people?' wheezed Ma Gracie. 'Eeeh, but that's terrible, girl. Family is everything. It's all we've got. The connections between us, that make us the same and make us strong. Are you on your own in the world then, lass?'

Cathy's mouth felt parched. 'I-I am, yes. I'm alone in the world.'

'Well, that's a shame,' said Gracie. 'A bonny, clever lass like you. There's no need to be lonely and alone in the world. But you're lucky. You've landed on your feet with Matty. Now you've got all of the Johnsons as well. You'll never be alone again.'

Cathy smiled at her weakly. She wasn't sure she liked what the old woman was telling her. Then there was an interruption as Matty came in with a tray of tea. 'And look who's just turned up as well!' he announced happily.

It was Alec and Ellie, both togged out in their Sunday best. They were smiling brightly in that smoky room, coming to pay homage to the old dragon lady. Cathy stood up to make room on the hard settle.

'You two know each other, don't you?' Gracie asked Cathy and Ellie.

'We're the very best of friends,' Ellie beamed. She was smiling bravely, full of glimmering hope. She was wearing some daft little hat that Cathy had never seen before. She was dressed like she was trying to look younger than she was. She had on a very loose cardigan that covered up what Cathy knew very well was showing underneath.

Old Ma Gracie cast a sideways glance at Cathy, and Cathy could see that the old woman didn't think much of Alec's lady friend. She looked like she was about to chew her up and spit her out. Gracie's expression was lit up with sheer malice. 'Come and sit down, then. We'll all have tea. We'll have a tea party like one big happy family.'

With Ellie sat beside her, Cathy felt like she wanted to protect her. She gave her an encouraging smile. Ellie looked terrified, frankly.

'You be mother,' Ma Gracie commanded Ellie. 'Go on, petal. You can pour the tea.'

The two sons looked as if a great honour had been bestowed upon Ellie. Why, usually their mam was the one to do such things! Alec looked quite pleased with himself as his girlfriend stood up to do the honours.

But she was awkward and hesitant. Cathy saw it at once.

'What's the matter?' barked Gracie. 'Is the teapot too heavy for you? Is it too hot?'

Cathy frowned. Surely Ellie was holding herself strangely? She was favouring her right arm. She couldn't heft the teapot up and she stood there wincing and wilting under everyone's attention.

'What is it, Ellie?' Cathy asked. She stood up to help her friend. 'Here, let me do it.'

Ellie shrank back gratefully, and let Cathy take over filling their porcelain cups with steaming dark tea. Ma Gracie clucked her tongue at Ellie's strange failure and Alec looked pinkly furious.

All Cathy could think, as she fulfilled her role as mother, was that Ellie had a broken arm. Its lumpy shape was hidden by her cardigan sleeve. But just look at the way she's holding it funny, her poor hand just hanging there. There's definitely something wrong with it.

She put down the pot and picked up the milk jug. In that very second she realised the truth of what had gone on. That bastard had gone and broken her arm!

Chapter 30

Though it was hard to get a moment alone with Ellie, Cathy did try. She coaxed her aside in the front lobby of the Johnson family home and hissed at her: 'What the hell have you done to your arm?' Cathy was fierce and concerned.

'What? Nothing . . .' Ellie's false brightness irritated her friend.

'I saw what you were like. You couldn't lift that pot. You're hurt – let me see!'

'No, Cathy,' Ellie had her arm behind her back and just that bit of movement pained her. Those big teeth of hers were biting down on her lower lip and her face was filled with anguish. 'Just leave it, will you? Don't make a fuss.'

'A fuss! But it looks like you've broken something.'

'It's just a sprain . . .'

'Did *he* do this?'

'W-what?'

'Your man. Alec, in there. Did he hurt you? Tell me, Ellie.'

'Nah, man, Cathy, divvent be daft . . .'

'Because if he did, I'll go in there and kick his fat arse for him!'

Her friend reached out with her good arm to put a hand over Cathy's mouth. 'Please, please Cathy, don't make things worse. It'll blow over. It's nothing really. If there's a fuss he'll get angry again . . .'

Cathy couldn't believe the dithery, frightened way her friend was carrying on. 'What's the matter with you? You're not like this.'

'What am I supposed to be like?' Ellie shot back. There was asperity and fury in her voice. 'You tell me! I don't even know anymore. But I depend upon him, Cathy. I've let him put a roof over my head. I . . . I think I love him.'

'You love a man who's broken your arm?'

'It's not broken. It's just a sprain . . .'

'Have you seen a doctor?'

'Yes, it's fine . . .'

'It should be bandaged or something. Let me see it.'

Ellie sounded cross again, barking out: 'Let it go, Cathy. I don't interfere in your life, do I? I don't tell you what to do. So don't you go telling *me*.'

Cathy had to leave it at that. They were on a visit to the old woman's house and their absence had been noticed. Matty came out into the lobby with his broad, gleaming smile and looked puzzled when he saw their stricken faces. 'Hey, what's going on here? Are you two lasses having a scrap?'

Cathy tossed her head, now thoroughly angry at Ellie for her passivity. 'Aye, just a little difference of opinion.'

'Well, best break it up,' he told them frowningly. 'Me mam's saying she's tired now and it's time to say goodbye.'

Frankly Cathy was relieved to get away from that candlelit mausoleum and the presence of that giant, malign old baby. She hated the way Gracie had both men dancing attendance on her, bringing her cigarettes and lighting them. She had them fetching photos from the sideboard to show the girls ('Look at my lads as babbies! Look how bonny they were – all except Alec!'). It revolted Cathy, the way she fired out these orders, just to prove she could make these men dash to do her bidding.

It was as if she was proving something to their girlfriends: 'I'm still the most important woman in their lives, and they would do anything for me. You'll never mean as much to them.'

Well, Cathy got that message loud and clear. Even though the visit was amicable on the surface, and fairly successful as these awkward things go, the whole hour she spent in that dingy room was riven with tension. She emerged into the teatime gloom feeling bruised from the severe examination by those pale blue eyes and brimming with concern for Ellie.

Alec had whisked Ellie away immediately, back off to her gilded cage in Boldon Colliery.

'I thought that went really well,' Matty told Cathy as they sat on the trolley bus, heading back into the docks.

'Really?' Cathy smiled at him. It wasn't his fault the whole thing had been so tense and such hard work for her. He seemed oblivious to everything that had gone unsaid under the surface, of that long hour. It was his essential sweetness that made him see things more simply than she did, Cathy mused, as she watched the smeared lights of the town go by. She marvelled that he had any sweetness at all to his temperament, growing up in an environment like that . . . But she knew that she must be very careful indeed, never to criticise his mother, his family, or the place he had come from. She knew this intuitively – such criticisms would not be met well.

'I'm glad you think it was a success,' she said simply, smiling warmly at him. Yes, he was a simpler soul than she. Remembering that was important. She mustn't befuddle him with her complex reactions to the world.

'Ah, me mam loves you, petal. I can tell!' He chuckled to himself, gazing up at the polished wood of the tram's ceiling. 'I remember how she treated some of my older brother's lasses when they paid a call. They went fleeing out of there in tears, some of them. She can be bloody horrible to anyone she takes against!'

'I got off quite lightly, then,' Cathy smiled. 'And what about Ellie?'

'The jury's still out on her,' Matty admitted. 'Mam finds her a bit shifty and dishonest. But then she never likes the kind of women our Alec goes for. She says he's drawn to scrubbers.'

Cathy's heart leapt up in rebellion and her face flamed. 'Ellie is not a scrubber!' She hissed the last word, conscious of others seated and strap-hanging, eavesdropping on every word as the carriage lurched along the tracks.

Matty shrugged at her. 'Well, maybe she's not. But that's what Alec usually goes for.'

'I'm worried about her,' Cathy admitted.

'Divvent worry! Our Alec might be a boastful pillock, but he always treats his women right. Why, he carries on like they're princesses!'

Cathy wasn't so sure that was true.

The rest of that week hurtled by, and Cathy was caught up in her usual routine of time at home with Teresa Sturrock, helping the increasingly idle woman to keep her house and cook meals for her. Then she had hours each day and night at the Robin Hood, where Ellie's appearances had become rather sporadic of late.

'It's not like her to be unreliable,' Noel glowered, doing her work of polishing all the glasses, right in time for opening. 'It's since she moved to that house. All the way over in Boldon Colliery! It's a different flamin' town! It's miles away!'

Cathy didn't say anything about Ellie to Noel. She wasn't sure how he'd react. She knew from other conversations that he didn't think people ought to interfere in what went on between a man and a woman. He hated anything that he regarded as women's chatter. 'There's a lot of bother caused by vicious gossip and women's chatter,' he often said. She would catch him staring beadily at the Women's Table sometimes, wary of the way their heads were pushed together, intent on discussing some pressing topic or other. He really didn't think any good ever came from women's blethering on.

Cathy felt differently, of course. She believed that men might think they had all the answers and they truly believed that they ruled the whole world. But Cathy knew the truth: that it was women who kept the world moving. They kept everyone fed and they looked after everyone's well-being. Women kept the hearts and souls of the people together. It was men who tried to blow them apart with their silly ruthless violence and greed. That was as much as Cathy knew, and she wasn't ever budging from that view.

She joined the women at their table by the fire on Friday night.

There was Winnie, looking exhausted after another shift at the biscuit factory. Ada was there, looking pensive, her mind elsewhere. Teresa was three sheets to the wind on cherry brandy since it was her birthday and Noel had treated her to free drinks. The women toasted Teresa with their own, less exotic drinks, and the whole saloon bar loudly cheered the old woman. She looked massively gratified to be the centre of attention.

'Have you and Sofia made your peace yet?' Winnie blurted out the question and Cathy frowned at her.

'Ah, there's been no falling out,' Teresa snapped at her fortune-telling friend. 'Sofia can just be a bit touchy sometimes. She's very continental that way.'

All the women rolled their eyes at Sofia's unfathomably foreign ways.

Ada Farley said, 'It's on account of you seeing one of the Johnson boys, isn't it, Cathy? Old Nonna Franchino will never forgive you for that. Not since they menaced her.'

Cathy didn't want to argue about it. She hated having to defend her boyfriend's family against the things they all said about him. She could see that if she was going to carry on seeing him, there were things that she was just going to have to put up with. It was like going out with someone in the public eye! Someone famous from the Music Hall! Everyone thought they knew all about the Mad Johnsons, and everything they got up to. But they didn't really. And very few had been into the inner sanctum. Very few had sat in that sepulchral living room and been examined by that old woman Gracie, done up in her bits of ribbon and lace.

Cathy didn't want to discuss any of it with the women tonight.

'Eeeh, I remember when Gracie Johnson still had the proper use of her legs,' said Ada with that faraway look as she thought back to the past. 'She used to wear a long coat with all these pockets on the inside. They said she had all kinds of knives in there. She'd go round ready to pull a blade on anyone who got in her way! She was vicious, they used to say. She slit a fella's throat once and pushed him in the river.'

'Ah, it's just old hearsay,' Teresa said tipsily. 'I never believed a word of it. They're just low and petty robbers, that lot. That's all there is to them.'

Cathy was boggling at the thought of Matty's mam going about the town in a long coat, slitting men's throats. The terrible thing was, she could picture it. Having met the old devil, she could half believe it! Gracie Johnson would look them in the eye as she put the knife in, Cathy was sure of it.

'You must make peace with Sofia Franchino,' Teresa told Cathy. 'She's been a good friend to you.'

Cathy knew she was right and winced at having the obvious pointed out to her by Teresa.

It came almost as a relief to her when Noel yelled out, 'It's busy at the bar, lass! Stop chin-wagging with them old witches and get back to work!'

She left the ladies and felt as if she was escaping their probing looks and questions.

Going out with Matty was turning out to be hard work, in some ways.

Oh, but he was worth it, wasn't he? She loved walking about with him. Knowing that he was her man. She felt proud of him, so big and tall beside her. And when he held her it was like being swallowed up and gripped securely in a way she had never really known before. She felt safe. She actually felt she could switch – for a little while anyway – the part of her brain that was always ticking away. It was always thinking about protecting herself, escaping, survival . . . all those things that had kept her alive. She had looked after herself for so long, it was hard making herself vulnerable to another.

'But your heart races like mad!' Matty marvelled, as he held her close. He was holding her close enough to feel her fast heart hammering through her blouse and her shawl. It was pattering against his own chest. It felt like the heart of a small mouse or a bird. Something tiny that he was holding in his hands, beating furiously against his palms in the seconds before he set it free. 'Why does your heart go as fast as that?'

It was later that night and, following Cathy's hours at the bar, they were taking a late stroll through the town. With them both having odd, irregular hours at work, this was becoming one of their routines. It was one of the things they both liked to do. The streets of South Shields late at night were quiet and almost empty in the frosty nights of February. The two lovers took advantage and walked miles around the winding lanes and thoroughfares. They lingered in the cavernous shadows under the arches.

This was where they paused tonight, under a vast vaulting arch of stone. The mildewy brickwork was frozen at her back as he kissed her and she could look up in rapture at the stalactites of ice clinging to the darkness above. She fancied that they were in some primeval kind of cave. The occasional roar of trains crossing overhead were the cries of the primordial beasts that wanted to eat them alive. Cathy found herself growing quite fanciful as they stood in the cold, her feet going numb and her face getting hotter and hotter with every kiss.

'Do you always bring lasses down here?' she asked him, breaking away.

'Of course not,' he frowned, though she knew it must be a lie.

'How many lasses have you been out with?' Cathy didn't even know why she was asking him. What business of it was hers? Really, she didn't care. She wouldn't have felt jealous if he'd had all the girls in town. She was just asking him things now – not because she was keen to know, but because she could feel he was getting carried away. She needed to slow him down . . . and she knew that asking him questions about the other lasses he'd had before would be flattering. Most fellas would find questions like that flattering. They liked to think they had a shockingly colourful past. Most fellas liked to boast about such things.

But Matty surprised her then. 'I've had less experience than you'd imagine, Cathy. I went to France, remember. I was nobbut a bairn when I signed up to go. Why, at that point I'd barely kissed a lass. I'd never seen one with nowt on, ever.'

Cathy had to smile at his reflective tone. He was thinking back and imagining himself as a younger lad, just a few years ago. He had come through so much in a short time and he looked amazed at himself, standing there with just a gleam of distant moonlight on his sharp features. By, he was handsome, Matty Johnson, she thought.

'And did you see girls in France?' she asked. 'Was there time for love and anything like that?'

He didn't answer her. He didn't want to talk about it anymore. She had said the dreaded word. Matty clammed up whenever anyone said 'France'. Instead he returned to kissing her with renewed vigour. He had his hands in her hair, mussing it up. He made her squirm against the hard frost of the brick wall of the tunnel behind her. She ached for him body and soul as he pinioned her there, in the darkest shadows they could find. His mouth was clamped onto hers and his tongue felt huge and strong as it pushed into her mouth.

Tonight he was more intent and more bold than he had ever been before.

She fought free of his kisses, gasping for air.

Their mingled breath puffed up in warm clouds between them.

Then he was saying, 'Let me, Cathy. Let me do it now. Come on, Cathy. It's the perfect time. It's the right time now. I'm ready . . . Let me, will you?'

At first she was befuddled, not quite sure what he was gabbling about.

'You know, Cathy,' he said. 'You know what you want. Come on, Cathy. It's been weeks. I've been good, I've been waiting. But I must have you now. Go on, Cathy, let me . . . let me come inside . . .'

He took both her hands in his and squashed her palms between his strong fingers. He drew them down into the pressing darkness between them. He cupped both her hands around his crotch and she could feel that hardness there. A wonderful, hot, alarming hardness. By, he was big! She was surprised at the contact. It was so sudden and he'd been such a gent, this whole time. Now he was guiding her hands to touch him . . .

'Just take it, Cathy, please . . .'

Then his own hands were clutching at her skirts, pulling them up. He was being too quick, too rough.

She pulled her hands away. Touching him was just making him worse. He was straining at his fly buttons from within and though the feel of him excited her, that feeling was starting to change. She didn't like how he was carrying on. That pulling at her dress, it was horrible. It was like he was another person, all of a sudden. She gasped when his fingers touched her bare thighs and slid their way upwards. The cold tugged at her and it felt like a bucket of water over whatever ardour she had felt. But still his fingers moved towards her steadily.

'No, Matty,' she told him firmly. 'Not here and now. This isn't the right place, Matty.'

'But Cathy, just a bit . . . let me . . . just . . .'

She pushed at him. 'Matty, man. Leave off! Listen to what I'm telling you!'

And he did. He listened. He eased back. The pressure of those busy fingers fell away. He took a step backwards. The kisses stopped. The feel of him melted away. Instantly she felt shivery.

'I'm not ready yet,' she told him. 'And look where we are! Under the arches! It's hardly very romantic, is it?'

There was a strange look on his face as they straightened up their rumpled clothes and turned to walk back to the Sixteen Streets. Yes, there was frustration and thwarted desire in his expression, all too plainly. But there was more. There was anger.

Cathy didn't like the look of that at all.

The Mad Johnsons all had anger within them. Tamped down. Ready to erupt. She didn't like the thought of that one bit.

He left her on Frederick Street, just after midnight.

One chaste kiss in the middle of the road, and then he turned to go, almost wordlessly.

She was really churned up inside, watching him go. She had such mixed feelings about it all. Part of her wished that they had simply done it, there and then, under those arches. In the dark, getting it over with.

The other part was hugely relieved that they hadn't.

Chapter 31

'Well, I think she's gone off him,' said Teresa Sturrock decisively. 'That's what I think. It's all over now.'

Her son beetled his shaggy brows and scowled at her. 'You don't know anything, Mother.'

She tossed her head, 'I know more than you think, my lad.' She was sitting at the dining table, fiddling with her rollers and pulling a hair net over the wisps of hair she'd pinned to her skull. 'And I tell you something, our Noel. It's all over between Cathy and that handsome Johnson lad.'

It was early Friday evening and Cathy had nipped out to fetch their weekly fish supper from Swetty Betty's. It had become a regular thing for the three of them to share a battered cod and some roe and a smattering of scraps on their chips, eating them straight from the paper with a mug of sweet tea.

Now, while Cathy was off up the street, queueing with everyone who shared the same Friday ritual, Noel's mother was taking advantage of the girl's absence. She was goading Noel with her suspicions about what was going on.

'Does she mention him anymore? Why, at first you could hardly get her to talk about anything else. She's barely said a word about anything for a week! Haven't you noticed?'

He kept his eyes on the sporting page of the *Chronicle*, but Noel had to admit that his wily old mother had a point. There was something odd about Cathy this week. Her irrepressible nature had let her down. But what had her unhappiness got to do with him? Women were up and down all the time, weren't they? That's what they were like. You never knew where you were with them. Noel found their whole sex utterly vexing.

'I'm telling you, lad. This is your moment.' Teresa patted her hair net, making sure everything was packed down tight inside. 'Oh, aye. You should strike while the iron is hot.'

He muttered, trying to make sense of the racing form and all the figures in front of his nose. But his mother's words were getting through to him. Damn her! She was actually managing to raise his hopes up. 'Iron is hot, by hang,' he grunted.

'Winnie was round this morning and she had a look in the teacup that Cathy had left unwashed on the side . . .'

'Saints preserve us,' Noel rolled his eyes.

'And Winnie says it's as plain as day. She's unhappy and she's about to finish with that lovely-looking red-haired lad. But she's still after some security. She's after a chap who can look after her.'

Noel glanced up to see his mother's squinty eyes boring into his. 'Oh, ha'way, mother. She's never gonna look at me. She never was gonna look at me!'

Teresa pursed her wrinkled mouth. 'That's not what our Winnie says.'

He swore and went back to studying form. But his heart was beating just a little bit faster.

Soon after that Cathy came in, clutching steaming parcels from the fish bar triumphantly. The old woman had the cutlery and cruet out ready, and she divided up the spoils fairly, quick as a flash. She buttered several rounds of bread and urged Cathy to take the lion's share of the glistening scraps, sprinkling them on her chips.

'Aye, aye, hinny,' Noel added. 'You like the scraps best of all of us.'

Was it just Cathy's imagination, or were the pair of them being extra nice to her, all of a sudden? Though it was true, she did enjoy the scraps more than everyone else – the little crumbs and nuggets of cooked batter that came dredged up with the fish. It's the story of my life, Cathy thought ruefully. I'm just grateful for scraps and crumbs of comfort!

The three of them sat contentedly, devouring their early supper with great relish. For once Noel had put his newspaper away in order to concentrate fully on their meal together. The radio was on and Teresa was in a sprightly mood, looking forward to an evening in town with some of her cronies.

'You two will be working all evening?' she asked her son.

'Aye, just the two of us all night,' said Noel. 'That Ellie's been off again for days. It's murder covering for her, with just two of us.'

'She'll be back,' said Cathy.

'She's not even sent a message this past couple of days.' Noel shook his head. 'It's not like her. She's changed since she's been over in Boldon Colliery and seeing that Alec fella. She's playing fast and loose with her job and letting me down.'

'I was thinking of taking a trolley bus over her way,' Cathy said. 'Just to give a knock and see how she is.'

'Maybe a good idea,' Teresa nodded approvingly. 'You know, I've said this before, but it's as true now as it ever was. Nothing good ever comes from moving away from the Sixteen Streets.'

Noel barked with laughter. 'Oh, Mother, honestly! You sound like one of the ancient old wifeys from round here. All that superstitious rubbish!'

She shook her head firmly. 'Nay, son. There's something in it. Certain folk belong right here, and woe betide them who try to deny it and move away. They don't have their people around them anymore. It's like they don't have their hearts rooted inside their bodies anymore. They become lost . . .'

Cathy was staring at her landlady. 'And that's what you think has happened to Ellie? That she's got herself lost?'

'Aye, I do, pet,' Teresa said sorrowfully, crunching up the last of her battered fish.

Noel stage-whispered to Cathy: 'Me mam's seen old Winnie today. She's gone all mystic, just the same as that silly old moo.'

Cathy couldn't help laughing.

That Friday was a very busy one at the Robin Hood. Perhaps the milder weather had drawn them all out of their boltholes? Noel couldn't be sure, but he was glad of the custom and Cathy was happy to be surrounded by noisy chatter and laughter. Keeping constantly busy was good for her. Keeping a fixed, warm grin on her face was the best way of convincing herself she was happy.

Because she wasn't, really.

There hadn't been anything from Matty all week. Not a peep! No sudden loud knocking at the front door. No little note pushed through the letter box. He hadn't suddenly appeared at the bar as she worked, though each evening she still held out hope that he would come sauntering in. He'd come in quite breezily and ask for a pint of mild, behaving as if absolutely nothing had gone wrong between them.

She sighed, her mind drifting as she filled a tankard from the pump for old Frank Farley. She kept thinking back to that hectic, almost frenzied moment she and Matty had shared under the arches last week.

Had she made a mistake?

She'd just about fought him off. She had denied him, right at the last minute. That's what had happened, hadn't it? Well, that's how he would surely see it. He was a bloke. Blokes got to a certain point in the proceedings and they couldn't help themselves . . . At least, that was what Cathy had always been taught.

Why, it was painful, really, to try to get a man to back down when he reached a certain point. When he was all full of passion. Cathy had been told that it could even be dangerous for a fella to be stopped in his tracks once he had gone so far. It could do great damage to him, to spoil his ardour when he was carried away!

Admittedly, it had always been men who had told her these things. She wasn't quite sure they were telling the strict medical truth.

But for years she had accepted the wisdom of what her previous swains had told her. You just have to go along with it. You can't make him stop. He'd be humiliated! He'd be crushed!

And that's just what she'd done to Matty, hadn't she?

It hadn't been right, though. It was cold and damp and horrible, right down by the docks. When the trains had hurtled over the arches, horrid showers of Victorian brick dust had come sifting down on them.

She actually thought something of Matty. She had fond feelings for the lad. She had assumed he felt the same about her. But there he had been, fumbling away and trying to get his hard, quick fingers into her drawers. It had all seemed so ordinary and banal and mucky. It was a huge letdown to her. She couldn't help but feel horribly disappointed in him.

Friday night went tumbling on through the hours and she kept on pulling those beer pumps, filling the pint pots with gushing ale. She kept that broad grin plastered to her face and did her usual banter with the regulars. She watched Frank and

Harry and Tommy grow more and more pie-eyed as the hours advanced. None of them were keen to get home, it seemed.

Is this what life was like for men and women? They got stuck together and grew to loathe each other's company? So that they stayed out all hours they could, getting kaylied, so by the time they were home again they could hardly see straight?

Maybe it was better forgetting all about love altogether, she thought.

When closing time eventually came, she rang the little ship's bell and set about the task of winkling out the stragglers and sending them home.

'Cathy! Cathy! Don't send me back home,' Tonio Franchino tried to put his arms around her neck. 'Let me stay here for a lock-in! Let me stay and keep drinking! I don't wanna go home . . .'

She prised his arms gently from around her neck, frowning at the state of him. She had kept an eye on him all evening, aware that he'd been getting hammered and sitting with a bunch of fellas she didn't recognise. There had been no sign of Sofia or her mother at the Women's Table tonight, acting as a deterrent to his making an arse of himself. But those two women hadn't been in the pub for well over a week, had they? Cathy had conceived the idea that Sofia was avoiding her.

'Why don't you want to go home?' Cathy asked him patiently.

'Ah, never mind, but it's no good. They will hate me! They will give me grief . . .' Suddenly his handsome features looked hangdog and defeated. All at once he seemed very small and shabby to Cathy, not at all the proud strutting fella she was used to.

She lowered her voice. 'Have you lost more money with your infernal gambling, eh?'

He reared up. 'No! What makes you think that?' He put on a wounded air. 'Lost money? How would I lose money?'

She realised that she had gone too far. It was Sofia who had told her about the gambling and the dreadful amounts he regularly threw away. He looked horrified to see that Cathy knew all about it.

'I'm going home,' he sniffed, pushing past her, lurching for the door.

'I'm sorry, Tonio,' she called. 'I didn't mean to be rude . . .'

He swung round on her and she was surprised to see that his eyes were blazing. 'It's none of your business,' he slurred. 'My God, Sofia's right about you.'

'W-what?' gasped Cathy.

'She said that you worm your way in with people . . . and make friends with them . . . and you make them think that you're to be trusted . . .' Now he was sneering at her. 'But you aren't really. You're only out for yourself, Cathy Carmichael! You carry on like you're a nice girl, but you're really hard inside. You're hard and cruel.'

Suddenly Noel was standing between them, looking angry. 'What are you saying to her, man?'

Tonio shook his head. '*Gaagh*. Nothing. Just forget it.'

Cathy found that she was standing with her mouth hanging open. She was astonished by the Italian man's outburst. Had he really meant it? Was any of it true? How on earth had he come by such a low opinion of her?

Watching Noel clumsily manhandling Tonio out of the saloon, Cathy thought to herself: is he right? All those things he was saying – am I really like that?

There was a noisy kerfuffle at the door as Tonio tried to turn back in order to tell Cathy a few more home truths. Noel was surprisingly firm with him, using his hefty arms to give the Italian a shove that sent him reeling out into the street. After that there was just a couple of quieter, wavering drunks to shoo out and at last Noel was locking and bolting the pub's front doors.

'By the 'ell!' he burst out. 'What a long bloody night that was!'

Cathy tried to smile, turning to carry out her usual cleaning up tasks at the bar.

'Nay lass,' Noel told her. 'You look wiped out. And the rubbish that daft bastard was spouting at you has got you shook, hasn't it?'

She nodded and couldn't help tears spilling down her face. 'Oh bugger, I shouldn't let some drunk bloke upset me!'

Noel studied her. 'You're more upset than you're letting on. You have been for days.'

'Aye,' she said softly.

'Right, we're gonna have a brandy. On the house. Me and you.' He lumbered to the bar and brought out a fancy, heavy bottle from France. 'I've been saving this up for a special occasion. Well, we'll crack it open now. And you, my lass, you can sit with me by the fire and you can tell me what's ailing you.'

Cathy smiled at him. It was actually a relief to have Noel – Noel Sturrock of all people! – being kind to her tonight.

Chapter 32

I'm getting sloshed, she thought! This brandy is really hitting the mark. It's after midnight, we're still in the pub. I've never drank anything as delicious or strong as this . . . and I'm opening up my heart to Noel.

He was a surprisingly good listener. Head cocked to one side, slowly eating a pickled egg he had fished from the jar. He didn't interrupt or interject much. He murmured occasionally, making noises of encouragement.

The words came spilling out.

Everything was jumbled up, just as it was in her head. She spoke of her settling into her new life with the Sturrocks, and how grateful she was to both mother and son for giving her this chance. She described what it felt like to have new friends and to feel accepted in a place.

But she also talked about how she felt that all of that assurance and comfort could be pulled away at any moment. She went around feeling that everything could be taken back from her, at any time. She would never take anything for granted.

'Eeeh, lass,' Noel tutted, and shook his head. He nibbled a bit more of his pickled egg. 'Are you hungry? Would you like one?'

She demurred and turned to the subject of Matty Johnson. Now, this really was ridiculous, her inner voice counselled her.

What was she doing, trying to talk about this with Noel? What would he ever understand about any of this? At the same time, she was compelled to relate the tales of her carefree nights out with Matty, and how he made her feel.

'Aye, he might be able to turn your head, and he's handsome and all that,' said Noel, munching on his egg.

'He really is handsome,' said Cathy.

'But a lad like that – does he really know how to treat a woman?' Noel contorted his face, as if he was really mulling it over. 'Would he know how to treat a real woman properly? A lad like that? Would he be respectful enough?'

But Cathy's mind was moving on elsewhere. She was thinking about her best friend, Sofia. She told him about Sofia's reaction to her walking out with Matty, and the crushing blow that had been to her.

'Ah,' murmured the landlord softly. 'Now that's a shame, lass.'

Cathy even told Noel about going to Tudor Avenue for a kind of interview with the formidable Gracie Johnson; how it had appeared to be some sort of test that she had seemingly passed. She had been deemed good enough, bonny enough, respectful enough to be connected to the Johnson clan.

Then – and this astonished herself more than anything – Cathy told Noel about the scene under the arches in the dark the other night. She told him about the moments she had felt that Matty was going too far. How she had rebelled and pushed him away. How she had rejected him.

'Is that how he must feel?' she asked Noel now. 'Would a man feel really angry about that?' She studied Noel carefully; his troll-like visage and his curious, piercing eyes. He was a man, wasn't he? Surely he could tell her – let her into the secrets of how a man must feel?

'I don't know about him,' Noel said at last. 'Every man is different. I can't speak for him.'

Cathy nodded, disappointed.

Noel went on, 'Though I do know that forcing someone, making a lass do something that they don't want to do . . . well, that's a wicked thing. I do know that much.'

'Oh, well,' said Cathy. 'It wasn't like that, exactly. When I told him I wanted to stop, he listened to me.'

'Aye, but he wasn't happy, was he? And he let you know that?'

She nodded. 'Yes, I suppose that's right . . .'

Noel's face darkened. 'It's the Mad Johnsons all over, man. I know their family of old. I know their kind. They always just take what they want, whatever it is. They think they've got a God-given right to seize just whatever it is they . . . desire.' His thick voice did a kind of hitch before he hit the word 'desire'. It was a strange, unfamiliar word coming out, Cathy thought.

'Matty's different to the rest of them,' she said.

'They're all the same,' Noel grunted, and poured them both more of the brandy. 'See this? This bottle came from Alec Johnson. One of the consignments he brings here. He gets it all nicked from the docks. It's dropped off a wagon somewhere down at the harbour. He charges me a pretty penny for all this.'

'I thought you got those knock-off bottles cheaper?'

He laughed bitterly. 'What made you think that? No, it's Alec who does well out of that transaction. I pay more than wholesale prices . . .'

'But . . .' she was puzzled.

'And I get to keep my knee caps, put it that way,' Noel sighed. Her eyes widened. 'Oh, Noel . . .'

He shrugged. 'It's gone on so long I hardly think about it. It's just the way it all works. My God, even the pickled eggs come from the Johnsons and you won't believe what I have to pay for them.'

'But that's so unfair!'

He laughed. 'Of course it is! But you see what I mean? They'll act like your friend all the time, but it's take take take. They'll screw everything out of you.'

The bluntness and coarseness of his words made her feel sick. Perhaps he was right. Perhaps Matty was no better than his horrible brother.

'I think . . .' she put in. 'I think Alec has broken Ellie's arm.'

Noel's eyes went wide. 'No!'

She quickly told him what she had observed in that dingy house on Tudor Avenue, and Noel looked shocked. He swore. 'That poor lass . . .'

'She wouldn't really talk about it properly, though. Not while she was there. So, I'm going to see her. I'm going to go to Boldon Colliery.' Suddenly lucid, through her tired fug of brandy fumes, Cathy was set upon a course of action. 'I'm going to go and see her tomorrow and check that she's all right.'

'Good lass,' Noel said approvingly.

Then all the brandy was finished, the fire had dwindled down to red cinders. It was time that the two of them were getting home.

The next morning, when Cathy's head was thick and throbbing, there was a loud banging at the front door.

'Oh help, will you get that, petal?' Teresa asked. 'I'm still in my night things! I'm not decent.'

Cathy was bilious as she opened the door onto a bright morning. She was amazed to see Sofia Franchino standing there with her baby in her arms, and a hectic brightness in her eyes.

'Oh now, look, I don't want an argument,' Cathy told her. Through her hangover she could still recall Sofia's husband's hurtful words of the night before. All that stuff he'd attributed to Sofia! How she'd said that Cathy was hard and cruel, making friends only in order to hurt them!

'No, no, I don't want to argue,' Sofia said. She looked straight into Cathy's face and there wasn't a drop of animosity there. 'I'm here as your friend. I need my friend. I'm sorry, Cathy, I haven't been kind to you . . .'

Cathy ushered her indoors. 'Whatever's the matter?'

Sofia wouldn't speak until she was sitting at the parlour table with a cup of milky tea in front of her. The baby sat burbling in her lap and Teresa Sturrock was hovering, keen to hear what all the drama was.

'Why don't you go and dress?' Cathy prompted her. 'Let me have a few moments alone with Sofia?'

The old woman went off muttering to herself.

Sofia picked up her china cup and sipped the hot tea. When she set it down again, the cup tinkled unsteadily against the saucer and she spilled some.

'Your hands are shaking!'

Sofia nodded. 'I've had an awful shock.'

Cathy was alarmed. 'What is it? Is it Tonio? Is it Bella? Everyone's all right, aren't they?'

'Oh, yes, everyone is fine.' She patted Cathy's hand. 'At least, for now we are all fine. But something has happened, Cathy. Something I prayed would never happen . . .'

The toddler wriggled in her lap, disturbed by his mother's distress. Instinctively Cathy reached over and took him into her own arms, to let Sofia drink more of her calming tea. She braced herself for whatever news was coming next. 'What has happened, Sofia?'

Sofia bit her lip. Her eyes were huge and beautiful as they stared at Cathy, but her distress was plain to see. 'I-I think . . . I have seen him, Cathy. I have seen *him* in the town. Yesterday, when I was on the high street . . . I think I actually s-saw *him*. He is here. He is looking for us. H-he has found us!'

Cathy was confused. 'What? Who are you talking about?'

But even as she asked, she was beginning to remember. It was all to do with their conversations last Christmas. Back then Sofia had explained a little about her family's past. She had told a story that had seemed at the time rather like a fairy tale. Privately, Cathy had dismissed it all as much too fanciful to be true.

'Don't you remember, Cathy? What I told you . . . about the man who would one day come looking for us? We always knew it would come true. I think I saw him, with my own eyes!' She was almost frantic, sitting at the parlour table with terror on her face. 'The Man in the Black Hat.'

Well, she was so serious and melodramatic about it that Cathy might have laughed. But she didn't. She reined in her initial response, seeing that her friend was genuinely upset and frightened. 'But Sofia, plenty of men wear hats. Specially in this weather. What you saw was just some bloke . . .'

Sofia shook her head fiercely. 'This was a big hat. Wide brim. A fedora. It's him. I know it is. He's come looking for us.'

'But . . .' Cathy tried to recall the details of the tale Sofia had told her. 'How on earth would these gangsters find you and your family? You said Tony threw a dart at random into a map of the world . . . Have they searched everywhere for you?'

'Oh, I don't know,' Cathy said. 'But his face was familiar, under that hat. I don't think he saw me, but I saw him. We were outside the big store. He was looking in the window and I thought: they have come at last to get us. Now we're all going to die.

'Surely not,' Cathy burst out. 'Why, even if this terrible man really was here in town, how would he ever find out where you live?'

Sofia looked bleak. 'We have a café in town, with "Franchino's" painted in large pink and green letters on the front. Remember?'

'Oh yes . . .' said Cathy. But she still thought the whole thing was absurd. 'A man would come all this way just because of a few gambling debts?'

'Oh yes,' said Sofia. 'This is all Tonio's fault. He has led us into ruin. My mother always said he would. She came with me to protect me. She always knew something awful lay ahead of us.'

Cathy stood up to make more tea. She was filled with purpose and pragmatism. She didn't like all this fatalistic wallowing one little bit. 'I'm sorry, pet, but I don't believe a word of it.'

'You think I'm lying?!' cried Sofia.

'No, no, I believe you think you saw what you saw, but I think it's a lot of old tommyrot. I don't believe this fella in the hat has got anything to do with you. I think it's just a coincidence and it's your mind playing tricks on you.'

'You do?'

'I think you're overtired, is what I think! Look at you! With the two bairns and your mother and the house to run. And you working at the ice-cream parlour, too. And all the money worries and Tonio still gambling an' that . . .' Cathy shook her head sorrowfully. 'No wonder you're seeing things and getting scared. It's just your mind, that's all, hinny. It's all in your mind . . .'

The Italian girl didn't look so sure. 'It's been going round and round in my head. I can't tell anyone. I don't know what Tonio would say. My mother would keel over and die if she thought they had found us. These people, they make the Mad Johnsons look like schoolchildren . . .'

Bringing back the hot, freshened teapot, Cathy decided to be firm with her friend. 'Now look, you mustn't let this take over your life. You can't go round full of fear. Just you go about your normal business and bugger them. If there really is a man in a big hat after you – then tell the polis! That's what they're for! If someone threatens you, set the polis onto them! But don't live in fear, Sofia. That's the worst thing you can ever do.'

Cathy's good sense seemed to be getting through to her friend. 'I hope you are right. I really hope so.' She gave a hesitant smile. 'I'm glad I stopped being so silly and came over and talked to you. You're my friend. I've missed you, Cathy.'

'I've missed you too, hinny,' Cathy told her. 'And, as it happens, we've got another friend in need of our help today. I was about to dash over to Boldon on the tram to check on her this morning. You can come with me if you like? You see, I'm terribly worried about Ellie . . .'

Chapter 33

They left the baby with Sofia's mother before catching the trolley bus on Westoe Road. 'Huh,' sniffed the old nonna, glancing up and down at Cathy.

'It's all right, Mama,' Sofia told her, passing her the dozing toddler. 'We are friends again.'

'Friends, not friends, friends again,' Nonna seethed. 'Life is complicated these days.' She was standing on the doorstep and little Bella was peering out from behind her.

'Where are you going now?' the small girl asked.

'To Boldon,' said her mother. 'Another friend of ours needs our help.'

It did indeed feel rather like a rescue mission, accompanied by a mounting sense of urgency as they clambered about the tram and took their seats. Neither of them had seen or heard from Ellie for several days. Cathy had seen her most recently, quickly filling Sofia in on events at the Johnson household. 'Eeeh, if you'd seen her struggling with that teapot before I took it off her. It was pitiful!'

Sofia was frowning. 'This is what comes of carrying on with men like that one.'

Cathy didn't reply to that. There was no reason to mention Matty and start up all that bother again. It was Ellie they were thinking of today.

The address was scrawled on a brown paper bag. Cathy had copied it down from Noel's papers. Before she had moved into her paid-for palace in Boldon Colliery, Ellie had promised them all that she would put on a proper housewarming party, and have them all over. She'd do a lavish spread and get in lots of drink – there was never any expense spared when Alec was involved. But that party and those invitations had never arrived. Not yet, anyway. It was just one more thing to give rise to awful suspicions about how Ellie was getting on.

'Here, this is it, look.'

The door was the shabbiest in the middle of a terraced row. Cathy and Sofia scurried along as the wind screeched through the canyon of the street. This part of town was so dark! It was quite different to home, being so low and buried and hidden in the shadows of the colliery and the slagheaps. Even the clouds above were dense with coke dust and smoke. The knifing winds couldn't blow them away; the darkness lowered over the streets and houses and wouldn't budge. It was a dark and dreary place to live, Cathy thought. Clearly, moving here from the Sixteen Streets was a step down in the world.

They knocked and kept on knocking until the door opened up the tiniest crack. 'Y-yes?'

Ellie didn't even sound like herself. She was hesitant and nervy. She kept the chain on the door as they tried to explain to her, 'Ellie, it's us! We were worried about you . . .'

She gasped. 'You shouldn't have come all this way . . .'

'It's not that far,' said Cathy. She glanced up at the smudgy clouds above and thought that, actually, she felt like she had descended into the infernal reaches of hell.

'At least he's not here,' Ellie said.

'Can we come in?' Sofia asked. 'We're here to see you. We brought stottie bread and some jam.' It was true, Sofia had hastily packed supplies into her basket before setting off. She thought it would be criminal to turn up empty-handed on a visit.

Ellie undid the chain and the door creaked open. 'All right, just for a while. But if he turns up, you must leave straight away.'

Cathy and Sofia exchanged a glance before stepping inside. Ellie was behaving even more strangely than they had expected.

They found the inside of the little miner's house dingy and unkempt. There were newspapers on the floor and dirty clothes scattered on the furniture. The curtains were drawn and mucky dishes were heaped on the tablecloth. The girls glanced around disapprovingly but knew better than to say anything. Best not to pass any comment at all.

'I've not had a chance to tidy round yet today,' Ellie said, and took them through to the scullery, to put the kettle on. 'I'll do you a brew, but you won't be staying long, will you?'

'We just came to see how you are,' Cathy told her. 'After seeing you at Gracie Johnson's, I'll be honest with you, pet – I was concerned.'

'Ha!' Ellie shrugged it off. 'You've no call to be concerned about me. I've got everything I need. I'm dead happy.'

'How's your arm?' Cathy was watching as the girl filled the kettle and set it on the stove. 'Did you get it looked at?'

'No need,' she snapped. 'It was just a sprain. I fell on it awkwardly. Slipped in the back yard. Easily done.'

'Hmm,' said Cathy.

They settled with their tea in the back parlour. Sofia had sliced up the stottie cake and spooned homemade blackberry jam onto each soft slice. There was no butter in the larder, so they had to do without. Cathy sniffed her tea and thought: the milk is on the turn, an' all.

'So this is your new home,' Sofia said warmly.

'Aye, this is me,' Ellie replied, just a touch defensively. 'If I'd known you were coming I could have straightened up a bit more. You're not seeing me at my best . . .'

That was true enough. Cathy had never seen her looking so dishevelled. Her unwashed hair was hanging down in straggles over what looked like yesterday's make-up, all smeared and cakey on her face. She was in an old housecoat that looked as if it might have belonged to her late mother.

The conversation inched along awkwardly and soon enough Cathy found herself bursting out: 'When are you coming back to work? Noel's being going on and on about you letting him down . . . We've been working our bums off without you there to help.'

Ellie sneered at the mention of their boss. 'That nasty old crookback. I shouldn't worry about letting him down. What's he ever done for me?'

'He's given you a job all these years,' Cathy said, surprised by her bitter tone. 'And he's concerned for you now.'

'Another one concerned, eh!' Ellie laughed harshly. 'Funny how you're all so bloody concerned about me now. Now, when I've got a decent fellow to look after me and a home of me own . . .'

Cathy didn't want to point out that her fellow really wasn't all that decent and that the home she was in wasn't really worth boasting about. Best to keep her lip buttoned, though.

Ellie's eyes flashed, as if she could hear what Cathy was thinking. 'Where was everyone's concern when I was living alone in that stinking room at Mucky Florrie's, eh? What concern did you all have for me then, eh? When I was crying myself to sleep every night? Out of loneliness and despair? When I was grieving after me mother and I had no one – no one at all! – why didn't anyone care about me then?'

She was getting upset, clutching a jam sandwich and mashing it into crumbs that dropped into her lap.

'Eeeh, Ellie man, don't get yourself hysterical,' Cathy told her. 'You always seemed so happy and sorted out . . . Why, no one knew you were lonely . . .'

'No one was bothered, that's why,' snapped Ellie. 'They looked at me and just dismissed me. I was just that big lass with the big teeth and big knockers at the bar. Noisy and strong and she can look after herself. She don't need anyone. That's how you all saw me.'

Sofia had fallen quiet during Ellie's outburst. Her heart was going out to the woman, though. She was surprised by the anguish pouring out of the barmaid. To her it only went to prove what she had always suspected: you never knew what levels of misery and pain filled up the lives of other people. Even the cheeriest soul you knew could be riven with despair on the inside. Sometimes they never let it out at all. It just poisoned everything they did.

'I am sorry,' Sofia said. 'I am sorry for your unhappiness, and I wish I had been a friend to you over the years.'

Ellie glared at her as if she had only just noticed she was in the room. 'What do I want with your sympathy? You're no pal of mine. Why, your bloody old mother assaulted my fella! He's still got a lump out of his skull where she hit him with her walking stick!'

Cathy shushed her. 'Now Ellie, don't be nasty to Sofia. She's come all this way with me. She brought you the bread and the jam.'

Ellie wasn't going to be pacified. 'Eyetie muck! I'm not eating that!' Then she was on her feet. 'Actually, I'd be happier if you both just left. Would you just go? Alec will be home soon and he won't like me having visitors from the rough end of town.'

Both women gasped. 'Won't like you having visitors?' said Cathy.

'Rough end of town!' Sofia cried. She was already heading for the door, angry at being called that awful word by the barmaid.

'We'll be off now, I think,' said Cathy, and ducked through the messy living room again. At the door she turned round to ask Ellie, 'Look, are you sure? You're sure you're happy here?'

Ellie had folded her arms and she nodded. But there was a look of great weariness on her face. 'Aye, he makes me happier than I've ever been in my life.'

'All right,' Cathy said. 'We'll take you at your word for that. And what about Noel? What about your job? Shall I tell him that you still want it?'

She pursed her lips, replying almost reluctantly. 'All right. Tell him that. Tell him I'll be in work tomorrow night. And tell him . . .' She took a deep, shuddering breath. 'That I'm sorry. For messing him about.'

Cathy nodded. 'All right.'

Ellie shooed them both. 'Now, get out, the pair of you. Before Alec comes home.'

And that was that.

On the trolley bus the two girls were subdued, both thinking their private thoughts. Sofia stared out of the smudgy windows at the darkened streets and the livid orange and black skies as dusk fell.

'Eyetie. My God. They don't let you forget, do they? You feel at home. You feel like you've been here long enough to belong. You go through a war with these people and all kinds of struggles and horrible things. All living in the same place. But still they will remind you – this is not your real home. You don't really belong here.'

Cathy tried to console her. 'Nay, pet. She was just raving and upset. Of course you bloody belong! You belong here more than I do. I'm the one who's the newcomer to the Sixteen Streets!'

The two of them smiled at each other, linked by their mutual trust and understanding and a liking for each other that had been there since the moment they first met. 'Ah, I missed you,

Cathy Carmichael, this past couple of weeks,' Sofia said. 'Let's never fall out again, shall we?'

Cathy promised wholeheartedly. 'In this life, we need all the friends we can get. Which is why it's so daft that Ellie's chucking her friends away.'

'She is silly cow,' Sofia growled darkly. She only ever dropped her English grammar like this when she was upset.

'That she is, but I think she's full of lies, too. I think she's scared of that man she's with.' Cathy had seen enough to convince herself that her suspicions were true. 'She's got herself in too deep with him and now she fears that she'll never get out. That's what I reckon is going on.'

'But how do we help her?' Sofia shrugged. 'How do you help someone who doesn't want to be helped?'

There was no easy answer to that. 'You just have to wait,' Cathy said. 'Until they come to you. That's all that you can really do.'

Sofia smiled at her as the bus bumped and lurched on its way to the arches. 'You're wise for your years, aren't you, Cathy?'

'I don't know about that,' she smiled ruefully. 'I feel like I've made a right bloody mess of my own life, to be honest.'

Here they were at their stop, at the very bottom of the Sixteen Streets. The hooters were blasting out and there was a shift coming out of the factory gates. All the lasses from the biscuit factory were surging out into the road with their hair up in scarves and their clogs knocking loudly on the cobbles. Their chatter filled the air like a great flock of starlings. Voices cried out greetings to both Cathy and Sofia as they mingled in the crowd.

'This is how you feel like you belong to this place,' Sofia told her friend as they toiled up the hill with all the others. 'When you're in the crowd with everyone. When they're all pleased to see you. That's when you can feel like you're truly part of the place.'

'Aye,' Cathy grinned. 'I think you're right.'

Chapter 34

It was a couple of nights later when Matty Johnson came to see Cathy at the Robin Hood.

'I don't really have time to talk to you,' she frowned. 'We're run off our feet tonight. And bloomin' Ellie has let us down again, too!'

Matt leaned over the bar slightly. 'He'll let you take a break though, won't he?'

'Aye, of course,' Noel agreed when things settled down a bit.

'Let's gan and stand outside, where it's quieter,' Matty suggested.

She put her woollen shawl around her bare shoulders as he led her out to stand at the side of the pub. This was where the brewery wagon parked up each week, with the massive dray horses waiting so patiently. Cathy loved to come out to see the beasts as the great big kegs of beer were being unloaded.

Matty sat down on a mildewed barrel and looked up at her. 'I'm sorry,' he said simply.

Why, it had been more than a week since she had clapped eyes on him. She'd been wondering if she'd ever see him again! Had he been so disgusted that she'd deterred his advances? Or was the lad ashamed of himself? All week she had been wondering which it was, but now she saw him in the flesh her questions simply melted away. He looked abashed, but he looked wonderful, as well. He'd put on his smartest jacket over a clean vest, especially to come and see her. Mind, his boots were still covered in clarts. He might have given them a bit of spit and polish.

'It's all right,' she told him. 'We were just going too fast, all of a sudden.'

His face was turning pink. 'See what I mean? I don't know how to do things. It's like I said, I don't have that much experience with lasses. Not with decent lasses like you, Cathy.'

She smiled at this. 'Oh! I'm glad you think of me as a decent lass, then.'

'I do! You've got class!'

'Class! Eeh, by!'

'That's what me mam said. After she met you. She turned to me and our Alec and said, "That Cathy Carmichael, she's got class. She's a special girl."'

Cathy was amazed. 'She said that, did she?'

'Aye. But she said it in front of that Ellie, Alec's fancy woman, and you should have seen her face fall. Me Mam's not had much good to say about her . . .'

Cathy's heart twinged a bit for Ellie, and she berated herself for being so glad of a scrap of praise from that peculiar old woman. At the same time she was glad to be accepted by her boyfriend's mother. She simply couldn't help it – she was pleased about that.

She got Matty to budge up on the barrel and said, 'What are we going to do, Matty?'

'How'd you mean?'

'Shall we carry on going out together? Is that what you want to do?'

He was so big and muscular and sure of himself but faced with a delicate question like this, he turned dithery. It pleased her to see him grow unsure. There was something tender in his expression in those moments that she really loved seeing. 'Of course I want to carry on. You're the best thing that I've had in my life in ages. Forever, probably!'

As they made plans for the coming weekend and spending some time together, Cathy realised she was playing it rather cool. She wasn't being too keen and dashing in to make everything right with him. Let him make the running, she thought.

'Right, I have to get back to work, or Noel will have my guts for garters. Are you coming in for a pint?'

He shook his head, looking about ten times happier than he had at the start of their conversation. 'I told me mam I'd run some errands for her while I'm over this side of town.'

She nodded her head, wondering what kind of errands he could run at this time of night? All the shops and offices were shut, weren't they? But then she dismissed the thought: don't think about things too deeply, Cathy. Maybe she should just go with the flow. 'Very well,' she grinned, and kissed him lightly on the cheek. 'I'll see you Saturday, and we'll make a fresh start, shall we?'

He beamed at her, and she remembered just how much she'd enjoyed his company in the time they had already spent together. She had relished being this lad's girlfriend, there was no doubt about it.

'Bye, Matty,' she said, waving him off as he set off down the street with a loping run. He hardly ever walked at a steady pace, she had noticed. He was so full of energy that it was like he was always holding back from breaking into a run. He's excited, she thought. He's actually excited that he's my boyfriend still.

She turned back into the pub, feeling rather pleased with everything.

*

It was a rowdy in the Robin Hood that night. There were a couple of unfamiliar faces, very drunk, and intent on causing bother. Frank Farley was in his cups – as usual – and he responded to the jeers. Usually he was a quiet drunk, only letting rip with his tongue (and some said his fists) after he went home. Tonight, however, he ended up in a fracas with these two younger blokes from North Shields. Fists and tankards flew and there was blood and shards of broken glass on the floor. A table was shoved over and suddenly Noel was amongst them, taking control of the situation. Once more Cathy was surprised by his strength and his commanding tone, which he could adopt in an instant whenever he needed to.

He booted out the unfamiliar fellas and they tumbled into the street. Frank Farley sat against the bar with his head in his hands and blood running down his purple face. 'Go and fetch Ada, hinny,' Noel told Cathy. 'She'll have to take him home and patch him up.'

'What were they even fighting about?'

'Gawd knows,' grunted Noel. 'They're drunks. They don't need a reason.' He straightened up the tables and chairs and called out to allay everyone's fears: 'It's all over now. Get back to your drinkin."

Cathy decided that, better than knocking on Ada Farley's door and dragging her over, she'd be best off helping Frank home herself. 'Whatever you think is best, lass,' Noel shrugged. 'Can you manage the weight of him?'

It wasn't a pleasant task. Frank was a dead weight with his arm over her shoulders, but it was just a hop and a step down the hill to his home. All the way there he muttered and rumbled about the bastards from North Shields and how he'd fettle them next time he saw them. 'Aye, Frank,' she told him. 'But for now, just keep one foot going in front of another. That's all you have to do for now . . .'

When Ada Farley opened the front door of number thirteen, she didn't look surprised to see Frank's dishevelled state.
'Fighting again?'

'They set upon him,' Cathy told her. 'It wasn't his fault.'

'Drinking himself daft *is* his fault, though,' said the buxom
matriarch of the Farley clan. Her three young boys were clustered about her in the hall and they helped manhandle their
dad into the house. 'Get him into the front parlour and put a
throw over him,' Ada said. 'He's not getting into bed with me
in that state. Cup of tea, pet?' she added, glancing at Cathy.

'I should get back to the pub,' Cathy said.

'Ah, a gobful of tea won't matter.' Ada led her through to
her parlour, and Cathy had to admit, she was intrigued to see
the warm, friendly home of the Farleys. It was a beautifully
kept place, full of old furniture and bits and bobs, just the same
as the Johnsons, but everything here was dusted and polished
to within an inch of its life.

Winnie was sitting there, hunched over her tea and waving
a greeting to Cathy. Cathy took her tea gratefully and hoped
Noel wouldn't be cross that she was dilly-dallying. Ah, so
what if she was? It had been a long night. Why, it had been
a long week!

'Will Mr Farley be all right?' she asked.

'Why aye. Our Tony and our Tommy will get his boots
off and get him settled. Put the fire bucket by his head if he
needs to be sick in the night. But what else can we do? He's
a hopeless case.'

'I see a bad end coming to him,' Winnie remarked loftily.

Ada ignored her prognosticating friend. 'Now you, Cathy
lass. I saw you tonight, outside yon pub with your chap Matty
Johnson. I suppose you're getting serious, are you?'

Cathy didn't like the idea of being spotted and spied upon,
but there was just something so kindly and benign about Ma

Farley that she didn't really mind. The woman's face was old before its time. Her body was lumpy and clapped out and she couldn't have been more than – what? Mid-thirties? Forty? It was so hard to tell. But giving birth to those little lads and a lifetime of toil had seemingly taken it out of her.

Cathy found herself opening up to the woman at number thirteen. 'It was going really well,' she said, and before she even knew it, she was telling Ma Ada all about their times together, the dancing and all the laughter and the long talks as they walked. She told her about meeting Matty's formidable mother and then even told her about the unfortunate scene under the archways.

Ada Farley's eyes lit up with a mixture of annoyance and compassion. 'Eeeh, lass. It's the old tale. And there you were, fighting for your honour, were you?'

'Well, not honour exactly. But I felt uncomfortable. I knew I didn't want to let him . . . you know . . .' Suddenly she stopped herself. What was she doing? Going into all of her business with a woman she didn't even know so well! Why, this was stuff she wouldn't even divulge to Teresa Sturrock, who was a much more familiar face. However, she thought, maybe it was because Ada was such a motherly figure. She was warm and she was ready to listen. She wasn't judging or banging on about what girls should or shouldn't do. She was nodding with infinite understanding, as if she knew exactly what Cathy had been through.

'It's the old, old story,' Ada said again. 'And it doesn't have to go the way the fella wants it. You get to have your say, you know. Don't get caught, Cathy. Not like I did! Look at me, and learn, lass! I gave that daft drunk fella snoring in the next room all his own way. Aye, I did. And I'm not ashamed, even though I'd been brought up in the ways of the church and everything. It happened and that was that. But here I am, all these years later and I've got a house filled with bairns! That's been my life and I'd not change it. Well, I'd not change most things in it. But just you hark on, Cathy Carmichael. Don't just go the way I did because you want to make some great galumphing fella happy for a few moments. It might shut him up, but it's not worth it in the long run.'

This lengthy speech seemed to wear the tiny old woman out for a moment or two. Both Cathy and Winnie were staring at her in amazement. It was as if she had opened up her heart a little, under her layers and layers of shawls and cardigans, and shown it quite plainly for them both to see.

'Thank you, Mrs Farley,' said Cathy respectfully. 'I appreciate what you're telling me. And I will be very careful.'

Gratified, the diminutive motherly woman nodded.

Then, because she was tired and trusting and not thinking about it, Cathy made a slip. She said, 'I don't want to get caught again.'

There was a beat and she realised just what she had said. Ma Ada's eyebrows went up. Winnie gasped as she realised what Cathy had meant. 'Again?' said the old traveller woman. 'What do you mean "*again*"?'

Ada Farley stared at Cathy with a sad expression. 'Are you saying that you've been caught by a fella before, lass? Are you saying that you've had a bairn already in your young life?'

Suddenly Cathy was up on her feet, putting down her cup with a clatter. 'I-I have to get back to w-work,' she said, and headed into the hall.

'Ah, don't rush away,' Ada Farley called after her. 'Anything you say here will go no further . . . You know that, divven't yer, pet?'

But as she dashed back out onto chilly Frederick Street, Cathy doubted that was true. Oh, what was she doing? Letting herself spill her guts out like that? You started telling a bit of the truth and, sure enough, all the rest of it followed. It was bad enough that she'd told Ada Farley one of the dearest secrets she had. But to do it in front of that daft, chattering Winnie, too! I must be mad, she thought. I must be bloody mad!

Cathy tottered miserably into the night, towards the amber windows of the Robin Hood.

If this gossip about her spread, it could change everything for her round here. With just a tiny misspoken word, Cathy might well have ruined her new life.

Chapter 35

She spent the next day or so trying to put her moment of indiscretion out of her head. How could she have been so stupid? She had been tired and overemotional, after Matty and everything, but that was no excuse. Cathy had gone and spilled her most precious secret and now there was no taking it back.

She walked on eggshells for a day or two, waiting for the news to break. Ah, she was sure that she could trust Ada Farley. It was that strange Winnie one she was wary of. Wasn't she known for traipsing round everyone's houses, drinking their tea and spreading tittle-tattle of all kinds?

And Winnie was thick with Ma Sturrock of course, too. That was the real worry. Of course Winnie was going to tell Teresa that the seemingly innocent girl she had taken in had a secret bairn stashed away somewhere. She was bound to!

Cathy spent Thursday and Friday feeling shifty and hunted. She was sure that Teresa was giving her funny looks. She felt certain that the old woman already knew about her! But Teresa said nothing. She carried on as normal, letting Cathy do all the housework and the cooking, feeling more and more scared with each minute that went by.

Then, by Friday night, Cathy was starting to think she had

been fretting over nothing. The storm wasn't going to break at all. Her shameful secret was safe . . .

But by Friday night she had something else to worry about.

The knocking came early in the evening. Someone was pounding at the front door like their life depended on it. It sounded like they had the hounds of hell pursuing them!

'What the divil's that?' Teresa Sturrock cursed, spooning up the gravy from a suet pudding Cathy had made them. She hated to be interrupted in the middle of eating – it always gave her stomach gyp.

Cathy threw open the door to a grey and windy street and was shocked to see Ellie there. The barmaid had the collar of her shabby coat turned up and a headscarf hiding her distinctive dishwater blonde hair. 'Can I come in, pet?' she asked, in a breathless voice.

'Why, of course!' As she stepped aside, Cathy noticed that the girl had a small fake leather valise with her.

The door thumped shut and Cathy pulled the curtain over it, glad to keep out the awful weather. 'Come through to the parlour and get settled. We're just having our tea.'

'Eeeh! Come to interrupt our meal, have you?' Teresa burst out. 'I get stomach pains and wind if I get disturbed, you know. What are you doing, calling at this time?' As she spoke, she kept in shovelling the delicious savoury kidney pie.

'Ha'way, sit yourself down, pet,' Cathy told her friend softly. She could see that Ellie was on the verge of tears. Down went the valise and off came the coat and the headscarf. Well! Ellie looked proper dishevelled in her wrinkled blouse and old skirt. Her stockings were laddered, Cathy noticed.

Ellie accepted a cup of tea and had taken no more than two sips before she burst out: 'I've ran away from him.'

Cathy stared at her. 'What?'

'You were right, Cathy, love. Everything you were thinking and saying. I was lying through my teeth when you and Sofia came to see me the other day. I longed to tell you the truth. But I was living a lie! It was all a load of rubbish!'

Across the table Teresa's jaw was still working as she chewed and enjoyed her meal. She was enjoying Ellie's scene even more. 'What was a load of rubbish?'

'My life with Alec,' Ellie said miserably. 'He's a bastard. He's a vicious little bastard and I was a fool for ever going with him. Why did no one warn me? Why did no one say what he was like?'

Cathy and Teresa exchanged a quick glance at this but didn't say anything. Cathy simply took hold of Ellie's cold hand. The girl winced as she did so, as if she was wary of contact, or as if the bones were hurting again.

'But what did he say?' Cathy asked. 'When you told him you were leaving?' She couldn't imagine Alec Johnson taking such news lightly. He would see it as a defeat, as a personal slight.

'I've not said anything,' Ellie admitted. 'I waited till he was out, doing whatever nasty business he does. Then I threw a few essential things in my bag and I ran out of that house. That horrible midden! It's been like a prison, ever since I moved into the hideous place. I hate that part of town with its black clouds and all those scowling faces. They looked at me like I was some kind of whore! I hardly ever left the house, because of the way they all looked at me!'

Teresa finished up the last of her meal and dabbed her thin lips with a napkin. 'So are you saying he's going to come home and find you gone?' She frowned. 'That's gonna upset the nasty little fella, isn't it?'

Ellie jutted out her chin. 'I don't care. He can be as upset as he likes. Them Johnson lads always get their own way. They're nasty bastards, the lot of them. It's about time one of them

learned they can't just take what they want . . . and keep it.'
Now the tears were running freely down Ellie's smutty, soot-
smeared face. Her shoulders shook inside her thin, dirty blouse.
She looked beseechingly at Cathy. Her words came out thickly
as she sobbed and her teeth got in the way even more than
usual. 'Will you help us out, pet? I know I've not been the best
of friends to you in recent times. I've been awful, I know, even
when you were trying to help. I was swanking about, full of
meself. And then I was pretending everything was wonderful!
But now I'm throwing mesel' on your mercy . . . Can I stay
here? Would you mind? Just till I get back on me feet?'

Both women were shocked and discomfited by the sudden,
urgent request. Cathy felt helpless. 'Why, Ellie, you know this
isn't my home. I have no rights here! I'm nobbut a waif and
stray in this house myself.'

Teresa bridled at this somewhat. 'You're more than a waif
and stray, Cathy Carmichael. You might have been homeless
and new in town when I first took you in, but you've more
than proven your worth. You've been like a daughter to me,
you knaa.'

Cathy blushed, amazed by the blunt, kind words. 'Thank
you, Teresa. That means a lot to me.'

'Aye, well, you know I'm not a soft touch,' the old woman
said, shifting uncomfortably on her cushions. She let out a
dainty burp. 'Oh, hell. Didn't I tell you that any upheaval
played havoc with my insides? Now look, I'm not some home
for runaway women. I can't just take in every lass who's got
nowhere to go . . .'

Ellie looked shamefaced, folding her arms over her stomach.
'I'm sorry, I shouldn't even have asked. But I've got no one
else. I think I've burned all me boats. But you know me, Mrs
Sturrock. You've known me and my late mam for years and
years, haven't you? You know I'm a decent sort.'

The old woman sucked her teeth and let out another belch, wincing at the discomfort. She was thinking that, really, Ellie wasn't a decent sort at all. She'd been living in sin with a man in Boldon Colliery. Really, she was no better than a woman of the street! And in her slipshod blouse and stockings this evening, that's exactly what she looked like as well.

'But if we take you in, lass, is that nasty man of yours gonna come looking for you? Is he gonna be banging on my door? I don't want that. I don't want trouble coming to my house!'

Ellie shrugged helplessly, sobbing again. She knew she couldn't guarantee what Alec would or wouldn't do next. It was more than likely that he'd come looking for her. He'd be absolutely full of bloody hell. 'He knows it's over, though,' Ellie said through her tears. 'He was sick of the sight of me. He said as much. He said awful things about me. Upsetting, cruel things. Why, he doesn't want me anymore. He said he felt lumbered with me. Nah, I bet he'll be glad to see me gone . . .'

Teresa and Cathy both stared at the girl. She was utterly broken and hopeless. They both knew that they had to do something to help her.

Cathy said, 'Look, she won't be any bother. She can come in with me. She can squeeze into my room.' She turned to Ellie. 'Are they all the belongings you've got, in that little bag?'

She nodded unhappily. 'I just took what I could carry. I don't want things anymore. That whole, horrible house was full of things and I grew sick of the sight of them.'

Ma Teresa looked doubtful. 'If she stays here, it can't be for long. You understand that, don't you? And I don't know what our Noel is going to say. You're lucky he's out working at the pub right now. If he was here I'm sure he would never agree to it. He'd send you off with a flea in your ear . . .'

'No, no,' Cathy said. 'He's kinder than that. Look how he's been with me. He accepted *me* here, under his roof, didn't he?'

Teresa gawped at her. 'Why, you fool! That's because he loves the bones of you! You daft wench, can't you see? Are you that bliddy blind, girl? My lad's crackers about you and has been from day one!'

This wasn't something Cathy could cope with, either now or any time. Teresa's strange outburst hung in the air for a moment and Cathy knew that she was meant to say something nice about Noel in return. 'You have both been like family to me,' she said stiffly. 'I couldn't have asked for anything more. But right now, what are we going to do about Ellie? We can't let her sleep on the streets.'

'Of course we can't,' grumbled Teresa.

'I'm so, so sorry to be a bother,' Ellie said. 'And I bet Noel already resents me, for letting him down at the pub, doesn't he?'

Teresa had to admit that this was the case. 'But you know Noel. He hates and resents most people he meets. The ones he approves of are few and far between!'

It was somehow decided that the best thing to be done was to get Ellie all dolled up and working again behind the bar of the Robin Hood. Surely that would be the most effective way of getting her back into Noel's good books.

'You can work for your bed and board,' Teresa said as she watched Ellie fill the tin bath and help the girl out of her clothes. 'Help! What's all this? Look at the state of you, lass!'

Her arms and her back were covered in bruises. Fading ones, the hues of bitter fruits. More livid ones, mauve and blue.

'So he beats you?'

'He gets off his head. He takes everything out on me. He never did it till I was in that horrible house of his in Boldon . . .' Ellie was hunching forward, so as not to reveal her swollen belly to Teresa. She was more ashamed of that than she was her bruising, Cathy thought.

'Nasty little man, I always hated him,' muttered Teresa. She said other things about the whole Johnson clan, in much more vulgar language. And then she left Cathy to finish undressing and washing the girl with sponges and warm soapy water.

The bruised girl closed her eyes and let her friend clean her. It felt like she was scrubbing away more than a few days' accreted layers of sweat and grime. It was like she was absolving her in some kind of ritual. It was a cleansing of the spirit almost, and the warmth and loving attention of it did her good.

'You're really showing plainly now, pet,' said Cathy, as the older girl stood up naked before her in the warm water. For a moment, under Cathy's frank and admiring gaze, Ellie was unashamed of herself and her condition. The feeling lasted for only a second or two.

Cathy wrapped her in a clean bath sheet and patted her dry. She combed out her lank hair and brought her clothes to borrow.

'Why, you look like a different woman!'

It was true. The ruined girl who'd come banging at the door for help had been transformed back into the buxom, confident, slightly brassy Ellie that they all knew.

'Are you feeling ready to get back behind that bar?' Cathy asked her, smiling. 'Do you feel strong enough? To go over there and give them all a surprise? Will you show them how strong you are?'

Ellie patted her hair and examined herself in the flyblown mirror in Teresa's parlour. 'Why aye. It's Friday night. And behind that bar is where I belong. No one's gonna take that from me. I know where I'm meant to be!'

Chapter 36

You would never have known that Ellie had suffered the awful tribulations that she had. Not in the way that she barrelled into the Robin Hood that evening with her usual aplomb. She was shining with freshness from her bath by the range and fired up with a gumption that Cathy hadn't seen in her for a while. She also had a fringed shawl draped artfully about her to disguise her belly.

The regulars were delighted to see her back behind the bar and she seemed to glow with the attention they lavished upon her.

It was one of their more festive, noisy Friday nights at the pub. Aunty Madge was plonking away at her piano, getting a singsong going. Ellie was even feeling brash enough to give them a song – a recent music hall number that had them all roaring with laughter.

Noel sidled up to Cathy at the bar. 'I've got to hand it to you, lass. You seem to be responsible for getting her back to work and as good as new. Well done, Cathy.'

She nodded graciously, not daring to break the news to old Noel yet that Ellie was seeking refuge at his own house. She could tell him that later, or better still, smuggle Ellie in somehow without him noticing.

Eeeh, why was life so complicated? Cathy was just thinking this when her Matty came swaggering into the saloon in a freshly pressed shirt.

'You're a sight for sore eyes,' he told Cathy, beaming.

'Get away with you, flatterer!' she laughed. She was glad they were back on an even keel, seemingly, after their nice talk outside the other day. She longed for her friendship with Matty to be uncomplicated. It was hard enough for him, coming back from the war and what with everything he must have carried back with him from the front. She realised that he had complications enough, as a survivor. He really didn't need other relatives or dramas getting in the way of him trying to live his life. He needed everything to be simple. Just him and Cathy. It had to be just about the two of them. That's how it ought to be.

Now he was leaning on the bar and frowning at Ellie, who was at the piano giving her all to a song that had been new last year:

'But I dillied and dallied, dallied and I dillied
Lost me way and don't know where to roam . . .'

Matty frowned as he accepted a pint of mild from his lass. 'So she's back over this way, is she?'

Cathy bit her lip. 'I suppose Alec's furious that she's run away from him?'

'It's all his daft pride, man. But yes, of course he is. He's off his head. He came home and she'd left an awful note for him, calling him all the pigs and bastards and all the names she could think of.' He sipped his drink ruminatively. 'Mind, she doesn't seem too damaged by the whole experience . . .'

Cathy wasn't having that. 'She's putting on a brave face. If you could see the bruises all over her body. Why, I was shocked and knocked sick by the sight of them. That brother of yours has been using her as a punch bag!'

Matty's face darkened with anger. 'Aye, that makes me want to give him a good pasting. Me own brother!' He tutted sorrowfully. 'I'm bloody well ashamed of him. So, where's Ellie staying now?'

For a second Cathy hesitated and bit her tongue. Instinctively she clammed up against the question. Her first duty was to protect her friend.

Matty raised both eyebrows at her. 'What, you think I'm gonna get the information off you and then go running straight to our Alec and tell him where to find her?' He sounded hurt as he stared at Cathy.

She pursed her lips. 'Of course I trust you. It's just . . . if I don't tell you, then you won't have to lie to your brother, will you? When he asks you if you know where she is?'

'Oh, aye, okay,' Matty said, as applause followed Ellie's rendition of the Marie Lloyd ditty. She took her bows enthusiastically. Cathy looked at Matty and he didn't seem at all mollified by her reasoning. He simply felt that Cathy didn't trust him enough. His colour stayed high, as if he was burning with shame for being one of the Mad Johnsons.

When Ellie returned to the bar, she was awkward in front of Matty.

'Now then, Matty,' she said. 'I don't want to hear about what your brother's saying about me. I'm sure he hates my bloody guts.'

'He's pretty upset,' Matty told her.

'You can just tell him that he can whistle for me. He had his chance and he treated me badly. As far as I'm concerned that little ginger bugger can go and boil his head!'

And that was the end of the matter, as far as Ellie was concerned.

Matty drained his pint and promised Cathy, 'I'll take you out on Sunday night. Shall we go dancing again?'

She kissed his cheek quickly. 'Ah, that would be lovely, pet.'

The rest of the night went by in a fairly ordinary fashion. There were no punch-ups or fracas or any untoward events to speak of. There was one odd moment when Cathy noticed old Winnie sitting at the Women's Table. She had dragged Noel down to sit next to her, and she was clearly bending his ear. The landlord, grimacing, was indulging her. Yet, as Cathy observed from afar, he seemed to grow intrigued by what he was hearing. Almost despite himself, he sat there, paying heed to what Winnie told him.

A trickle of dread ran down Cathy's spine. She stopped in her tracks and cold fear filled her mind. She could surely guess what that interfering busybody was telling him! That particular secret that Cathy had ineluctably let drop at Ada Jones' the other night. Winnie was wasting no time at all in spreading that little nugget of shame about!

Even as Cathy stood there watching them, both Winnie and Noel turned to glance back at her. As if it couldn't be any more obvious who they were gossiping about! Cathy swore and the pounding of her heart filled her ears till she could hardly hear anything else.

Well, that was that, then. Cathy returned to polishing glasses with a redoubled, furious effort. Now Noel would know that Cathy had once been pregnant. He'd listened to those flamin' jungle drums and heard the latest. And so what would he say? What would he think? He would know his waif and stray wasn't pure like the driven snow. He was supposed to be infatuated with her – according to his bloody mother! Well, let him hear the truth! Maybe it would put him off her at last?

But what if he chucked her out? What if she was left, like Ellie, with nowhere to go?

*

Much later that night, the two girls were huddled together for warmth in Cathy's bed. The house was still and quiet by now. Teresa had put out as many of the cats as she could find and she had lumbered off to her own room, slamming the door on the day. Some time after that they heard Noel letting himself into the house and crashing about tipsily downstairs.

'He's still having his after-hour lock-ins, then,' Ellie said, lying on her back and staring at the pale ceiling. 'He's been having those as long as I can remember. As long as I've been working there, anyway. Him and his closest cronies, abusing the licensing laws. Eeh, he'll never change.'

Cathy said, 'It's a wonder he doesn't get in trouble with the polis or the brewery . . .'

'There's usually a polis or two in there with them, man. He keeps them sweet with free drink! He's not daft, that Noel.'

They listened to him drunkenly muttering on the stairs and the landing, unsteadily making his way up to his attic. Both girls held their breath and pulled the candlewick bedspread up to their chins as they sensed rather than heard him passing by Cathy's bedroom door. There was a faint pulse of flickering light from the lamp he was carrying as he made his way to his room. Was it Cathy's imagination or did he pause directly outside her door? As if he was debating whether to knock, or to shove his way inside? Or perhaps he was standing out there and indulging himself in mucky thoughts? Or sending up a little prayer that she would start to fall in love with him?

It was only a second or two, and then he was lurching off again, the gaslight fading and the door to the top room slammed shut.

'Thank you for letting me stay here,' Ellie whispered to Cathy. 'Even with old Noel shambling about on the stairs, I feel safe here.'

'You were really scared of Alec, weren't you?'

'I still am! No one knows what he's capable of. No one knows what he's really like. And the people he knows, Cathy! The types that he has running around, doing his dirty work for him. Why, they're the scum of the earth! No one knows what all the Mad Johnsons are really like.'

Cathy wasn't having this. 'Not all of them. My Matty's a decent chap. He won't have anything to do with nothing wrong.'

'Don't you believe it, and don't be naïve, pet,' Ellie snapped.

They lay on their backs in the midnight silence, stifling the tension that had risen between them. Cathy really didn't want to argue with Ellie because she had been through enough. For her part, Ellie didn't want to argue with the girl who had given her sanctuary. She was content to let Cathy find out about Matty for herself. Let her make her own mistakes!

'What are you thinking now?' Cathy asked her.

'That we ought to get ourselves some sleep,' Ellie said.

But there was something yet that Cathy wanted to ask her friend. 'Ellie?'

'Uh-huh?' Already she was drifting.

'When I was helping you in the bath earlier, you were holding the towel over your tummy. When Teresa came to help with washing your hair . . .'

Ellie's laugh was uneasy. 'Well, I was being modest, wasn't I? I didn't want her seeing me Mary-Ann!'

That wasn't it, Cathy knew it. She could picture quite clearly the way that Ellie had held herself and covered herself and drew her knees up. When she had stood up with water streaming off her bruised body, she had paused before clutching the towel to the swelling of her belly. For a second she had quietly gloried in her nudity, letting Cathy gaze at her.

'You were hiding your tummy from Teresa, but not from me. You're really showing a lot now, aren't you?'

Ellie said, 'Aye, I know I am.'

'What are you gonna do about it, now you've left him, then?'

There was a long pause in the darkness. 'I don't know. I just don't know what I'm to do, Cathy.'

'We're all here, you know that. To help you.'

Ellie was quiet then, and when she spoke again, her voice was thick with tears. 'Thanks, lass. I don't deserve a friend like you. I was a horrible bitch to you when we first met, wasn't I?'

Cathy couldn't help giggling. 'Aye, you were an' all.'

'Well, I should have known better,' Ellie whispered. 'I should have known you were a good girl, who'd be a fine friend to me. And you'd have more sense than I do, even though you're ten years younger than me!'

'Ah, you've got sense, Ellie . . .'

'Have I? Me? Letting myself get knocked up by a fat little weasel like Alec Johnson? I've got nae sense at all, Cathy. I've been a naïve little fool, that's what I've bloody been.'

'You're not a fool . . .' Cathy protested.

'Oh, but I am,' Ellie sighed.

They fell quiet then and drifted towards sleep.

And I was once such a naive fool as well, wasn't I, Cathy found herself thinking. Once upon a time – not all that long ago – I was a daft little naïve lass of the kind that Ellie was just scoffing about. I was that girl and I was caught out. All those memories, so carefully held back, were tumbling to the forefront of her mind.

She hardly ever let herself think about this. But as she fell asleep that night, sharing her bed with Ellie, her thoughts and her dreams and her prayers were filled by the baby she had left behind in the north.

Saturday breakfast time saw Noel descending on the parlour with a furious look on his face.

The two girls and Teresa were tucking into a hearty breakfast of fresh bread and black pudding, fried eggs and a vast pot of tea. Ellie was slathering her stottie cake with soft yellow butter when Noel stumped into the room and the two of them locked eyes.

'So, we're putting you up as well, are we, now?' he thundered.

'Your mam kindly offered me a place to stay,' Ellie said.

'It's my house! I'm the man of the house!' he roared. Then he swung round on his mother, who looked flustered and upset by his shouting at this early time in the morning. 'Mother, what are you doing? What are we running here? Some kind of home for fallen women?'

'Eeeh, our Noel!' Teresa cried. 'That's a bloody awful thing to say!'

He growled, almost like an animal with his hackles up. Surveying the two girls in their night things he spat: 'But that's what they are, you knaa'. The pair of them are strumpets!'

Cathy's eyes blazed. 'Just you take that back, Noel Sturrock. You just give your nasty tongue a rest from its wagging!' She was fighting back. She knew that going on the offensive was the best way of fending him off. But inside Cathy was quailing. This was her worst fear coming true. This was everything she had dreaded. Now she was sure her secret was about to come out.

'I know about you,' he growled at her.

'T-there's nothing to know,' she said, her nerve failing her. 'Just stop now, Noel. Stop causing a scene.'

But he wasn't to be pacified. 'You, Cathy Carmichael. You're no better than you ought to be. I've heard all your secrets now. Have you heard the news, Mother? I had it straight from no lesser source than your precious Winnie, that bloody old witch!'

'What are you talking about now?' Teresa cried, plainly upset by all these unnecessary ructions.

'Noel . . .' Cathy whispered. 'Don't! *Please!*'

'Our lovely Cathy's just another fallen woman,' he shouted gloatingly. 'She's a flamin' harlot! And she's one who abandoned her own bairn! That's right, Mother. She's had a bastard and she's chucked the bugger out and abandoned it! That's the kind of lass we've let into our lives and our household. So, what do you think of that, Mother?'

Chapter 37

It was all out now, wasn't it? Just look at bloody old Noel Sturrock's face as he berated her at the breakfast table on Saturday morning. And the look on his old mother's face! It was so upsetting to see.

'Eeeh, pet. Tell me it's not true!' Teresa wailed.

'It's all true,' Noel said disgustedly. 'She's had a bairn when she was nobbut a bairn herself. And she's left it behind her, back where she came from in the north!'

Teresa was staring at her, but it wasn't with the appalled horror that her son had expected. There was nothing in Teresa's eyes but compassion. 'Come here, pet,' she told Cathy.

'We should chuck her out into the street,' Noel was shouting. 'The pair of them! People will think we're running some kind of bloody brothel!'

His tiny mother raised her voice against him. There was something steely in her voice that cut through his bleating outrage. 'Hush your mouth, lad! Have some sense, will you?' Again, she said to Cathy: 'Come here and give me a cuddle, lass.'

Cathy had found herself doing just that. She went to the woman who had taken her in off the street, all those months ago, and she sat in the chair next to her. It was slightly awkward, with her being twice Teresa's size, but she submitted gladly to the woman's consoling hug. The tremulous, skinny arms went about her and Teresa whispered into her hair: 'I just knew there was some kind of sadness in your past. I knew you were running from something terrible. Eeeh, you poor girl. You don't have to tell us the story. You don't owe us anything, lass.'

Cathy hugged her friend back and fought the tears that were threatening to overwhelm her.

Ellie was in floods. She had put down her buttered stottie and sat staring at Teresa and Cathy. Her own heart ached to feel a love like that. It was as if Cathy had found a new mother for herself.

Noel stared at the three of them in dismay. 'Aren't you furious with her, Mam? She's kept this disgusting secret from you . . .'

His mother fixed him with a basilisk stare. 'Disgusting secret, nothing! Why, you understand nothing about women or love or anything at all, Noel. You understand bugger all about life or what can happen to a body. But you're bloody well quick to judge folk, aren't you?'

Muttering angrily, Noel had left the women to it. He would never understand their ways and, what was more, he didn't want to. He left the room hissing the word 'harlots' under his breath.

Teresa told Cathy, 'I want you to know that you've always got a home here with me. I knew you were a good'un, the first time I clapped eyes on you. But I also knew there was some secret sadness you had. If you want to talk about it, that's fine. If you don't, that's all right too.'

'Thank you,' Cathy smiled, sitting up again. Her neck was cricked from bending to cuddle the tiny woman.

'And the same goes for you, Ellie,' Teresa had addressed their guest. 'You will always have a place at my table, too. Whatever my daft son says.'

Ellie sobbed and grinned and hardly knew what to say. 'Thank you, Ma Sturrock. I'm so grateful for that. You'll never know how grateful.'

The Sunday night dance was at a place called the Albert Hall, upstairs in a tall building on Fowler Street. It was a much rowdier do than the one at the Alhambra, where everything had been so exotic and elegant. Here, on the bouncing floorboards of the Albert Hall, the lads and lasses jostled each other as they whirled about and stamped their feet. The band was an Irish one, and the music was all jigs and fiddles and reels. The men had their shirts unbuttoned and their sleeves rolled up. All the women's hair came shaken loose, with Cathy's no exception.

It might have been a bit rough and ready, but she enjoyed it nonetheless. As Matty held her and whirled her around, he laughed with sheer joy. She hadn't seen him like this yet. It was as if these were his own people, and he was in his natural element. The drink was hard liquor, not some sweet fruit punch, and it kept flowing as the night went on. Cathy felt queasy at first but gave herself up to the experience. Her head swam, and her feet seemed to have a mind of their own, knowing just how to dance to these old country tunes.

It was good to get her mind off things at home.

'So what's happened now, then?' Matty asked her as they took a breather.

She couldn't tell Matty what Noel had said. She didn't want him knowing anything about her secret past. She could hardly get into the story without having to admit what it was all about. And the whole point of a wild night of dancing like this was to forget all your worries and woes, surely?

'Never mind me,' she laughed during a break from the dancing. 'It's just the usual nonsense at home, with Noel throwing his tantrums and kicking off.'

'Eeh, him,' Matty frowned. 'He's a funny little creature, isn't he? I've always thought he's got a nasty streak in him. People have said all sorts of horrible things about him all his life. No doubt some of them are true. Look, if you need him bashed up or given a warning to teach him a lesson . . .'

Cathy's eyes widened. 'What?! What are you saying?'

He shrugged diffidently. 'These things are easily organised. If you need that strutting popinjay putting back into his place?'

He was serious! Cathy stared at him in shock – he really was offering to have Noel beaten up for her. 'Aw, Matty,' she said, trying to hide the disappointment in her voice. So he really was like all the other Johnsons in the end, wasn't he? He was just the same as the rest.

He mistook her tone for gratitude. 'Hey, it's all right, lass. Divven't you worry. I'll not have a little scrap of a man upsetting my girl, will I? I'll punch his lights out meself if need be.'

'No, no,' Cathy protested, as the band whipped up the room into a fresh new whirligig of music and stamping feet. 'You really, really don't have to do that.'

Matty took her in his arms and danced her back into the thick, pounding pulse of the night.

On Monday, Cathy installed herself in a glass booth at Franchino's with Sofia. They sipped the strongest coffee Tonio's machine could provide and opened their hearts to each other.

Sofia was still raging with paranoid discontent. Her husband was letting her down. He was failing her and his whole family. The money he was bringing home was pitiful. Their business was doing better but the money was vanishing. They weren't losing it to the Johnsons anymore but the money was being squandered anyway. It was down to Tonio's shady nights of gambling.

'Still?' Cathy asked.

'It's no use talking to him.'

'Do you still love him?'

Sofia seemed shocked by the question at first. 'Of course I do.' Then she blinked. 'I don't know . . . I hardly know anything anymore. I feel like he is letting us down . . . he's not the man I once ran away with . . .'

Cathy nodded. 'What does your mother say?'

'She knows how he gambles. She knows we have problems. But she holds back from being too involved. He is the man of the household. She respects that, but she puts curses on him when he isn't looking. She wishes he would come back to us. He even has less time for the bairns . . .'

It was funny hearing the local word 'bairns' in Sofia's strong accent. It was touching, somehow.

Then a look of alarm passed across the Italian woman's face. 'And all my mother can talk about at the moment is the man in the black hat!'

'Not this again,' Cathy rolled her eyes. 'I thought you'd decided that it was just your mind playing tricks on you, when you were unhappy? I thought you'd put that thought behind you?'

Sofia shook her head. 'No, no, Cathy. It's different. My mother . . . she saw him for herself! With her own eyes! She saw the man in the black fedora here on Ocean Road!'

After their hot, strong cortadito Cathy said her goodbyes and headed for home. She had managed to mollify Sofia slightly, but there was no doubt about it – there was panic in her friend's eyes when she talked about these Neapolitan gangsters and this man in the black hat. But really, it had to be nonsense, didn't it? All of it? Even with the coincidence of the old nonna thinking she had seen him too. It was all a load of hooey, Cathy thought. Did people really keep vendettas going for year upon year? Did they really travel thousands of miles to see them through to their deadly conclusion?

Cathy couldn't see how they could have the patience. To her, hatred and revenge seemed like exhausting things. Who had the energy to maintain such emotions, when the rest of life was so bloody tiring?

But maybe hatred was the thing that gave some folk strength? Maybe it sustained them somehow?

She would never understand all that carry on. Get on with your own life, was Cathy's steadfast philosophy. You've got enough to do, living a decent life of your own. Let others do what they have to do, and don't get in the way. That seemed to her to be the best way of carrying on.

But Sofia had seemed nervy, back there at the ice-cream parlour. Why, it had been like she was expecting that man from Naples in the black hat to come walking in at any moment . . .

It would be hard to live your life on a knife's edge, thought Cathy, as she strode energetically up the hill to the Sixteen Streets. You would just have to put it all out of your head. You couldn't sit there every day, imagining enemies coming after you. You'd go off your rocker, wouldn't you?

She shook her head to clear it. She waved and nodded at a few friendly faces who recognised her as she cut through the ginnels and back alleys to Frederick Street. Eeeh, it was nice to be greeted warmly by folk. It made all the difference.

'Hallo, there, Cathy!'

It was Winnie, with her wild white hair flailing about in the breeze. She came hurrying over to Cathy looking like a parcel of dirty washing tied together with string. In a flash Cathy remembered that she was furious with this old biddy. She reared up and towered over the old woman. 'What were you thinking of? Gossiping about me behind my back? Stirring up trouble?'

The old woman looked alarmed. 'Ah, now, Cathy! No, I wasn't! And you can't prove that I was!'

Cathy glared at the old travelling woman, lowering her voice threateningly. 'If I ever hear you spreading tittle-tattle about me again, I'll break your fecking neck, all right, hinny?'

Winnie's face went slack with shock. Cathy took note of that with some satisfaction, and marched past her and up the cobbled street.

She hated violence and she hated threats. She thought hatred and revenge were a waste of time and energy. But by the heck it felt good to scare the life out of that miserable witch.

Cathy had but a moment of guilty pleasure before she arrived back at the Sturrock household and into the midst of another upheaval.

Teresa was weeping in the hallway as soon as Cathy let herself indoors.

'What's the matter? What's happened? Has there been an accident?' Cathy was alarmed by the noise and the fuss that Teresa was making. She had never seen her so upset. 'Calm down, love. Get your breath back.'

Teresa really had to fight to get her words out. Her chest was heaving like she had run ten miles without stop. 'Cathy, it's the polis. We've had the polis at the door today! They came about an hour ago . . . and there was only me here. Eeh, Cathy! I can't believe it! It can't be. It's too cruel . . .'

Now Cathy was starting to feel panicked. 'Tell me! Tell me what's gone on!'

The old woman managed to stop wailing long enough to tell her: 'It's about Ellie. They came calling here at our door . . . and it was about Ellie.'

'But where is she?' A cold hand grasped hold of Cathy's heart. 'She's all right, isn't she?'

Chapter 38

After her Sunday night at the Albert Hall, Cathy had been exhausted. It was late and her head was still spinning from the dancing and the spirits.

Had Ellie been in her bed when she had crept upstairs at last?

Cathy had been asleep just as soon as her head had hit the pillow. Her dreams had all been about Matty and Noel. Matty twirling her around and making casual threats of violence; Noel berating her at the breakfast table about her lost child.

Had there been a hummock of bedclothes beside her? A dip in the mattress? A moan of sleepy protest as she had slipped into the bed?

Furiously she tried to think back . . . Yes, yes, surely Ellie *had* been there on Sunday night? She was so used to her friend sharing her room by now that she hardly even noticed that she was there.

And then the next morning – this morning – Cathy had woken with a thick head and, luckily for her, a day off. She had blinked crossly and muzzily at the brightness of the sun coming in. She had slept in and Teresa had been yelling at her up the stairs.

Now Cathy could remember clearly. She had been alone in the bed on Monday morning. But there was nothing so strange about that. She had slept in, so Ellie would have been up hours before, surely. She'd have got up quietly and given herself a quick scrub with the cold water from the jug by the window. In the clear morning light she might have had to break the film of ice on the water. It was that cold these early mornings! Yes, there had been nothing so very odd about not seeing Ellie this morning.

So then, that made the last time Cathy saw her yesterday morning, when Cathy had baked them stottie bread in the oven and fried up rounds of black pudding. Then Noel had had his awful scene, trying to upset them all. That was the last time Cathy had seen Ellie, when the older barmaid was witness to all that carry on. She had shed a few tears on Cathy's behalf and was concerned when Cathy brushed it all away, determined not to let Noel get at her.

Ellie had helped her dress for her dance at the Albert Hall! She had tied ribbons in her hair and stared at her reflection. 'If I'd had your looks and your confidence, Cathy, I reckon my life would have been a whole lot easier.'

Cathy had taken her hand in hers. 'You're a bonny woman. And you're confident! Of course you are! I was intimidated when I first met you at the Robin Hood.'

Ellie shook her head. 'It's all put on and fake. Like the hairpiece I wear! I make myself brash like that because that's how I've had to be, working in places like that, living in places like I have. You have to be ready to give as good as you get.'

Cathy nodded and let Ellie comb out her dark red hair. 'Aye, I understand that.'

'But your confidence is different, Cathy. You don't have to fake anything. It's like deep down you really know who you are. You are sure of yourself. It's a lovely thing to see.'

'Ah, tush . . .' Cathy had smiled, not quite following what Ellie meant. 'I've made a few mistakes of my own. As you'll have gathered by now.'

Ellie was struggling to put her thoughts into words. 'But you're not daunted by life, Cathy. That's the important thing. You'll always be happy, deep down, whatever happens. I just know you will.'

It was a strange little scene, and Cathy would find herself returning to it in her mind in later years.

It was right before Matty came calling to take her off for the dance. Cathy had had to urge Ellie to keep out of sight, so that Matty wouldn't clap eyes on her, staying there at the Sturrocks. It felt like subterfuge, but it prevented the two of them being in an awkward position.

Cathy said goodbye to Ellie and went hurrying down the stairs to meet Matty.

And now she thought about it, that was the last time she had seen Ellie alive.

'It's true, I thought she was asleep on Sunday night. Under all the covers . . .' Cathy said in a hollow voice. 'And I was so tired myself, I never even checked. I thought, well, I can tell her all about the dance tomorrow . . .'

But Ellie hadn't been there at all. She had been missing since early Sunday evening, as far as Teresa Sturrock could work out.

'Cathy, lass, sit down,' Teresa told her on Monday teatime.

'What's happened to her?' Cathy felt a slow creeping dread stealing over her. 'Has she run away? Why were the polis here? Tell me!'

And the child, she thought. Her unborn child. It's not about Ellie, is it? Whatever has happened to her, it's happened to the baby as well.

Teresa looked distraught, gripping the back of a dining chair with both clawed hands. 'Th-they've found her,' she said.

'What do you mean?' Cathy tasted bile in the back of her throat.

'It was bairns playing who found her, or so the polis say,' Teresa gabbled. 'First thing this morning. Lads playing about, up to no good in Westoe Cemetery, at the top of the hill . . .'

Cathy's hands flew up and she pressed them over her mouth. There was a moan trying to escape from her.

'Aye, lass. She was there. On the graves. She'd been lying there all night, the polis said. She was soaked through and frozen to the bone.'

Cathy couldn't get her head round it. Try as she might, she couldn't make sense of what was being said to her. 'But what was she doing outside? She had a place here . . . We made her welcome . . .' Her eyes darted to fix on Teresa. 'Well, she'll have pneumonia or something. Staying out all night like that. Where is she? The infirmary?'

Teresa's whole face quivered. She bit her lip and told her friend flatly, 'She's dead, Cathy. They found her lying there stone cold and dead among the graves.'

'*What?*' Cathy was on her feet, springing out of her chair like a jack-in-the-box. 'No! She can't be!'

And the *baby!* It was almost too terrible to think of. Cathy fought for her breath. And the baby was dead as well. Before it had ever had chance to live.

Teresa forced herself to grind out the words. To tell her friend the last few details she knew, painful as it was to do so. 'They say she'd cut her wrists, Cathy. Both of them, very deeply, right up to the crook of her arm. She was lying in a pool of her own frozen blood inbetween the old headstones. They say that there was no doubt about it.'

Cathy sat back down heavily, like all the strength had drained out of her.

'She definitely meant to take her own life,' Teresa concluded.

'No!' Cathy sobbed. 'She wouldn't! She'd *never* do such a thing, not when she was . . .'

'But she did, Cathy lass. She took herself away from here. She was thinking of us, really. She wouldn't make a mess here in our house and frighten us. She went off to the graveyard and did it, when nobody knew where she was. You were off out dancing. It was a quiet night for her. She must have been very unhappy. Or she could see no other way . . .'

'I refuse to believe that,' Cathy said. 'She was full of life! She was strong! She was . . .'

The older woman came round the table to cradle Cathy in her arms. 'Aah, we never know what's going on inside of other people's hearts, Cathy. Not really. We're all a mystery to each other, I think.'

It was arranged that Teresa and Cathy would visit the police station the next day to identify the body of their friend. As they made their way there, wondering how such an awful task had befallen them, they realised that Ellie simply had no one else in the world to come and see her.

'How dreadful to be left so alone,' Teresa said, as they came within sight of the forbidding building with its tall windows. 'I remember her mother and how the two of them were so close, living in that one room for years. Ellie was devastated when her mother was taken. Maybe she never really got over the sadness of that?'

But Cathy was still refusing to believe any of it. There was no way that Ellie would take her own life. There was simply no way. What was more, her religion wouldn't allow it. Having shared a room with her, only Cathy knew about the crucifix the girl wore and the prayers she intoned almost soundlessly, kneeling by the bed before lights out. That was proper religion, that! People like that didn't go taking their own lives, did they? They didn't dare chance the hellfire!

The polises were gruff and businesslike. Stepping into the greenish tiled corridors of that place was frightening and overwhelming. It was like stepping into a murky pond, Cathy thought. They were swimming into a place of echoes and slimy depths, where all the criminals and ne'er-do-wells were brought to face judgment. And here, hidden at the back, on large stone slabs, the bodies of victims of all sorts were laid out under clean, pale sheets.

An attendant listened to their request and took them to an antechamber and drew them over to a particular table. Without fuss or ceremony, he lifted back the top of the sheet.

Teresa gasped and Cathy held her breath.

'Yes, yes. That's our friend,' Teresa said.

Ellie's eyes were closed, but she didn't look as if she was resting. There was a twisted anguish in that face. Her prominent teeth were clamped down on her lower lip, and they gave her an absurd, rabbity look. It looked as if her jaw was rigid with terror.

'That poor girl . . .' Teresa Sturrock whispered. Her voice sounded shrill in that dark, antiseptic room. 'What kind of a life has she had? She worked hard and had nowt at all to show for it.' The old woman shook her head. 'Our Noel should be here. He should have come with us.' But there had been neither sight nor sound of Noel at home tonight.

Cathy was calm enough to deal with the official business: all the talk of inquests and death certification and the funeral home expenses.

'Death costs a pretty penny,' Teresa sighed when, at last, they were free to walk out of that forbidding building. 'I suppose, since she has no one else, it'll be us who'll be footing all the bills?'

They walked in the frosty night towards home. Just a couple of days after Cathy had gone off to the dance with Matty. Just two days after Ellie had set off alone for her final hour on earth. Only two days ago.

'I can't stop seeing her face,' Cathy said. 'I don't think I'll ever stop seeing that face. She looked flamin' terrified, didn't she?'

'Hush now,' Teresa told her. 'Whatever pain that lass was in, it's over now. She must have been very sick and unhappy inside to do such a horrible thing to herself.'

Cathy didn't say anything as the pair of them ambled slowly back to the Sixteen Streets. But she still didn't believe a word of it. Whatever the police said – and they were quite convinced that Ellie had taken her own life – Cathy refused to credit it.

Then she was jolted by a sudden thought.

'Where was the knife?' she suddenly asked aloud, as they toiled up the steepest part of Frederick Street. She put a hand to her temple and looked frustrated, like she wanted to go back and ask more questions. 'If she cut her own wrists there must have been a knife with her. Where was it? Did they find it? Where did it come from?' She looked at Teresa. 'You must check to see if one's missing from your scullery.'

Teresa looked ill at the thought. 'One of *my* knives!' She clutched the front of her furry coat. 'Oh, what a terrible idea. Oh, Cathy. You make my belly go cold . . .'

'But they never even mentioned a knife,' Cathy said, picking up her pace and urging Teresa to walk faster. 'Isn't that weird? Shouldn't they have said?' And they hadn't mentioned her unborn child, either, she thought. It was as if they had barely examined her. She was just another dead girl. Another poor girl that no one really cared about . . .

'We're not policemen, Cathy! We don't need to know stuff like that! Why do we need all the grisly details of it? That girl lay dying in the churchyard because she was so unhappy. She was at her wits' end and none of us really knew about it. And then she did something truly terrible to herself. There's no going back and changing things. It's too late now, Cathy. She's dead and gone, and there's nothing that anyone can do.'

Cathy stopped for a breather and stared out over the docks and the smoking rooftops. Night was coming in over the harbour and the sonorous hooting of the big ships underlined their mournful mood. Cathy shook her head and told her landlady: 'She never did herself in. You know it and I know it. You think the same as me, don't you, Teresa? You know it's true. She had too much to live for. She would never have killed herself. Our Ellie was *murdered*.'

Chapter 39

At the noisy wake for Ellie Mackenzie, nobody talked about her pauper's funeral. That had taken place quietly, almost unnoticed. It had to happen on unconsecrated ground, away from the churchyard where her body had been found. In the eyes of the law and God, she was a suicide and so they took her poor body and put it away somewhere anonymous and quiet.

Only Cathy raged and complained about that. And only Cathy went round saying that Ellie had been pregnant. No one else liked to mention it. The dead girl became even more wicked in the eyes of the world at large: taking her own life so violently when she had a young'un on the way.

'Cathy man, you can't go round making accusations about murder!' Teresa Sturrock warned her. 'You'll get your own self in bother.'

Cathy wouldn't be mollified. 'I don't care about that. And I know what I know! It was that bastard Alec Johnson behind this. Whether he did it in person or not and stuck that knife in her arms. He's the one responsible, you mark my words.'

But no one else would believe such a thing.

The dead girl was quickly put away in the earth under an unmarked grave and the world rolled on.

'The least we can do is offer her a noisy send-off,' Noel said. His eyes were gleaming bright. He looked febrile, upset. Cathy was gratified to notice that he had shed his own tears over the girl who had been his barmaid for so long. 'What do you say, Cathy? Shouldn't we hold a proper wake?'

It was something that the regulars at the Robin Hood were very good at. They could make a loud and joyful collective noise, and it would blot out all the smaller, complicated, private feelings. All the niggling second thoughts and doubts that any individual might have could be quashed under the hullabaloo caused by the many.

The wake was on a Friday night, some days and weeks after the death of Ellie. Sofia had been drafted in to help out at the bar. Cathy was responsible for training up her friend and was finding the task more difficult than she had expected. Either Sofia was slow to pick things up, or Cathy lacked the patience and skill displayed by Ellie when she had spent time passing on all of her skills. Possibly the latter was the case, Cathy thought. Even though Ellie had been bluff and brash at times, and had even seemed territorially unfriendly at first, underneath it all she had been generous and kind. She had artfully taught Cathy everything she need ever know about running this place.

Why, Cathy could have taken over running the Robin Hood single-handedly tomorrow, should she need to.

But now here she was, trying to get Sofia to learn to pour a decent pint, only an hour before the wake began.

'I will manage,' Sofia said tersely. She was all dolled up for the night, as was Cathy. They were wearing their best dresses – Cathy in emerald velvet, which suited her colouring best of anything she had ever worn. Sofia was in a black frock with a plunging neckline that showed more of her large, pale breasts than anyone, aside from her Tonio, had ever seen. When she had reported for work that night Noel's eyes came shooting out of his head.

'We are glamorous tonight for Ellie's sake,' Sofia had announced. 'It is our tribute to her.'

It flashed through Cathy's mind that Ellie had never been all that kind about Sofia or her family, or any foreigners at all in fact, but that was hardly worth mentioning now. The woman's daft prejudices and faults had all died with her. Now it was time to preserve the memory of everything that had been good in her. It was all about celebrating her life, Cathy thought. She had to remember that, and to quell the fury she still felt at Ellie's violent, horrible demise.

At six o'clock, Aunty Madge plonked her dextrous hands down on the piano keys and the place started to fill up. 'My Old Man Said Follow the Van' had the first of its many airings of that night. Everyone remembered, not so long ago, Ellie in full voice, having memorised all the words to that silly, rambunctious song. The whole pub sang it for her now.

People drank quickly and with relish. It was as if they were dousing that Friday night in as much spirits and beer as they could pour into it. They were celebrating their long-loved barmaid, but there was also a feeling that they were marking the ends of many things: the war, the flu epidemic, and the winter itself. A feeling of putting the blazing torch to all these terrible things was somehow in the air. Whatever it was, everyone got themselves good and sloshed pretty early on.

Cathy was run off her feet for the first couple of hours. The first time she took a break she found a stool by the fire, close to the rowdy Women's Table. She was greeted by a wrinkled mixed-race woman with wispy scarlet-tinted hair and it took her a moment to remember who she was.

'I'm Florrie,' the woman laughed at her confusion. 'You've only met me a couple of times, love. I don't come in here much. I was Ellie's landlady for many years. She had a room in my house at the top of Frederick Street.'

'Of course!' Cathy smiled, sipping a glass of water. She'd already downed too much alcohol tonight and was trying to slow down. 'Ellie often said how grateful she was to you,' Cathy lied. 'You gave her somewhere to live for all those years.'

A shadow passed over the Caribbean woman's face. 'She should never have moved out from my place. It's always a mistake when people suddenly get up and leave the place they are used to. When they fall under a spell and follow a bad man . . .'

Cathy nodded readily. 'I said the same myself. I knew no good would come of it.'

Florrie had tears rolling down her soft, fat cheeks. 'I used to look after her when she was a little lass, did she ever tell you?'

Cathy had to admit that she hadn't. Ellie talked about her own childhood as seldom as Cathy did.

'Her mother . . . well, she had to pay the rent. And there were certain times that she had to have the use of her room alone. And so the little lass came to sit in my room with me. We would sing and play cards and dress up her doll. She was such a lovely little thing. It was always a surprise to me when she grew up so big and hard and tough. She never really had a kind word for me, once she was grown up.'

'She certainly had a tough side to her,' Cathy admitted. 'Ellie didn't like to let people get close.'

'It was a very decent place, my house,' Florrie made sure that Cathy knew. 'It was nothing sordid and nasty. Cathy's mammy had only very respectable gentleman callers. Very nice, clean gentlemen. There was nothing bad in it. Lily, they used to call her. I always thought it was a lovely name.'

'I suppose, when she got in with Alec, Ellie was only doing what her mother had done,' Cathy said. 'She was just doing what she had been taught.'

But Florrie shook her head. 'Ellie made the mistake of depending on one man. That is a very bad move for a woman. It is something you must never do. I never did – and look at me! I have my own house and my own life. No one ever tells me what to do.'

I bet they don't, Cathy thought ruefully. Then she noticed that there was a crush at the bar, and Noel was getting exasperated with his novice barmaid, Sofia. 'I'd best go and pacify him,' she said.

'Ah, Noel,' chuckled the honey-skinned woman from the top end of the street. 'You probably don't know this, but he was one of Lily's regular callers. Well, when he was little more than a lad. Can you believe this? His mother sent him up to mine. With a handful of money! Like she had sent him off to the corner shop to buy bread and milk! He had a handful of coins to give Lily, and his mother's instructions. She was to turn this unlovable, ugly boy into a proper man. I'd let him into the hall and he'd scowl at me, like I knew he was up to no good. He's always been a shifty little bugger! I'd sit with young Ellie playing dollies' tea parties in my parlour. And that bloody crookback would be with the mother in their room . . .' Florrie broke off into peals of laughter and sipped her beer. 'It's why he never dare put a foot wrong with me. I know all about him. I know how he broke his duck, and who it was with. Old Lily told me every grisly detail afterwards!'

Smiling, Cathy left the old woman to her drink and the company of the others at the Women's Table. She wasn't sure if she had taken a liking to Florrie or not. She enjoyed her warm, raucous humour, but there was something sour and nasty in it, too. She hated that relish for gossip and mucking about in other people's dirty wash baskets.

*

The demand for drink was fierce, and the three bar staff were kept working solidly for hours, without any chance to think or talk or reflect upon their missing colleague. When Noel said, 'I can hardly hear mesel' think!' over the pounding noise of the piano and the cacophonous singing, Cathy patted him on the back. Carelessly she said, 'Ah, just think of all the profit rolling in!'

Instantly his face turned white with anger. He looked furious, then stricken. She was shocked to see his eyes fill up with tears. Once again Cathy was amazed to see how piercingly blue those eyes of his were. 'Out of my way,' he said gruffly, shoving his way through the bar into the back.

Oh God, she'd gone and upset him now! It was one of those moments when Noel's capricious finer, softer feelings rose to the surface. She followed him into the back and found him sobbing noisily over the eternally filthy sink.

'She's really dead, Cathy! That lass! That lass I saw nearly every day of my life! They've put her in the bloody ground! She was so miserable she cut her own wrists and died alone!'

His words were bursting out of him and it was like he'd been keeping them trapped inside for days. They were rank like vomit, seething out of his belly and showering over her as she took him in her arms. She could hardly believe she was doing this, but quite instinctively she pulled him into an embrace and squeezed him tight. Her, hugging Noel! Who she found so repellent! He who became so forbidding and snarling, that time when she'd done so much as touch his hand.

And all that ranting and raving he'd done at her, that Saturday morning! When he had exposed her secrets so savagely. He had called both Cathy and Ellie harlots and had treated them like dirt! But it seemed like that was now all water under the bridge. Ellie's death had put all that shame into perspective for him, perhaps. Cathy didn't know; sometimes she just didn't know where she was with Noel.

Now he was like a giant bairn, going to her embrace and sobbing at her neck, till she felt all his slobber and drool running down her exposed cleavage.

'She's never coming back, Cathy. It's not like some huff she's in, or a sulky strop she's thrown. Now we'll never be able to ask her . . . We'll never really know what was wrong or what we could do to make it better . . . Eeeh, and a bairn as well, Cathy. Her baby inside her. It's the worst thing I've ever heard. The bloody pity and shame of it all! Why couldn't any of us help her?'

In his snotty, messy, blurting explosion of grief, Noel had got it exactly right. They were too late. There was absolutely nothing that any of them could do to help Ellie now.

Back in the saloon bar, having extricated herself from the landlord, Cathy sat between Teresa and old Nonna Franchino. She took another drink and listened to all the noise building around her.

'I knew it, I knew it,' the old Italian woman said. 'I told you so. I warned you all what the Mad Johnsons are like.'

And on her other side, Teresa Sturrock looked bleakly into the flaming hearth. 'I used to dislike the lass. And her mucky mother. But you know, in recent times I changed my attitude towards her. I saw her differently when she became a friend of yours, Cathy. I thought she was all right, really.' Teresa smiled sadly and looked more serious than Cathy had ever seen her. 'I suppose people can always surprise you. Whoever they are.'

Chapter 40

After the evening fizzled out, Cathy sent everyone off home. 'I'll stay and tidy and lock up,' she told them. Even Noel went shambling off, worn out by the evening's drinking and emotions.

Cathy was glad to get some time on her own. Moving around the familiar confines of the Robin Hood, collecting up glasses was its own act of remembrance of Ellie. How many times had the two of them scooted round tidying this place up, late at night?

She shed a lonely tear or two for her friend, once she was alone. The clock ticked and it was well after midnight. The clinker shifted in the fireplace and Cathy's ears were ringing with all the music and loud chatter of the evening. When she heard someone step into the room through the back bar, she thought she was hearing things.

But she wasn't.

'Matty!' she gasped, almost dropping her dustpan in shock. 'You shouldn't be in here!'

He looked a real picture to her. A proper sight for sore eyes. He was in that smart jacket again, with a white collarless shirt underneath. His red hair was plastered down on his head like he'd combed it with water, trying to make himself even more handsome for her.

'I couldn't keep away,' he said. 'I knew what was happening here tonight. I didn't know whether to come or not . . .'

She shook her head. 'You shouldn't be here after hours.'

He burst out almost angrily, 'You've been nowhere near me! I've sent messages . . . I tried to call round. Why wouldn't you see me, Cathy?'

Her eyes widened. 'I . . . I couldn't see you. Not after what happened to Ellie.'

He lowered his gaze. 'That poor lass. But what's that got to do with seeing me?'

Her face hardened and she jutted out her chin. 'Because your brother did it. He killed her, Matty.'

He drew in his breath like she'd burned him. 'Nay, lass. That's not right. You can't mean that.'

'But I do, Matty Johnson. Your rotten brother is responsible for what became of Ellie. Whether he physically did it himself or paid someone to cut her wrists or drove her to do it herself. It's all down to that slimy fat sod.'

'Cathy, you're upset.' Matty took a step forward.

'There's been nothing from him! He didn't even send flowers!' She was getting herself upset again. 'He's wicked, Matty. He didn't care . . .'

Matty's hands reached for her. He was aching to take her in his arms. 'You don't know anything about it, lass. You don't know what went on between them. My brother's no murderer . . .'

'Isn't he?' she snapped. 'I think you're being naïve, Matty.'

'Nay, lass,' he said again, stealing closer.

There was a space between them that seemed to bristle with a live electrical charge. 'What did you come here for tonight, Matty? What were you hoping to get?'

He swallowed thickly. 'I came to see you. I knew you must be upset, and alone.'

She tossed her head defiantly and her thick hair swung about her shoulders. The motion of it made the breath catch in his throat. He stared at her dress and the paleness of her bared shoulders. 'I don't think I want to see you, Matty. I can't stomach the sight of any of your family.'

He refused to believe it. He inched closer. 'I don't think that's true. I think you've been wanting to see me. It's been tearing you up inside.'

She hesitated. 'I-I've missed you, Matty, I won't deny it.' She seemed to be fighting some kind of invisible battle with herself. 'And I won't deny that I love seeing you now. I almost forgot what it is to look at you. To talk to you. But I don't think I want to go with you anymore, Matty. I just don't . . .'

He gritted his teeth. 'But that's not fair.'

She almost laughed. 'What do you sound like? Them's like a bairn's words.'

'You can't blame me for what happened to Ellie,' he said.

'I'm not . . . I just . . .' She seemed full of thwarted desire right then. Her bonny face was twisted up with anguish.

Matty told her: 'I tell you what I think. You're punishing yourself for still being alive. You're guilty, still being here in the world when Ellie isn't. Isn't that it?'

This insight of his made Cathy gasp. She stared right into his eyes. 'I . . . Yes . . .'

'But Cathy, man. Denying yourself happiness is never gonna bring her back. Making yourself miserable and lonely is never gonna do you any good. Why are you so intent on making yourself pay? You were a good friend to her. You don't have to be unhappy . . .'

'Matty, I just . . . I don't know . . .' There! There it was! The uncertainty in her. The wrangle she was going through. It was like a chink in the armour of her defences. Matty saw it and, without thinking about it, sprang at her. She was in

306

his arms all at once, surrendering to his embrace. He clasped her to him and was almost alarmed at the heavy way she was breathing. It was like he'd pursued her across clear country and she was worn out with running.

'Oh, Cathy,' he said, and couldn't hardly hear himself talk for the pounding of blood in his ears. Suddenly the stuffy saloon bar was much too warm. Perspiration was flowing down his back. His face felt wet with it. He kissed her and the tears on her face mingled saltily with his sweat. 'Oh man, lass. I've waited and waited for this.' He snatched deep kisses, one after the next, like he was plundering her. She wriggled and moaned in his arms.

'We can't . . . not here, Matty . . .'

'Aye, but we have to,' he said urgently, pressing his face into her wonderfully fragrant hair. My God, he thought, what does she smell of? Spices? Woodsmoke? Is this the natural scent of her? He nuzzled into her pale neck and she gasped with the pleasure of it. Automatically his fingers went to work on the run of little hooks and eyes that went down the back of her velvet frock.

'You can't undress me here,' she breathed, shocked at the very thought of it.

'Where else have we got to go?' he smiled. 'Where else is there for us? We'll be okay here . . .' Now there was a devil-may-care look in his eyes. She recognised it at once. Why, it was enflaming him even more, being in this public place after dark! Kissing like mad and pulling her dress all open at the back. It was all making him hotter than ever, doing it in a place he shouldn't. He was huffing and panting like a stallion. She could picture the steam and the froth of sweat on his bare hide . . .

His strong hands went round her thighs and he half lifted, half pushed her backwards towards the Women's Table. 'You *can't!*' she said, almost laughing. But he picked her up and laid her down on the table in all the beer spills by the fire. He towered over her with shadows licking at him and his expression was a strange blend of emotions. He looked almost angry as he studied her. He reached out and pulled at her loosened dress.

Now she didn't resist or protest. She let him bare her breasts and was proud to be seen by him in the firelight.

His breath seemed to go still within him. When he spoke again, his voice sounded darker and deeper than she'd ever heard it. This was right. This was it. This was just the moment she wanted. 'I'm going to have you right now, Cathy,' he told her. 'Is that okay? I'm going to have you at last.'

She smiled at him, feeling nothing but bold and joyous and ready. 'Ha'way, then,' she said challengingly.

He dropped his smart jacket to the spit and sawdust floor. He loosened his collar and cuffs and wrenched the shirt off with one tug. His broad chest was covered in auburn curls. She had glimpsed them before, but their profusion delighted her. They went all the way down his stomach and then further.

Matty kicked off his heavy boots. Eyes locked with hers, he unbuttoned all the flies on his britches. Down they came, with very little ceremony. The crown of his thick red cock came springing up from the cup of his hands as he displayed himself proudly to her.

'Matty . . .' she said, marvelling at him, sitting up on her elbows. It was touching, the way he was showing himself off to her before they went any further. She watched him roll down and kick off all the rest of his clothes until he was completely naked. Confronting her unashamed in the golden silence of the Robin Hood.

He came to her and they were kissing again, hungrily, unstoppably. He pulled at the dress to get it off her. His hands were up inside the skirts but his fingers on her bare flesh felt nothing like they had, that cold night under the arches. This time they were welcome. He was welcome doing all of this. A low, delighted animal groan escaped her parted lips.

He reached for her and she felt his clever fingers slip inside her. Her thighs tautened. 'Now,' she hissed. 'Matty, I don't care about anything. Just do it now.' She surprised him by grasping his hard cock in one hand and guiding it to her, pressing its tip into her.

'Oh, Cathy . . .' he moaned.

He was hardly all the way inside her before there came a great crash from the bar. There was a huge cry of rage.

They both froze in that instant of bliss. They knew they were caught.

'*You . . . filthy . . . bastards . . .!*'

It was Noel. Of course, it was Noel.

He had crept back into his pub. Through the back. Creeping silently like a disease. Like poison in the veins. Why had he been so quiet? Did he know he'd be surprising a scene he wasn't supposed to witness?

He was there. He was ashen with shock. His mouth was slack with horror. But his eyes had dancing points of light. Glee and delight. Cathy saw those lights. She saw his wicked pleasure as she hoisted herself up. She didn't even cover her breasts. She was so shocked by the moment she simply lay there. She felt Matty go out of her, shrivelled and alarmed. He pulled back, still looking magnificent in the firelight. Her Matty! Naked and appalled, caught at the very moment of his triumph!

'I should thrash you both,' Noel growled at them. He had the broom in his hands, as if he intended to do just that.

Cathy came to her senses somewhat, pulling her dress back over her nakedness. She was damned if she was letting him get a longer look at her!

309

'Get your things, you!' Noel shouted at Matty. 'Get your filthy rags back on!'

Matty didn't hurry. He dressed himself with no undue haste. He stared back defiantly at Noel the whole time. 'Don't blame the lass,' he said at last. 'Don't sack her. She loves her job here.'

The landlord of the Robin Hood sneered at the lad, taking great delight in watching him struggle into his breeks. 'Ah, shut your gob, you. Who are you to tell me what to do? Dirty animal. How dare you tell me anything? With your mucky arse out in my pub! How dare you?' Then he glanced at Cathy, who had got up from the table now and was retreating across the room, shrinking like a shadow in the dawn. 'And you! Behaving like a *whore*! After we've been mourning and thinking about Ellie!'

Matty pulled on his jacket. He jammed his feet into his boots without fussing with the laces. 'Leave her alone, Noel. Like I say, it wasn't her fault.'

Cathy wasn't having this. 'Nay, Matty. It was both of us. We both wanted it. We couldn't stop ourselves.' She glared at Noel. Suddenly she felt spiteful with frustration. 'Do you hear me, Noel? We couldn't help ourselves. We had to have each other. Do you know what that's like? Do you even know what such a thing feels like?'

He stared back at her, eyes wide like he could hardly believe she would be so cruel. Taunting him! Her who'd had all her breasts hanging out just moments ago. Daring to ask him if he knew how desire felt!

'You cruel and nasty lass,' he growled at her. Then he threw down the broom with a clatter.

'Get home, Matty,' Cathy told her fella.

'Are you going to be safe with him?' He jerked his head at the distraught Noel. There was contempt in his handsome face.

Why, I'm used to feeling the whole world's contempt, aren't I, Noel thought miserably. He felt like he was sinking into a morass of despair. There in his own bar, in the very heart of his world. This dirty pair had ruined it all! They had made the place stink with the spice of their sweat and their sex!

'Of course she'll be safe with me,' Noel said harshly. 'It's you she wasn't safe with.'

Matty glared at him coldly. 'What's that supposed to mean?'

Ah, but then a crafty look came over Noel's grotesque features. He glanced at Cathy. A calculating look lit up his bright blue eyes. He was going to offer a way out. He was going to cover her shame. Why, he was offering her the hand of forgiveness really. And this is how he did it: 'He was attacking you, wasn't he, Cathy? That's what was happening here?'

Both Cathy and Matty stared at the little man in horror.

'What?' Matty growled.

'No!' Cathy burst. 'No, that's not true!'

Suddenly Noel was excited. He gabbled at them: 'Yes, yes! I walked into a terrible scene! I caught you! I made you break off! Cathy, Cathy lass, I saved you, didn't I?'

She shook her head, appalled by his words. 'No, Noel!'

Noel looked very pleased with himself as he told them: 'He was *raping* you, Cathy. That's what I came in and saw tonight. I stopped him! Why, I think I might have saved your life, girl! You should thank me!'

'My God, you're mad!' Matty shouted.

'It wasn't rape,' Cathy protested. 'Can't you understand? I wanted him! I wanted him to do it!'

There was a beat of heavy silence. 'Oh, really?' Noel asked. 'But if you'd wanted it, that would make you a wanton. A whore. A jezebel. I couldn't have one of those working for me. Sleeping under my roof. I just couldn't, don't you see? And if the whole town knew you were tupping some lad like this and doing all the filthy things with him . . . Well, your life would be ruined round here, wouldn't it? If word got out? If they all knew just how slack and easy and rotten you are?'

Matty took an angry step towards him. 'You little bastard . . .' he began, and Noel darted back behind his bar.

'Get away from here, Matty Johnson!' he jeered mockingly. 'Or else! Or else I'll let the whole town know what you were doing here tonight!'

Matty was torn. He longed to reach behind that wooden barrier and tear that little crookback limb from limb. He looked at Cathy and she had a strange look on her face. She looked defeated and exhausted. Why, that little streak of nothing had managed to get to her. She even looked ashamed. Ashamed of the pair of them and what they had been doing here tonight!

Matty felt like roaring with frustrated anger.

Noel told him: 'If you don't get out of here now, I'm going to tell all the world that you were taking her by force. I'm going to say to all and sundry that you was raping her!'

There was a moment's agonised pause. Matty exchanged a terrible glance with Cathy. Something horrible had happened here. Noel had cankered everything between them.

Matty turned on his heel and hurried out of that place. He thundered off into the darkness and the night.

Noel was left looking at Cathy, who was silent.

She looked so defeated and lost.

'Ah, now, pet,' he said. 'Don't be upset. He's gone now. He's ran away. He can't get at you anymore.'

Chapter 41

Cathy slept through much of the following morning.

She woke in her darkened room at the front of the house and, as the events of the previous evening came back to her, she let out a groan.

It had all gone so horrible wrong.

Matty! Matty storming off into the night.

She had stood there covered in stale beer spills from lying on the Women's Table. Her face was burning bright with fury and firelight. Watching Matty go. She had never felt so close to him as she had for those precious few torrid moments. And now he was gone.

Noel Sturrock had capered like a demented goblin. He was triumphant at her upset; he was delighted at her being brought so low!

Had they even said a word to each other after Matty had charged off? She couldn't remember. There was a roaring in her ears, like all she could hear was the angry turbulence of the sea.

She had made her way back here. To the place she laughingly called home. How could she ever be settled here again?

Everything had gone wrong.

She felt heavy and achy. She hadn't had enough sleep. She felt like she hadn't had enough sleep for years.

Oh, but part of her could still remember what Matty had looked like. What he had felt like. That part of her still felt lit up and excited. That part of her didn't give a hoot about that sneaky, perverse Noel and what he had said. What kind of a man was he, that he came bursting in and gloried in wrenching two lovers violently apart?

She washed herself in cold water from the jug by the window and pulled on a skirt and jumper, hardly looking at what she was choosing. Downstairs there was Noel and his mother to face.

What on earth was she going to say for herself?

Noel would be bound to rub things in . . . He would delight in making it all worse, of course.

But, as ever, these things had to be faced up to. Cathy squared her shoulders and lifted up her chin. She had never been a coward. She refused to be ashamed of herself.

And she was alive, wasn't she? Ellie Mackenzie no longer had the chance to make a fool of herself, or to make trouble for anyone. Poor Ellie would no longer ever make love to anyone. But here Cathy was, and she was alive! And, by God, she wasn't going to live her life feeling ashamed of anything.

Downstairs Teresa was solicitous and kind. She fussed around bringing tea, treating Cathy like she was made out of fine china.

'Where's Noel?'

'Nipped out early.' Teresa bit her lip and she spooned out extra sugar into the hot tea. 'He told me, Cathy. He said what went on.'

'Oh,' Cathy said, and sipped her tea, biding her time. She almost gagged at the sweetness of it.

'Oh, you poor girl,' Teresa shook her head. 'You should get the polis in. Get the Johnson lad reported. He must be like an animal! A monster!'

Cathy frowned and shook her head, trying to clear it of confusion. 'What? Who?' But her thoughts caught up just a moment later. Of course. Matty. Noel had already started spreading his poison, beginning with his own mother.

'Eeeh, love, it's not your fault,' Teresa sighed. 'Some men are just brutes like that. And I know you thought something of your Matty. Eeeh, what a terrible thing.'

Cathy lowered her eyes. 'Is this what Noel told you?'

'He said he saw it all.' The old woman's face was twisted in mingled pity and disgust. 'He walked in at just the right moment. To save you . . .'

Cathy shook her head slowly, marvelling at the gall of the man. 'Aye, I guess he'd tell you that.'

'But Cathy lass, you mustn't be ashamed. There was nothing you could do, was there? You were just unlucky. Thank God my son was there for you. See? I told you, didn't I? I always told you he was devoted to you. He'd do anything for you, Cathy!' Teresa's voice was quavering. She was getting emotional as she counselled her friend. 'You must never think that this . . . thing . . . that happened last night would lower your value in Noel's eyes. He still feels the same way about you, even after that. And even after knowing about, you know, your secret bairn as well . . . I'm sure he does feel the same way about you, even with all of that . . .'

The girl had to turn away, feeling her gorge rise. This was all so twisted up. Everything was topsy-turvy. She was so tired and upset she could hardly even tell which way was up or down anymore.

She needed to get out of here. She needed to talk to a friend.

Sofia listened with huge, sympathetic eyes.

They sat together at the Franchino dining-room table and talked late that morning. 'We'll have mama's limoncello,' Sofia said. 'It's good for shock.'

'Is it?' Cathy asked.

'It's strong,' Sofia said.

She was trying to take in the story that Cathy had been telling her. Part of her was very shocked at the way Cathy had surrendered herself to Matty. She was amazed that her friend would be so brazen and sinful. She held her tongue and listened carefully, trying not to betray her discomfort.

When it came to the part about Noel's bursting in and everything he'd shouted at them, Sofia looked even more shocked.

'That must have been terrible!'

'It wasn't my finest hour,' Cathy admitted.

'And Matty just ran out of there?'

'What was he going to do? Noel had him tied up in knots of words. He was threatening both of us.' She found her own words sticking in her throat. 'What am I going to do, Sofia? I don't know what to do. Noel's gone and told his mam that Matty attacked me. He'll be spreading that story all around the town . . .'

'I reckon he will,' Sofia said. 'And you know, it might be the easy way out for you. For your reputation.'

Cathy looked scandalised. 'Sofia, man, no! And what then? Let everyone think that poor lad is a rapist?'

Sofia poured them another tot of medicinal liqueur. 'Maybe that's for the best, Cathy?'

'What?!'

'What have those Mad Johnsons ever done for you, Cathy? What good has ever come from being involved with them? This should teach you forever, I should think. Let the world think he took advantage of you. And you'll be in the clear. You can move on with your life.'

Cathy could hardly believe what her friend was saying to her. 'I don't think you understand what I've been telling you. I wanted him, Sofia. I still want him.'

'Do you? Do you really want to be part of that family? Them who murdered Ellie?'

Horror and confusion slammed into Cathy's mind once more. She had an almost instant headache as she tried to think it through. At one level she knew that Sofia was talking sense. Or at least, she was reminding her of truths she had set aside.

'It was Alec who did for Ellie. Matty is a good man, I'm sure of it,' Cathy insisted.

Sofia looked dubious. To her, a good man would never have behaved like Matty had last night! He'd had his wicked way with Cathy in the middle of the empty pub! Sofia could still hardly believe it.

'I have to see him,' Cathy suddenly said. 'I have to talk to Matty.'

'Maybe you should leave it a day or two . . .'

Cathy shook her head, getting up woozily. 'No. If Noel is putting these lies out there and telling the whole town, Matty will think I'm just letting him do it. He'll think badly of me, I know it. I need to see him today. I have to go over to Tudor Avenue.'

Sofia watched her turn to go. She jumped to her feet. 'I can't let you go over there alone.'

Cathy was relieved to have moral support. 'What about the kids?'

'Mama's got them today. She knew I'd be tired after working last night. I've got a free afternoon.'

So it was decided. They would take the trolley car across to that insalubrious part of town. Sofia would accompany her friend into that dark place. Sofia could hardly believe her own bravery. But, like Cathy, she was good at facing up to things. She was good at facing her fears. She had to prove to herself that the Johnson clan didn't scare her like they did her Tonio.

The trolley bus rattled and jangled through the busy back streets of town. The two women didn't talk much aside from asking the clippie for tickets. There were too many folk pressed close by for them to continue their conversation. What they had to talk about was too intimate and shocking for public discussion.

At last they arrived at the stop by the park next to Tudor Avenue. Cathy's unerring sense of direction led her straight to the correct door.

'It looks like a proper midden,' Sofia said, frowning slightly as she thought of the right word.

'Aye, it does,' Cathy agreed. Then she rapped loudly on the front door. She was trying not to remember the last time she had been here. She was trying her best not to think about poor Ellie standing there in the lobby, hiding her broken arm. Looking so brave and pathetic as she pulled at her sleeve, denying there was anything at all wrong with her. But Cathy had known the truth! She had known that Ellie was lying to herself and covering up damage and hurt . . .

Oh God, Cathy thought. Maybe Sofia is quite right. No good can ever come from getting mixed up with the Mad Johnson boys. It's true, isn't it?

There came a clatter from the inside of the door then and it creaked open abruptly. A huge, broad figure stood revealed in the frame. It was Jan, the middle brother. The one who barely ever said a word; the one that the brothers hardly even treated as human.

'We need to see Matty,' Cathy spoke up boldly. 'Is he in?'

Jan's brow furrowed as he processed her request. 'Aye. He's in his room. He was out late. He's tired.'

'Aye, we know he was out late,' Cathy said. 'Can we come in?'

The man mountain at the front door looked bewildered. House guests hardly ever came calling at the Johnson house. The clan was fiercely private. No one who wasn't family came in through those doors. His brows knitted together in consternation. 'Why?' he asked.

'On account of we want to see him!' Cathy burst out. 'Can't you just let us in?'

For a moment Jan looked stricken and anguished. He simply didn't know what to do. His whole life he had been conditioned to believe that his home was sacrosanct. It was his family's castle and outsiders must never be admitted. He was used to hiding things and keeping secrets, even when he didn't understand what those secrets were, or why they must be kept hidden. Cathy's forthright request had knocked him sideways.

'Jan?' came an imperious, squawking voice from the direction of the living room. 'Who's out there, man? What are you doing? You're letting a bloody awful draught get into the house!'

'It's a lass,' Jan shouted back. He grunted at Cathy. 'What did you say you were called?'

Cathy told him, and the message was relayed to the old woman in her dark sitting room. 'Oh, let her in,' Gracie Johnson bellowed. 'Don't leave her standing out there.'

Jan behaved like a gigantic, mute butler, as if he was working in a grand stately home. Cathy followed him into the Johnson house, sparing a glance and a reassuring nod for Sofia, who felt terribly nervous entering her enemies' den.

'Ah, Cathy, love,' said the old woman. 'It's been too long since you were round.' Gracie was in her nightdress again, all ribbons and lace. Sofia stiffened and stared goggle-eyed at the old woman.

Cathy's voice didn't return the old woman's warmth. 'I wanted to come over. But I couldn't. I just couldn't, not after Ellie.'

The old woman stared straight into Cathy's eyes and asked, 'Who?'

Cathy could hardly believe it. 'Ellie! The girl who was my friend . . . She's . . . she's died.'

'Oh,' said Gracie. Her nose wrinkled as if she'd caught a whiff of something unpleasant. 'The one Alec was knocking around with. Yes, I heard she'd come to a bad end. Alec was distraught, of course.'

Cathy couldn't believe it. 'He was, was he?'

'Why, of course he was! He thought a lot of her. Though I don't know why. But love is a mysterious thing, isn't it?'

The two visitors stared at the grotesque old woman and they could barely credit the incongruity of her going on about the nature of love. What could she know about such things? She was a heartless, nasty old beast.

'Ellie was my friend,' Cathy said. 'And she only came to a bad end because she was mixed up with your son.'

The old woman laughed. 'You might believe that, but you'd be hard pushed to prove it. Look, girl. She was just a strumpet. You know she was. She took handouts from our Alec. He looked after her. She put herself into that position. No one forced her.'

Cathy stepped closer to the horrible woman. She could see the flecks of spittle on her chin and the peeling make-up on her face, like a clown's almost. 'She was my friend. And I know . . . I just know that your Alec killed her.'

Suddenly all of Cathy's thoughts about Matty and herself and their situation had fled. Her mind was focused absolutely on poor Ellie. All she could think about was how they had mourned her last night. Her hangover right now felt like a nauseating reminder that Ellie's life had been wasted and she was never coming back. And it was all because of these people – Gracie Johnson and her wicked kin!

'Killed her!' the old woman hooted with laughter. 'Why would he go to all that effort? Yes, he wanted rid of her. That was no secret, nor no surprise. But our Alec's clever. He wouldn't dirty his own hands with that trollop's blood. He'd let her do it to herself and then he was free, wasn't he? He didn't want her hanging round his neck, and who would? She was an albatross, that one! She was a fat old bucktoothed tart, that's all she was!'

Sofia let out a cry of surprise then, as Cathy burst into violent life. She simply couldn't help herself. Even Cathy hadn't known what she was going to do. In the next few seconds there were cries of confusion and terror from all sides as Cathy launched herself at Gracie.

'Cathy, no!' Sofia cried, horrified.

Jan came lumbering forward with a shout of rage.

But he couldn't even get close for a few moments. Spitting with rage, Cathy had flown at the old woman in her armchair and sent it tumbling backwards. Now they were just a struggling, shrieking mass of lace and pale pink blankets.

Gracie was shrieking and thrashing around, her voice emerging in a panicked gurgle. Cathy had her skinny throat in both hands.

Sofia was over there faster than Jan and she could plainly see what was happening on the front room floor. Her friend was coldly and deliberately throttling the life out of old Ma Johnson.

Chapter 42

It was all too easy. It would take just the tiniest bit more effort.
All she had to do was squeeze her fingers a bit harder, until she
felt that old woman's throat constricting and her fists would
close almost completely around it. That's how easy it would be
to finish her off.

Gracie wasn't putting up any kind of fight now. All her
strength had gone out of her and she was lying still in all her
bedclothes. There were shouts and screams all around, filling
up the room, but Cathy couldn't hear a word of it. She was
intent on what her hands were doing.

'Cathy, man, no!' Sofia was pulling at her shoulders. 'You're
not to kill her! They'll hang you!'

She couldn't make any sense out of Cathy's words. Their
import had nothing to do with what she was trying to get done.
She just had to stop this callous old woman saying horrible
things and then the world would be a much better place. That's
all there was to it.

The lumbering Jan was trying to get hold of her too. He
made a strangely high-pitched noise of distress and his massive
hands clamped over Cathy's. But he couldn't stop those hands
squeezing.

'No, Cathy!'

There was one voice that cut through her madness, however. He shouted from the doorway and the beloved familiarity of his voice brought her to her senses.

'What? Matty?' she gasped, and suddenly let the old woman drop like a dead weight into the mound of lace and knitted woollens.

Matty was over there in a flash, inspecting his poor mother. 'Mam? Are you all right?' But his mother was insensible. Her eyes were squeezed shut in pain and her whole face looked closed in and unreachable. Was she dead already? Her son lifted her up and shook her gently. 'Mam, wake up!'

Sofia took hold of Cathy, who was dumbfounded with shock at what she had done. 'Cathy, come away. Let's go over here, away from her . . .'

The giant Jan let them go. His attention was on the tiny, crumpled figure of his mother and his brother's attempts to revive her.

'Cathy, what were you doing?' Sofia gasped. 'You could have killed her!'

'I wanted to!' Cathy gasped vehemently. 'By God, I really wanted to!'

'Hush now,' Sofia urged her. 'Don't go saying that. They'll have you carted off if anyone hears you saying that.'

'The world would be better off without her and all her clan,' Cathy said, and even she was horrified at the harshness of her tone. It felt like she was watching the whole scene from above, quite removed from herself. She felt distant and fearless as she observed Matty gently patting his mother's face until she revived. She drew in a strangled, painful breath and her two lads hoisted her back into her chair.

Then Matty was turning to the two lasses. His face was pale with shock and his words came out raggedly, like he was fighting for his breath. 'What's been going on here? What were you trying to do?'

Cathy stared at him. She locked eyes with him and almost lost her composure. In that moment she just wanted him to take her in his arms again and tell her that everything was all right. She wanted to beg forgiveness off him; say it had all been a mistake. She would have said anything to make things right again between them.

But how could that ever happen? She had tried to strangle his mam!

Now Gracie was coughing and spluttering. She was less purple in the face. It was clear that she was going to be all right.

'I just came here for a talk,' said Cathy. 'I came to see you, Matty. But then there was talk about poor Ellie . . . and your mother, she . . .' Cathy was sobbing by the time she struggled through what she wanted to say. She couldn't make any of it make sense. Hysteria was rising up in her own throat and she was finding it hard to speak through it.

Matty saw things very simply. 'You tried to kill my mother, I saw you.'

Sofia had her arm around Cathy and was trying to turn her away, back to the door. 'Come on, love,' she murmured. Then she told Matty: 'I'll take her away. Out of your sight. There'll be no more trouble here . . .'

Behind Matty, Jan was standing up and his face was dark with upset. 'Aye, get her away! Get her out of here before we get our hands on her!'

Sofia had to snap back at him: 'There's always disaster when the Johnsons are involved! Someone always gets hurt!'

Matty was still fixed on Cathy. 'Why did you do it? Cathy, it was a terrible thing to do. What's my family ever done to you?'

Then there came a feeble cry from his mother on her chair. Her pudgy hands were flapping in the air. She was alive but she needed his attention. Matty turned away from Sofia and Cathy. 'You'd better go,' he told them, over his shoulder.

In that moment Cathy knew that she had ruined everything between them forever. There was no going back from this.

She remembered very little about the journey back across South Shields to the docks and home. Sofia took charge of everything and Cathy was a shambling wreck. She stared at her own hands and couldn't help thinking, in an appalled kind of way: these might have been the hands of a murderess. That old cow had been asking for it. She really had deserved it. But Cathy had completely lost her mind! She had relished the feeling of her fingers closing around that windpipe. It had felt like wrestling with that large bird in the roasting dish at Christmas; the sensation had been horribly similar.

'What was I thinking of?' she asked Sofia, in a hollow tone.

'You weren't thinking at all,' her friend told her. 'Something else took over. It was like you were possessed by rage . . . and everything else boiling up inside you. All the frustration and hurt and everything. All the frustration going back years. You almost went too far.'

Cathy glanced sideways at her friend. 'Thank you for being there. For stopping me.'

Now they were off the tram and clambering up the steepest part of Frederick Street. Somehow the horror of what had transpired was set aside, and so was their fear of what that terrible scene might incur in the future. The repercussions of the attempt on Gracie's life were something that neither girl fancied thinking about just yet. Instead a kind of hilarity took over them.

'That old monster didn't expect that!' Sofia said. 'You should have seen her face when you dived at her! Suddenly she went backwards, arse over titties with you bang on top of her!'

It was sheer hysteria and relief pouring out of her at last. Sofia couldn't help herself, starting to laugh loudly. She had to stop walking and she had tears rolling down her face.

Cathy stared at her in appalled horror. 'It's not funny!'

'It is! It is!' Sofia protested. 'If you'd seen her face! It's like she's always had her own way. No one has ever even disagreed with her! And what do you do? Jump on her and send her flying! You got her by the throat!' Now Sofia was wheezing, clutching her sides and keening with laughter. 'Oh, oh, it's too awful. I'm going to wet myself!'

Cathy was shocked. 'I can't believe you're laughing . . . laughing at . . .' But it was much too infectious for Cathy. Now she was off, as well. She picked up the Italian girl's hysterical mood and was off. She too could conjure up the outraged face of Gracie Johnson and Sofia was quite right: it was bloody funny.

'Eeeh, just imagine,' Sofia laughed, as they clutched each other and hung onto each other in the middle of the street. 'What would Ellie have said about that? Wouldn't Ellie have laughed, watching all of that carry on?'

Cathy had to agree, Ellie would have loved it.

Sofia had to get home to feed her bairns and the rest of the family.

'I'll see you tonight at the pub,' she reminded Cathy. They were both due to work together. It had slipped Cathy's mind completely. She hadn't seen Noel since that shameful scene in the saloon and she was dreading it.

Come to think of it, she hadn't been inside the pub since that business with Matty.

Was that only last night? It seemed impossibly long ago.

And she had ruined everything. It was all spoiled.

That anger! That fury! The way it had come boiling out of her. Sofia was right. It must have been waiting inside of her, waiting for its moment and the right target. She really could have murdered Gracie with her bare hands. Only Cathy knew how near she had come to doing just that, and how much she had relished that thought in the moment.

Maybe I'm really losing my marbles? she wondered as she let herself into number twenty-one.

She found Noel and his mother having an early tea at the table. Fish paste sandwiches that looked pretty unappetising to her. When Cathy wasn't around to put food on the table, the Sturrocks went back to eating any old rubbish.

They were surrounded by Teresa's cats, who were all waiting for tidbits. When Cathy entered the room, everyone looked at her expectantly.

'We wondered where you'd got to, lass,' Teresa said, getting up arthritically to fetch another cup and saucer for her.

'We were worried,' Noel said. There was concern in his voice, but he didn't quite meet her eye.

'I . . . I went out with Sofia for the afternoon.' Cathy took her place at the table.

'Oh aye, that's a good idea,' Teresa said, pouring her a very stewed-looking cup of tea. 'Getting some fresh air, eh?'

Cathy smiled awkwardly.

There was a pause as they looked at their cups and the bland sandwiches. A look went between mother and son and Noel cleared his throat. 'Look, lass. I said some unfortunate things last night at the pub. I was upset, naturally, and some things came out wrong.'

Cathy stared at him across the messy table. She kept her mouth shut, unsure of where he was going with this. She wasn't going to make it easier for him, either.

'Cathy,' he sighed. 'I would never say anything to upset you. I'd never say anything against you. I think you're a smashing lass, you know that.' Teresa seemed to nod in satisfaction as he said this, as if she had coached him in what to say. He went on: 'Now, I think we're all agreed about what went on in the

Robin Hood last night. It was a terrible scene. That lad . . . that animal . . . he tried to do something absolutely disgusting and brutal to you, didn't he?'

Cathy took a sip of tea. Its bitter tang was really awful. She didn't say anything, or nod or respond in any way to what Noel was saying. She let him continue.

'He almost had his way with you. He almost ruined you, lass. But then, I came in, didn't I? I interrupted everything just in time. He had to stop. And you were saved, weren't you?'

Both Noel and Teresa were staring at her now. Cathy locked eyes with both of them, and understood what Noel was getting at. In his own clumsy, selfish way, he believed he was being subtle. Maybe he was. Cathy hardly knew anymore. All she knew now was that she was being offered an olive branch – of sorts.

If she agreed to Noel's version of things, then she could stay here. Life would go on as normal. She would have a roof and a bed and a job and a family of sorts. All she had to do was agree that she had been attacked by Matty. She had to deny him. She had to abandon any hope of ever being with him.

Or she could tell the truth.

But it was too late for that, wasn't it?

Matty was never going to want her now. She had gone to see him, hoping they could still be together. Hoping that they might run away together, even.

But there was absolutely no hope. Not now.

Cathy set her teacup down and sighed. 'Thank you, Noel. Teresa. Thank you both. I don't know what I'd do without you. You're like my family, aren't you? My true family. I've done nothing but bring trouble to your door . . .'

'Nay, lass,' Teresa protested. 'We love you. Don't we, Noel? We love the bones of the lass.'

'Aye,' he said. 'We do. And I'm so proud that I was able to save your honour last night. It's the proudest moment of my life!'

'Thank you, Noel,' Cathy told him.

Oh, but she felt cold inside. Why, in one afternoon she had narrowly avoided being a murderess. And now she was a cold-hearted liar. What kind of an awful person was she turning into?

Chapter 43

'And the latest that I've heard is that he was told by his mother to get to Newcastle to oversee bits of their business over that way, in the big city.' This was Winnie, gossiping at the Women's Table at the Robin Hood. She leaned forward confidingly to inform Cathy of the latest news about Matty Johnson, but Cathy was in two minds whether she even wanted to hear it or not. 'It sounds like she's just got him out of the way,' Winnie went on. 'Out of sight, out of mind.'

'Aye,' smiled Cathy tightly, and put all of the women's empty glasses onto her tray. 'Well, he's a grown man. He can choose where he wants to live.'

'Naw, he's doing exactly what his hateful old mother is telling him. Just like all them Mad Johnson boys.' Winnie glugged down the froth of her milk stout and plonked her empty onto Cathy's brass tray. 'There you go. I know how fond you were of him, hinny. But you're best off cutting him out of your heart completely. From what I hear tell, he's taken up with some rich widow woman in Newcastle. Soon as he got there! He's not daft, eh?'

Cathy felt a pang, somewhere in the region of her heart, at the very idea of Matty taking up with someone else, just these scant few weeks since she had last seen him. Oh, she had done her best to push him out of her thoughts, and mostly she had succeeded. She knew it was all hopeless now.

Maybe in a while, she kept thinking to herself. If she let some water go under the bridge? Maybe one day they'd find themselves washed up together in the endless ebb and flow? They'd remember what they had once been to each other?

But that was a fool's game, she knew. And she knew that Matty and his entire family would never forgive her for trying to throttle the life out of his rancid old mother. Just as she would never really forgive any of them for what had become of poor Ellie.

It was a really tangled web and she didn't want to hear about any further knots. Certainly not entanglements with rich widows in Newcastle. She wouldn't relish hearing any more from that gleeful mixer, Winnie.

'Same again, lasses?' she asked the Women's Table. It was a quiet Thursday night and Cathy was content to wait on them during a lull in the evening.

There was the usual gaggle of women by the fire: Teresa, Ada Farley, Winnie, and Sofia's mama. The small group had become a regular fixture and Cathy felt obscurely proud of making them feel so welcome here and strengthening the bond between them.

Returning to the bar, she let Sofia pour their pints. In her few weeks of practise, the Italian girl had become a dab hand at the beer pumps.

'Winnie's still going on about Matty and telling me stuff,' Cathy groaned.

'Just tell her that you've moved on,' Sofia said. 'Tell her you don't want to know anything about it.'

Cathy nodded, but a part of her really did want to keep on hearing about Matty.

She returned with the tray of fresh drinks and grinned at them all with a cheeriness she didn't quite feel. 'These ones are on the house!' she told them.

The women whooped at this, but Teresa looked worried. 'Eeeh, lass! Whatever will Noel say, with you giving away all his drink?'

'Ah, he can afford it, the old bugger. I saw him counting out all his paper money from the till a little while ago,' Cathy chuckled, swishing her velvet skirts as she moved away.

'That one!' she heard Teresa tell the others. 'She behaves like this whole place belongs to her! She's like the queen of the Robin Hood, ain't she? Mind, I don't notice my son complaining much . . .'

That was a point. Where *was* Noel? He'd been at the bar with them, not ten minutes since.

Cathy found him through the back.

He had company.

'Oh, er, Cathy lass . . .' he said. His voice was high and strange with nervousness. She had never heard him sound like that before.

He was in the stockroom, where it was dingy, smelly and cold. There were two fellas with him. He must have let them quietly in through the back door and they were supposed to be delivering crates of bottles. Nothing so unusual there, then. Money was changing hands. A great thick wodge of paper notes was being passed from Noel to the shorter of the two men.

Alec Johnson.

Cathy realised that she was holding in her breath. It was like her body just refused to breathe.

That balding, tubby little twerp of a man. He was there in his serge green suit and his mustard-coloured waistcoat. He was red in face from exertion, from carrying in those cartons of glinting bottles. When he saw Cathy standing there, he gave a smile that was more like a hideous sneer. 'Oh, hello there,

Missy. Nice to see you again. I see you've filled out a little. What a lovely figure you have.'

Cathy flushed scarlet as she felt his unwanted attention crawling all over her. 'Noel,' she said, and her own voice sounded odd to her. 'Are you really still doing business with this horrible man? After everything that's happened?'

Noel looked ashamed, as well he might. He hung his head and murmured: 'I've nay choice, lass. They've got all the power. I *have* to buy from them.'

'You don't have to do anything you don't want to,' Cathy snapped, bridling at his weakness. 'Just think about what he's responsible for. Just think about our lovely Ellie!'

But Noel stood there frozen, like a little boy getting told off by his mammy. He was hopeless.

Cathy was left to face Alec alone. And by, she could have turned on him and scratched his eyes out. He'd have been no match for her. But he had a great big looming figure beside him. A man who stood taller even than his brothers Matty or Jan. Smugly, Alec saw her take note of his massive companion.

'Ah, you'll not have met my Uncle Jed, will you? He's helping me out. He's from Newcastle. He's standing in for our Matty. Say hello to Cathy, Uncle Jed. She's the nasty little bitch who almost strangled your big sister, Gracie.'

Uncle Jed took a step forward into the light and Cathy gasped in dismay.

He was huge and grey-faced and terrifying. But what was more, he was wearing a large-brimmed fedora.

'You're the man in the black hat!'

Alec Johnson frowned at her. 'What are you on about?'

The giant in the hat growled. His voice seemed to begin right down in his boots. 'What are you talking about?'

They were interrupted all of a sudden by Sofia, appearing in the lit doorway. 'Cathy, what are you doing back here? I—'

And then she stood there, transfixed. She was appalled and terrified at the sight of the man in that hat.

'Oh my God,' she said. 'It is *him*.'

Cathy had never heard such fatalistic dread in anyone's voice before.

'What are you two on about?' Noel hissed.

'That's what I'd like to know, too,' Alec frowned. 'Uncle Jed, do you know these two?'

Uncle Jed shook his massive head. 'Nuh-huh.'

'But it is *you*!' Sofia was behaving like she was seeing a terrible phantom. 'You have plagued us for years! I saw you. My mother saw you. You are dogging our footsteps. You will destroy us!'

The slab-faced Johnson uncle looked confused. 'I don't even know you.'

'Are you Italian?' Sofia asked. Then she slipped into some fluid, gabbly language that Cathy didn't understand. It was Neapolitan dialect and left the huge man looking more perplexed than ever.

'What's wrong with the girl?' Alec asked Cathy.

'It's a vendetta,' Cathy said. 'She thinks he's come all the way from Naples to get her and her family.'

'What?' Alec barked out with laughter. 'I've never heard the like! Our Uncle Jed's from Jesmond! Why, coming here's the furthest he's ever been in his life!'

Sofia seemed to take in the import of his words. 'So he's not Italian?'

'He's not the man, Sofia,' Cathy told her. She was glad but impatient with the girl. 'You've just been seeing some bloke from Jesmond going around the town in a big hat.'

'What?' They were all amazed then, as Sofia cracked the tense scene by laughing helplessly, almost hysterically. 'All that worry! All the sleepless nights I've had! Thinking we were

334

finished! Thinking that we'd have to run away – again!' She looked appalled and delighted and relieved, all at the same time. 'It was all for nothing! He is just some bloke! From Jesmond! Who happens to have a hat!' She shook her head at her own craziness. 'Oh, wait till Nonna hears about this.'

Noel was staring at his two barmaids in amazement. 'You're both absolutely crazy.'

'Perhaps we are!' Cathy tossed her headful of dark auburn curls at him, then turned to the Mad Johnsons with renewed defiance. 'Well, if you're about finished with your business here, I suggest the two of you go and bugger off into the night, hey? We don't want your sort here.'

But Uncle Jed's massive feet stayed planted on the stone floor. A conniving look came over Alec's rat-like face. 'Oh, we aren't quite done yet, are we?'

'We aren't?' Noel asked nervously. 'Ah, come on, lads. I paid you top whack for those bottles. I paid over the odds. Everything I can spare! I don't even need thirty bottles of spirits. They'll last me a year! What else do you want from me, Alec? Just leave us all in peace, eh?'

Alec took his time. He fetched out a cigar and toyed with it. 'There are still scores to settle, I think.'

Cathy stared at his piggy eyes and realised what he was getting at. Her bowels turned to water. There was violence in the air. This man was getting excited at the very thought of it. She watched as he snipped the end from his cigar and lit it, pompously, puffing away. In a mild, almost disinterested voice, he told his uncle: 'Smash all the bottles, would you?'

Uncle Jed grinned. It was a ghastly sight. 'The ones we brought tonight?'

'Aye, those first. Then all of the rest of them. Everything in here. And then break open the beer barrels. Spill everything out!'

'No!' Noel screeched, flinging himself forward. It was as if he were being propelled by an invisible force. 'No, you can't!' He was prepared to fight tooth and nail to protect his beloved pub.

'Smash them, Uncle Jed!' shouted Alec, and Jed had already produced a nasty-looked metal rod from inside his long coat. He swung it round like he was playing golf, knocking the hanging light so that all the shadows tilted joltingly back and forth. With destructive glee the massive man started laying into the bottles of whisky, brandy and rum they had transported here so carefully tonight. The noise was shocking and seemingly endless.

Noel was howling with protest the whole time as the spirits gushed and flowed. Cathy tried to grab him, to stop him flinging himself desperately in the path of the remorseless Uncle Jed. The cruel, twisted end of the crowbar flew up again and again, and it was a miracle it never caught Noel in the face as he tried to throw himself onto it, to protect his assets.

Alec was laughing uproariously at the whole scene. 'And when you've smashed everything, Uncle Jed, break this hunchback's arms and legs, would you? The little bastard's getting on my nerves.'

In his distress Noel hardly heard what Alec was saying. But Cathy did. She knew they were all in terrible danger from these men. 'Sofia!' she screamed at her friend. 'Go and get help!'

In all the chaos and the mess, the men hadn't noticed that the Italian girl had backed her way instinctively to the stockroom door. She was open-mouthed with shock. Her ears were ringing with the hideous sound of breaking glass.

She turned to go.

And was met by four wild, worried faces.

They had come to see what all the perishing noise was about.

'Here, what's going on?' cried Ada Farley, appalled by the sight that greeted them as they arrived at the stockroom door.

It was the women from the Women's Table. Ada, Winnie, Nonna and Teresa.

This made Alec Johnson laugh even harder. 'What use are you old biddies going to be? Against us fellas, eh? You haven't got a hope in hell, have you?'

Chapter 44

But they did have a hope in hell, it turned out.

'Eeeh, man! Did you see us! Did you see what we did?' Ada Farley was amazed. She thought she was dreaming. She supped from a full pint of stout and struggled to get her breath back. 'Why, we proper fettled them two rough buggers, didn't we?'

The other women could hardly disagree. They all sat by the fire in the quiet pub in a stunned silence.

'That's learned them a lesson and no mistake,' said Winnie.

'And if they come back again,' muttered Nonna grimly, cradling her deadly walking stick. 'We'll give it to them all over again.'

Cathy was providing her startled heroines with free drinks in the aftermath of the Mad Johnsons' suddenly departure. As the glasses clinked and the dark beer was triumphantly consumed, she was still struggling to take in what had happened.

How had they gone from terror and despair to this?

Why, one minute that vicious ginger Alec was sneering in triumph. He was telling them he was going to break all their arms and legs. And that ghoulish-looking uncle was glaring at them hungrily like he was prepared to eat the lot of them, like an ogre in fedora.

Then the women came dashing in and they were furious. Nothing would stand in their way. Even if that fella was seven foot tall and armed with a crowbar, he was still no match for the women of Frederick Street.

They were united and undaunted. It was as if all the fear, frustration and worry of the past few months had mounted up and up inside their hearts and souls. It was like all that exhausted, bitter, pent-up emotion came pouring out of them in one great big tidal wave. They screeched and hurtled across the room in the direction of their friends' assailants. Noel Sturrock was flung aside to safety as the older women flurried through the stockroom like a flock of harpies from the old Greek legend. They were all claws and wicked talons, intent on ripping their enemies into bloody shreds.

The Johnsons were so surprised that they simply stood there, unable to defend themselves. That wicked crowbar was plucked from Uncle Jed's tight grasp and chucked into a corner.

Later it was jokingly said that what had aggravated the women into such a state of primal fury was seeing the waste of all that booze. Oh, they had a good laugh about that one! And it was true that the sweet smell of spoiled booze was sickly and pervasive. But Cathy knew that what really spurred the women into action was their seeing Noel, Sofia and herself in need of help. The older women rose up as one and came dashing in to save their souls, and Cathy had never been as glad to see anyone in all her life.

Alec shrank back instinctively as Nonna Franchino lashed out with her cane. He had a vivid memory of just how that had felt. Ada Farley's large, strong hands – veterans of a thousand and one wash-days at the tub and the mangle – closed around Alec's lapels and she shook him hard like she would an errant lad of her own. Winnie swung the handbag that contained her portable crystal ball and it connected heavily with Uncle Jed's colossal knackers. The giant thug from Newcastle howled with pain and it was wonderful to hear!

Teresa Sturrock didn't manage to land many punches but she jumped up and down and hollered and whooped in the most blood-curdling way. 'This is for Ellie Mackenzie!' she screeched at the top of her voice, and then added a few truly filthy words that she would never admit to even knowing.

Cathy had watched in astonished joy as the two men turned frantically towards the back door and tumbled out into the cobbled lane.

How the women laughed to see them go!

'Aye, and don't bloody bother coming back!' Sofia shouted after them.

As they sat at the Women's Table, chewing over their triumph and laughingly congratulating themselves, Nonna Franchino was wearing a strange look. 'So that man in the black hat was not the man we thought?'

'No, Mama, we both mistook that giant great galoot from Newcastle for the man in our nightmares.'

Nonna tossed her head and clucked out tongue. 'How stupid we are. To lie awake with nightmares and dread! Thinking our lives are over! Our happiness is finished! Just because we have thought we were menaced by a single man. And in the end it was just a hat! Just a hat!'

For some reason, this plangent lament struck all the other women as very funny. The ancient Italian woman looked piqued as they laughed at her. 'I will bray you all with my walking stick!' she warned them, and no one was quite sure whether she was kidding or not.

As they finished their drinks, Noel shambled over with another round. He looked so relieved and ashamed of himself they couldn't help feeling sorry for the landlord. 'Thank you.

Thank you so much,' he said. 'You stopped them destroying everything. You saved the pub.'

Cathy had never seen him look so humble or heartsore.

'This is our pub!' Winnie burst out, raising her glass. 'For the first time we women felt welcome here. And we weren't about to let some runty little bugger ruin that for us! And nor were we about to let him hurt you or Cathy or Sofia!'

'There's been enough hurt around here in recent months,' said Ada Farley, contemplating the murky depths of her beer.

'Aye, very true,' said Noel Sturrock. Then he turned to his diminutive mother. 'What do you say, Mam?'

She sat there on her stool by the fire, smiling oddly. She had a faraway look in her eye. Her hair had come free of her hairnet and was all frizzed up. 'Hmm?' she said. 'What's that, son?'

Noel opened his mouth to repeat himself but he suddenly saw that something was very wrong with his mother.

She keeled over senselessly onto the bare floorboards.

It was the exertion and the excitement of the night, of course.

Later Noel and Cathy were kicking themselves for letting the old woman get herself into the middle of that dangerous scene.

'Ah, rubbish,' Teresa dismissed their worries. 'I loved every flamin' minute of it! Would you deprive an old biddy of her excitement, eh?'

She sat up in her bed for several days after the siege of the Robin Hood, getting her strength back and gloating over their triumph.

'Has there been any word from them Mad Johnsons?'

Noel shook his head, taking her dinner tray from her lap. She had barely touched anything. 'Not a dicky bird from them.'

'Aye, maybe we've taught them a lesson at last. They can't just take, take, take. People fight back, in the end. Why, they must have had hundreds of pounds off you through the years, eh?'

He nodded vaguely. 'Summat like that. Now look, Mam. Stop roving over it all. You're getting too agitated – you have to rest.'

Noel was terribly worried about her. That new young doctor had come by to take a look. No expense spared, Noel thought. He'd pay anything to get his mother back on her feet. The young doctor had listened to her and looked her over. He had frowned and prodded at Teresa Sturrock and then he told her son: 'Well, she's worn out. Her heartbeat is very irregular. She's not in a good way, I'm afraid to say. I'm surprised she's lived to the age she is, to be honest.'

Noel felt affronted by the doctor's vague, unhelpful words. 'Should she be in hospital? I mean, what can you do for her?'

The young doctor blinked and shook his fair fringe out of his face. 'Well, now, I don't think there's anything much to be done for her. Not unless we could take out all her tired old organs and replace them with new ones. But that's not an option, I'm afraid. No, Mr Sturrock, I'm telling you that your poor old mother is just worn out. She's not long for this world. I'm sorry to state it so brutally plainly, but I think you're best off preparing for the end. And making her as comfortable and happy as you can.'

'Oh,' said Noel in a hollow voice. 'But she isn't even all that old!'

'I believe she has had what is called a hard life,' the young doctor said.

'Aye, I suppose that's true.'

The doctor left his card and his bill and was gone.

Cathy had been standing by the teapot with the tea unpoured, taking in that whole scene. 'Oh, Noel. I'm so sorry.'

The front door went bang and the two of them were alone in that parlour. The silence gathered around them and it was like a little rehearsal for when the old woman was gone. Just the two of them left at number twenty-one with a whole host of hungry cats.

'Aye, lass,' Noel nodded. 'I know you'll be sorry. You love her just as much as I do, don't you?'

They took turns sitting up with her.

Teresa was a practical woman. She wasn't daft. She knew what was coming. She sipped her beef tea and she did as she was told. She eked out the last of her mortal strength and bided her time till the end. She had visitors and she would let them stay a little while, and then she would wave them off gladly.

Her room wasn't a gloomy place, with death hanging around greedily at the door; there was laughter and chatter, sometimes quite loud, when she had the strength.

Sofia brought her a dish of her husband's signature ice-cream: fior di latte. She spooned it into the old woman's mouth for her and Teresa declared it: 'The food of the gods! Nectar! Eeeh, that's lovely, pet.'

Sofia told the tale of how her husband Tonio had gambled with the Neapolitan gangsters all those years ago, and it wasn't just cash he'd taken away from their table – it had been their grandmother's recipe for this ice-cream, too. That had been worth just as much as money to the Italian hoods – the Grapelli boys – who had forced them to flee their homeland.

Teresa had laughed, 'Oh, you tell me such stories! Such nonsense!'

Ada Farley, also visiting, piped up: 'Ah, we've all spent all our lives round here, telling each other stories, haven't we? Tall ones and sad ones and stories that, even though we all know them, still need a good airing now and then.'

'Aye, hinny,' Teresa smiled. 'That's true.'

Then she waved all her friends out of her room for the last time.

*

Later that day, she was left alone with Cathy.

Cathy was like her guard dog. She fed her, washed her, dressed her. Teresa wasn't ashamed or upset by having everything done for her. She was proud. She was relieved and proud to be getting looked after by this girl who was like a daughter to her.

'I knew as soon as I saw you, lass, at the top of Frederick Street – not even a year ago! – I knew you were like the daughter I'd never had.'

Cathy sat by her, smiling, and stroked her tiny hand. 'Aye,' she said. 'I know, pet.'

'Listen,' Teresa told her, inching straighter in the bed so she could look the girl in the eye. The effort cost her, Cathy could tell. 'Lass, you have to listen to me.'

'Lie down. You need to rest,' Cathy told her.

'Nay, let me say my piece.'

'Go on, then.'

'I told you, you've been like a daughter to me. And I'd love to give you everything I have. I'd love to pass it down . . .'

Cathy shook her head. 'I don't want anything. That's not why I look after you or . . .'

'Shush, man,' Teresa snapped impatiently. 'I don't have much time. I know that and you know that. And I would like to see you with a bit of security. With a bit of stability in your life. When I go, there'll just be you and Noel here.'

Cathy didn't want to hear the rest of it, intuitively knowing what was coming next. However, she let the old woman talk.

'If you want security in your life, then you can have it. You can have your job and your home and everything, forever. You can have more than that.'

'Oh?' Cathy smiled at her.

'Look, I know he's a bugger. And he's nowt to bloody look at. And I know he's got a flippin' awful temper on him. Yet despite all of that, his heart is good, Cathy. His heart is made out of gold and he loves you with all of it. You know that, don't you? Noel loves you to death, hinny.'

Cathy simply stared at the earnest, wrinkled old face. 'Aye, I suppose I do.'

'Then make an old wifey happy on her deathbed, won't you, pet? And take his hand? Won't you make my son's whole life worthwhile? Won't you give his existence a bloody point at last?'

Cathy threw back her head and laughed. 'You're really twisting my arm, aren't you?'

'Of course!' Teresa grinned. 'I know I'm laying it on thick, but I mean every word. Underneath everything, underneath all the bloody awfulness, my son's a good man and he adores you. Just marry him, Cathy, and you will get everything. You'll get the house and the pub and the life you're looking for.'

'Am I?' Cathy wondered aloud. 'Is that what I'm really looking for?'

'Oh, aye,' Teresa flapped her tired hand. 'Why, I told you that right at the start, didn't I? You belong here in the Sixteen Streets, Cathy Carmichael. And as Cathy Sturrock – as my lad's wife – you'd be at the heart of the place forever. You'd be landlady of the Robin Hood Public House on Frederick Street. No one could ever take that away from you. I can see it all, long after I'm gone . . .'

Cathy smiled. 'Have you taken up telling the future then? Like that bloody Winnie?'

'Ha!' Teresa laughed weakly. 'I dunno about that, but I can see a little of what will come to pass. If you take my son's hand and marry him, he'll make you queen of our world, Cathy. You'll be our Queen of the Sixteen Streets. Now, what do you say to that?'

The End.

Acknowledgements

Thanks to Jeremy, my family, agent Piers, editor Rhea and all at Orion.

Credits

Elsie Mason and Orion Fiction would like to thank everyone at Orion who worked on the publication of *The Runaway Girl* in the UK.

Editorial
Rhea Kurien
Sanah Ahmed
Sahil Javed

Copyeditor
Clare Wallis

Proofreader
Laura Gerrard

Audio
Paul Stark
Jake Alderson

Contracts
Alyx Hurst
Dan Herron
Ellie Bowker

Design
Tomás Almeida
Joanna Ridley
Nick May

Editorial Management
Charlie Panayiotou
Jane Hughes
Bartley Shaw
Tamara Morriss

Finance
Jasdip Nandra
Nick Gibson
Sue Baker

Production
Ruth Sharvell

Sales
Jen Wilson
Esther Waters
Victoria Laws
Rachael Hum
Anna Egelstaff
Frances Doyle
Georgina Cutler

Toluwalope Ayo-Ajala
Sinead White
Ellie Kyrke-Smith

Operations
Jo Jacobs
Dan Stevens

Also by Elsie Mason

The Biscuit Factory Girls

Can Irene find a new home by the docks?

Newly married to dashing RAF officer, Tom, Irene Farley leaves behind her safe countryside life to move in with his family by the docks in South Shields. Little prepares her for the devastation the Jerry bombers have wreaked on the Sixteen Streets or that they would be living under her mother-in-law's roof, alongside Tom's brothers and their wives!

Irene's only escape is her job at the local Wight's Biscuit Factory packing up a little taste of home for the brave boys fighting for King and country across the channel. As the threat of war creeps ever closer to the Sixteen Streets, the biscuit factory girls bond together, because no one can get through this war alone . . .

The Biscuit Factory Girls at War

Home is where the heart is . . .

Beryl was the first Farley clan bride, finding a home in the arms of loving, attentive, elder son Tony. Yet even now, wrapped in Tony's embrace, Beryl has never quite been able to forget the past she ran away from, nor the shocking family secret she tried to bury.

With Tony away fighting the Jerries alongside his brothers, it's up to Beryl and her sisters-in-law to keep the family afloat. Hard, gruelling work doesn't faze her, but the sudden arrival of a devastating letter does . . .

Will Beryl be able to hold her family together and face up to her past? Or will the war take away the one thing she holds most dear – the one person she never thought she deserved?

A Wedding for the Biscuit Factory Girls

The third novel in the heart-warming and heart-wrenching WW2 saga series set in South Shields

Her wedding day should have been the happiest day of Mavis Kendricks' life. Marrying handsome Sam, the youngest of the Farley boys, means joining the Farley clan, and there's nothing Mavis has ever wanted more than a family of her own. But the appearance of an unexpected guest ruins everything . . . and brings back painful memories Mavis would rather forget.

It's not long before the war-torn streets of South Shields are buzzing with rumours. One of the biscuit factory girls, funny little Mavis has always been a bit of a mystery. As far as anyone can remember, Mavis and her twin Arthur have been orphans. So who was the grand old lady at the wedding? How do the twins own their own house? And just what is Mavis hiding? On the Sixteen Streets, nothing stays a secret for long . . .